THE
HITMAN'S DAUGHTER

THE
HITMAN'S DAUGHTER

CAROLYNE TOPDJIAN

Copyright © 2022 by Carolyne Topdjian
Cover and jacket design by Mimi Bark

ISBN 978-1-951709-58-7
ISBN 978-1-951709-84-6
Library of Congress Control Number: available upon request

First hardcover edition February 2022 by Agora Books
An imprint of Polis Books, LLC
44 Brookview Lane
Aberdeen, NJ 07747
www.PolisBooks.com

For my mom and dad,
who always let me daydream with my earphones on;

And for Jason,
who is always ready to play the music super loud with me.

Three may keep a secret, if two of them are dead.

—Benjamin Franklin, 1735

I. INVITATION

Though the hotel was constructed in 1921, the haunting didn't occur until seventy years later. On the fourth of August, 1991 at half past three in the morning, every television set in each of the four-hundred and thirty-nine guestrooms of the Château du Ciel switched on preternaturally. By this time, the hotel's revenue was already suffering from the market crash four years prior. Fortunately, not many guests were checked in to experience it. But those few who were—seeking a nostalgic rendezvous or unparalleled privacy—would tell you the same story. They awoke to the sounds of their televisions blaring and an infant crying.

The former nuisance they would shut off with a click of a remote, but the latter would prove difficult to pin down or drown out. Was it coming from next door? Upstairs? The corridor? After a few noise complaints to the front desk, the guests would eventually drift back into a troubled sleep. And with bags under their eyes and a sour taste on their tongues, all would check out hours later.

Some would moan they felt ill from acute heartburn or intense migraines. Others would claim they rose in the morning with streaks of white in their hair or spiders crawling in their bed sheets. They'd blame the Château: its poor wiring, its dusty vents and acidic wine selection. A handful would demand refunds and threaten never to step foot inside the hotel again.

And for a little while, that was the case. The Château in all its grandeur fell into ruin. The era was forgotten. So was the mysterious baby. Until the invitations arrived in the post.

The season has come
for an unforgettable celebration...

Ring in the New Year in opulence
at our Centennial Diamond Ball

Black & White Attire
Champagne Cocktails
Eight-Course Dinner
Dancing
Orchestra

Château du Ciel:
Soar in luxury, remain forever.

Part I

MIDNIGHT COMES

ONE

December 31st, 2020

In room five-oh-eight, Mave Michael Francis gazed longingly at her uniform folded atop the dresser and ignored the 9mm pistol it cushioned. Simple, unremarkable, white blouse, black pants; both pressed perfectly by a colleague working laundry and nothing like the whisper of beaded chiffon currently wrapping her figure. The gown left her feeling naked. Vulnerable. Though only her shoulder and back were bare to the world, it was enough. Certain rules had been ingrained in Mave from an early age. Blending in was critical.

Without her uniform, without her thick-rimmed glasses and her pasted-on smile, Mave wasn't just a shopgirl with a quirk. She was a marked misfit—in this ostentatious dress even more so, and just hours before her dreaded birthday. She picked up the gun, a second-generation family heirloom fitted with a silencer.

The handle was near-frozen in the folds of her knuckles and the barrel swayed left to right. She used two hands to steady it. Her fingers weren't long enough for a comfortable grip. Much like the dress, the gun felt entirely wrong on her. But she didn't set it down. Just as she didn't change out of the gown. On the eve of her birthday, masochistic choices and a sour mood were usual symptoms, an annual rite of passage. In a few hours Mave would turn twenty-five—the same age her mother had been when she'd—

A knock at the door drew her from her spiraling thoughts. "Who is it?" she called, stashing the pistol beneath her uniform.

"Good, you're still here!" Bastian's voice drifted from the hall-way.

Mave shoved everything into the dresser and moved for the doorknob. Odds were, Bastian needed her to find something. She swung open the mahogany door and looked up at the concierge. Barely clearing five feet, Mave often gazed up at people but with Bastian it was more pronounced.

"Hey, what's up?"

Bastian whistled and pressed a gloved hand to his heart. "Mercy, Mave! That you?"

She self-consciously brushed her temple. *Did he notice?* Her sensitivity to colored contacts meant she had to switch to glasses to alter her appearance—except in her rush, she'd forgotten her frames in the bathroom. Hopefully Bastian would be too distracted by the dress to pay any attention to her eyes—another insecurity and hint of her strangeness. Eight weeks into her employment at the Château and, so far, no one but Birdie had remarked on it. Heterochromia iridis: one iris the color of the sea, and the other, a muddied bronze. It helped that old wiring left most of the hotel in shadow—restricted staff hallways included.

"Security!" Bastian sang, momentarily switching to his Islander lilt. Sure enough, his appraisal travelled south of her neck. "All those rich boys are going to break down the door of the shop!" Bastian was a harmless flirt. His infectious chuckle filled the corridor.

Mave imagined she resembled a high-end call girl despite the compliment. Her lipstick shade was Secret Escort Red. *At least I'm not a common whore. Cain would be proud.* She tamped the unwanted sentiment and mirrored Bastian's grin. "Not bad yourself. Wow, is that a double Windsor knot?" *Good. Deflect.*

Bastian looked down and admired his tie. If there was something Mave had in common with the concierge, it was charm.

In Bastian's case, however, she guessed it was genuine and not a learned survival skill.

"What did you misplace?" Last time it had been a courier slip that had gotten lodged in the slides of his desk drawer. Mave flared her nostrils, tried to clear her mind and get a read. From early on, Cain had nicknamed her sixth sense hound-dogging—like the innate reflex of a tracking bitch. But Bastian interrupted before she could pick up any mental scent.

"Nothing. For you." He held out an envelope he'd removed from his inner breast pocket. Standard letter-size, unmarked, ivory stock.

Mave furrowed her brow. He wasn't here for the hound-dogging? Uniform or not, two months had been long enough for word of her weird ability to spread throughout the hotel. After all, a part of her appreciated the distraction of helping strangers. Missing possessions were an itch. They demanded she scratch, follow, seek. Or else their prickle would develop into a full-blown rash, (a mental malady she didn't care to suffer).

So yesterday, when the chef had misplaced a purchase order for fingerling potatoes, he'd dropped by the shop and Mave had directed him to the clipboard hanging on the wall next to the walk-in freezer. The day before that, when a guest lost her room key, the front desk advised she swing by the shop, and Mave recommended she search under the passenger seat of the silver BMW parked in the visitor lot. Her tips were the reason people sought her out.

"Go on, take it." Bastian wagged the mysterious envelope and checked his watch. "Ay! Got five minutes to check on a flower delivery for nine-nineteen. Then place an order for dry cleaning. *Then* find cat litter for the violinist." He heaved a sigh. "Don't ask," he added before Mave could verbalize her amusement. She had yet to witness Bastian anything but easygoing. Then again, before this week, he'd never had to cater to more than a handful of guests. The Diamond Ball was a last-ditch effort to keep this fossil of a hotel from sinking into oblivion. And provided Bastian's to-do list, it was working.

As Mave accepted the letter, Bastian spun away with a wink, then tossed over his shoulder, "Oh, and Birdie said not to be late. Something about natural lighting."

"What natural lighting?" She was due to meet Birdie in the chandelier-lit shop in fifteen minutes.

"I know," Bastian's globular eyes grew even rounder, "storm's already started."

Right. That too.

Meteorologists were warning of a complete whiteout set to sweep across the state overnight. As if supporting winter's terror, the wind chose that moment to moan through the old vents. Or maybe that was the Château's infamous ghost: the Spirit of Dead Poets. He was rumored to prefer the library, but perhaps he'd ventured upstairs for the occasion. Maybe he'd lost his invitation to the Diamond Ball and had a bone to pick. Lord knew Mr. Hendrick had been raving enough about this night for even the dead to lament missing out.

Not only was the dusty hotel fully booked for the first time in decades, but weeks earlier the online waitlist for the New Year's gala had tipped into triple digits. Either way, the weather advisory had been clear: an incoming ice blizzard was smothering the last sunset of the year.

Bastian circled his phone in the air. "You believe it? Cell lines died an hour ago. Mr. Hendrick thinks it adds to the 'romance' of the night—snowed-in for the festivities." He exhaled a groan. "How am I supposed to work strapped to my desk and the landline? Anyway, don't you be late—you know how Birdie gets."

And Mave did. The hotel's resident artist of forty-some years, Elizabeth "Birdie" Everhart was an eccentric, determined shrew. How else had Mave agreed to sit for a portrait? In this dress? On New Year's? On the most despised day of all days, her birthday?

One grand in payment, that's how. She widened her fake smile. Anything for a dollar. Like father, like daughter.

With a last wave, Bastian left. Mave shut the door and pulled in a deep breath, which only caused the dainty dress to pull snug against her breasts and reinforce her doubt. *Enough.* She snapped the rubber band on her wrist. *Quit sulking. Get it done.*

Envelope in hand, she slipped into the adjoining bathroom. Space was limited in staff quarters and if she sat on the toilet and leaned forward, she'd bump her nose on the facing wall. Mave leaned on the sink instead and ignored the monotonous drip of the tap. She scanned the frame of postcards she'd taped to the mirror. Collected over the past four years, each was addressed from a maximum-security prison—a daily testament of everything she strived to avoid. The only problem? Even as a law-abiding citizen, she had no clue how to avoid a criminal lifestyle.

No crumbs. No ties.

For as long as she could remember, she'd kept a low profile, moving from one state to another. She'd stocked an emergency kit exactly as Cain had taught her. A bottle of bleach, hair dye in Strawberry Sunset, colored contact lenses (good for an hour max before her eyes became bloodshot). Just in case. You could never be too careful. Not to mention the gun, the bullets. On special occasions like tonight, she would pull them out, inventory everything and reminisce about her spoiled roots.

With a sigh, Mave tore the envelope's seal. She dreaded a new postcard to display. Eight weeks was a record, even for her father.

She blinked. *Not from Cain.* The envelope held a monogrammed notecard.

Change of plans. Come to my studio first. -B.

Rubbing her forehead, Mave tossed Birdie's note into the wastebasket and rested her cheek on the mirror—onto the single photograph taped to the center of the glass. Too bad her gift couldn't help her sense how to find something useful. Like a purpose. Like a home.

"How long?" she whispered to the picture of her long-dead mother. "How long till he tracks me this time?"

Six addresses in four years. Mave had done everything she could to evade him. She'd dropped her last name, deleted all social media accounts even though they were under aliases, changed IP networks, banks and her email to become untraceable. Maybe that was the problem. Her father knew her disappearing tricks too well. He'd taught her every single one.

Her toes grew numb against the black and white tiles. Two months ago, when a tourism recruitment officer had offered her a job in a secluded hotel in Colorado, it'd seemed like kismet. And now…was it time to pack up and leave this mountain resort already? Her mother's portrait remained silent. Mave refocused on the evening—a priority problem.

She debated her options. *One: hide inside my room tonight, piss off Birdie, and get fired in the morning for leaving the boutique unattended on the biggest night the hotel's had in years.* (She could already hear Mr. Hendrick hollering about thousands of dollars in lost revenue.) *Two: suck it up and do my job. Earn some much-needed cash. It's just one night. Just one dress.* Birdie had insisted she wear it for the portrait and had dropped it off a few days ago. And what Birdie wanted, Birdie got.

Mave took a last moment to smooth her cropped hair with her fingers, combing her bangs askew over her brow. With her mother's image masking her reflection, she slid her clear glasses onto her face. *There. No more moping.*

She stepped into a pair of five-inch stilettos, steeled herself, and exited the safety of her room. As she locked her door with the antique, tasseled key, Mave recited the first two lies of the evening: *Just one night. Just one dress.* She rolled her lips together. *What could possibly go wrong?*

Less than five seconds after she'd stepped into the elevator cramped with guests, Mave's breath quickened and her stomach tightened. Riding up to Birdie's suite versus climbing eighteen flights of stairs in heels had seemed like a reasonable choice—until the doors had sealed her inside a car saturated with cologne, hairspray, sweat, and the hint of mold that lingered throughout the Château.

Muzak offering monotonous cheer from overhead speakers was not helping Mave's anxiety. Doing her best to deny her claustrophobia, she gritted her teeth and counted Mississippis in her head. One by one, the other passengers got out on their respective floors until she was alone.

Just as the bossa nova began to waver in her ears, the car chimed its antique bell, slowed to a stop, and rolled open its gilded cage. Mave had to resist a forward dive to safety. She exited onto the twenty-third floor.

Scalloped shells. On the wallpaper, on the carpeting, on the lumpy wingback, oil paintings, and deco tile-work. Each level of the hotel had a design motif and this one, it would seem, was regurgitated cockles and clams. *Might explain why it remains eerily unoccupied. Affront by sealife.* That, and Birdie's reputation for harassing any temporary neighbors. Rumor had it the artist had bought the entire penthouse floor in the early eighties. Mave referenced the wall signage for directions and turned down a long, empty corridor.

Despite more than one tour from Bastian, this enormous hotel remained a labyrinth to her. Left turn. Right turn. Another right turn. Built by a French investor during the Roaring Twenties. Over six hundred thousand square feet of regal opulence nestled in nature, Bastian had recited from the website. Four-hundred and thirty-nine guestrooms recognized for hosting numerous international celebrities, industry moguls, and diplomats since the Château first opened its doors. That was before its decline. Before its ornate railings crept with rust and its crown moldings chipped and splintered. Now the hotel was lucky its annual hunters' gathering—its only grace from bankruptcy—attracted a low-maintenance crowd each September. According to Bastian, the outdoorsmen didn't give a shit about tarnished silver or cracked plaster. Their only requirements were soft beds, cold beers, and accommodation for their portable meat lockers.

Halfway to her destination, Mave's confidence faltered as the scalloped wall sconces flickered and dimmed. Their buzz of electricity filled the hall like a hymn of wasps. She hugged her arms tight across her middle, fighting a chill, and picked up her pace. Likely the ice storm was damaging more than just the cell towers this evening. By the time she reached the double-doors of Birdie's studio, her imagination had declared a state of winter apocalypse outside. Mave knocked briskly.

"Birdie?" She neared her lips to the seam between the doors. "It's Mave Michael! I got your note!" Did the old woman change her mind about the portrait? Mave tried not to think of her meager life savings. Someday she'd own more than a travelling toothbrush in a transient's room. She'd live in a permanent home that she'd decorate with bright colors, fresh peonies and fairy lights. She raised her fist to knock again when a faint response came.

"'M-in."

Mave waited a beat, turned the knob, and found it unlocked. Like every other door in the Château, this one announced her entrance with a crackle and creak.

Two steps into the dark studio and rather than calming her jitters, Birdie's cluttered space heightened them.

Burnt spotlights hung haphazardly from the ceiling. A naked mannequin stood facing the corner like a shamed youth suffering punishment. Canvases of various sizes—mainly incomplete portraits—were piled against the drawn velour curtains, shoved against easels, worktables. Mave shuddered under the portraits' collective stare and did her best not to trip over anything. The floor was littered with wrinkled tubes of paint, rags, plastic bags, ripped sketches.

"Hello?" *Was Birdie in the adjoining room? Was that a Barbie doll's head?* Sleet pattered the windowpanes. An illusion of skeletal children tapping their fingertips on glass harassed her logic. "Yoo-hoo, I'm here!"

As she wandered deeper into the artist's atelier, another sound—a cough?—floated through the wall. She bumped a mason jar with her foot, and a mysterious inky mixture spilled and stained the rug black. Not that anyone would notice. For Mave—whose meticulous organization overcompensated for her inability to find her own possessions—this studio was her worst nightmare. It was a miracle Birdie could find a brush much less complete a painting in this chaos. No wonder the woman frequented the hotel's boutique. Over the past two months, Birdie had been constantly consulting Mave. Where was that stick of charcoal? That bottle of glaze? Her book of preliminary sketches or scrolled-up drafts? At certain moments, Mave had suspected Birdie was merely testing her skill. How else could a hefty glass muller used to grind pigment have ended up hidden inside a plant holder just outside the shop?

"Mave Mm—!"

Her attention snapped to the call.

Birdie's cry travelled from the connecting room "—*no*."

A thud.

The brassy ring of a rotary telephone cut short.

Mave's blood spiked with adrenaline. Something was wrong.

Uncaring of her steps, she scurried through the wet stain and thrust open the door to a drafty, unlit sitting room. The space was narrow and deep. "Birdie? Where are you?" *How many rooms within rooms were there in this suite?* "Birdie!"

Always case out a joint before entering, her father's voice warned. *Know your weapons. Your exits.*

Rubbing her biceps to keep warm, Mave squinted into the darkness and conducted a mental inventory. Tall stacks of horded magazines. Tufted couch. Trunk box. Standing vase. She flinched at the sight of a girl with hunched shoulders across the room—then exhaled. Her reflection in the facing mirror copied her actions.

Focus, she chided herself. *Your birthday is making you melodramatic. You need this money. Find Birdie.*

Next to the couch, a paneled door was cracked ajar.

As she hurried toward it, her heel caught and raked something soft—a fallen wig. A sense of urgency goading her, she carried on and entered into a subzero bedroom. Movement stirred in the corner of her eye. A figure in black.

Breath caught, Mave spun and saw... no one. Her eyes playing tricks again.

The heavy curtains ballooned and billowed. Grains of ice resembling coarse salt blew over the carpet. Mave shivered and huddled.

In her haste to shut the balcony doors, she didn't notice Birdie. Not until she tripped over the old woman's ankles and into a pool of blood.

TWO

Scrambling onto her behind, Mave gagged on a scream and pushed back with her heels—*away, away,* away from the old woman's wounded, crumpled body. Her stilettos scraped into the carpet.

No, no, no.

She recoiled against the nightstand, her pulse whooshing in her ears.

So much blood. Leaking. Blooming out. Like before. Like the morning she'd discovered the truth about her father's profession.

NO.

She clapped her hands to her mouth only to be reminded that her one palm was slick with blood. She frantically wiped them along the side of the bed. Her smears sullied the duvet. Wrapping her arms around her middle, she clenched her eyes shut. Her breathing grew more and more erratic. Her head swam with the monster, transporting her to the unwanted past.

("Hey, dad! I'm back!")

She'd been twelve. It'd been raining all week and the motel room had smelled of damp cigarettes.

Stop. Breathe. Listen, her father's voice ordered in the here and now. *Find a way out.*

("Know you said to wait for you downstairs, but I really need to pee." Mave yanked off her rubber boots and knocked on the bath-

16

*room door. Inside, the sink was running. "And you're like taking for-
ever... Hey, Dad! Are you shaving?")*

Come back. Be present.

*(The suitcase lay open on the stripped mattress. Mave frowned
and gnawed on her lip. It still tasted of syrup from the diner's three-
ninety-nine pancake special.)*

Don't go there, M&M. Stay here.

*("Dad, I'm coming in, okay?" Why wasn't he answering? She
wiggled the knob.)*

DON'T—

A bite at her wrist—Mave gasped and her eyes shot open.

Her teeth chattered. Her fingers pulled at the elastic band.
Snap.

She was in suite twenty-three-oh-one of the Château du Ciel.
Snap.

It was the day before her birthday. It was New Year's Eve.

Good girl. What did I teach you? Look. Listen. Learn, Cain
Francis trained. *It's nothing like before. You didn't hear a gun firing.
No shot. No gun, M&M. In fact, she may still be—*

Birdie lay on her back, legs bent, mouth agape, eyes frozen in
Mave's direction as if she were still crying out for her. And then
she blinked.

"Birdie!" With renewed purpose, Mave broke from the clutches of memory and crawled to her, her vision blurring with tears.

There was time. She could save her. Her knee struck hard,
chiming plastic.

The landline. Grabbing for the phone, Mave yanked on the
handset lying off its cradle and thrust it to her ear. Her ragged
breaths overlapped the silence. Struggling to revive the connection, she helplessly spun zero on the dial without success. She
dropped the antique.

Think. The cell lines were down. It would take too long to
run back to the elevator. And there was a chance Birdie had already called for help. The telephone was lying nearby. She'd heard

a sound earlier—a voice, a cough. Help would be arriving soon. "Okay," she wheezed. "I can do this." Cain had schooled her in first aid—had taken special care to drill her on gunshot injuries. Had Birdie been shot?

No. Yes. Doesn't matter. She's breathing. Apply pressure to the wound.

Between the encroaching shadows, multiple bloodstains, and Birdie's dark sweater, Mave struggled to locate the injury. For a moment she simply trembled her hands over the woman's body.

Birdie's wig cap sat crooked on her scalp. Her thinning hair was matted and streaked. The bleeding from her waist seemed more critical. Wagering a guess, Mave flittered her fingers over the wet stain at her stomach. Sure enough, a cut bloomed. One hand atop the other, she gingerly pushed into Birdie's clammy, tender flesh.

She couldn't stop shivering. Was she making it worse? Her fingers flooded and her knuckles darkened.

"It's g-going to be okay." Mave licked the tears off her upper lip, unsure which of them she was trying to placate. "Do you hear me—Birdie? Can you hear me?"

Birdie's jaw twitched once. Twice. And her reply came not by sound.

Mave sucked inward. *A scent!* Birdie was sending her a message—had lost an object—

"I'm right here, Birdie. Tell me."

… something red.

Without releasing pressure, she leaned closer to Birdie's chest, ignoring the hint of turpentine wafting from the artist's skin—ignoring the sound of pounding in the background.

… a red leather book… packed in a dark … tight …

Before she could fully place it, the object's metaphysical scent, and her read of its owner's longing, vanished.

Mave willed her body to cease its trembles. She studied Birdie's face for any signs of life.

Wait. I didn't see where yet. I didn't—

She inhaled stream after desperate stream, pulsed her lungs to no avail.

"Hey—"

Mave jumped. A flashlight's beam blinded her eyes.

"—hold it right there!" a man hollered.

Two security guards stomped into the bedroom. She'd seen them on occasion. Penn and Teller, she'd named them in her head. Dressed in matching black suits, one had dark hair slicked into a ponytail and was markedly larger than the other.

Mave resumed shaking. She tried speaking words. A nonsensical syllable escaped her throat.

The smaller one, Teller, approached first, one hand at his hip, the other aiming his flashlight at Mave. "Let go and slowly back away from Ms. Everhart."

She was still pushing on Birdie's stomach. Obliging Teller, she gave up her sorry attempt at first aid as the giant—Penn—put on gloves and took over assessing Birdie's injuries.

Teller's attention stayed on Mave. "Are you hurt?" His brow deepened, a thick slash across his stern, turtle-boned features.

Mave wanted to yell at him. Tell him he was too late. She barely managed to shake her head.

Finding her with nothing but bloodstains, he muttered, "Nice and easy," lifted her by her armpits like she was a small child, and distanced her from the body.

Mave rested her spine against the cool wall and drew her knees to her chest. Sequins dug into the backs of her thighs.

Another person arrived uttering curses, shut the balcony doors, flicked on the Tiffany lamp on the nightstand. Mave squinted, eyes burning. She didn't—couldn't—look at Birdie anymore. She stared into space, at nothing in particular.

There was talk of securing the room.

Teller barked into his radio. The police couldn't come yet. Zero visibility. The ice was too thick, had already downed multiple trees.

They needed cranes, chainsaws, plows. Roads were out of commission for at least another two days.

The semi-functional part of Mave's brain wondered why they were calling for police and not an ambulance.

Because, M&M: ambulances are for the living, not the—

"Struggle took place," another male voice, a real one, interrupted. "Cord's damaged, ripped from the wall."

"Would explain why front desk lost the connection," Teller said. "Hey, careful not to move that. You know the drill. Don't touch anything, period." Apparently this wasn't their first time handling a dead body. But considering Teller's graveled bark, it might be their first bloodied, resident VIP.

Mr. Hendrick's bulbous face came into her line of vision, his beefsteak jowls sagging and drained of their usual ruddiness. He was kneeling in front of her, lips moving, words exiting. The groomed edges of his mustache merged into his frown. Mave blinked and remembered to listen.

"... clear she's in shock," Mr. Hendrick announced to Penn and Teller.

I'm not, she argued without voice. *Just because I walked in on a dying, gory body that reminds me of when I was a kid and found a stranger shot dead in a bathtub... I'm resting. Just resting.*

He wrapped a clean blanket around her shoulders. "Ms. Michael, we're going to have to ask you some questions. Are you able to stand, to walk?" Without waiting for her reply, he gently helped her up by her elbow. "That's it—blanket on. Come with me."

She wanted nothing more than to leave this cluttered nightmare and never return. Mr. Hendrick waved a silent command at Teller who joined them as they exited the suite. In a daze, she permitted them to guide her: left turn, right turn, left turn. On and on. Buzzing sconces. Dancing scallops. At last, they entered a service elevator.

Mave widened her eyes. Her heart leapt to her throat. *Please, no, not another box.* The mental protest manifested too late. The doors slid shut and, with them, the remains of her mind followed suit.

Downstairs, the jubilee had commenced. Guests in tuxedos, draped in silks and furs sauntered the lobby. They primped, chatted, flirted, flaunted their cleavage and puffed their chests. A singer's croon carried from the grand ballroom. Sinatra. Laughter. Clicking heels. Unnoticed among the revelers, Mr. Hendrick ushered Mave to the hoteliers' private offices with Teller trailing behind.

The offices were empty. All hands were on deck.

Mave sat numbly in a leather club chair as Teller and her boss advised her to stay put—rest. Did she want a change of clothes, a sweater perhaps? Mave nodded robotically. Mr. Hendrick had a few calls to make next door, would be back in a moment. Teller, meanwhile, (who Mr. Hendrick addressed as Tag), was ordered to find Birdie's personal maid, ensure the suite was sealed, and fetch Mave some clean clothes—all with absolute discretion.

Mave wasn't sure how much time passed. A minute spanned eternity. She slipped off her stilettos and curled up her feet. She picked at a bead on her gown. Less than a week ago Birdie had marched into her shop with a garment bag, on a mission to see Mave dressed up. Today the woman was dead.

Not just dead. She'd been stabbed seconds before Mave had entered the studio.

God, what if the killer had been hiding inside the suite the entire time? A shiver passed through her body. She fumbled for a fancy bottle of mineral water from a side table and drained it in one go. Her thirst was insatiable. Wiping her mouth with her wrist, she reached for another bottle.

Eventually someone from housekeeping delivered warm facecloths. With a stunned expression, she mentioned Mave could wash up in the employees' restroom. Mave blinked at the bloodstains streaking her hands. She looked better dressed for Halloween than a New Year's black-tie event.

Inside the restroom, she wiped her face with the towels, scrubbed her knuckles raw, and did her best to avoid her zombie-like reflection in the mirror. Having filled a wicker basket with the dirtied cloths, she returned to her club chair outside.

The blanket was still there. She pulled it to her chin, cloaking her ruined dress. A window from an office nearby let in the storm's roar. The more Mave focused on the white noise, the more her eyelids grew heavy. One unnerving question after another pushed to be heard inside her mind. It was too much, too soon. She didn't want to hear them, consider them. She didn't want to think, period.

Her head dipped to the armrest.

It was a lucid dream; it had to be. The storm from the office still moaned in the background. Plus everything seemed dimmer and brighter than in real life. The bells above the shop door jingled too sharply. And Birdie Everhart's shadow rolled before her too densely.

Mave checked the time just as she'd done a week ago: five minutes before closing.

Birdie strode inside indifferently, her refined confidence impressive even as it announced her privilege to the world. Mave set aside her drawer of stamps and meager receipts. "Birdie?"

Dapples of pink streaked the old woman's upper cheeks and her mouth was pursed in a severe line. Mave smiled, hoping to diffuse her obvious stress. "Is everything okay?"

"My muller."

Mave shook her head and grew distracted by a hint of ash lacing the air.

That part was wrong. There had been no scent in real life.

She sniffed, and the sensation dissolved. "Huh, I'm sorry, what?"

"Don't mumble, Mave."

Birdie had spoken those very words. Mave relaxed her shoulders and dismissed any discrepancy. She was re-enacting the past in a dream after all.

"Now, are you capable of finding a stolen item? Or simply things I've personally lost?"

"I'm not sure." Mave pushed up her glasses and smoothed a wrinkle from her blouse. "No one's ever asked me that before. I suppose if the stolen object belongs to you, then I should still be able to"—she chose her words carefully—"guess its location."

"Excellent. My muller, it was taken. Or maybe misplaced by that new maid I hired. I told her to stay out of my studio but they never listen."

Another wave of ash bloomed, and Mave absently brushed her knuckle across her upper lip. The ice storm felt like it was raging in the back of her skull. She wished its white noise would die.

Mistaking her confusion, Birdie impatiently added, "It's a grinding tool made of glass similar to a mortar. I need it to refine my pigments into powder."

"Okay, I'm sure I can help." She pulled in a deep breath and wrinkled her nose as the ashy odor tickled her sinuses.

"What's wrong?"

They were off-script again. "Nothing." She cleared her throat, determined to erase the errors of dream from reality. She had to maintain order, remember last week exactly as it'd happened. "Just clear your mind like all the other times"—Yes. That's what she'd said—"and focus on the tool itself."

A vein ticked in Birdie's temple but she did as Mave asked. Seconds later the artist's connection to her muller appeared in Mave's inner eye. "Come with me." Mave's steps faltered as she recalled her slight gaffe: when she'd originally tracked the item, she'd shown open surprise. But dream-Birdie seemed not to notice. Her eyes widened as Mave rounded the counter and exited the giftshop. The storm grew louder out in the galleria. She ignored it and rolled up her sleeve.

The doorway bells hadn't stopped ringing before Mave held the muller in her hand. The glass tool was browned with soil from the plant pot it'd been buried in, directly outside the shop. Birdie's jaw slackened. She clearly hadn't been in on the prank. Mave doubted her hound-dogging would have worked otherwise. She passed Birdie her tool and dusted her hands.

Birdie inspected the muller as if she'd never seen it before. The streaks in her cheeks darkened and a dangerous heat built behind her gaze. Mave tucked her hair behind her ears. "Is there anything—"

The old woman spun and stalked off without so much as a thanks, her stolen item clenched in her fist.

As Mave watched her disappear, the potted palm fluttered in her periphery, its leaves forming silhouettes of razors. The scent of ash wafted from behind, nudging, calling. Her shoulders stiffened again. She struggled to resist, to remain grounded. But in the end, her need to track overruled reason. She turned slowly, her tongue blotted dry, and reminded herself: this was a dream. Even if its improvised parts felt real.

Her heart raced. The reflex to cough battled with her need to swallow. *Swallow, swallow, pull.* Mave's breath clipped as her connection to the scent grew taut with its source.

There: an indistinguishable figure reeking of ashes hovered just in front of the shop's door. Mave stared in disbelief. None of this made sense. It wasn't a lost object she'd tracked, but a person. It was there and not-there, as if filtered behind a screen.

Just a dream.

Mave tilted her head for a different angle, and like another set of eyelids obscuring her vision, the mesh of darkness followed. She couldn't see beyond it—could only process *through* it. "H-hello?" she exhaled.

The figure froze as if caught unaware.

This isn't right. Mave retreated a step. *I need to wake up. Please wake up.*

The shadowy figure quivered and extended its hand toward her, seeming to push at the mesh. Was it checking to make sure Mave was really there? That *she* could see *it*?

She nodded without meaning to. "I d-do—I see you," she whispered. And for some reason, the confession caused the figure to flinch and for Mave's heart to fire like a shotgun.

She jerked awake. Anxiety spun in her stomach and her neck was stiff from being bent at an awkward angle. How long had she nodded off in the chair? An hour, two perhaps? She sat up roughly and massaged a kink in her shoulder. She'd had a strange dream—a bad dream—but already its details were melting from her consciousness.

Birdie's visit to the giftshop. The muller she'd tracked and then...

Hushed voices carried and Mave turned her neck. Mr. Hendrick's office door was ajar an inch. Enough for shreds of his conversation to be overheard.

"... briefed Sheriff Mor ..." Tag's murmur carried. "... from a state penitentiary taped ..."

She straightened her spine. Her inner alarm tripped and the remains of her stupor fell away with her blanket. With a quick scan to confirm she was alone, she crept behind the office door.

"—told her what Jordy heard and about her bloody boxcutter," Tag said, "plus those postcards. Course, Morganson wouldn't say nothing so I called a buddy of mine works traffic control upstate. Get this: that girl's full name is Mave Michael Francis, daughter of Cain Francis."

"Who?" Hendrick said. "Should that name mean anything to me?"

Tag snorted. "Not unless you need to get someone whacked. Cain Francis is a gun for hire. Or was. Been in the slammer going

25

on four years now, doing time for murder one, multiple counts."

If Edward Hendrick gave a response, Mave didn't hear it. Thoughts reeling, knees folding, she slid into a crouch. *What box-cutter? How? What did her father have to do with—*

"I know." Tag dropped his tone and Mave had to strain her ears. "… father's a *hitman*, a fuckin' contract killer. Apple don't fall far from the tree, right? Had us all fooled. How much of a background check did you do on this girl?"

"Don't give me that ex-Marine bullshit," Hendrick hissed. "This is a hotel, not the bloody White House. And the tourism agency gave her a glowing recommendation: experience as a key holder, courteous, neat. The shop's inventory has never been more accurate. Are you one hundred percent sure you're not wrong about—"

"She's got an FNX-9 9mm with a suppressor in her dresser. Serial number scratched off."

Mave's heart pounded wild against her ribcage. *No!* What were they doing snooping through her belongings? Acid churned in her stomach. Then she remembered. Hendrick had instructed Tag to bring her clean clothes. From her dresser. Where she'd stashed her father's pistol beneath her uniform. She'd stupidly agreed to it.

A misunderstanding. That was all. She'd explain. Mave kneaded her forehead where a dull ache was forming.

"Goddamned Birdie—this is a PR nightmare," Hendrick griped. "Where's Charlie? Bastian can take him a bottle of the vintage Barolo, the ninety-four. Anything to keep him soused. And Parissa, too," he thought aloud, speaking overtop Tag when the guard offered to deliver the wine himself. Mave had no idea who they were talking about—additional VIPs from the sound of it. "We can *not* let any guest catch wind of this. Not tonight. There's too much riding on this weekend. The mayor. The investors— Christ. What if they—"

"Let me do my job. All due respect, you want damage control, first thing is to retain the girl until Morganson gets here."

NO. Nausea rolled in her gut. She bit her lip, suppressing a cry.

"You're absolutely certain Mave is responsible for Birdie's death?"

Her jaw fell open. She cupped her ribs, struggled for air.

"Evidence don't lie."

What evidence? she inwardly screamed.

"All right. I've heard enough." A chair scraped the floor. "Let's get this over with."

Before Mave knew what was happening the door to the office swung open, and Tag gaped at her crouched behind it.

THREE

The hotel director, the security guard, and the shopgirl: it was an illogical staff meeting in the offices of the Château du Ciel—the start of a bad joke. Tag insisted she cooperate until the police arrived. Mave insisted she get an explanation. She had a right to defend herself and managed to articulate this, and not much else, to the men.

"Two things on-scene, kicked just under Birdie's bed." Tag's gaze stayed glued to her as if, at any moment, she might produce another pistol from thin air. Though she had gotten up from the floor and back into the club chair, the ex-Marine hovered over her, legs parted, arms crossed. Like a prison guard. "First is a boxcutter. With blood on its blade."

Seated on the chair opposite Mave, Mr. Hendrick checked his watch for what seemed like the hundredth time in the past minute. "Once the police make it here, they'll be able to confirm—"

"It was used to slash Birdie in the stomach," Tag interjected. "And it don't take a genius to know whose cutter it is."

Dread pooled in Mave's gut. Even before he said it, she knew what was coming.

"You always put your initials on stuff?"

Not on everything. But loose supplies from the shop, items that could walk away—scissors, stapler, tape dispenser. X-acto knife. They were normally sorted in a drawer beneath the counter. And all were marked with her neat print: MM.

"I'm—" her voice cracked. Just in case someone were to borrow anything (*like a boxcutter to stab Birdie*), Mave would know which item belonged to the boutique. "I don't like to lose things." There was a logical explanation for everything. None of which resulted in her murdering the Château's resident artist. If only they'd listen. She turned to Mr. Hendrick. "Please…"

His eyes were downcast, too dark to read in the weak lamplight.

"I had nothing to do with this. I was just"—*trying to earn extra cash*—"in the wrong place at the wrong time." (*Twelve years old—a motel bathroom—a bullet wound puncturing the forehead like a socket for a third eye.*) She plucked the rubber band on her wrist.

"Second thing we saw," Tag said as if she hadn't spoken, "was some fancy artist's tool about the size of my fist." He demonstrated by clenching his hand, his knuckles sharpening into pale peaks. "Kind of like a glass knob."

Fancy artist's tool.

"Also got blood on it. And white hairs."

Birdie's crooked wig cap flashed in her mind. *Glass knob.* Her thoughts jumped to the muller Birdie had asked her to locate last week. The one Mave had dug out from a potted palm directly outside the shop. It couldn't be…

"Sure. You know just the tool I'm talking about, don't you?"

She'd never mastered a poker face. *Can read you like the breaking news at the bottom of my screen*, Cain Francis used to reproach. *Gotta try harder than that.*

"Figure Birdie gave a fight, startled her attacker." Tag's stare bore into her cheek. She struggled not to scratch her face. If she wanted to get out of this mess, she had to control her roiling anxiety. "Stabs weren't enough, so the killer improvised. Know what the coroner's report will say?" Mave chewed the inside of her cheek as Tag continued spewing his morbid theories. "Killer used a bludgeon to finish the job. Fits the noise Jordy heard and the bleeding from Birdie's skull."

"Jordy?" Her voice sounded windswept, hollow.

Tag put his hands on his hips. Beneath the flap of his suit jacket, a baton was visible. "He's working front desk tonight. He answered Birdie's phone call for help."

It couldn't get worse. But it did.

"Jordy heard your name when he asked Birdie who was up there, hurting her."

"Wait—*what?*" Just as quickly, the mistake crystallized: she'd called out hello, announced her presence in the studio, and Birdie had replied—yelled for her from the bedroom. "That's not what happened!" She dug her nails into the armrests, spun her head from one man to the other. "I was just in the next—" Her tongue tripped as her words raced to be heard. "That makes no sense!"

Calmly M&M, her father's voice warned. *You act like a caged animal, that's exactly how they'll treat you.*

She released the armrests and wrung her fingers together on her lap. The beds of her nails were darkened. It would take multiple scrubbings to get all the blood out. (Cain had worn gloves. Always. Six bottles of bleach had been stored beneath the kitchen sink, just as precaution.)

"I barely knew her," she said more evenly. "I mean, why? What would I gain from wanting Birdie"—*say it*—"dead."

"You tell me." Tag eased his glower a notch, openly curious. Mr. Hendrick leaned forward, as if also on edge for her response.

"This is ridiculous," she burst out. "No matter what you've heard about—" She snapped her jaw shut before mentioning Cain Francis. "I'm *not* a coldblooded killer."

"Here's the thing." Mr. Hendrick furled his brow. It was the first thing he'd said since Tag took over the conversation and spun it into a biased interrogation. He tented his fingers and touched them to his lips, observing her like one might contemplate a poisonous flower. "Even after everything, I'd like to give you the benefit of doubt. Except"—

Except you're genetically programmed.

Except you're professionally trained.

"—the video footage."

Without her needing to ask, Tag filled her in. He evidently enjoyed the sound of his own voice. "Before the murder, you're the only person caught entering Birdie's studio."

She blinked, her brain slow to process this latest blow.

He said caught. *You're caught. Red-handed in every sense. Everything they were telling her was wrong. Twisted.*

"You hear what I just said? Hours of footage show the halls of the twenty-third floor empty"—Tag pointed at her—"till you."

Stop, she needed to shout. Another mistake. One thing after another painting her in guilt. But how?

"The cameras," she looked to Mr. Hendrick, willed him to recognize the truth, "they must have a blind spot. You have to believe me. Birdie was already injured when I found her."

Edward Hendrick regarded her with pity. "Look, Ms. Michael—Mave—"

"I came through her studio. I heard her shout my name but that's because I was in the next room. I went to find her and"—*a flutter, a figure in black*—"wait—I thought—when I first entered the bedroom I saw someone." *Yes, good. There.* Someone else— the real killer—was still floating freely around the hotel. Let them chew on that.

"Who?" Tag asked.

"Well…" A person wearing dark clothes? What *had* she seen apart from the billowing curtains? "I don't know."

"What'd they look like?"

Mave strained to recall the moment she'd first stepped inside Birdie's bedroom and felt movement in her peripheral vision. But it'd been too dark. Too cold. "I didn't—I'm not sure."

"Man or a woman?"

"I…"

"Where'd they go? How'd they leave?"

She stared at her hands, gripped her knees tightly. She sounded foolish, desperate, even to herself. Yet she had to try. She opened her mouth to tell them. "The balcony was—"

Tag's loud snort cut her off. "You expect us to believe someone climbed the walls outside? Twenty-three stories up, on tonight of all nights? There's a motherfucking *severe* storm—"

"Tag," Hendrick reprimanded.

"—only thing climbing out there is ice."

Mr. Hendrick raised a hand, ordering Tag to simmer down. "Wait," his tone was far gentler than his security guard's bark, "if you didn't visit the suite to hurt Birdie, why were you there?"

To make money. A pipe dream. "Birdie hired me." Mave swallowed, wishing for another bottle of water. "She wanted to paint my portrait. Offered to pay me."

"I see."

Did he?

A hint of disappointment crossed his features. "So you knew about Birdie's money."

Huh?

"That she kept plenty of cash on hand in her safe."

Was he asking her? Telling her? "Well, I guess." Everyone knew Birdie was rich. "I mean, I hadn't really…"

"That why you went up there?" Tag said. "To rob her?"

"What? No! I told you she invited—" *The note.* "There's a monogrammed card in the wastebasket of my bathroom." It took effort to keep her voice steady. "It's a handwritten note *from Birdie* asking me to visit her studio." She took a giant breath. "Just ask Bastian. He delivered it to me himself."

Mr. Hendrick gave a slight nod. "I'll have someone check and bring it here." But his disillusioned expression contradicted his agreement. Between front desk's statement, the boxcutter used to slash Birdie, the glass muller she'd handled, the video footage, her *history*…there were one too many strikes against her. One too many coincidences. She had guilt smeared all over her. The realization caused her nerve endings to charge with heat. What would happen when the police arrived?

First degree murder.

Would they arrest her, trap her inside a tiny cell until a predestined verdict made it permanent? The more she imagined it, the more her body hummed like a live wire. If she hadn't kept those horrible postcards—if she hadn't agreed to have her portrait painted—if she'd only stayed in her room tonight. Mave stood, her head dizzy from the abrupt movement.

"Where do you think you're going?" Tag growled.

She waited for the room to settle in her vision. "I need, I need to move," she answered weakly. "Get some air." *Away from you.* She turned to leave.

"Afraid I can't let you do—" The remainder of his objection fell on deaf ears. Instinct took over.

As Tag reached to restrain her, she drove the heel of her palm into his face.

fOUR

The force of the crunch travelled up her arm, stunning everyone in the room. Mave included.

Don't let them touch you: one of her father's rules of survival.

Tag wobbled back a step, eyes bulging and blinking. He dabbed his knuckles to his nose. Blood dripped and flecked his upper lip.

Oh god—I think I broke it. Her palm stung.

Tag sniffed, shuddered as if clearing his head, and came at her again—this time with his baton clenched and features contorted. Mave reacted.

Ex-Marine or not, the security guard never stood a chance. Not against the daughter of an assassin who'd been primed since youth to be a weapon.

Fueled by fear, her brain had no time to digest the flow of her body. It moved independently, channeling muscle memory—hours of one-on-one martial arts training with her father.

Block, base, over, up, swing.

It was over in seconds.

Her breath hitched. "I'm so sorry—" She trembled with adrenaline, scrambled down to Tag's figure collapsed at the foot of her vacated chair, and used the end of his tie to blot his nose.

The irony didn't escape her. For someone with a hitman for a father, she'd lived a relatively sheltered life. The only time she'd hurt anyone was years ago on a crowded public bus—a man had groped her from behind and had disembarked at the next stop nursing a black eye.

Tag moaned. She shook her head. "I can't—I won't be—"

Mr. Hendrick swore, pulling her focus. His back was pressed to the wall, his eyes clouded in fear. He fumbled with a two-way radio and called for backup.

Penn.

Mave scolded herself. No time for regret. They'd made up their minds, targeted her. Would cage her like they did her father.

With another kick in her bloodstream, she darted out from the offices and past the reception desk. A few guests stared and twisted their necks in surprise. Mave didn't give them the opportunity to inspect her. The soles of her feet slapping Italian marble tile, she sped toward the end of the lobby.

Her legs knew where they were headed before her brain registered their destination: downstairs along the galleria, the library. Moments later she rushed past its French doors and into the shadows of its tall bookcases.

On a night when everyone was busy celebrating, the hushed space was predictably abandoned. It always was. Mave threw herself into the chair she normally used during her breaks—the wingback furthest from the gloomy stone hearth. No fire was burning this evening. And in her hurry, she hadn't bothered with the light switch. Probably a good thing. Despite her wariness of the dark, she was better hidden this way. Besides, with its arched ceiling and deep interior, the library was more cavernous than claustrophobic. Its rumored ghost had drawn Mave from day one. She'd found as long as she avoided the black-stone hearth—which, no matter a fire, oddly emanated cold—the supposedly haunted hideaway was always empty and calming. And compelling. Like an airborne sedative laced its plumes of dust.

She lifted her knees onto the worn leather seat and hugged them. It was noticeably draftier this evening. Every sound seemed amplified: her slackening breath, the tinkling beads of the chandelier, the hissing vents, the occasional murmur of passersby in the galleria. She bit her trembling lip. Before she could stop them, fresh tears were spilling down her face.

She didn't want to hurt anyone. Ever. Not Birdie. Not Tag. Not even that creep on the bus years ago. *Birdie.*

The grief she hadn't allowed herself to feel in the offices now broke over her in full force. She'd barely known Elizabeth Everhart beyond their patron-employee relationship, and yet her heart wept for this woman. Birdie had never been unkind toward her, even when brusque. Deep down, Mave had respected her sharp mind and doubly sharp tongue. She'd admired her unapologetic vigor and finesse. Birdie had been a fighter. Right until the end.

(—*no!*)

The memory of the old woman's cry gripped Mave. Her vision blurred and her nose became stuffed. No one would believe her. Why should they when she had Birdie's blood on her hands? When she'd physically taken down an ex-Marine in front of the hotel's director? The staff here barely knew her. To them, she was nothing more than the new girl, the one who could conveniently help them find their misplaced wallets. That's it. Not even Bastian could speak of her innocence and offer her a solid character reference. She'd made sure to keep it that way—another Cain Francis Rule of Survival. *Protect yourself. Always be a step ahead, an arm's length away. That way, no one's ever in reach to hurt you. You understand?*

The few times she'd tested that rule, things hadn't gone well. Like the summer she'd opened up to a woman she'd befriended at a coffee shop, she'd found her calls blocked mere hours after she'd confessed about her odd ability to track the lost objects of strangers. Or the time she'd slept with a guy she'd met at a used bookstore and let it slip her father was in prison, she'd been dumped and discarded the morning after. Mave buried her face in the crux of her elbow, struggling to find a way out of this nightmare. Her mind whirled.

How much longer till police gained access to the Château and questioned its staff? How much longer till they examined the incriminating evidence and arrested her? One day? Two, tops? She couldn't hide in the library forever. Her only chance was to get moving and piece together the truth—one she had no hope of learning if she was penned up prematurely by Tag. It'd been the right decision to run. But escaping security had been the easy part. Now if she wanted to keep her freedom, she had to uncover the real murderer and present a solid case to the police that cleared herself of guilt. Mave sniffed and removed her tearstained glasses.

Her head was marginally clearer. She needed evidence. *Real* evidence. She had neither stabbed nor bludgeoned Birdie. A true criminal had. Someone had stolen the boxcutter from the giftshop, had outsmarted the hotel's cameras, and had timed the killing perfectly to implicate her. Mave ground her teeth as the realization hit.

Birdie's note had ordered a last-minute change in location, ensuring Mave was in the studio in the timeframe of the murder. Both weapons—the glass muller and the boxcutter—would have her fingerprints on them. Mave hadn't just been in the wrong place at the wrong time. She'd been framed. She shook her head in disbelief. But why? Who'd do such a thing?

Safety is an illusion, M&M. Danger is always lurking, biding its time until the right moment presents itself.

Birdie's history here—a woman that difficult and rich—she was bound to have rivals, enemies who might have been lured back to the hotel for the holidays. One final fête to return the Château to its former glory. A chance to revisit the pains of the past, old grudges, deep-seated jealousies.

Her mind flipped through the faces of guests and staff who'd recently dropped by the boutique. Only Birdie's stood out—a seasoned beauty with no expiration date, all the boldness and bite of a diva from classic cinema. *A step ahead,* she scolded herself. She'd gotten too comfortable in the shop, had let down her guard helping others, and look where it had—

"Mave Michael!" A baritone command from the library's entrance yanked her from her thoughts. "Time's up." As it turned out, she wasn't hiding at all.

She didn't have to view Penn's giant build filling the doorframe to imagine it there. She stood, her bulky glasses dropping from her lap. Her nerve endings reignited with coldfire.

"You come out now," Penn called, "and I'll tell 'em you played nice." His voice remained where it was—hadn't advanced. "And don't pretend you're not in there. There's a camera to your upper left." Mave tilted her head and squinted at the ceiling but it was too dark to make out any detail. "Smile," Penn sang, as if spying her every move. When she didn't respond, his sigh travelled the length of the room. "You're in the reading nook furthest from the fireplace."

She frowned. *Not bluffing.* But then why didn't he just come in and get her? He literally had her backed into a corner. She tiptoed closer, around a freestanding bookcase, and spotted him. All six foot six of him.

It was the most peculiar thing. He just stood there at the library's threshold, his baton held ready and his thick neck craned forward as if he were searching the room's shadows for a person beyond Mave. *If you know I'm here, why not sneak in, catch me unaware?* He continued scanning for something his eyes couldn't place. Too many hiding spots. Not enough light. In fact, the switch for the chandelier was inside—another reason for him to enter. Yet he remained glued to his spot. Thank god. He was built like a linebacker. Sure, she'd gotten past Tag, but Penn was nearly double her width and height—another species of threat altogether. The small of her back dampened with sweat. She didn't dare look away. What was he waiting for?

"Game's over. You got caught," he said. "But you don't come out now, and I promise, life's gonna get a whole lot worse for you."

But I didn't do it. Her eyes heated. *I'm innocent.*

The hiss of the vent seemed to grow stronger and the chandelier's strands clinked like wind chimes. Or was that her senses over-sharpening into delirium? The hair on her arms rose on end. Several things happened at once.

Darkness groaned. Penn swore loudly. And an object thumped by Mave's feet.

She jumped in her skin, her hand pressed to her heart.

"The hell was that noise?" Penn swayed his head, straining to see inside.

A book lay on the floor.

"Hey! What are you doing back there?"

Must've accidentally brushed it, she tried to rationalize, *caused it to fall.* Her heart continued its wild patter, unconvinced. Penn didn't seem about to charge, so she snapped up the dusty hardcover. She half-expected to hear the groan again but nothing happened. It was just a book.

She angled it toward the glow from the doorway. *The Fall of the House of Usher and Other Works.* Poe.

A theory popped into her head. Could it be that simple?

She glanced back at Penn, guarding her exit like a bull being held back by imaginary rope. Fear. But not of her.

Since first hearing about the Spirit of Dead Poets from Bastian, Mave had considered the story to be a rumor circulated by management to attract tourists—a fake haunting to add another layer of romanticism to the Château. In all her breaks spent in the library, she'd never encountered anything remotely ghostlike. *Until now.*

She immediately shut out the idea. Hound-dogging or not, she didn't believe in poltergeists. Admittedly, visiting the library had always given her a peculiar chill and sense of being watched, (especially when she'd first explored its stacks), but she'd grown accustomed to the feeling. In hindsight, it'd probably been her unconscious reaction to the security cameras.

Penn shifted uncomfortably. His tongue prodded the corner of his mouth. All he needed to do to disprove her theory was take a step forward. Instead, it was Mave who approached him. Slowly.

Cautiously—the heavy hardcover in her grasp.

He licked his lips. "There you are. That's it," he said, having spotted her at last. The pinch in his face relaxed. He held out his hand and signaled her forward like a traffic controller. "It's for your own good." Though she was seemingly cooperating, his gaze continued to dart around the dark library. The looming bookcases. Spiral staircase. Swaying chandelier.

Mave saw her opportunity. Closer. A bit closer. She had only one shot.

"Catch!" She pitched the book at his face. In the time it took him to swat the fluttering pages of verse, she dove and slid through his legs. A stitch tore under the arm of her dress.

"Oh no you—"

She scrambled to get to her feet, managed to rise to her knees, and Penn's meaty grip locked on her calf.

fIUE

Mave didn't even have to turn around. With an average-size man, it may not have worked. But given their height difference, they were positioned perfectly. She hammered her elbow into the security guard's kneecap, thrust her skull back and nailed him square in the groin. Stars exploded in her vision.

Penn grunted as he buckled and released her calf. She didn't stick around to check on his injury like she'd done with Tag. A racer from her starting block, she sprung up and bolted down the corridor.

Another two hundred yards and the hallway would split into a T. Centered there, a double-sided staircase would lead back to the main lobby. Multiple rabbit holes to elude the fox. Once out of sight, she could calm down and formulate a plan to save herself. While debating which route to take, Mave snuck a glance over her shoulder.

Penn was up, limping after her. And he looked none too happy about it.

Faster, Cain Francis growled between her ears. *You need cover. Now. Blend, dammit.*

People. Snatching her hem to her knees, she took the stairs two at a time and sprinted toward the growing reverberations of the waltz. Partygoers gradually swelled with the sound, congesting the antechamber outside the grand ballroom. Whether or not he'd been instructed to keep a low profile, Penn chose not to yell after her. Though conspicuous in her haste, she managed to rush past the onlookers and reach the first set of double doors without trouble.

"Darn red wine," she laughed when a woman blinked at her stained gown with concern. Mave snuck inside without waiting for her reply.

It was her first time in the grand ballroom, and despite herself, she was struck with wonder.

Le ciel. The sky.

The ceiling soared into a dome of moonlight, crowned with ornate cornices and floral frescos. Rows of chandeliers shimmered from tile work. Crystal everywhere caught candlelight, pulsed like stardust. Moving inside the space was like floating through…"Diamonds," Mave marveled.

She grabbed a champagne flute from a passing waiter. Her lips reflexively tightened. She'd rather drink sewage water than swallow a drop of alcohol, but it helped to have something in her hands. A quick scan for escape routes and an even quicker decision: she made a beeline for table number thirty-one.

Six chairs were temporarily unoccupied; the other six supported tipsy tourists distracted in conversation. In the romantic lighting, no one noticed as Mave's hands grazed a chairback, then another. Without stopping she exchanged her champagne flute for a shawl of black Chantilly lace, then palmed an iPhone and swept the shawl overtop it. A few steps farther, she slid the lace onto her shoulders and adjusted it to cover the bloodstain on her dress.

Penn must have entered the ballroom by now. Whether or not he'd spotted her…

Mave glided deeper into the belly of the fête, feigning interest in her cell. *Eyes in the back of your head, M&M.* Without need of a passcode, she accessed the phone's camera and switched it to mirror mode. Her hurried strides traced the perimeter of the crowded dance floor. She wasn't the only person without shoes. A few women had already abandoned their heels and opted to dance barefoot. A stout man in his forties wearing a HAPPY NEW YEAR top hat headed toward her. Blending in or not, she wasn't ready to waltz with a stranger. She abruptly switched direction, dipped her head, and avoided all eye contact as a jazz number commenced. Revelers spinning cheek-to-cheek switched to the swing. A lift and tilt of the camera's screen revealed Penn.

He'd spotted her, was tunneling through the crowd, his large figure demanding space and parting throngs of guests like a reaper in a wheat field. Not good.

Mave ceased her attempt at fitting in and accelerated toward the stage. Left—right. Past the orchestra, at the back of the ball-room, the catering door swung open. Mave tramped on the train of a woman's dress, mumbled an apology, and made a dash for it.

A waiter carrying three wine bottles exited the kitchen and froze in his tracks. A hefty waitress appeared at his side, spotting Mave next. "Excuse me, miss, you can't—"

"'S'okay, work here!" Mave blurted as she raced round them and into the busy kitchen. She barely avoided bumping into a man in an apron, swerving just in time but losing her shawl. Someone shouted a string of colorful curses. Dishes shattered and cutlery clattered. Mave didn't dare stop to assess the damage she'd caused. She'd worry about cuts to her feet later.

The room was a blur of steaming trays and white uniforms, counters arranged with plated art: chocolate delicacies, pink boules, caramel lattices. She hurriedly sought an escape. Three more doors. Three more wagers.

The first would connect to the delivery dock. Nothing there but recycling and garbage bins. Her second option: a fire exit with a crash bar funneling one-way to the great outdoors, (*no thank you*; not unless she wanted to freeze to death in the storm). That left the third exit: a generic EMPLOYEES ONLY route with an over-sized doorframe.

She'd lost her bearings. What else had Bastian shown her on this level, the cigar lounge? She'd gladly take second-hand smoke over a dumpster or hyperthermia.

Hedging her bets on the third door, Mave jumped for a short-cut. She scooted over a stainless-steel counter, something saucy wetting her hip, and cringed from the racket of more glass breaking and yells protesting her trail of wreckage. She collided with the imposing door, palms out, pushed on its brass handle—and frantically pumped the latch when it held. A check over her shoulder showed Penn skidding into the kitchen. *Pull!*

She yanked. The heavy door thrust forward and Mave released the breath she'd been holding. With a reverse jerk of the handle, she rushed into shadows.

A drop in temperature—chairs stacked tall, perched precariously on dollies to form a maze—she zipped through them and found herself in another, smaller, ballroom, this one empty. Even in darkness, the space was in obvious disrepair. Three arched windows rattled and filtered a haze from the ice storm. Mave could only see five steps ahead. Behind her the EMPLOYEES ONLY door jostled.

Run, run, run. Past a lidless grand piano upended on its side. Past a pillar with exposed wires curling out from its belly. Bits of crumbled stucco nicked her soles. She could only pray another escape route stood on the far side of this room.

Penn's lumbering steps echoed behind her. "Hey! Stop!"

She fled faster. There: another door, another crash bar, this one designated off-limits with a RESTRICTED AREA sign.

Parts of this Château are unsafe to wander, Bastian had warned on their first tour.

What lay beyond? Another crumbling hall? A boiler room? Outside? She couldn't last scantily dressed in a blizzard but neither could she endure being arrested and imprisoned. Not like her father. *Please…please don't be locked.*

In one continuous motion, she reached and slammed her way

through the mysterious doorway. Temporary relief flooded her system. She was still inside the shelter of the hotel—granted, disoriented in its bowels. The door behind her latched with a double click similar to a gun cocking. And Mave faced a new problem: absolute blindness.

Where am I?

Wind howled. A musty scent clogged her nose. Trying to catch her breath, she switched on the flashlight on the phone still clutched in her sweaty palm. Before her was a long, unmarked corridor lined with oil lamps. What glass remained intact was smudged with soot and grime. *Keep going.*

Her steps swept dirt and splinters of wood—pricks that caused her to hiss in pain. Everywhere, wallpaper puckered and peeled. Dust bunnies the size of her skull (*not* rodents, she insisted) skirted the chipped baseboards. She picked up her pace and glanced back. So far, no sign of Penn's pursuit. Had he spotted her breaking into this space? Scurrying ahead, the confirmation came just as she reached a split in the hall.

A sharp beam hit her back. Penn's flashlight.

Stiffening, she clicked off the phone and ducked left. The sudden crackle and sputter of his radio gave her a start.

"*Got her yet?*" barked a stuffed-up voice through the walkie. Tag. Mave pressed her back to the wall. They'd find her. Everything she was doing was too loud. The grate of her lungs. The thud of her chest.

"Gimme five," Penn rumbled. "Got her cornered past Queen's Hall, inside the old railway aisle."

Railway aisle? Beyond a passing comment about ongoing renovations, Bastian hadn't mentioned anything about a train during their tours. But a vague memory surfaced.

She'd skimmed online posts about the town's history before accepting the job in the giftshop. One had mentioned a train line that extended to the Château. A century ago, before the explosion of roadways, it had driven tourism and commerce to build railways direct to the most prominent hotels. If she recalled correctly, the Château's line had been shut for at least fifty years.

"'Member, we're dealing with a deadly con," Tag replied. "Use your Taser."

Any residual guilt Mave held for breaking the guard's nose vanished. Anticipating an agonizing jolt of electricity, her muscles flinched and fired. She stumbled down the dark hallway with her hands thrust forward.

"You got nowhere to go!" Penn goaded as if sensing her flight. "Locked in! Don't matter which way you turn. All ways in here lead to a dead end." The distance of his voice had lengthened. Maybe he'd ventured down the alternate hall. The beam of his flashlight was no longer visible. (Which meant she could no longer make out her pathway.) "No need to make this harder than it …"

She flitted away as fast as she could, willing her steps to be silent. The draft's whistle grew louder, drowning out the sound of her panting. Her shoulder skimmed the wall. The corridor curved. If her path led to a dead end as Penn claimed, why did it feel like she was approaching the howling mouth of a doorway?

But moments later the bend in the hall stopped and she met a wall. Mave frantically shuffled her hands across its rough surface. Brick. Boxed in. Her skin broke into renewed sweat.

Stay calm, M&M.

But how could she control her claustrophobia in complete darkness with a giant-man minutes from Tasering her? Lightheaded, her nails rapped metal bars.

What—?

She traced a crisscross diamond shape, then another. Anxiety overruling caution, she risked flashing the phone and released a sharp breath.

She stood before an elevator shaft. The bars she'd felt were from its rusted cage, cracked ajar on one side. Penn's footsteps returned within range. There was nowhere else to hide. Elevators would be the death of her.

She squeezed through the gap in the cage and onto the floor's ledge. The hem of her dress lifted in the draft and goosebumps crawled up her legs. As she balanced on her toes, heels in the air, she held out a hand and groped for support. The iPhone slipped from her grasp and perhaps five seconds later, clanked onto a surface below. It was little consolation: it wasn't a bottomless drop.

Her hand brushed a thick, braided cable. She gave it a tug to test its stability just as a glare caught the corner of her eye. Penn's flashlight? Was he closing the gap? *Now or never.*

Muscles flexed, jaw clenched, she gripped the cable, extended her other hand, and dropped her weight from the floor. Swallowing a cry, she clung for dear life as the arches of her feet pressed together and sandwiched the cable.

Easy-peasy, she tried to convince herself amid panicked pants. *One-Mississippi, two-Mississippi—just like gym class. In a normal school. Five-Mississippi, six-Mississippi...had I attended a school.*

She carefully slipped down the cable, inch by inch. Her biceps started to burn. She imagined plummeting to her death. Her skull cracking. More blood seeping. The descent felt like forever, until her feet touched cold cement.

She released the cable and fell onto all fours, resisting the urge to kiss the filthy ground. Her knuckles were still curled, inner skin, hot with blisters.

Get up, her father's voice ordered. Never the gym coach, always the drill sergeant.

Suppressing a groan, Mave fished through discarded nails and lumps of loose cement until she found the phone, cracked but otherwise functional. She'd lost track of Penn above and took a moment to inspect her surroundings.

She was in an abandoned, square basement. If she jumped, she could touch the ceiling. The walls alternated between decaying cinderblocks and plywood that had turned grey over time. No signage anywhere, though a few spots held flakes of paint.

Beyond the elevator shaft stood a single doorway boarded up

with planks—the source of the wind. Mave approached the doorway and recoiled from fluttering cobwebs. Batting off the sticky threads, she paused.

Penn had called the corridor above a railway aisle. Is that where she was? The closed-off passage to the defunct train line? Not seamlessly closed off, she noticed. A space the width of her hand existed between the two lowest boards. It would be tight, but the upside of being small was she could probably pass. Penn, on the other hand, would have zero chance of maneuvering through the boards without a sledgehammer. If this was indeed an old railway landing, she rationalized, that meant the tunnel must lead out.

She ducked, awkwardly straddled the boards, and wrung her body through like a clumsy contortionist. Along the way, her dress caught on a splinter and tore at her waist. Not ideal considering the little heat from the railway aisle disappeared altogether on the other side of the square room. Crawling through dust, Mave coughed, found her feet, and lit the phone.

She'd entered a decrepit, arched concourse. Organic ironwork ornamented a gateway.

Elbows tight to her ribcage and mobile outstretched before her, she crossed the threshold and stumbled down a short flight of stairs. Whether or not the cell lines remained dead aboveground, she had no hope of catching a signal this deep. Besides, who could she call without a passcode? The police? She had a decent amount of battery life left, but soon, she'd have to conserve the phone's energy and light.

Around her, damaged brickwork alternated with exposed ducts and broken pipes. The wind continued its sigh, occasionally whistling ominous notes as if someone were blowing into a hollow bottle. Her teeth began to chatter. The bottom of her feet stung. As her adrenaline sputtered and ebbed, exhaustion hit. The walk ahead of her could be long. Another labyrinth. She needed to rest for a moment, catch her breath.

Finding a small niche in the brick, Mave folded herself inside, huddled into a ball, and turned off the phone. Just a minute to warm her hands, she reasoned, puffing into her fists; a minute to adjust her eyes to the dark. Then she'd continue. She'd sneak her way back inside the hotel, find food and clothes, investigate in secret and lay low until the blizzard cleared.

As her consciousness melted into the darkness, she imagined a glittering countdown, the eclipsing secondhand of a clock. In the distance, the orchestra strummed "Old Lang Syne." And Cain Francis brushed her forehead with his graveled whisper.

Happy birthday, M&M.

SIX

JANUARY 1ST, 2009

It was midnight when the deadbolt spun and her father returned. Ever since she'd stumbled upon the dead body in the bathtub six months ago, she'd stopped wondering about his whereabouts. It was essential to pretend, deny, suppress at all costs. She didn't ask. He didn't lie. Tonight, along with his usual duffel bag, he carried in with him a cardboard box the size of a coffeemaker.

She paused the episode of *Friends*—the one where there was a blackout and Ross was trying to confess his crush to Rachel—and rolled off the couch to go heat his dinner in the kitchenette. Neither one of them reacted to the idiot crying *Happy New Year!* from a nearby fire escape. Silence was their routine. Her father detested greetings nearly as much as inane questions like *how was your day?*

Mave stared at the microwave's buttons, a plate of cold spaghetti and meatballs in-hand. They'd been in this furnished apartment for nearly two weeks and she still didn't know how to operate all its appliances. She spun the dial and accidentally hit the reset button for the clock. *12:00-12:00-12:00* blinked. She sighed, missing the microwave in their previous rental. Their old place had been infested with cockroaches so they'd had to switch buildings rather suddenly. At least that's what Cain had told her. Mave had never come across a roach in the entire three months they'd resided there.

"It's okay, already ate," Cain said, noticing her fiddling with the

buttons. He unlaced his boots. "Go sit. Got something for you."
She gave up trying to fix the clock, put the plate in the fridge, and
moved to the dining area. She sat with her legs folded on the chair,
elbows on the table, and propped her chin in her hands.

Cain removed his coat and gloves and stored everything neatly
inside the closet. She loved that about her dad. He hardly ever lost
anything. He was the tidiest person she knew.

He wore a Henley shirt in charcoal this evening. Matching grey
jeans. The average working Joe costume. She never knew what to
expect when he took off his coat. Some nights he'd return and peel
off his jacket to reveal a janitor's uniform. On others, he'd wear
hospital scrubs or a suit and tie. Cain Francis was a master chame-
leon. With an everyman face and build, he blended like nobody
else. The right costume could make him look tougher or kinder,
taller or shorter, older or younger. Even his eyes could shift colors,
mirroring the blue or green of his shirts. Mave often wondered
what he would settle on without the disguises. What style would
he prefer if left to his own devices: scruffy and relaxed; clean-shav-
en and sharp? Stirred by a yearning that always burned brightest
on her birthday, tonight she also pondered what had made her father this way.

What had his parents been like? Had her grandfather home-
schooled Cain? Taught him how to fight like Cain was teaching
her? She swallowed back her curiosity. Questions about the past
always ended in the silent treatment and a vein ticking in her father's forehead. She didn't want to feel that loneliness—to hit that
impenetrable wall. Not tonight. She picked the wood's grain on the
table with her thumbnail and did her best to hide her frustration.

He seated himself across from her and slid her the box he'd
been carrying. "Happy thirteenth, M&M." He leaned back and
crossed his arms in wait. Any emotion in his eyes was shuttered,
but the edges of his mouth held a curl. She knew that curl. It was
the same look he'd worn when she'd landed her roundhouse kick
last week.

Biting her lip, Mave rose onto her knees and pulled open the folded lid. Despite her melancholy, her face broke into a smile. She carefully lifted out a hydrangea in a glazed pot. The petals blushed pink and darkened to purple at their edges. She stuffed her face into the blooms, imagining a sunset, and inhaled. Sweet tang. Dark earth.

"Thought you'd like to brighten up the place." Cain's gaze never left her face.

Had he bothered to ask her what she'd wanted for her birthday, she would've requested that cute bottle of strawberry perfume she'd seen at the drugstore. Or the fancy eyeshadow palette zipped inside a heart-patterned case. But this was better. The beige apartment with its blank walls was in desperate need of cheer, and besides, Mave didn't know how to apply makeup. She figured, over the past year, the emergence of bras in the hamper and tampons beneath the bathroom sink had been an adjustment enough for Cain. Baby steps. She glanced around the drab furnishings, seeking the perfect spot for the flowers.

"Hang on," he said, "one more thing." He stuffed his hand into his pocket and dug out a birthday candle. Careful to avoid the plant's leaves, Cain perched it in the outer rim of dirt and lit the flame with a plastic lighter. "Make a wish."

Mave closed her eyes and blew out the candle. Each year she wished for the same thing. Not that it mattered. They kept moving anyway.

The realization killed the glimmer of hope she'd begun to entertain. The flowers no longer seemed cheerful. She saw them for what they were: an empty gesture, another type of lie. The plant would never take root here. Never. She wanted—no—she *needed* to watch them grow someplace permanent. But a real home was a gift Cain couldn't give her. Her cheeks warmed and her nostrils flared.

She sat on her hands to keep from smashing the pot against the linoleum tiles.

"Hydrangeas were your mother's favorite," he said, interrupting her brooding with a rare sentiment. He knew. He understood. And if he couldn't make it happen, he'd give her this: a memory.

Longing stirred deep inside the walls of Mave's chest. It was so strong, it pushed against everything else in her abdomen: her stomach, her heart, her lungs. On a rollercoaster of emotion, she untucked her hands from her seat and traced a petal.

"Pink ones?"

Cain gave a single nod.

She rested her cheek on the table and stared at the flowers. A fantasy of her parents on their wedding day materialized: a younger Cain in a tux, his arm wrapped around his bride's waist; Valeria Francis smiling and clutching a glorious bouquet of pink hydrangeas.

"How come there aren't more pictures of her?" None of her as a bride. None of her as a kid. Had she been an only child, too? Had she felt the itch of lost things like her? She knew next to nothing about her mother, apart from how she'd been killed in a car crash by a drunk driver. Even then, Mave's single memory of the tragedy was of her father.

On the afternoon of her death, Cain had come to pick her up from the sitter for the first time. He'd worn a ballcap with a logo of a bird. He'd lifted her to his chest and held her too tightly. And his skin had smelled of chlorine.

As far as Cain Francis was concerned, from that point on he and Mave had become a finite bloodline of two. Any questions she voiced about any other family, he evaded.

Her father lowered his head onto the table so he could meet her gaze. "You're all the picture I need." He reached out and brushed her bangs from her eyes. They stayed that way a minute. Mave was afraid to blink and have the moment end.

Cain slid a paper napkin on the table toward her. When he spoke next, his voice had lost any warmth.

"Clean yourself up and go to bed." He stood, leaving her alone with the napkin fluttering under her breath. Mave shut her eyes as the refrigerator's motor gurgled awake. Only then did she realize her lashes were wet.

SEVEN

JANUARY 1ST, 2021

A hiss of air. A bed of brick. Mave rolled and tugged the covers over her shoulder. *Hang on. I shouldn't have a—*

Her eyelids snapped open. She focused on blackness, the fog of sleep clearing from her brain.

Lesson one: when you napped inside a closed-off tunnel, you had no idea of the time of day when you woke.

Lesson two: if you acquired a blanket from thin air during said-sleep, chances are you weren't alone.

She jerked upright and, heart thrumming, shuffled for the mobile digging into her hip. Her surroundings lit up as she squinted at the cracked screen: January 1st, five to seven in the morning. She'd slept through the night—still curled inside the niche in the wall. Alert. Still barefoot and dirty, her tattered clothes in place.

Sour bile laced her gut. She ground her teeth, kicked herself for dozing off, and inspected her arms and thighs as Cain had taught her. No trace of needle pricks or harm. No Penn, no police, pursuer or threat. Everything was as she remembered it before she accidentally crashed. Except....

Her brow furrowed. She brushed the white terrycloth now bunched at her waist: a bathrobe she'd mistaken for a blanket. *Château du Ciel* was embroidered in gold floss on its breast pocket. *How'd I get this?*

A shiver travelled her spine. She didn't believe in sleep-tele-portation, dream incantations, or spontaneously appearing spa wear. Someone from the hotel must have discovered her, tucked her in and then, what—left? Back through the elevator shaft? But why? Who'd do such a thing? As unsettling as it was, she wasn't about to refuse an offering of warmth.

She stood and slipped on the robe. It wrapped her hip to hip. Dropping the phone into the pocket, she knotted the belt and burrowed her chin into plushy cotton. It smelled of lavender. She hugged her arms around her middle.

Where was she? How was she going to get out, avoid blame for murder? A hysterical wheeze scraped her throat.

Slow down. Breathe. Easier questions.

She eagerly inhaled the lavender, rubbed her eyes, and eased back her panic.

When had she last eaten? Yes, she could answer that. Yester-day, early-afternoon; she'd snacked on an apple. For a moment, she considered retracing her steps aboveground, back to the kitchens. But it was too risky. Assuming she could even scale the elevator shaft with her blistered palms—assuming security wasn't now pa-trolling the restricted railway aisle—Penn had claimed re-entry into the second ballroom would be barred. Locked in, he'd warned. There was only one sure way to freedom. She blew out a shaky breath.

Get back inside and dig for the truth. Onward.

Ignoring her stinging feet, she flashed her phone and wan-dered deeper into darkness. The ground was cold, filthy; nothing but pipes, rusted rails and rotting railway ties vanishing into obliv-ion. What she wouldn't give for a pair of winter boots. Sneakers. Matching terrycloth slippers. At this point, she'd even take her abandoned stilettos from the break room, (heels she'd had to train herself to balance in at age fifteen, much to the displeasure of Cain Francis).

Eyes and ears open, M&M.

Every few yards Mave flashed her phone. The absence of natural light distorted the perception of time. Without the cell to correct her, she might have mistaken five minutes for fifty. The trek was unwelcoming, each new stretch of tunnel as dilapidated and deserted as the last. Overtop the whooshing silence, the draft would shift, a random pipe would moan, and Mave would shiver. It wasn't until a half hour passed that something varied: an animal scampered by her ankles.

Rat.

She jerked her light in its direction, tripped and rear-ended into a pipe. Mave focused on the vermin, a cry caught in her lungs and, just as quickly, relaxed.

Against the brick to her left—now as still as a garden gnome—the reflective eyes of a tabby cat gleamed back at her. The stray blinked, bothered by the beam, and darted away.

Mave hurtled after it. Given her empty stomach, she wasn't averse to becoming a freegan and, who knew, the fat cat might lead her to a dumpster or better yet, to a forgotten door into the Château's galleria.

Mave pictured the giftshop: the vitrines, the snow globes, silk scarves and souvenirs; a basket of Belgium chocolates at her fingertips. Wistfulness bloomed inside her chest. Over the past few years she'd loved working in giftshops, the one at the Château in particular. She figured it was the solitude combined with the transient guests; the scent of mints and confections wrapped in fancy papers; the tinkle of bells whenever someone entered. She sighed, reaching a split in the tunnel, then frowned and slowed her pace.

She'd lost track of the cat.

Dismissing her feline guide, she shifted to find the ground rails and paused. A delicious scent teased her nose.

She cocked her neck forward. No hound-dogging necessary. The draft ahead was unmistakably saturated with dregs of bacon fat. Maybe she was beneath the hotel's restaurant. Or breathing in the exhaust from the kitchens. Neither particularly made sense in a train tunnel, but what did she know about century-old engineering and construction?

She followed the scent down an alternate tunnel crawling with thick, black cables like the roots of a tree. The smoky flavors drew water from her mouth. A few steps in, and ambient light began to blend with the beam of her phone. She zeroed in on its source.

Twenty feet beyond, several bricks were missing and the wall had a narrow break. She tucked away the mobile and snuck closer. Seconds later, the drone of a woman's voice drifted, growing louder, clearer with each step Mave took. Chinese. She couldn't understand a word, but she recognized the speaker's intonation—a news reporter from a television or radio broadcast.

She approached at an angle, hunkered low, tightly clutching the lapels of her robe. The smell of bacon thickened, coating the roof of her mouth. It had to be coming from beyond the break in the wall. And layered beneath it, another distinct tang: cigarette smoke. Mave pressed herself to the brick.

"…huā hé jù huì jiāng chí xù dào zhōu mò. Qǐng chá kàn wǒ mén dè wǎng yè hé diǎn jī chá xún zuì xīn jiāo tōng…"

She bit her lip, crept low to the ground, and inched her neck forward toward the mysterious crevice. Her eyes widened.

Not a crevice. A cave. A well-stocked, plugged-in cave full of hoarded things: books piled high along floor-to-ceiling pipes, two computer monitors connected to a subwoofer—one displaying a toggling screen of the hotel's hallways and quarters. And amidst it all, a shirtless man with his back turned, frying bacon on a portable cooktop.

Mave gawked from her hiding spot. Thankfully the Chinese news broadcast switched to a pop song and drowned out her pounding heartbeat.

He stood over his pan, took a drag of his cigarette, and absentmindedly scratched his head of thick, brown hair. *Who are you? What is this place?*

Though only visible from behind, he was obviously thin and

fit: broad shoulders, subtle cords of muscle wrapping his ribcage. Threadbare jeans hung from his hips. Mave made a conscious effort to snap her mouth shut and swallowed. Wrist to shoulder, his right arm was inked with symbols and branch-like patterns. He dropped his cigarette butt into a soup tin and pulled out a remote from his back pocket. The radio shut off. He slid the pan off the burner.

What was he doing…stirring? Then she saw.

"Ah! Shit." He blew onto a piece of sizzling bacon, batting it from one hand to the other. More choice words in perfect English escaped his lips before he threw back his head and swallowed the strip in a single bite. Her curiosity burning alongside her pulse, Mave wished he would turn so she could see his face. She may have spotted a flash of beard, but it'd been too quick to be certain. He licked his greasy fingers and stilled.

"Don't act shy now, māomī," he said, startling her further. "We both know you're here to steal my breakfast."

He knew she was starving? Still, Mave thought with affront, she wouldn't go as far as to steal. Not yet. Goosebumps pebbling her skin, she gathered her courage to come out from behind the wall. Granted, he appeared a healthy male a head taller than her, but her father had prepared her for moments like this. If he tried anything funny, she could take him. Just like she'd taken on Tag. And Penn. She shoved away the unpleasant memories of the security guards before they could spiral into alarm.

Straightening her spine, Mave stepped forward just as the stranger dropped a strip of bacon to the ground. She was so puzzled, she didn't notice the cat zipping for the handout until it was too late.

She tripped. The cat yowled. And the half-naked man twisted to find Mave splayed on her hands and knees.

Part II

POEM FOR A KILLER

1. WHAT LIES FORGOTTEN

Girls disappear all the time. From late-night parties, dirt paths, and residential roads across the world, they vanish. We look for them. We look some more. But there is always another report, another unexplained absence, a new girl missing with a fresher scent to catch. And so it goes.

Eventually, a number of girls are forgotten.

EIGHT

FROM THE RED BOOK OF THE DEAD

MARCH 3RD, 1991

Dear Rie,

Arrived a few days ago. It's exactly like you described! A gorgeous mountain retreat on steroids. The silverware at dinner alone is worth more than my meal plan back home, and my dust allergies have yet to forgive you (even if my student loan officer is high-fiving you). I mean, I knew your family was rich, but wow. This place. I keep thinking I'm in a dream.

I've been super careful given the contract. You're the only person who knows I'm here. My stepmom thinks I'm doing an internship in NYC for the semester. (Pretty sure she was drunk when I convinced her, so yeah. Same old, same old.) Can you believe it? All of our guesses were way off. It's not a mistress. It's his sixteen-year-old daughter, Caroline. She's four-months pregnant!

Makes sense, I guess, why he hired me on top of the OBGYN he's got on-call. Mr. Law thinks I can sympathize and act like a good role model, like a surrogate big sister or something. He kept mentioning how important it is for Caroline to be around a responsible, level-headed young woman—one who knows the value of maintaining a wholesome reputation. (Yeah, he seriously used the word *wholesome*.) It's like he thinks I'm an old-school lady's companion. But hey, I'll take it.

Before leaving yesterday, he set me up in a huge suite. We're talking almost four times bigger than our old dorm room. At first I thought it was a mistake. A king-sized, four-poster bed draped in fox fur is hardly what I'd call a bunk for the hired help. But the suite adjoins Caroline's, so it's more than convenient. Plus I get the impression no one's lined up to take over my room. Most floors seem to be empty. In the evenings, the hotel is dead-quiet except for the wind. Every time I pass through the lobby, I can hear my steps echo. It's eerie. Maybe it's the rainy season? Does the hotel get busier in springtime? I'll have to ask your mother next time I see her and thank her again for the referral.

I know technically I'm not supposed to write to anyone—can't tell you how many times in the past forty-eight hours Mr. Law has drilled me on "maintaining the utmost discretion" and "the consequences of breaking my NDA," and on and on—but I figure you don't count, right? (Just in case, though, don't mention Caroline or this letter to anyone, okay?)

I admit, even though things are breathtaking here, it feels a bit lonely. Mr. Law says the phone jacks are all being replaced, so the lines keep going dead. And there's no TV in my room. It doesn't help that I've been listening to Caroline cry for the past two days. Nonstop. I get that it's her hormones but still... So far she's been very standoffish despite her tears, almost skittish. Even though we're only four years apart, she seems so much younger. Then I think to myself: knocked up, junior year. Ouch. I can't imagine how horrible that would feel—to have my entire future upended in a heartbeat. I'm afraid to press too much. My *Nursing Practice and Theory* textbook didn't exactly prepare me for this.

If it were you, what would make you feel better? And before you say sex and a hit of X, the only guy I've seen lurking around here is your brother. And my access to drugs is limited to raspberry leaf and ginger root. So unless you have a pregnancy-safe herbal mix for tripping...

Write me back, okay? But be sure to address your letter to the old concierge, Rahul. He's been nice enough to act as our smuggler. Something about his crinkly warm eyes makes me trust him. Your brother though, he's another story.

MARCH 13ᵀᴴ, 1991

Dear Abee-cakes,

Can't believe it was my idea for you to take the semester off. Partying is not the same without you. I miss you already and so glad you secretly wrote.

Okay, first: whatever you do, do not bring up the hotel's lack of hustle and bustle with Birdie. My mother has attachment issues. She hasn't left that place for over a decade and, I swear, it's like she's developed a distorted notion that the hotel is a reflection of herself. Underrated glamour, sophistication in hibernation… Who knows what garbage Dom has been feeding her ego? Have you bumped into Dominic, by the way? If not, you will soon. He drops by the Château regularly to check in on Mother. And by check in, I mean he's banging her even though he's her employee and young enough to be her son. (I know. I'm gagging.)

Which brings me to warning two: if you think Charlie is bad, wait till you meet Dom. He's a horrible flirt, and unlike my annoying brother, he has this preppy Tom Cruise thing going on that tempts you into flirting back. But he's also Birdie's plaything which—I don't know about you—kind of kills the buzz. He'll jump through whatever hoop Mother lays in front of him as long as his paychecks are signed. It's pathetic. Thank god you have Rahul on your side. He's a real gem. And don't be fooled by his polite, work-horse demeanor in front of guests. I know a fellow mischief-maker when I meet one.

Caroline Law. Wow. I don't really know the girl, but I'm familiar enough with her uptight father. Let me guess: he dumped Caroline under your care with strict instructions, then left without so much as a goodbye to his mess of a daughter. No wonder she's devastated. Like I already told you, Immanuel Law is a super right-wing politico—never a wrinkle on his shirt or a hair out of place. Actually, he and Mother became "good friends" before I was born. Pretty sure they were an item back in the day and have been hooking up, on and off ever since. (Yes, another age gap. Not as extreme as Dom, but Mother has a type. Likely her shrink labels it a twisted Oedipal complex).

Caroline must feel so lost inside. And being secluded in the lap of luxury probably isn't helping. No girlfriends or social life. No boyfriend. If there's one thing I learned from my time up at that hotel, it's that it can swallow you up if you're not careful. Just look at Birdie.

MARCH 22ND, 1991

Dear Rie,

So excited to hear back from you! Outside of these walls, you're my only contact with the world. I thought I'd be settled in by now but the opposite is true. I can't get used to all this lavishness in nature. It's like I'm trapped in a castle at the turn of the century. How did you spend your summers here? I know you were just a kid then, but didn't you feel cut off from everyone? The more I experience this hotel, the more it seems like I'm wandering inside a bubble. Ironically, Caroline keeps a snow globe with a miniature of the Château on her nightstand. I find her gazing into it often. I wonder if she feels it pressing on her, too. The quiet.

Okay, maybe I'm being dramatic. Except having no functional phone is starting to get to me.

Since Mr. Law has been away for a stretch, I naively visited the front desk and tried requesting that we be moved to another, more "modern" set of rooms. You'd think a hotel that splurges on dried rose petals in its soap could at least offer its guests HBO. But turns out Mr. Law left instructions with staff: under no circumstances are we allowed to transfer suites; we are to stay in *these* particular rooms. Isn't that weird? No one will tell me why. And I can't help but think it's because Mr. Law is a control freak.

When I signed my contract, he made it clear that phone calls were strongly discouraged. Only this seems a bit over the top, right? Like it's assumed I'll be tempted to blab if I call anyone. Maybe I'm exaggerating again. I'm half-tempted to ask Rahul for help. Except the concierge's desk is smack in the middle of the lobby with no privacy whatsoever. And I don't trust the rest of the staff. They have shifty eyes. For all I know they're on Mr. Law's payroll, too. What about your brother? Is he reliable? You think I could ask to borrow the phone in his suite?

Mind you, I don't want to give him the wrong idea. I've caught him staring at me a bunch of times—mostly during my evening walks. I think he's noticed my routine and started waiting for me. He always seems to be in the mezzanine, smoking by himself in a group of armchairs, a tumbler of whiskey dangling from his fingertips. He never speaks to me. Just stares. Honestly it's a bit creepy. If he wasn't your brother, I might be worried.

NINE

JANUARY 1ST, 2021

A scramble of movement. A streak of fur. In the time it'd taken Mave to roll to her feet, he'd ducked, slipped a mask onto his face, and transformed into a porcelain monster: four eyes, three noses, and two mouths flanking a frown. In his left hand, he raised a spatula like he was about to swat a fly. Stunned for words, Mave didn't bother pointing out that his pan of hot grease was a better weapon. On the balls of her feet, arms spread, she was tensed like a surfer approaching a tidal wave—caught between the need to flee and to ogle the danger before her.

"Get out." His eyes were coal-black through the holes of his mask, nothing like the lifeless fake ones jutting from his left and right temple. It was like staring at a grotesque sculpture: one head, multiple faces. She remained mesmerized, stunned—a sting in her knee where she'd skidded.

The mask had a horseshoe-shaped cutaway that revealed his real mouth and chin, and she'd been right. He had a beard. Though at the moment it was hard to tell where the facade ended and the man began. His monstrous disguise was at odds with his unmarred torso. Even with her gaze pinned to the mask, it was hard not to notice the rest of him. Flexed. Inked.

"I said get out." Fierceness flashed in his eyes.

Excellent advice. He was mad—all edges. She ought to run. *And go where?* Her legs were primed, a clear path to the tunnels at her back. It was only logical she escape him. But Cain Francis had made sure Mave's logic had been molded differently than most.

Watch the way his spatula trembles, M&M. How his lungs pull in too quick. It was almost as if *she* were the threat. *Masked*, Cain's voice pointed out, *he's the one hiding. From you.*

She tilted her head and narrowed her eyes. "Why? Are you"— her voice cracked and they spoke overtop one another—"afraid of me?"

"—deaf or something?"

She kept her gaze fixed on him, either held in his stare or too afraid to look away. Perhaps both. "What is this place?"

"Nowhere." Even with his mask and spatula still raised, he gave the impression of a child caught in an act of mischief. Following a gut instinct—her father's careful teachings to filter prey from predator—she ignored his pose of threat and turned her inspection to her surroundings.

The piled books had labels on their spines, library codes. A Tiffany lamp sat atop a room service cart doubling as a desk—paper pads, hotel stationary. Everything was familiar, right down to the white damask duvet bunched on a mattress in the corner.

"You're stealing from the hotel? Wait," she touched the embroidered monogram on her breast, "are you the one who left me this?"

The scratch and static of a walkie-talkie distracted them both. Mave spotted the radio at the same time as he dropped the spatula.

"Shit. Okay," he mumbled to his feet. "Bad idea... would happen..."

"*Oasis Spa to custodial, over.*"

She choked on her breath. "Is that the *hotel* channel?"

He quickly reached for the radio, switched off its volume while muttering in neither English nor Chinese. Spanish? He dragged his hands through his hair. "You're still here. Why are you still here?"

Any number of good reasons. In fact, now that she'd gathered her wits, Mave had no intention of leaving. Whoever he was, not only did he have food and electricity, he had security cameras streaming on his computer and access to staff radio lines. How much of the footage had he witnessed last night? What did he know?

She stared at the images of the Château on the computer screen flipping from hallway to hallway and held the lapels of her robe. Its softness beneath her fingers offered her a wary hope. He'd blanketed her inside the cold tunnels, (whether or not he cared to admit it). She was about to ask him for more help when something else caught her eye.

Mave opened and closed her mouth like a fish. She moved to the second computer, the one with a sleeping monitor.

"Hey, hang on, you can't just—"

She picked up the thick-rimmed glasses, half-folded and dangling from the corner of the flat screen, and peered into its clear lenses. *Can't be.*

"How'd you get these?" Her voice shook. She struggled to recall where she'd dropped her glasses.

"Those aren't—it's not what you—" The answer materialized in her mind at the same time as he snatched the frames and tossed them aside. "You need to leave."

A series of connections formed in her mind. The library. The glasses. The rumors.

"What? Stop looking at me like that."

All this time—all those breaks in the library when her unconscious had hinted someone was watching her—she'd dismissed it as an effect of the hotel's superstition, but now...

"It was you."

"You're not making any—"

"You're the fake ghost from the library." As if she didn't have enough evidence, she reached for a book and waved it in the air for him to refute.

"What?"

"The Spirit of Dead Poets. You're him. The one who groaned yesterday and dropped Poe at my feet."

He scratched behind his porcelain ear. "No idea what you're on about. You're clearly lost and confused. Look," he seized the book from her and dropped it onto another pile, "what do you want?" He crossed his arms. Mave wasn't convinced.

"Can you take off that mask?"

"Easy. No. That all?"

She needed answers. Who was he really? What did *he* want? Maybe she could offer him a trade. She angled her head toward him, cocked her chin, and drew in a deep breath.

"Jesus," he sighed and rubbed his temples. Mave ignored him and concentrated on getting a read. He cleared his throat. "Hate to interrupt, but mind telling me what the hell it is you're doing?"

Beyond the scents of bacon and cigarettes that saturated the space, there was nothing. Not even a blip. He was blank.

She pulled back and huffed in frustration. "Seriously? You're not looking for *anything*?"

He shook his head. "Again. No idea what you're talking—"

"Haven't you lost something special?" She blinked at the stacks of books surrounding them. "Like, I don't know, a first edition of Walt Whitman you need to find?" Once again, she found herself wishing she could see his entire face. As it was, the only thing on view from his neck up was his mouth twitching into a tight smile.

"First off, if I did have a rare copy of Whitman, I wouldn't be so stupid as to lose it. Second"—he shrugged, distracting her with the movement—his shoulders, his arms—"don't own things. Don't lose things. Anything else before you go?"

"Can you … ?" She gestured toward his chest, hoping the shadows kept him from spotting the sudden flush on her cheeks.

Bracketed beneath the mask's gaping frown, his mouth opened. He slowly circled his head as if trying to read her mind. "*Can I…?*"

"I mean…" It was the middle of winter. "Don't you own a shirt?"

He glanced down at himself as if surprised to find his bare chest a topic of conversation. He scratched his head. "Technically, I don't own anything—like I said."

She tried not to gape. "But aren't you freezing?"

"You always this uptight?"

"I can practically see my breath clouding." She ignored the snub, aware she was rambling to appease her nerves. "Did you know there's an ice storm outside? Like record-breaking. How can someone not want to wear a coat, let alone a shirt during an ice storm?"

He shrugged those stupid shoulders again. "Don't like doing laundry." But he leaned around a pile of books, rifled and threw on a hoodie. "There. Happy now?" Without waiting for a reply, he spread out his palms and cautiously reached for her like she was a delicate, jittery creature he was trying not to startle.

"What are you doing?" Cain's *don't-let-them-touch-you* rule seemed to evaporate with the remainder of her thoughts. His gentle hold on her elbows sent a jolt of electricity through her body. She was so sidetracked by the sensation, his warm hands, she almost missed the fact he was steering her out.

"Thanks for your visit." His voice had dropped, his words scratching. "Don't come back. And don't tell anyone you found this place or met me here. Got it? Not a word. Not a soul. *Ever.*"

Rather than frighten her off, his parting sentiment sparked an idea. A cruel one. She couldn't. But she was also out of options.

Mave got as far as the threshold to his hideout before digging in her heels and resisting his push. Either he'd seen on-screen what she'd done to the security guards or he wasn't brash enough to try to out-muscle her. Her stomach knotted. She barely managed a whisper.

"And what if I do tell?" It was wrong of her. He'd helped her with the bathrobe and in return she was threatening to expose his secret.

Still grasping her elbows, he stiffened behind her. "What did you say?" A standoff. Neither one of them dared move.

Mave's heartrate picked up. She was certain he could hear it galloping through her skin. "I know the way in here," she lied. She had a terrible sense of direction. Without a cat or scent to follow, she'd be lost. But there was no other choice. No going back. "You're a thief. A con," she continued, hating every word. "What if I tell everyone—starting with Mr. Hendrick?"

His breaths fell on the crown of her head. She counted them. At thirteen, she'd given up on his response, was ready to turn, take it all back. But he spoke.

"And thus I clothe my naked villainy / With odd old ends stol'n out of holy writ, And seem a saint, when most I play the devil."

Her mind spun. Was he speaking in riddles? In verse? She reviewed what little she'd learned about him. "Whitman or Poe? No wait, that's—"

"Shakespeare. What do you want?"

She couldn't do this alone. And one thing was certain: he was an outcast. Just like her. No normal person would be holed up inside a decrepit tunnel listening to Chinese radio on New Year's Day. She thumbed her terrycloth, hedging her bets. The library. The bathrobe. The security footage. "I didn't kill her."

For a beat, he ceased breathing altogether. "I don't care." His jaw sounded clenched. "What do you want?"

"Help me. Help me and I won't tell anyone about you or where to find you. I promise. I just need access. In private. Your security footage. Your radio. A way back inside. Anything you have—anything you know to help me prove my innocence."

"Innocence? You're blackmailing me and you expect me to believe—"

"Please."

Whether it was the desperation in her voice or something else, he released her elbows. Mave spun to find him with his lashes lowered, contemplating her proposition. She tried not to fidget as his gaze travelled her face, pausing over each of her irises before settling on her mouth.

"I help you sneak around, find your proof, and you forget we ever met." He leaned close enough for the tobacco smoke of his hair and clothes to drift, close enough to cast her in his slice of midnight. "Deal?"

She locked her knees to stop their tremble. "Deal," she said before he could change his mind.

He remained where he was, in her space, no doubt resenting her, trying to flex his muscles and intimidate her. He was oblivious to her upbringing. Mave sucked in her ribs and squeezed her fear into a tight ball. This wasn't her first pissing contest. She lifted her chin.

"Well then," he shifted back with his palm out, inviting her to reenter the depths of his strange world, "after you, Mave Michael."

TEN

Mave angled past him with her hands on her hips, hoping to hide her newfound anxiety.

She eyed his empty frying pan and the hollow of her stomach rumbled. She bit her lip. Without a word he reached beneath his service cart and pulled out a demi-baguette wrapped inside a linen napkin. He held it out for her to take, then began rolling a new cigarette.

Too busy ripping into the crust with her teeth, she didn't bother asking him how he'd come to obtain freshly baked bread. Stolen or not, right now nothing tasted better.

"So what should I call you?" she asked between bites. "I mean, what's your name?" She spotted a barstool—one likely belonging to the cigar lounge—and made herself comfortable. She strained to pin down who he was, his motives, why he lived this way.

He lit his cigarette with a silver Zippo and flopped back-first onto his mattress, arms spread like a Christ figure. Rather than respond, he stared at the ceiling.

Strong silent type. Fine.

She swiveled to his two computer screens, hoping to get started with the security footage. Both monitors were asleep. She leaned forward, hit the keyboard, and blinked at the login prompt. "Holden Robert Frost?" she read mid-bite.

His head rolled in response as she swallowed a too-big chunk of bread. She could use some water but was afraid to push her luck.

"Don't touch my stuff."

"You prefer to be called the Spirit?"

"I prefer you went away."

His reply sounded like one Cain would give: that of an antisocial criminal. She lowered the bread to her lap, her appetite suddenly gone. Her eyes widened. What if he was more than a thief—what if he was guilty of darker deviancies. Like Cain. "Yesterday evening—did you—where were you?" she stuttered before she could edit the accusation.

His laughter built slowly, as if he were picturing killing Birdie in his mind, trying it on for size. "Ah, fuck," he muttered to the ceiling, "day just gets better and better." He took a drag of his cigarette while ignoring her.

She crossed her arms. "Well?" She pressed on principle, her anxiety replaced with affront. But his reaction was enough to tell her she'd been ridiculous to ask.

He turned his head to her again, his humor spent. "Right here," he drawled. "Or do you need to check the timestamps on my browser history to believe me?"

She batted the smoke filling the space and attempted to save face—as if she hadn't just demanded his alibi. "Mind putting that out?"

He looked her straight in the eye, brought his cigarette to his mouth, and pulled a long, deep drag. The wind whistled through a nearby pipe. She struggled to keep a neutral expression as the tip of the cigarette flared and frayed. She wanted to look away. Wanted to act unaffected, unaware of his every move. Even when he puckered a long, lazy kiss of smoke into a ring.

She bit off another chunk of baguette. "Nice trick." She used the dinner napkin to wipe the crumbs off her face. "Anyone ever tell you it's incredibly gross?" Why then did it provoke her curiosity for more? Clearly, it'd been too long since she'd been alone with a man. Her standards had plummeted to a new low.

"Exactly why I avoid people." He smiled dryly, his dark eyes veiling secrets.

She wished he wouldn't. She wished he'd take off that awful mask. At least then she wouldn't feel as if she was conversing with a potential monster. Was he scarred? Just eccentric? She didn't know what to think. His lifestyle was appalling. "So, what, you just live here?" Four grey walls. Stolen junk everywhere. No windows for miles. If it weren't for the lamplight, she'd likely be screaming by now. "Why?"

"Enough questions." He sat up. "I agreed to help you sneak around, not tell you my life story."

"So you're saying you've been down here a long time?" He couldn't be that much older than her. And given the amount of hotel contraband surrounding her, it seemed he'd been settled here for a few years, minimum.

He pressed his thumb to the center of his temple like he had a headache, smoke billowing around him.

"Fine." She crossed her arms. "I need your password."

It was obvious he'd raised an eyebrow beneath his mask.

"The security footage," she clarified, eager to return her attention to the computer screen. "Apparently I'm the only person recorded entering Birdie's studio yesterday, but I find that hard to believe, seeing as someone else killed her. Another person had to have walked those halls."

Perching the cigarette between his lips, he shifted next to her. She made to get up and give him his stool, but he put out his hand. "Stay." He leaned across.

Mave pressed into the backrest, her feet not touching the rung, and pretended to relax while battling her over-sensitized nerves. Up close, the tree branches inked on his forearm were designed from fine script. Poems. The verses rippled as he typed his password too quick for her to follow. Thankfully, he shifted upright, giving her space to breathe again.

"Give me a date and time. Footage is only good for forty-eight hours."

"What? That's it, two days?"

He exhaled a stream of smoke. James Dean would be applauding from his grave. "Unless it's uploaded to an archive in that time span, the recordings are erased."

"So I can't watch a week's worth of footage from the twenty-third floor?" She'd been planning on studying Birdie's frequent visitors and drawing connections.

"No one can."

She sighed and helped herself to a Château du Ciel notepad and pen. Cops in movies always jotted down leads—crafted profiles with photographs, clippings, maps and pushpins, charted elaborate connections on giant whiteboards. In comparison, the three-by-five paper on her lap seemed pathetic. "Okay, I guess," she tapped the pen nervously, "could we go backwards then? Start with last night, midnight and make our way to the morning of the thirty-first?"

Holden flicked his stare to her hand. She ceased rapping the pen against the notepad. Annoying him wasn't going to help her cause. "Please?" She tacked on a smile as incentive.

He ran her the tapes from yesterday. Twice. Both times, apart from Mave, Mr. Hendrick and security during the incident, the sole person to have walked the twenty-third floor was a dark-haired woman.

"Housekeeping," Holden said when she asked. "Birdie's personal maid."

"How do you know who everyone is?" She recorded *maid* on her sad little notepad.

"Don't. Birdie's been hiring and firing cleaners for years and no one else bothers with the penthouse. She rooms on the same floor. That's where she's leaving from—here." He paused the footage, freezing a bird's-eye view of the housekeeper exiting her room. Mave added the time to her notes: five minutes to midnight.

"And she heads to the service elevator—not to Birdie's suite. Huh. Any chance her room interconnects with Birdie's studio?"

"Birdie's quarters are in an entirely different wing, so no."

"And this captures the entire floor?" She found herself thinking of the cameras' potential blind spots again.

"Not exactly. Only the elevator banks and entrances to the occupied spaces are captured: Birdie's suite and the maid's room."

Mave chewed on a hangnail, her subconscious nagging her. Something about the footage was off. "Could someone have tampered with this recording?" It appeared flawless, and yet....what was it that bothered her?

"Doubt it. Hendrick updated the hotel's security system less than a year ago. The cameras aren't exactly high def, but still, hacking in isn't like uploading a clip on YouTube. To fool around with the recording, you'd need all sorts of tricks to bypass the firewalls."

"Isn't that what you're doing?"

He shot her a look that bordered on offended. "Don't hack. Just stream."

"How?"

"We're not discussing me, remember?" He found his makeshift ashtray, the soup tin, and stubbed out the remains of his cigarette.

"Right." She reviewed her thoughts aloud, hoping to draw out the source of her suspicion. "Yesterday, while they were keeping me inside the offices, Mr. Hendrick asked Tag to find Birdie's maid. He must have been referring to this woman." Her suspicion veered in an alternate route. What did the housekeeper know? What had she told management? "Do you think she'd be willing to talk to me?"

"Depends." He crossed his arms, the indigo lines on his forearm flexing. "You got something to blackmail her with, too?"

She deserved the slight, and yet—Mave gritted her teeth. His bitterness stung more than it should have. "I get it." She flung the notepad onto the service cart. A single lead was useless. It was all useless. "You don't want to be helping me any more than I want to be in need of your help. But I'm stuck, okay?"

She rolled and unrolled the end of her belt. "I'm sorry I forced you into this situation. Really, I am. But you have to understand, trapped inside this hotel there's a real murderer on the loose. And whoever they are, wherever they're hiding, they've framed *me*." Before she could stop the words spilling from her mouth, she was relaying all that had happened to her in the past twenty-four hours. The invitation. The blood. The interrogation and subsequent chase. She didn't quit until all her fears and frustrations were vented. He listened without interrupting and she soon ran out of breath.

The darkness in his eyes had deepened, intensifying his grotesque mask.

Mave dipped her head to hide her face. Silence hung, thick as the leftover smoke. Apparently she'd shocked or bored him enough that he had no reply. No *that's awful*. No *sucks to be you*. Nothing.

He shuffled next to his mattress. After a beat, a familiar square tissue box extended in her line of vision.

"They're three-ply," he said, "with lotion." She snorted as she quickly accepted the box and wiped her eyes with her head turned.

"Thanks." Like everything else here, it belonged to the hotel. He probably had a housekeeping trolley stashed nearby, fully loaded with toiletries.

"So," he put his hands in his pockets and rocked on his feet, "your dad's a hitman in prison, today's your birthday, and you want to snoop around the hotel, ask some questions to clear yourself of murder." A one-sided curve like a comma teased his lips. "Did I catch that right?"

Apparently, a rant meant she'd lost all her filters. She nodded, not trusting her mouth to betray her again.

"It's okay," he said, trying to catch her eye. Mave kept her gaze averted. "Hey, my biological father was a junkie and my grandfather was a royal prick who nearly drowned me in a bath when I was a baby." That did it.

She met his stare, lost for words, desperate for a read on him.

"Learned to swim at an early age." He released his smile, kindling warmth inside the hollow of her chest. She had to remind herself: the masked man before her wasn't a harmless, friendly stranger. What was he doing down here surrounded by all these books? And the computers, the radio…

"Well," he cleared his throat. "You saw the footage. What next?" He picked up her discarded notepad. "No one but the maid's on your list."

No one but the maid. Her vague suspicion from a moment ago crystallized into understanding. "That's it!"

"What's it?"

"Birdie's in her suite the entire day, right?" She pointed to the footage of the housekeeper still paused on the computer screen. "And apart from me, this woman is the only other person seen wandering the floor."

Holden looked unimpressed. "So what?"

"So, the maid leaves her own room in the morning, comes back, and then later, just before midnight, she leaves again and uses the service elevator. See? At no time is she anywhere near the doors to Birdie's suite."

"Yeah, we already established—"

"Where's Bastian?" She stood, unblinking at the screen as if it might reveal more secrets. Her blood spiked with the revelation. "He's missing in this video. If no one but me visits Birdie's studio, how on earth did Bastian get a hold of that handwritten notecard from her? How did he have a conversation with Birdie that same afternoon, when Birdie was apparently complaining to him about the lighting?"

The studio had been a mess, darkened with the blackout curtains drawn. No white canvas was prepped, waiting on an easel. No riser, chair, or backdrop had been arranged.

(*Mave Mm—!*)

She swept her palms over her ears to clear the echo of Birdie's cry. One thing was certain: Birdie had never been expecting Mave to visit her yesterday.

"Bastian gave you a note ordering you to the studio." Holden caught up with her hunch. "So you're saying …"

She took the notepad from him and wrote *concierge* beneath *maid*. Recalling Birdie's strange final thought, she also added *red book* to her list. "I'm saying I need to speak with Bastian—ask him how he got that note. I need to revisit the penthouse, retrace my steps, and find this woman." *And this book.* It must have been important for Birdie to covet it moments from death. "You know a safe way inside the hotel, right?"

"Sure, but you got a problem first."

That was putting it mildly but she obliged. "What?"

"Look." He reached down and tapped a few keys. Live footage of the Château streamed on-screen again. "It's barely been a few hours since the Diamond Ball ended. Everyone is still passed out in their rooms. Barely anyone, anywhere. You go aboveground now and you're sure to get spotted on camera."

He had a point. Even with a crowd last night, Penn had eventually tracked her inside the library. How could she saunter the hotel's halls without being watched? An empty stairwell flicked on the computer screen, confirming the risk. Too many eyes. Not enough cover. Unless…

"Do you know where to cut the power to these cameras—is that possible?"

Holden flashed a wicked smile. "All breakers lead to the hotel's main electrical room in a sub-building."

"Can you take me there?"

"Yeah. And since it's your birthday, I know just the guy with a key to get in." He reached for his walkie-talkie. "Might as well have some fun."

She hadn't expected his response to lessen her anxiety—to spin it into another type of nervous energy altogether. Somehow it had. Her entire skin felt flushed.

Holden brought the radio to his mouth.

"Wait, what are you—"

"—to Bastian, over."

Mave needed more time to plan—to get organized. Any warmth she felt drained from her body.

ELEVEN

FROM THE RED BOOK OF THE DEAD

APRIL 2ND, 1991

Dear Rie,

Did you get my last letter yet? I met the infamous Dominic Grady and boy, you weren't kidding. If you hadn't given me a heads up, I likely would've ended up wasted and in his bed, and all before nine p.m. He is *extremely* charming. I mean—that cute little accent—can you blame me?

He caught me during my evening stroll, introduced himself, and invited me for a drink in the cigar lounge. I was going to politely turn him down after what you wrote. I'm not sure what got into me. I'd just finished listening to Caroline's post-bath weep. Again. I guess I was feeling especially exhausted from caring for someone who exists under a constant grey cloud. One drink couldn't hurt, right? (Wrong.)

Forty minutes later he had me tipsy and giggling like an idiot at his jokes. I told him all about the nursing program and my plans to work in pediatrics after I graduate, maybe pursue midwifery. He's so easy to talk to! He's not at all the hoity toity playboy I expected. I mean, yes, he has a better manicure than me, wears designer suits on a Sunday, and obviously has connections. He also has a pager. What is so urgent in the art dealing world that requires a beeper? Anyway, we were so deep in conversation that I didn't notice your brother had wandered into the bar.

Next thing I knew, Charlie was hovering over our table, glaring down at Dom. From his smell and wobble, I'd say he was already drunk. Dom smiled and said something flippant. I can't remember what exactly. But the energy in the room had changed. I swear we were only talking, Rie—maybe some light flirting but nothing to explain what Charlie did next.

He snatched Dom's glass, shot back the martini, and slammed it back onto the table. We both jumped and stared at the crystal stem, now cracked from the force. Blood trickled from Charlie's palm.

Not to sound full of myself, but was he was jealous? Of me? Was he thinking Dom was cheating on Birdie? Rahul showed up—I suspect the bartender alerted him of trouble brewing—and godsend that he is, Rahul quickly diffused the situation.

If he hadn't come in when he did, I'd hate to think what Charlie would have done next.

APRIL 14ᵀᴴ, 1991

Dear Abs,

Let's just say I'm more than familiar with Dominic Grady's charisma. I guarantee you, had my brother not spoiled your tête-à-tête, Dom's next move would have been to have you drop by his suite for a convenient reason.

This is partly my fault. I should've prepared you better—briefed you less on the hotel and more on its dysfunctional VIPs (a.k.a. my family). Sad but true, Charlie's drunken temper and overreaction are nothing new—especially when it comes to girls who aren't trust fund drunks (or paid by the hour, ugh). He has a lousy record. Flashing his platinum card can only get big brother so far. I'm sure witnessing Dom work his charm on you was like rubbing salt in his wound. Oh, and if you hadn't already guessed, Charlie is a devoted mama's boy. I haven't visited Mother at the Château for a few years, Parissa, for even longer, but Charlie never misses a chance to latch onto her heels. It's pathetic, really. He and Dom are alike in that way.

Also, between you and me, Mother's threatened to cut off Charlie. He's always been a bit of a hothead, and since he flunked out of school last spring, his hissy fits have worsened along with his spending habits. Now with his leash tightened, he's stressed out to the max. He's up there licking his wounds and sucking up to Mother. I have no doubt his little martini glass performance was intended to reach Birdie's ears—except what Charlie doesn't realize is that it'll paint *him* in a poor light. Not Dominic. Meanwhile, from what you've told me, Charlie's getting hammered every night, biding his time until a solution to life's problems falls into his lap. Typical.

The last time Birdie was in the city, she chewed me out for Charlie's erratic behaviour—as if I were guilty for not babysitting my older brother! Isn't that nuts? Sure, I may enjoy partying and late-night adventures, but I'm not the one knocking out teeth and attracting lawsuits. Just this past winter Charlie had another tantrum, picked a fight with the wrong guy, and got himself banned from a big-wig social club. I'd bet anything Birdie is still pissed. Losing your shit behind closed doors is one thing, but tarnishing the family name publicly? That's a no-go with mommy dearest.

This is my really long way of saying no, I don't think you can trust Charlie. Or Birdie. Or Parissa for that matter (even though, out of us all, my sister hates "country living" and is unlikeliest to visit). If you haven't already figured this out, I'm an anomaly among my family.

As for the rest of them: stay clear. All of them are two-faced.

THE HITMAN'S DAUGHTER

April 5th, 1991

Dear Rie,

I realize it hasn't been that long since my last letter but, apart from Rahul, you're the only one I can tell this to.

Mr. Law came back this morning. At first I thought he was simply an overprotective father, but now, after spending a bit more time with Caroline and seeing the two of them together, I suspect he's emotionally controlling her for his own gain. Everything is *yes-Daddy* this, *of-course-Daddy* that. She's desperate for his love and approval and clearly terrified of losing whatever shreds remain. He, on the other hand, is a bit scary with his authoritarianism. I heard him through the door earlier, snapping at a maid. Something about the do not disturb sign and her breaching his daughter's privacy—that he'd have her fired for incompetence. Ten minutes later he asked me to recite a daily log of Caroline's meals and exercise regime and my mouth dried up. Is he always this stern?

The worst part is, I now understand Caroline's hopelessness. She let it slip after another bout of crying—Mr. Law is *forcing* her to give up her baby once it's born. She has no choice. NONE. He doesn't believe in abortion or recognizing bastards—Caroline's words. And get this: the whole reason she's up here with me acting as her glorified babysitter is to keep her pregnancy a complete and total secret from his social circle. I don't even think the baby's father knows she's pregnant. Mr. Law's gone as far as to have the OBGYN visit in private afterhours, and when I asked to meet the doctor to debrief, he ordered me to review my NDA—said that all his employees are required by contract to remain anonymous. Is it even legal to practice medicine covertly?

Seriously, this is messed up on so many levels. What century is this? It's *her* body—her right to choose! I don't care what patriarchal authority Mr. Law feels he's enacting—no man should control or get to decide the fate of a woman's pregnancy. But when I encouraged Caroline to express her outrage, you know what she said? "It hurts Daddy more than it hurts me." It took all my will-power to keep from shouting at her. How can she be so pitiful? So brainwashed?

While a big part of me is disgusted, at the same time, I don't want to make an already stressful situation worse. This girl is ma-jorly lost and heartbroken. If I'm to get through to her—if that's even possible—it'll take all my patience and sympathy. I'm keeping my mouth shut. For now. I need this gig. I mean, it's not like any-one but you misses me and *anything* is better than moving back in with my stepmom. And you said it yourself: Mr. Law's reference will open a lot of doors. Not to mention it's too late to re-register for the semester.

So here I am, doing my best to bite my tongue and focus on the positive. It's a job with amazing pay and, in a few months, I'll have paid off my student loan and will never see Caroline or Im-manuel Law again. This is the career experience I was looking for. It shouldn't matter that it prickles my feminist sensibilities, right? Go on, tell me I'm being melodramatic. Or silly. Or paranoid. Tell me this bad feeling in my stomach about Mr. Law is all wrong.

TWELVE

JANUARY 1ST, 2021

She stepped with care, her newly-charged phone highlighting each footfall. She needed to preserve her slippers. But given they were constructed from takeout cups and aluminum foil, she wasn't sure how much longer her effort would matter. The right one was already tattering. "Couldn't you have stocked some spa slippers, too?"

"I don't do open-toe footwear. And stop flashing that thing," Holden said, indicating the cell's flashlight. "I'm seeing spots."

Refusing to stumble in total blindness, Mave filtered the beam through her pocket and followed him through the tunnels. The thickening darkness only heightened her worry. Did he have night vision? Was this rendezvous with Bastian a mistake? Could she trust either of them? Almost immediately, her father's voice responded with a resounding *no*.

They were travelling to the library's vents where Holden claimed they could enter the hotel in secret. There, they'd arranged to meet Bastian for a master key to the Château. Holden also claimed when Mr. Hendrick had updated the surveillance system last spring, he'd cut costs in underutilized spaces. Evidently the cameras weren't set to capture the aisles between bookshelves.

"How many other people know about you?" she asked his back.

"I'm the Spirit of Dead Poets," he said in a bored tone. "Hopefully everyone who's ever worked or stayed at the hotel."

"That's not what I—" She sighed and changed course. *Pick your battles wisely, M&M.* "He'll come alone?"

"Yeah."

"How can you be so sure?"

"Look, you need to stop with the micromanagement." He slowed and pointed to a pipe. "Watch your step here."

"Micro—?" She scoffed as she hopped over the pipe and skipped closer to match his pace. "Well maybe I'd ask less questions if you didn't avoid giving answers."

"What does it matter? Just think of it as borrowing a skeleton key. No one gets hurt. And everyone leaves happy."

The issue of trust returned to the forefront of her mind. What did Holden Robert Frost want? He seemed more accommodating since she'd spilled her story and shown her vulnerability. Yet her intuition warned of a hidden agenda. Aside from her sad attempt at blackmail, his motives remained unclear. She couldn't risk letting her guard down. Not again.

"So, do you go aboveground often?" She forced her tone to be casual. She'd spent the past few years convincing strangers she was a harmless girl with a quirk. She could manage small talk with a three-faced mole-man. "What do you do all day by yourself?" She imagined him reading Shakespeare in shadows, peeping on guests, chain-smoking.

"No. And same thing you do. I work."

She hadn't expected a real answer. "You're not …?" *Homeless? Psycho-emotionally imbalanced? A thieving con?* Surely stealing a baguette from the kitchen hadn't been his first and only crime. She squinted at the knapsack he'd slung over his shoulder before they'd left his hideaway. And yet he'd shown signs of kindness, too. He'd fed a stray cat. And her.

He shot her a look over his shoulder. Between his mask and the crawling shadows, it was impossible to read. "Please don't stop.

The suspense is brutal." Sarcasm then. (Unlike her eyes, her ears worked fine).

She struggled for a way to ask him more about himself without coming off as insulting.

"I just thought—aren't you unemployed?"

"No. Self-employed," he answered cryptically.

She held in a growl. Trying to get him to open up was proving difficult. She gave up temporarily and switched to another topic. "What do you know about Birdie Everhart?"

"She was old and rich."

"Beyond the obvious."

"Only know the obvious. I wasn't exactly her confidante."

"Well who was? She must have had people she was close to, had regular contact with, besides her maid." Even Mave had relied on her father for most of her life. "What about family?"

"She's got a son who visits now and then."

Mave wasn't expecting that answer either. She'd gotten the impression Birdie had never had children. She certainly hadn't mentioned a son during her visits to the shop. The topic of conversation had always been something lost. Something found. Or Mave herself. Far from behaving like a lonely elder who took any opportunity to ramble about herself, Birdie had done the opposite. She'd directed all sorts of personal questions at Mave, (which Mave answered politely while skirting any details about her past). Birdie was one of the few people who knew Mave's favorite color was green and that she hoped to own a house one day and paint her bedroom walls a shade of Granny Smith apples. *Chartreuse*, Birdie had said.

"A son." *Okay. Progress*, she thought. Or maybe it was Cain she was hearing. Sometimes her voice and her father's got scrambled in her head. "Is he here? What's his name?"

"Charlie? No idea. Don't keep tabs on—"

"Oh, wait!" She'd heard that name before. "Mr. Hendrick mentioned someone named Charlie." She'd have to add him to the list of people to question. "And Parissa. Who's that?"

"Parissa Everhart. Birdie's eldest." Contrary to his opinion, Holden was full of useful information.

"What about their father—did Birdie have a husband?" She'd been wrong about the childless part, after all.

"Divorced widow. We're here." He came to a sudden stop and she barely avoided bumping into his back. He unzipped his bag and pulled out a crowbar. Mave bit back any additional questions as he carefully jimmied a square metal grate from the wall. He bent and pulled forward a milk crate. "You'll need a boost." As he readied to climb inside, she raised her light for a better view. Her stomach dropped.

Their shoulders would skim the edges of the duct. How deep did the vent run? Would it tighten once they were inside? What if it was crawling with rats? She hadn't thought this through. "Holden—wait—" Her breath cut off prematurely as she stared into the void. He turned to her, at home with the darkness.

"Mave? You okay?" His haughty tone had vanished.

She shook her head. "I don't think I—I'm afraid of—claustrophobic," she gasped. Memory crashed through her. Reality splintered: the car trunk slamming shut, her father whispering. ("Keep quiet or they'll find you.")

She flailed her fingers over her wrist and snapped her elastic band.

"Whoa, hey." Holden reached forward, startling her as he enveloped both her hands in his. A part of her registered his warmth, his smoke—a campfire in the middle of winter. "Mave?"

A shudder passed through her body. Drawing air deep into her lungs, she tore her gaze away from the black hole in the wall.

"We're going to do this together, okay? You and me. But first you have to trust me. Do you trust me?"

Her vision wandered the glow on his neck, his collarbone, the frayed tip of his hood's drawstring. No. She didn't require Cain's voice to warn her this time. She ought to pull away—deny his comfort. She'd known this strange man for all of thirty seconds and trusting him would be beyond foolish. Except she was out of options. She could either rely on his word or continue to wander aimlessly for hours—maybe days. She snatched her hands back and tucked them into her armpits.

"You want to get inside the hotel safely, right?" He peered down at her. "It's what you want: to ask Bastian questions?"

She did. Desperately. The proof was hidden inside the walls of the Château. She needed it. Birdie needed it. She may have been brash and entitled, but Birdie didn't deserve to be gutted and left to bleed out like a monster. Unexpected grief threatened to disarm her. Mave cursed the prick in her eyes and nodded.

"Here's what we're going to do." He spoke softly. "I'm going to go in first and lie on my stomach, all right? Then all you need to do is hop up after me and slip onto my back. Won't have to move a muscle. And you can keep your eyes closed the entire time. Picture something that makes you happy. Think you can do that?"

Happy. Like shaking a snow globe in the giftshop. Sparkles dancing. Crystals floating.

"I promise, Mave, it's not far."

He spoke her name like a note from a poem. Despite her wariness, the depth of his voice cut through her fear. She nodded again.

"Okay, I'm going to disappear inside for a second. And then you're going to come in after me. We good?"

She nodded. It seemed to be the only movement she was capable of. He stepped onto the crate and slid into the vent in one fluid motion. The soles of his boots stuck out, reminding her of the ache in her feet. Her paper slippers wouldn't last much longer—another thing she had to take care of sooner rather than later. "Okay," he whispered. "Your turn. Come on up."

With her light trembling and her mind centered on snow globes and the truth, Mave stepped onto the crate. *On the count of three. One... Two...* Before panic could overtake her, she heaved her weight into the duct.

It was harder with Holden in the way but not impossible. The duct was wider than she'd imagined (though not enough to cure her of anxiety). She clumsily climbed over his body, her knees digging into his calves and thighs, and flattened onto his back like he'd instructed.

Sparkles dancing. Crystals floating.

"Mave."

"Yeah?"

"You're choking me."

"Oh. Sorry." She eased her hold around his collar

"Also you're going to have to turn off that light." When she hesitated he added, "Trust me. Just close your eyes and think of your happy thought, remember?" Doubt raked her body, scraped her lungs. But she was already inside—had already taken this awful risk. She clicked off the flashlight and shut her eyes.

He moved in a military crawl for them both, his muscles clenching and his ribcage torquing under her weight. The experience of molding her body to his might have been thrilling or awkward or sensuous were she not terrified of the walls collapsing, the air running out and slowly suffocating to death.

Her sips of air grew shallower by the second.

"We're here," he said. "You can open your eyes now."

Mave blinked and focused on a diffused square of light—the exit overhead. She could nearly smell the dusty book jackets. The candlewax. "Okay—please—out."

"Yeah I know. But you have to slide back a little. I need to get out from under you or we won't fit."

"Okay," she gasped, concentrating on the exit. *I can do this.* They'd made it. The library—freedom—was a foot away. She just had to let go of him.

"Mave? The sooner you ease back, the sooner we can get out."

Uh-huh. Of course. She nodded and suppressed a nervous laugh. Just yesterday morning she'd been stacking postcards and polishing vitrines. Today, she was stuck to the ribcage of the Spirit of Dead Poets in a duct beneath the library's floorboards. The absurdity helped. She'd no sooner released him than Holden had pushed up through the vent cover. The exit was clear.

She scooted out behind him and swallowed her heart back into her chest. The floor-to-ceiling bookstacks seemed to have grown taller since yesterday. Holden silently replaced the vent cover, a grate of vines. If she hadn't been watching him do it, she would've missed it altogether. No wonder she'd never suspected his presence during any of her visits here. Minus the deceased part, he was a ghost in every sense of the word.

"What now?" she whispered. The constant darkness stirred her impatience. Was there anywhere in this hotel with lighting over a couple of watts? "Is he here yet?" It took all her discipline not to whip out the iPhone and cast it like a flare. She stood on her knees and peeked over a row of books instead. "The chandelier isn't lit. Does that mean he's late?" As if sentient, the crystal beads overhead began to clink in a draft. That familiar sense of being watched combed her skin with pins and needles. Mave spun to the opposite side. Nothing beyond more books and cobwebs awaited her. "Holden?" She turned.

He was no longer by the vent cover. In fact, he was no longer anywhere. "*Holden.*" Her eyes strained to see through shelves. Where had he disappeared to—another set of bookstacks? She crawled on her hands and knees to the end of the row. *Holden, where on earth are—*

Movement stirred to her left.

There.

A mixture of irritation and relief swept over her. Holding her breath from the dust, she craned her head into a gap between books and inspected the neighboring aisle. But it wasn't Holden's mask that materialized.

THIRTEEN

A hand in a white glove appeared before Mave, followed by a double-breasted navy suit with gold buttons. She knew that uniform, its owner.

Bastian placed a brass key onto the bookcase between them and slid it toward her through the gap. "Need it back by midnight," he whispered. Mave snapped her mouth shut and swiftly pocketed the key. Bastian bent down to the shelf vacant of books. His eyes bugged upon spotting her. "*Jeesam.*" His upper lip held beads of sweat. "Mave, how are you—you can't be here. That key is for—"

"I know. The Spirit brought me here."

He regarded her like she had a snake for a tongue. "*What?*" He muttered a curse in Creole and checked over both shoulders. As far as she could tell, they were alone. For now. Someone could walk into the library at any moment. She pulled in a deep breath and got straight to the point.

"I need your help," she whispered. "You remember that note you dropped off to my room yesterday? I need to know how you got it."

"Heh? What note?"

Her stomach tightened. What if he denied ever delivering it? But just as quickly, understanding dawned in his eyes. "Oh you mean that envelope from Birdie?"

She exhaled relief. "Yes, when did she give it to you?"

He waved dismissively. "In the afternoon. I think. Dropped

it off when I was away from my desk. What does it matter? More important things—"

"Wait, I thought you said you spoke with Birdie and she handed you the envelope."

"No, I was running around and swung back to the lobby for a delivery address. I found the envelope on my chair. Had your name on it."

She still didn't follow. "How'd you know it was from Birdie?"

"She left me a voice message saying to give it to you."

"You mean you never picked it up from her in person? Never spoke to her directly?"

He shook his head and shifted his eyes nervously. Was he looking for Holden? Or someone else? *A person looks away when he lies.* She was quick to dismiss her doubt. Bastian had to be answering truthfully. His account explained why he hadn't been spotted anywhere on the security footage. It also confirmed she'd been set up. The killer could have easily slipped him the note when no one was looking. But the voicemail?

She studied him closely. "Do you remember anything else Birdie might have said in her message—anything at all?"

He shook his head again. "Just what I told you: she asked you not to be late, that she needed natural lighting to work."

"Do you still have it, the recorded message?" Maybe he'd missed a nuance. She was desperate.

Bastian scrunched his face. "Think so, but she left it on my cell and I couldn't find my phone this morning." He absently patted his breast pocket. "And the lines are still down so...." *Awfully convenient*, her father's voice noted. "Hey, know you're in a jam, but any chance you can tell me where I lost the damn thing?"

"Your cellphone?" Even amid her anxiety, Mave appreciated being made useful. At least it got her mind off her problems for a few seconds. She closed her eyes, inhaled, and waited for the connection to rise. It was surprisingly difficult given Bastian was standing a mere two feet away, a willing participant in her search.

She pulled and pulled in the scent, tracking, coaxing it out from hiding…

She sighed and slumped her shoulders. "Sorry." She wiped her forehead. The stress of her predicament was too much. "All I can guess is that it's sandwiched in a soft place. There's peach and green fabric? A bed skirt or a curtain? And it's up high. No windows."

"A curtain with no windows?" He seemed to be sharing her confusion.

"Did you run an errand for a guest yesterday, maybe visit their room upstairs?" she tried. "It's someplace definitely," she struggled to describe what she'd sensed, "old fashioned. Maybe you could ask Mr. Hendrick about the decor."

"About Hendrick," his tone dropped, "there's something you need to know." A wave of dread spun in her stomach. "He's been asking for you all morning. Claims you're missing and offered any staff with info on your whereabouts a bonus of one thousand dollars."

"*What?*" Her muscles coiled, readying to flee.

"Shh, I'm no snitch." Offense etched the lines of his frown. "It's one thing to lend out a key but—this is different, okay? I wouldn't sell you out." He scanned over his shoulder again. "Listen, Jordy's got a big mouth. He's crying foul to anyone who'll listen, saying Birdie didn't die of natural causes. Mave, what happened last night?"

With few options remaining but to confide in him, she gave an abbreviated version of the events that had led to her current exile. "Someone set me up, made it look like I killed her."

"Shit," he sighed and spread his hand over his chest. "You really found Birdie like that?" He blinked as if dazed. "And now everyone's fooled, whispering stories while Hendrick thinks you're—" Something—perhaps the sting in her eyes—made him stop and clear his throat. "How you getting by?"

"Bastian, you believe me, right?" She swallowed. "That I didn't do this horrible thing?" She couldn't bring herself to say *murder* again.

The anxious edge to his expression momentarily softened. "I know a good soul when I see one. Your whole time here, you've done nothing but help people." Worry deepened the creases on his face. "This is wrong. You should've come to me sooner. How'd you end up hiding with…" The chandelier did that odd rattle again. With an upward glance, he grew distracted.

"Bastian, please," she redirected, "all that matters now is the truth. I need more information on the Everharts—the guest list. Do you know anyone here this weekend who had it in for Birdie?"

She could read the words running through his mind: half the Château's visitors and its personnel fit that description. Even so, a sudden awareness ironed the pleats on his forehead. "Dominic Grady."

"Who?"

His eyes widened. "Birdie's art dealer. Big tipper, arrogant looking. Gave off a creepy vibe. Yeah," his words quickened, "they had an argument a couple of days ago. People heard shouting. Birdie was upset."

Mave licked her lips and shifted her legs. Her knees were starting to protest their current position. "What were they fighting about?"

"No idea. But it got loud enough for a noise complaint from the twenty-second floor. By the time I reached Birdie's suite though, they'd finished their spat. Dominic stormed out right when I was knocking on the door—just about ran me over. Not even an 'excuse me.'" He huffed.

"Okay, Dominic Grady," she repeated to commit the name to memory. "Now what about Birdie's son, Charlie. I heard he's staying here. Any opinion on him? Or her daughter, Parissa? Last night Mr. Hendrick wanted you to deliver them wine to soften the news. They must have heard, right? How'd they take it? Are they both still checked-in?"

"Slow down," he said, flashing his palms. "Sure, they're both here. Everyone is. No one can go anywhere with all the ice and downed trees. But I can't imagine either of Birdie's children doing this. Everything I've heard so far, this was"—he cringed—"violent. Downright psycho shit. To be capable of bludgeoning anyone, let alone your own mother." Horror flittered in his eyes. "Listen, all I know is Charlie turns into a puppy when his mother's around. And Parissa? She's way too…" he frowned, searching for the right word, "posh. Isn't the type to get her nails chipped."

And the method had been too dirty for a professional hit. Unless that too had been staged—a messy stabbing then hit to the skull. She chewed on her lip and considered Bastian's opinion. "How about…are either of them married?"

"Parissa is, yeah. To Nicholas Vaughn. Business mogul. Owns a bunch of overseas telecommunication companies. And before you ask, yes he's checked-in, but"—he shrugged—"I have to be honest, Mave. This sounds like grasping at straws."

"No, it has to be someone Birdie knew—someone she'd invite into her suite. What about her personal maid? She was wandering around last night."

"Who, Katrina?" He clicked his tongue. "Nah, don't see it. She's a new hire, way too jumpy, poor thing. Has bad arthritis in her knees."

She had to fight to contain her frustration. Bastian was trying to be helpful. "Fine. You tell me: apart from Birdie's art dealer, Dominic Grady, is there anyone else who might be capable of murder?"

He swept his knuckle across his lip. "No," he said too quickly.

Her internal lie detector instantly leapt. "You're sure?"

"Yeah. Sorry." His eyes shot up to the chandelier again. "Look, I'm not—I should leave before anyone notices—catches us here." His complexion seemed ashy. It was possible he was holding back another name, protecting someone. He'd claimed it himself: he wasn't a snitch.

She nodded. She would ask Holden about it. *If* she could find him.

"And Mave, you have to..." His words, a warning even in their restraint, trailed into silence. She leaned forward and read his lips. ...*to be careful*, he finished. His breathing had quickened and his eyes seemed imploring. She struggled to unpack the reasons behind his message without matching his nerves. *The Spirit*, he mouthed. She'd barely inhaled the air required to ask for details on Holden when Bastian pressed his finger to his lips. *Shh!* He shook his head. "It's not safe," he whispered.

"Bastian?" He was starting to look ill. Didn't he know Holden was a fake ghost? "What's going on—what are you talking about?" Before the concierge could answer, his radio blared a rush of static that caused them both to jump. Mave cursed and pushed her heart back into her chest.

"What time is it?" He turned down the volume on his walkie and wiped his face. "It's gotten worse," he mumbled, "have to get out of here."

"Wait." She needed more. "What's gotten worse? What do—"

"I can't—" He pulled on his collar to loosen it. "Oh god—I'm sorry, Mave, I—" He seemed to choke on his words. He careened back and bumped into the shelf. Mave could hardly decide what to make of his jitters when he straightened and darted from her sightline.

"Bastian!" She clambered to her feet, shuffled a few steps and blinked into darkness. She wanted to go after him but beyond these aisles, a camera could expose her. She stilled like an animal perceiving danger. A pressure in the air—that sense of being watched—had intensified. What exactly had Bastian fled from just now?

Her body knotted in response—knees, stomach, shoulders. Dread wrapped her bones and pricked her pores. "Who's here?" Shapes of inanimate objects crowded her. Nothing moved. Yet all her senses had heightened. Like a super-antenna, they picked up a single transmission: she wasn't alone.

"Hol-Holden... is that you?" She held her breath and waited, not expecting a reply. But it came.

A squeal of metal resonated from deep within the room. Mave spun her head in the direction of the noise. Her eyes grew wide and the hair on her arms stood. Door hinges? Except there was no door in that direction and the sound didn't cease. In fact, it seemed to grow louder.

She dug her nails into her palms.

Freezing up is for prey, Cain warned. *Unless you care to be eaten, I suggest you move.*

She ordered her lungs to stop heaving and slowly crept toward the sound. She waited. The metallic grinding continued to cut the silence.

One step, then another. Inch by inch Mave forced her feet into motion and edged out from the cover of the bookcases. In the middle of the library, flanked by reading desks, she stopped.

No alarm blared. No security jumped out. No authority barked through a bullhorn. Only that squeal like a rusty screw incessantly spinning. She narrowed her focus across the room. The fireplace. The sound seemed to be coming from there. She hugged her ribcage and approached the one part of the library she normally avoided—the black-stone hearth.

Her heart drummed and flooded her with adrenaline. A few feet away, where the coldness threatened to set permanently in her flesh, she spotted it. The damper rod beneath the mantel was somehow turning on its own. Around and around it squeaked, in desperate need of oil. What could be causing it to spin—a pressure within the flue? The wind from outside? Her teeth at risk of chattering, she reached out her hand. Closer. Closer still.

Silence.

She held the knob between her thumb and forefinger. As if it had never been spinning. As if she'd imagined the entire thing. She blinked at her trembling hand. *What am I doing? I should be—*

A sudden stink of ash filled her nose. She shut her eyes, feeling dizzy. It was that smell, the same one from her dream in the office.

She let go of the knob and turned at the exact moment a blast of cold air pierced the fabric of her robe.

Mave screamed. Or she tried. Her body was paralyzed with the force of the vision—because that's what it had to be. Nothing like this could be real.

Not Holden. Not a dream.

Before her stood the monstrous ghost of a young woman—her face hidden beneath three pairs of hands, stacked atop one another. Masculine hands, growing out of the back of her skull. Blinding her. Muffling her. The thick fingers interlocked, nails caked with soot. Smothering her mouth. Her nose. Her eyes. The crisscrossed knuckles were like the teeth of a zipper above her pale swan-like neck.

Mave couldn't process any more. Her sight began to blur. She jerked away, her legs obeying a deep reptilian reflex. *Out-out-out.*

The iron railing of the staircase appeared out of nowhere. It clipped her temple. She hardly noticed the strike, the flare of fire and pain.

The smell of ashes overpowered everything.

ҒOUᴙTEEN

Dear Rie,

Both Mr. Law and Dominic left the Château earlier this week and things are somewhat back to normal. And by normal, I mean Caroline is back to clamming up and weeping on schedule; Charlie is back to drinking and staring at me every night; and the weather outside has returned to rain, rain, and more rain. Can't blame me for going squirrely, right? Please don't get mad. But I did something you might not like.

I visited Birdie in her studio—just to casually ask how you were doing. She told me you'd left for an impromptu trip to Cabo with friends. She seemed miffed about the semester not being done and your upcoming finals. Anyway, I realize now why you haven't written me back. You probably haven't even read my most recent letters since you're away. But more stuff has happened. I'm starting to freak out and need your advice bad. (Rahul is a sweetheart and all, but let's be honest, he's a bit removed from reality and can't possibly imagine what this is like.)

Ever since Mr. Law left, I've been paying more attention to Caroline's ticks and habits. I noticed how she's always keeping her left arm covered or tucked away. I'm not proud of it, Rie, but between her constant tears and the howling wind, my thoughts took a dark turn. I grew suspicious and worried. Her health is my *one* responsibility. What if she was self-harming? So I did what I had to. I crept into her suite late last night, drew back her blanket, and examined her arm while she slept.

There's no mistaking it. They taught us the signs in my practicum—prick marks in the crease of the arm. Caroline has them. They're healing but definitely there. I know for a fact she's not diabetic. So old scars can only mean one thing: Caroline was using hard drugs. She's an addict. And get this, a little further along her inner bicep, she has a tiny tattoo of a heart with the initials BP. So I figured the dedication was the safer topic of her two secrets.

"Who's BP?" I asked her this morning. Maybe it's her mysterious boyfriend, right? I was nervous she'd flip out—call me out for unethical practice, snooping or whatever. But she didn't so much as flinch. All she would say was, "He's dead." Then she pressed her lips together. Super tight. Like they were sewn together. Combined with the emptiness in her eyes, it was heartbreaking, Rie. It's like she's totally numb, lost to all feeling except those pockets of release when she's totally devastated.

How can I help her? I *want* to help her. But I feel so overwhelmed. I only skimmed treatment on this kind of stuff. God knows when the doctor will be back—even then, it's against the rules to meet him—and the rate of relapse with intravenous drugs is huge. I'm not even sure if I should bring it up with Caroline. Like that one time I mentioned addiction to my stepmom? She ended up going on another bender. So maybe it's best to pretend I didn't notice. Because what if I make it worse? It'll be the baby who'll pay for my mistake.

FIFTEEN

JANUARY 1ST, 2021

"She walks in beauty, like the night..." The drawl echoed in her thoughts. *"Of cloudless climes and starry skies..."*

Mave's body tensed. Was that real? Or in her mind. All in her mind. This entire hotel—all shadows and whispers—it was making her lose her grip on reality and imagine poems. Not just poems.

"And all that's best of dark and bright / Meet in her aspect and her eyes..."

Her shoulders rolled back, her pulse rising.

"You awake?"

Holden. *No such thing as ashes or ghosts.* Yet her eyes remained shut. What if she was wrong and the monstrous spectre was still out there?

No. It had been another lucid dream. That was all. She was overstressed. Had slept poorly. The trauma of finding Birdie had worn her out and left her mentally exhausted. What more could she expect when she'd been forced to revisit her past—had been painted as a killer? In hindsight, it was inevitable. All those rumors about a haunting in the library had broken her psyche. Bastian had frightened her. Her imagination had sped into overdrive.

Mave warily cracked open her eyelids. She blinked at the ceiling first, then focused on Holden's mask. She was still in the book-stacks, laying on her back, not far from where she'd first climbed out from the vent. Holden reached down to help her sit, and she flinched and rose without trouble.

"You okay?" He stood and relaxed against a shelf, hips out, ankles crossed. Unlike Bastian, he obviously sensed nothing sinister nearby. "Seem a bit shaken."

"No. I mean, sure." She touched her temple. "I'm fine." It was tender. Perhaps bruised by the floor.

"Bad dream?"

"Yeah, I…" *Had a mental breakdown.* She swallowed. "Fell asleep. Guess I was more tired than I realized." Too tired. She couldn't afford to lose herself like that. She scanned three-hundred and sixty degrees. There was nothing out of the ordinary. *Only Holden, see? No such thing as a ghost with her face caged in men's knuckles. Holden is the fake spirit.* She licked her lips. "What just happened?" She forced herself to her feet and straightened her robe. "Was that you?" Maybe he'd staged a mishap to spook Bastian like he had yesterday with Penn.

"Byron. Great British poet, though I prefer Percy Bysshe Shelley."

"What?" It took her a second to realize he was referring to the poem he'd recited to wake her. "That's not—where have you been?"

"Had to get something. Bastian give you the key?"

She slipped her hand into the pocket of her robe and spun the metal between her fingers. She nodded. At least she hadn't dreamed that part. "Get what?" She inched closer to better see him. "Listen, you can't just vanish and expect me—"

"Here." He ducked to his knapsack by his feet and drew out a pair of boots. He held them out for her. The stiletto button-laced knee-highs looked like they belonged to a wealthy dominatrix.

"How did you …" They were lighter than she expected.

"Just figured, you know"—he shrugged and tilted back into his relaxed pose—"you can't sneak around in those for much longer." They both eyed her sad slippers that were peeling aluminum foil.

"But where did you find women's boots…?"

He cocked his head.

"On second thought, never mind." Turning a blind eye was what she did best. *See no evil. Hear no evil.* Repressing the reminder of her sins with Cain, she lit her phone. The soles of the boots were blood-red even in the bluish beam. "What size are these?"

"Uh," he raked his hand through his hair, "extra-small?"

She flicked him a look of irritation, slid off her paper slippers, and thrust them at him with her phone. "Take these but *don't* litter. There's a recycling box by the desks." No mess. No disorder.

He scratched his beard, seemingly trying and failing to hide his amusement. "Don't I have to separate the metal and paper first?"

Ignoring him, she lifted her hem and slipped on the boots. They were too big, but comfortable. She tied the laces extra-tight. They would do—a vast improvement from treading on takeout cups. "All right. Let's go." The sooner she left this library, the better.

He took his time dragging his eyes up from her legs. "Wait. You'll need this, too." He reached into his knapsack again and removed a black woolen coat.

"What? No. This isn't right." She held together her robe's collar, thinking of her tattered dress beneath. "I can't just take other people's clothes."

He batted out the coat's wrinkles. "Mave, you might as well be wearing a white flag that reads fugitive."

She glanced down at herself. Remembering Cain's rule about blending in, she awkwardly unknotted her belt, shucked off her sleeves, and swung the bundle of terrycloth at him. She crossed her arms, waiting. Rather than trade her for the coat, he threw aside the bathrobe and aimed the phone's light on her. She put her hand on her neck, horribly conscious of her dress—sheer, stained, ripped. "Can't leave it like that," she said of the robe, hoping to redirect his attention. "It'll alert Mr. Hendrick of theft from the spa and get linked back to you."

"That so?" The excuse sounded weak even to her. "Good thing no one ever finds me unless I want them to."

"I did."

"True," he said with an edge. "You're the exception, the first person in a long while to enter my library." The twin flames of his irises grew intense. Beneath her palm, the pulse in her neck jumped. What did that mean: the exception?

She glanced at the bookshelf, pretending to read a few titles—anything to avoid him and his hints of haunting. *I dreamed that part. Too much stress, remember?* She fiddled with a lock of hair behind her ear.

"What makes you do it?"

"Do what?" Curiosity won. His stare was unyielding. She couldn't release herself from his draw even if she wanted to.

"Come here. Every day. Ten past one." Bit by bit, word by word, the distance between them grew smaller. "You sometimes pick out a book. Jane Austen. Virginia Woolf. Agatha Christie. Though most times you just sit in that chair farthest from the fireplace and study shadows—your left eye like a warm sip of cognac, your right, a whirl of cool saltwater."

"*How...*" She swallowed. An unwelcome swell of butterflies spiraled down her chest. Excitement or nausea, she couldn't tell.

"You like to twirl your hair when you're worried," he continued, as if compelled to confess, "that short strand behind your ear."

She drew in a shaky breath and crossed her arms. All this time, all her breaks, he'd been watching—searching through her disguise. For what? Why her? She lifted her chin, afraid, offended. "I visit for the quiet." Her whisper had grown labored. "And it's not polite to spy on people. In fact, it's downright creepy."

"You got me." He studied her mouth, leaned in like he was about to share a secret. "I don't give a fuck about being polite."

She couldn't help it. The air between them crackled.

"Holden?"

"Yeah?"

"Can I have that coat now? I'm cold." Another lie. Her blood beat fire. A ruffle of movement. Without leaning away, he held it open for her. Mave willed her feet to move. She slid her arms into the silk-lined sleeves. His fingers brushed along her collarbone, grazing her neck as the coat settled onto her shoulders. She paused, eyes shut, and lingered at his touch.

Sheets of hail had yielded to flurries. Everywhere, glasslike trees hung in defeat of nature, their branches snapped and splintered in tangles. The Château's stone exterior was coated in frost and its steep, copper rooftop fringed in seven-foot icicles. As her calves tunneled into snow, Mave raised the collar of her coat and tucked her hands into her armpits.

"This way," Holden said, his words blowing wisps. He marched forward, knees raised. Beneath the cut-out of his mask, his beard collected snowflakes. It wouldn't take long for their footsteps to fill in. "It's slippery. Careful."

Though heeding his advice, twice Mave lost her footing in her designer boots, and twice she barely avoided falling face-first by clutching onto Holden's waist. Eventually, he reached back and tucked her beneath his arm. Their closeness caused her to stiffen but she didn't protest, far too eager to steal his heat and balance. About two hundred yards out, they arrived at the small sub-building patched in grey brick.

Holden released her before the doorway marked AUTHORIZED PERSONNEL ONLY. Shivering from the sudden loss of his warmth, Mave stuffed her hand into her pocket for the key. She needn't have bothered. "It's already unlocked," she mumbled a second later. She threw him a questioning look but he was preoccupied, brushing snow from his legs. She inched open the door.

A blinking overhead light revealed a narrow shelter with a vertical duct and old gauges with missing needles. A few feet opposite the entrance, an inner steel-cased door held signs cautioning of high voltage. The hotel's main switchboard must have been behind it. She stepped inside cautiously with Holden following.

The light above flicked on and off, over and again. She looked to its switch on the wall as if she might find a child playing with it. A dull warning plagued her. Between the fluorescent flashes, an energy seemed to be collecting, coiling as if readying to strike. She shuddered and threw off the paranoia.

"Okay," she sighed as she chafed her cold hands together. *Let's be quick.* She reached for the rusted lever of the inner door. It rattled inside her grip and stuck from the other side. Mave caught her breath. *Unlocked. Light switched on.*

They barely had a second. She yanked on Holden's arm and rushed them behind the duct just as the inner door opened and someone stomped out.

SIXTEEN

Boots clomped. A shadow rippled across the floor marked with cautionary tape. Their breath held, Mave and Holden waited until the sub-building's main door opened, shut, and whoever had been inside relocked the door and left.

Mave exhaled with her hand pressed to her chest. "Did you recognize them?" Thanks to his height, Holden had snuck a glance at the last second. He shook his head and slipped out from hiding.

"Only saw him from behind: bow-legged guy in a black parka, had his hood on. Probably maintenance. He was carrying a toolbox."

"Then let's hurry—in case he comes back." They snuck into the inner room.

Several large panels with bundled cables were mounted to the wall. It would take more than a minute to sort through them. "You check that bunch," Mave pointed, "and I'll do these ones." She pushed up the cuffs of her coat and scanned the twisted grey wires running from her first panel, struggling to make heads or tails with the connections. "Wonder what they were doing in here?" she mused aloud while checking tags and fuse box numbers. "Maybe the storm caused an outage on a floor or wing?"

Holden cursed under his breath. "Disabling the cameras. That's what they were doing."

"What?"

He held up a handful of bright yellow cables. Mave shuffled next to him and blinked. They hadn't just been pulled from the fuse box. They'd been cut.

"Newest wiring in here, which makes sense given Hendrick's update to the security system. Someone had the same idea as us and beat us to it."

"Wait…that person who was just in here?"

He nodded. "Seeing as he did nothing to fix the problem, safe bet."

"But that was another employee, someone with a key. Why would another staff—" She drew in a sharp breath as Cain's voice filled in the answer.

He's up to no good. Doesn't want to be caught doing something he shouldn't. "So you think…"

"Yeah." Holden's dark eyes glinted. "That guy who just left might be your killer."

Falling snow had all but covered their suspect's footprints. Mave anxiously followed the trail while it still existed—before the man in the black parka reached the hotel and disappeared for good. But rushing seemed impossible. With nearly every step, she slid and flailed in her heels. The hard fall was inevitable.

"*Ow,*" she cried.

"Shit." Holden bent to help her but she was quick to get back on her feet.

"It's okay, I'm fine." She brushed off the snow.

"Those boots are useless." He scowled. "You're going to break something. Here," he shifted his knapsack, leaned over and offered his back, "hop up and I'll hurry us the rest of the way."

The idea of straddling his torso caused her stomach to tighten. "No."

"Quit fooling around. He's getting away."

She shook her head. "No."

He straightened and flashed her a funny look through his mask.

"I barely know you," she added defensively. She shouldered her way past him, her steps glaringly clipped and shaky.

"You had no problem with it earlier this morning."

"Inside the vent was different."

"Different how?"

"I was…"—*in denial*—"in distress." No more excuses about his beard, his smoking, his hidden face or caginess. Mave bit her bottom lip and tottered her arms for balance. She found Holden Frost attractive. Way too attractive. She couldn't afford to worsen that vulnerability, put herself in a position where she gave up control. Not if she could help it.

"Tell you what," he blew into his hands and rubbed them together, "you let that guy get away, cops come and arrest you, will that be enough distress for you?"

What are you doing? He's right! she screamed at her flip-flopping emotions. *You need to move at triple this speed. Now.*

"Mave."

She'd managed to wobble no more than few feet ahead. "Okay. All right." Her cheeks warmed despite the cold.

"Good. Let's go." He bent over again.

Fresh anxiety laced her bloodstream. Doing her best to ignore it, she jumped onto his back and gripped his shoulders. Holden tucked her close and got moving. Unable to resist, she burrowed into his body heat. More than once already, he'd asked for her trust—had come back for her in the library. But it still wasn't enough. He was obviously dangerous and she needed the truth.

"Why are you doing this?"

"Gee, don't know." He mumbled to his boots. "Not a fan of the great outdoors. Prefer to get underground before nightfall."

"I mean helping me. It doesn't make sense."

He lifted his chin, his breath forming clouds. "You're blackmailing me, remember?"

Except it was more than that and they both knew it. Even before they'd met, he'd studied her in secret. Mave swallowed. If she wanted his honesty, she'd begin by offering her own.

"I was bluffing," she whispered, knowing he could hear given her lips were so close to his ear. "I was never going to tell Mr. Hendrick about you." There.

His stride barely faltered. Between the swish and crunch of his footsteps, the silence was painful. A part of her kicked herself for giving up her only leverage. If he dropped her and took off … She waited, longing to read his face beneath his mask. But he only quickened his march with renewed determination. The nerves in her stomach rocked.

"I just told you there is no blackmail. Why are you still carrying me?"

He tipped his head back and spoke to the clouds. "Really, Mave? Now?"

"Yes, now."

"I don't know." He sighed. "Good manners?"

"You don't do polite."

"Shit. Right." He shrugged, causing her to bob. "Boredom? Entertainment? You keep it interesting."

The words struck a nerve. "Like a freak?"

"Said the girl to the masked mole from the dungeon."

She scoffed, both seeing his point and cursing that stupid mask that concealed his face. "Why, then?"

He bent his head, trying to glimpse her better over his shoulder. "That what you think you are: a freak?"

"Don't change the subject." She wasn't ready to discuss her self-image with him.

"Who says I am?" He focused forward again. "Maybe that's why I'm helping you; because you have a twisted idea of how the world sees you."

She watched his feet, the sting of his explanation merely deepening. "So you pity me."

"Jesus, Mave! Wrong. Besides the fact that pity isn't in my vocabulary, I *admire* you, all right? Your dad's fucked up, you have a lynch mob after you, and yet here you are worried I might litter." He blew out a breath. "You're not who I thought you'd be. Maybe I like that. Maybe I like *you*. Now can you please stop distracting me so we can get the fuck out of this snowdrift and find Birdie's killer before we die of frostbite?"

"Oh." It was the longest she'd ever heard him speak. He *liked* her? "You can't die of frostbite," she whispered, hoping he'd forget the last thirty seconds of their conversation.

As if he'd been feigning the risk, his warm hands cupped the backs of her knees and hitched her closer.

The tracks wrapped around and led to a service entrance at the rear of the property. Careful to remain shielded, Holden lowered Mave behind a van buried in snow.

"That's him," he whispered as they hunkered next to the vehicle's frozen tire, "the guy I saw." She squinted through the veil of blowing snow, flakes peppering her lashes.

He stood just outside a backdoor, leisurely puffing an e-cigarette despite the storm. Though his profile was hidden behind his hood, something teased her subconscious: his bowlegged stance, his average height. With a gloved hand, he patted his hip and unclipped something from beneath his parka.

"Turn around," she breathed, willing it to happen.

He did. Mave felt her mouth gape. She nearly rose to accuse him. *Nearly.* Only Holden's hand on her shoulder kept her anchored behind the van.

The murmur of Tag's conversation pulsed with the wind as he spoke into his walkie. "… broken into and … blew circuits. Didn't know what the hell they were doing. Fucking amateur. Caused a total blackout…"

Did he mean someone else tampered with the cables—or was

he simply lying to protect himself?

"... *think she's behind it?*"

Mave cut a glance to Holden, needing to confirm he was hearing this, too. *Hendrick*, Holden mouthed with a nod, indicating the speaker on the other end. She refocused on Tag. Despite the chill, heat crept up her collar. Tag looked bitter, dangerous. Maybe it was the cold. Or his taped nose and two black eyes.

"Yeah, I managed to—" He spun around, pulling his words with him. Mave shifted to the edge of the van's bumper with Holden shadowing. "...nearly covered up with the snowfall," Tag informed the hotel director. "Definitely saw her small footprints. I'd say she—" He shifted again and Mave ground her teeth.

Who was *she*? Was he referring to her? Blaming her for cutting the security cameras? Sourness rose in her gut.

"*Only an hour or so before the sheriff gets here,*" Hendrick replied. "*Whatever you do, don't let her get*"—static stuttered—"*need her spoiling all my plans with police tape.*"

The sheriff was due that quickly? What about the road closures? And exactly what plans was Edward Hendrick orchestrating? Mave's head was spinning. The hotel director was sounding shadier by the minute.

"*...staff meeting in the grand ballroom in ten minutes for phase two.*"

"All right, copy. See you in ten." Tag took a hit of his e-cig, picked up the toolbox by his feet, and with a last squint at the troubled skies, returned indoors.

What did he mean by phase two?

"Mave?" She'd almost forgotten Holden crouched behind her. "Wanna keep following him?"

She shook her head. "I've got a better idea."

SEVENTEEN

A side door had avoided freezing shut, shielded beneath a canopy fringed with icicles. They slipped through unnoticed. Without its buzzing lamps and hissing vents, the massive building felt strangely still, as if holding its breath against the snow.

Holden took out his radio from his knapsack, and they listened to updates over the staff channels. As Tag had said, the cut wires had killed more than the cameras. A blackout was affecting all floors. The emergency generators had kicked in for limited lighting and heating in common areas. Otherwise, all functional fireplaces were being lit, and housekeeping was being deployed with complimentary heated blankets, chocolate truffles, and scented candles to all guestrooms. It seemed Edward Hendrick had anticipated this outage. Winter romance was all the rage and he was busy profiting—prepping staff in the grand ballroom while the majority of guests nursed hangovers in their suites.

That also meant the hoteliers' offices would be empty.

"Mr. Hendrick's been acting overly nervous since yesterday," she whispered as they crept through an abandoned wing of meeting rooms. "First the bounty on my head. Now all this talk of phases and damage control."

"So Tag's *not* your guy? Because it sure as hell sounded like he was trying to convince Hendrick that you were involved. Turn here," Holden directed, navigating them along another hallway. She pointed her flashlight and dodged a credenza.

Holden was right. Since the moment Tag had discovered her in Birdie's suite, he'd been against her. Except it didn't make sense. If his entire goal was to arrest her prematurely until the sheriff arrived and made it official, why would he want to disable the cameras and blame it on her? "He clearly implied he saw my footprints," she recalled, "why?"

"Who knows," Holden said, "maybe he's planting more evidence to make you look guilty."

She pursed her lips. From the crime to the bounty, something didn't fit. Prior to the electrical room incident, she would have pegged Tag as an overzealous rent-a-cop: an alpha male with a chip on his shoulder who salivated at the prospect of enforcing rules. But her own father had been an expert con who'd fooled people for years. Anything was possible. "Okay, let's suppose you're right. Why kill Birdie? Why frame *me*? Before any of this happened, Tag and I had never met. He didn't even know me."

Holden slackened his pace and tilted his head. "Sure about that?"

She opened her mouth to say yes and paused.

Be smart, Cain warned. *Why was that guard so quick to blame you?*

Tag had conveniently searched her room and rifled through her personal belongings. He'd discovered Cain's postcards and gun. He'd dug into her background, exposed her family history—all in a couple of hours under the guise of investigating Birdie's death. But who's to say he hadn't known Mave's true identity in advance?

Holden palmed her flashlight's beam. "Too bright," he whispered, diverting her. "Lobby and offices are just beyond." They stilled at the boundary. Mave's shoulders inched upward as idle chatter drifted from beyond. Early-bird guests were up and about. "Hang back," Holden suggested. "I'll go first, distract them. You count to thirty, then head straight to Hendrick's office. Whatever you do, don't twirl your flashlight and draw attention to yourself, don't look around or hesitate. You got it?"

"Wait—what about you?" His mask alone broke the first rule of blending in.

"Don't worry about me. You just get inside—lock the door behind you. If there's any trouble, I'll knock three times." It was as good a plan as any.

She nodded. Her back pressed against the wall. She blinked and found herself alone. Cloaked in blackness, her breathing grew shallow.

How had he disappeared so quickly? *An illusion of the dark*, her mind resolved. The Spirit of Dead Poets was good at disappearing. Too good. Her hearing sharpened and she counted to thirty as planned. The chatter rose, then grew distant. The guests must have moved on. Nothing stood out apart from the pound of her own pulse. A distant shuffle and murmur drifted but it might have been her imagination. Mave sucked in a deep breath. It was time to break into Edward Hendrick's office.

She turned the handle and stumbled inside in one ungainly movement. A tremor of wind cut across the sash window, and her spine quivered in reply. She was in.

Teeth gritted, she eased the door shut and pawed her pocket for the cellphone's light. Hendrick's imposing walnut desk beckoned from the center of the room.

She scurried forward and yanked on its top drawers. Calculator, staples, greeting cards, a roll of antacid and, ironically, a jar of hot sauce. Nothing remarkable. She tried the bottom drawer and it stuck. *You're hiding something. What is it?*

Mave swept the desk for a makeshift pick. Paperclips were handy, but too thin to be of any use. Fountain pens, a leather agenda, sticky notes proved equally inadequate. She rifled through paperwork in a leather tray. Based on the sheer volume of mundane messages and printouts, Edward Hendrick was a paper-person. Her fingers grazed a brass letter opener. *Bingo.*

She wedged the knife into the gap between the lowest drawers. A few careful wiggles and digs, and she caught the inner metal clasp. Chewing on her lip to the point of swelling, she eased the clasp upward a hair. *Nice and easy*, Cain tutored. She could almost feel her father breathing over her shoulder. Growing up, Houdini lessons had been her reward. If she'd passed her spelling and math tests, Cain would show her tricks. How to palm a card. How to hide an object under her tongue while maintaining perfect speech. The bottom drawer released. "Yes," she breathed. Eyes flicking to the door, she lowered the flashlight and began rummaging.

Inside were hanging files full of blueprints—page after page of site plans of the hotel, legal documents and correspondence marked confidential. Even cursorily, drawings of the basement and train tunnels tempted her. But now wasn't the time to read for details. *Hurry already!* Muttering a prayer for a long staff meeting, she haphazardly snapped photos and froze.

Hinges creaked.

She flicked up the phone's flashlight and found the office door gaping wide.

"Holden?" Her whisper came out hoarse. Her masked lookout didn't appear to be there. No one did. *No one human and alive.*

She quashed the thought and snapped her elastic band. This wasn't another nightmare. She gripped and pointed the letter opener. "Who's there?"

No footsteps. No sound of life apart from her own rapid breathing. Mave didn't dare blink. In her haste, she'd forgotten to lock the door. The force of a draft had swung it inward. That was all. She raised her chin and confirmed a current against her cheek. Yet the blood in her veins kept racing. Her heartrate intensified, squeezing puckering gasping. What if she'd been awake in the library, after all. What if she was in denial this entire time and the haunting was—

Stop it. Just stop. She was being ridiculous, fearing nothing but dust bunnies. She edged a step backward and a breath brushed her neck.

"Boo."

She spun and rammed her hip into the desk.

"Quit your disco ball moves. You're giving me a headache." Holden sat on Hendrick's chair with his palm raised to block the flashlight in her grip. His mask and hood still cloaked his head.

"Are you trying to—" She ran out of air, unable to complete her rebuke about cardiac arrest. "Don't ever sneak up on me again, you understand? How did you just—"

"Secret passageway."

"*What?*"

"'Kay, you got me. Used the door."

Maybe she wasn't going insane. Not entirely. But it was hard to tell when he was treating this as a joke. She glared at him and tossed aside the letter opener. "Right. Just forget it." She'd reached her limit with Holden Frost and his disappearing/reappearing act. Bruise throbbing, she swerved and hustled past him to the door. "I'm done here. Let's leave before—"

"Wait." He grabbed her wrist—or he tried.

Without thinking, Mave knocked him flat onto the desk with her hip between his thighs and her hand cinched to his trachea. Her other hand—the one Cain would use to aim his gun—she readied to pinch.

"Don't," she spat.

He responded with a strained nod, his eyes rounded and animated with heat.

She released him and stepped back, brushing her coat smooth. So what if she'd overreacted? She was stressed and tired of his antics. Holden rolled upright and gasped a lungful of unrestricted air. "It's not safe," he rasped.

The gravity in his tone cut through the drumming of her pulse. "What do you mean?" Sticking around was a terrible idea. She needed someplace safe to review the photos.

"Front desk came back early. Five and half more minutes, then we'll be clear to move out."

She shook her head, torn. She could be wasting her one and only chance. "I need to get to Birdie's suite. The sheriff is—"

"Not here yet. Trust me." His voice softened. "More than half the entrances into this place are frozen shut and there's a blackout, just like you wanted. Even when the sheriff arrives—*if* she arrives—she'll be too busy wandering in the dark to investigate properly."

Mave took a deep breath and tried to draw on her patience. What was Holden's game? Yet, beneath her irritation, she was more relieved for his company than she cared to admit. Better him than Hendrick or Tag. Or that nightmare from the—

She refocused on Holden before the memory of the ghost could gather in full force. He was leaning on the desk, his cool composure restored. She crossed her arms. "Why five and a half minutes? What happens then?"

"Jordy takes a nap," he said, for once providing a direct answer.

Her brow hitched as she processed his words. "Are you telling me—Holden, did you *drug* the front desk?"

"Shh, keep your voice down."

"Don't shush me," she hissed. "They're going to think *I* did that."

His body language remained blithe as he poked at Hendrick's things, picking up a paperweight, then a pair of reading glasses. "Circumstantial. No cameras. And the kid'll be fine in a few hours."

"Tag won't care! He's using whatever he can to frame me."

"So you're back to thinking he's the killer?" He came out from behind the desk and continued his casual inventory of the office.

"Yes. No." She rubbed her forehead. "I don't know, okay? I just have this feeling—he's too eager to see me locked up." She thought aloud, "Maybe he and Mr. Hendrick are in this together, pulling some sort of scam. I found all these blueprints in the desk." In fact, she ought to double-check she'd taken enough photographs—but she found herself fixated on Holden's reaction instead. He didn't seem at all fazed by her discovery.

He uncapped a crystal decanter and sniffed its contents. "Okay, well…" He moved on to the hotel director's framed art. "If there's anyone here with an ear to the ground, it's Bastian. When you met, did he tip you off about either guy?"

"Not exactly. He mentioned this other man, Dominic Grady, Birdie's art dealer. He's convinced Dominic is shady. What are you looking for?"

"Information. Loose change. Right, Dominic Grady. Anyone else?"

"Sort of. He tried to warn me about…" *The Spirit—it's not safe.*

"Go on. About what?" He paused and blinked at her. "Mave?"

You. She couldn't bring herself to say it. If she was going to rely on him to help her through this mess, she needed more information. "He sort of hinted about another danger."

He straightened, giving her his full attention. "Yeah?"

She bit her lip. Here in the hoteliers' offices, reality was firm. Whereas *there*, in the hidden nooks and crannies of the bookshelves… She'd begin with a simple question. "Why does everyone stay away from the library?" At least she'd assumed it was simple. Holden remained silent. She narrowed her eyes. "What aren't you telling me?"

His mask wasn't enough to conceal his hardened expression. "Not everyone's welcome."

"But *I* am? What does that mean?" She shoved her hair from her face and huffed. "Penn—that big security guard, he seemed so scared he just froze at the doorway. And Bastian, he acted like—" She clamped her teeth together and paced in a circle. He'd acted like the haunting was real. They both had. No matter how outside the bounds of logic—dream or not, she'd experienced it—that tortured woman. Her long neck. Those blackened nails. Mave shook her head. How could that be when (one) it was madness, and (two) Holden had admitted he was the fake spirit.

Except for now. He stared intensely ahead.

"Can you at least take off that horrible mask?"

123

"No."

"Why the hell not?"

He blinked slowly. "Prefer not to be seen." A watcher—not the watched. But there had to be more to it.

Mave released a sigh bordering on a growl and stopped pacing. She wished she could be a proper psychic for once and read his mind. "You've asked me to trust you." Her voice had dropped, her frustration clenched like a fist in her chest. "Well that's a two-way street. What's your deal, Holden Frost, really?"

He shrugged. The tightness in his shoulders revealed he was more affected by her question than he was trying to let on. "No deal. Just a guy who sees the system for what it is: a prison. Found an out. Prefer my own company. That so bad?"

"What system?"

"Society. The shackles, the daily grind, nine to five doing something you hate, to feed a family you don't want, to live in a house you don't need." He exhaled like he'd gotten a burden off his chest. "Two and a half more minutes."

Who was this man? Where was his family—his roots? He'd mentioned a grandfather. "Fine. Tell me about yourself to pass the time."

"Like what?"

"Like I don't know, where were you born?"

A faraway look melted his gaze. "Ninth floor."

"Wait, what? As in *here*? You were born at the Château?"

"August fourth, nineteen ninety-one." His Adam's apple bobbed. "Now you know my name. My home. My birthplace and birthdate. That's more than I've told anyone." His voice grew grainy. "That enough?"

Understanding washed over her. He wasn't withholding information to keep her out. He was withholding information because it hurt him to remember. Mave's irritation at being shut out fizzled into guilt. She knew the effects of bad memories firsthand. She wouldn't make him recount them. Not unless he was ready.

"It's enough," she whispered. She eased back a step and pouted. That hadn't gone as planned. In fact, nothing had. Too many questions still shrouded the truth.

EIGHTEEN

FROM THE RED BOOK OF THE DEAD

MAY 22ND, 1991

Dear Rie,

Finals are happening and I haven't heard from you in weeks. Not a peep. I'm starting to get worried. Are you even getting these letters? How are you not back from Cabo yet?

I went to visit Birdie in her studio again. She was in a meeting with Dominic and brushed me off. Then from the hallway, I over-heard her telling Dom that you were just looking for attention. Get this: your mom thinks you're "off galivanting until you're satisfied with some childish display of rebellion." But it can't be that. It's not like you're a flake. I know you better than that. What if something's happened to you and you're lying dead in a Mexican ditch? Where are you, Rie? Please be okay. Please write me back, okay? I need you.

NINETEEN

JANUARY 1ST, 2021

She climbed the emergency stairs with Holden and tried not to think of the young man slumped facedown at reception. Her stomach tied itself into knots. What if Jordy didn't wake up? It was her fault he was collateral damage. She'd been the one to recruit Holden. And now innocent people were getting hurt. Is this how Cain had felt at the beginning? *Unlikely,* she corrected herself. Cain was incapable of guilt. Or worry for his victims. By the time she reached the landing of the twenty-third floor, Mave was burning inside and out. She couldn't remember the last time her legs had felt this limp or her lungs had worked this hard.

"Okay," Holden checked the wall signage as they both caught their breaths, "Birdie's studio—this way."

"No. Wait." Now that they'd arrived, she wasn't sure she could go through with it. The idea of sauntering into a crime scene and inspecting a dead body—she pressed on her chest. "Katrina first," she stammered.

"What about all that stuff about the sheriff on her way? Checking the suite for leads before the police get here? You said—"

"Katrina first." She didn't wait for his agreement and stomped past.

"Hold your horses, Nancy Drew. You're headed the wrong—"

The hall's emergency lights switched off, cloaking them in complete darkness.

Not again. Mave stumbled to a stop and groped for the nearest wall. "What just happened?" she breathed.

A clink and spark followed, and Holden caught up to her with his Zippo lit. He scanned in both directions. "Backup generators alternate floors every ten minutes. Saves energy. Come on," he nodded in the opposite direction, "maid's this way."

He steered her left when she was going right. With each twist and turn, Mave managed to calm her nerves—or at least squeeze them into submission. She couldn't afford to freak out because of a few shadows. Or a corpse sealed in a suite nearby.

They arrived before an unmarked mahogany door. "This is the one. You go on," Holden advised. "I'll stand watch again." He leaned against the wall and put out his lighter. The only way Katrina would see him was if she were to lean out into the corridor with a flashlight.

Mave faced the door in blackness, knocked three times, and brushed flat the lapels of her coat. Nerves swilled in her stomach. She was about to raise her fist to try again when the door swung open. The dark-haired, fifty-something woman from the video stood before her in wavering candlelight.

"Katrina?" Mave was expecting her to be in uniform. Her casual clothes seemed mismatched and dishevelled.

"Yes?" She raised the flame of her candle and weighed Mave up and down. Her eyebrows were over-plucked and her eyelids, heavy, making her seem together surprised and disdainful. "Who are you?" A light East European accent threaded her speech.

Mave thought it best to avoid giving her name. "I work for Mr. Hendrick. He must have already told you."

Katrina's lips thinned and her eyes glistened. New hire or not, she must have been upset over Birdie's death.

"You know, last night?" Mave gently prodded.

But instead of grief, the maid's frown morphed into anxiety. "You tell that impatient man I'm packing as fast as I can." She shook her head pleadingly. "Where does he expect me to go in this weather?"

Wait—she was leaving? "Sorry, there must be a misunderstanding. I'm here to ask a few questions."

Katrina wiped her nose and paused. Her expression slipped into wariness. "About what?" Bastian had mentioned she was jumpy. Perhaps this was her typical nervous disposition.

"By now, you must have heard about your employer's"—*how to phrase it*—"passing."

The maid fingered her necklace, a thin gold chain. A somber classical tune drifted from her room. "Listen, I'm not sure why Edward sent you. I already told them everything I know earlier this morning."

Them who? Didn't she want to help find the truth? Deliver justice? This was not going as smoothly as she'd hoped. Mave tried a polite smile. "Well, as it turns out, Mr. Hendrick has some of his facts wrong. I'm here to review things, help straighten them."

"Why would he send...?"

Mave's smile fell as Katrina gave her another once-over. The maid's heavy eyelids suddenly pulled wide as she recognized Mave. "I don't want trouble." She retreated a step.

"No, wait—" Mave leaned into the doorframe before she could shut it. "I'm doing this for Birdie. She deserves to—to rest in peace. *Please.*" It was partly true.

Katrina glanced down, lost in thought. "You must not have known her very well," she mumbled, seemingly conflicted. She turned away, leaving the door open. *Good enough.* Mave didn't wait for a formal invitation. She stepped inside after her, keeping the door ajar in case a hasty retreat became necessary.

The room was a windowless, small salon that presumably adjoined a bedroom. A dozen or so wicks flickered and a nocturne played from a pocket radio. Katrina set down her candle on a side table crowded with picture frames. And a rotary telephone. Mave froze. The maid's hand held a slight tremble as she reached for her radio instead and switched off the music.

Mave sighed. "Thank you. Think we're all a bit shaken. False rumors, you know?" She smiled again but Katrina didn't respond. "So...." This was harder than she'd imagined. She licked her lips and made an effort to stand straight—innocent and tall. "I was wondering, when did you last see Birdie?"

"Day before last," she replied, her gaze unfocused.

"What about yesterday?"

The furrow in her brow deepened. "I was off. Went to bed early and was asleep when it happened. I never would have imagined—" She pinched the bridge of her nose.

"When did you find out?"

She gave a small shake. "This morning. When security broke into my room and woke me."

"They broke in—why?"

"I was very tired. Couldn't hear them knocking. They thought I might be in trouble and let themselves in." Her gaze fluttered to an armchair as if in search of something. She shivered. "My shawl—excuse me a moment..."

Mave's guard went up as Katrina scurried out of sight into the next room. "You want a blanket?" she called out, "it's cold, no?"

"Oh, that's okay, thank you. I'm wearing a coat." She bit her lip, indecisive. Maybe Katrina was being nice because she wanted to help. Or maybe she was misleading her as she searched for a weapon. Mave crept closer to the exit, instinctively logging items within reach to defend herself if needed. Telephone cord. Candlestick. The maid's shuffles drifted through the wall—the pull and close of a drawer. Then another. A stream of anxiety spread in Mave's gut. This wasn't good. She was taking too long—but Katrina returned a second later with a pashmina wrapped around her shoulders, seemingly in innocence.

"That's better." She hugged her arms. "You were saying?"

Mave pried her eyes away from the bedroom door, clearing the suspicion from her face. "Just about security." She swallowed. "What time did they visit you exactly?"

Katrina shrugged. "Two-ish," her eyes flicked to the upper right, "two-forty."

"You mean…" She must not have been following correctly. "You were in your room asleep the entire evening?"

"Yes." She fiddled with her necklace again.

"You never left, even for a few minutes to celebrate?"

"Celebrate?" She stiffened ever so slightly. "No, why?"

Because the security camera caught you leaving your room at five to midnight. "Just trying to place everyone," she sidestepped. "Tell me about the other day then, December thirtieth, when you saw Birdie."

"Not much to tell. I went to her suite to clean."

"How did she seem?"

"To be honest," her frown deepened, "grumpy."

"Did you two talk about anything?"

She shook her head quickly.

"The weather? Plans for the holidays?"

"No."

"But you said she seemed grumpy. How?"

Katrina grew flustered. "I don't know, I suppose she just— didn't say hello or goodbye."

"How long did you stay?"

"Not long."

"Why?"

"She had company. I returned later when her suite was empty, finished cleaning and locked up." The response sounded rehearsed.

"You have your own key?"

She blinked rapidly. "Yes, I need one. To clean."

Mave fought to keep her voice and questions neutral. "You mentioned company. Who was visiting when you first went to clean?"

"Edward."

Mave cocked her head, her suspicions of Edward Hendrick re-kindled. "What were he and Birdie talking about?"

"I'm not sure. It sounded businesslike. Something about a missing signature and a deadline."

"A deadline for what?"

"I don't know." She fidgeted with her shawl. "Look I don't want Edward to get mad. He's already ordered me to...." She drew in a large breath. Her nerves were palpable. She clutched her shawl tight to her breast and absently traced her wrist. Mave opened her mouth to assure her of her trust but got distracted by a sudden scent. *Gold—dangling—a charm shaped like a doll.* It was there and gone like the thought itself. She hadn't sensed enough to locate the missing jewelry.

"He's heartless," Katrina whined. "Without this job, I don't have anywhere else to—" Her voice broke and she wiped her dewy eyes.

Something about her show of emotion—it seemed genuine, and yet a hint of alarm pricked Mave's skin. This woman had already lied to her once.

"You mean Mr. Hendrick won't let you stay here?"

She shook her head, her lips pressed firmly together. "He says I'm not a permanent employee of the hotel—only contract." She sniffed. "Birdie hired me privately and now that she's gone, I have to"—she shook her head again as if inwardly arguing with herself—"to get out immediately."

Mave shifted uncomfortably as a sudden urge to flee from the room itched the soles of her feet. Except it was obvious Katrina was hiding more than she was revealing. One last question, Mave told herself, then she'd go. "Did Mr. Hendrick visit Birdie regularly?" For that matter, why was Katrina lying about leaving her room overnight?

"Now that you mention it"—she blinked—"yes. I saw him in the hall at least three other times last week. Maybe more. And you know, he looked nervous. I'm sure of it. Like I said, I don't want to make him—"

Radio static hissed from the next room.

Mave flinched, her attention snapping to the sound. She stared at the open bedroom doorway as her stomach dropped. The shawl had been a diversion. She looked back at Katrina accusingly. Color had risen to the maid's cheeks. "Wait, I can explain. Please—"

"You left for your radio," Mave whispered, her heels already reversing toward the exit. "You called security."

"I—I'm sorry. I need the money, I—"

Mave bolted out the door.

The emergency lights had relit in the hallway. Holden was no longer standing guard and behind her, the maid's door slammed and its deadbolt cracked in the silence. At least she wasn't being chased. *Yet.*

She neared the junction at the end of the hall and skidded to a stop. She gaped at the wall sconces.

Was she dreaming, or were their lights pulsing? Then she sensed it: footsteps. Her panting took on a new inflection.

Out of this corridor, M&M. Now.

Her mind reeled to think of an escape route. The main staircase was blocked. *Another emergency exit.* But in which direction? She turned the way she'd come as another row of lights flickered in sequence—stoplights in warning. Someone was tramping the alternate hall, closing in. Hunters on both sides.

"Mave, over here," a voice rasped.

She reflexively spun to the call and spotted Holden. He was in a nearby service alcove with a vintage ice machine and a dumbwaiter. Before she had any chance to draw breath, he'd slapped the *call* button on the wall panel and flung open the lift's door.

"Quick! Get inside."

TWENTY

Mave's legs stiffened and her shoulders pinched. *In there?*

The dumbwaiter's stainless-steel carriage couldn't have been more than a few cubic feet, top to bottom. Holden was already folding himself inside and reaching back for her hand. A light gleamed in her peripheral vision. Her eyes volleyed from the dumbwaiter to the bend in the hall where someone with a flashlight was seconds from rounding the corner.

"Mave. Now," he whispered.

Get in, M&M.

With a last rattled look over her shoulder, she cursed her claustrophobia and flung herself after Holden. He all but lifted her onto his lap. She pulled in her feet tight as he yanked the door shut and sealed them inside the snug space.

Both their chests heaved and his warm breath drove into her shoulder. He wrapped his arms around her and tried twisting to make more room but it was near impossible. She dug her fingers into his forearm, silently ordering him to be still. Together, they waited.

Patter like footsteps passed outside. It was hard to be certain how many people they belonged to—one or three or five.

Mave kept her eyes glued on the faint light seeping around the door's edge. The backup generators would give out in another minute or two. (*One Mississippi. Two Mississippi.*) Panic bubbled.

What if security heard them in here? What if they jammed the door, trapping them in this tiny box permanently? Hadn't she read a news article about a waitress found dead in a dumbwaiter? Or what if someone called the lift from another floor, causing a malfunction that dropped them—

Holden undid a button on her coat. "Mave." It ought to have loosened the feel of the tourniquet around her chest. "Relax," he whispered. "Another minute and it should be clear."

She nodded and closed her eyes. Inhaled. Exhaled. "Just—tell me something—anything." She needed a distraction. "Why Chinese radio?" It'd been puzzling her since the moment they'd met.

He shifted slightly so that her side was pressed to his chest. "I'm trying to learn Mandarin."

Her heart kept up its wild thump. "Huh?"

He brushed a hair from her face. Her breath hitched and she opened her eyes. They'd adjusted to the dark. There was just enough glow for her to make out the pores of his porcelain mask. And his irises. Up close, they perfectly matched, veined like the translucent wings of a black moth.

"Professional development. I'm an online translator."

"You…" He was an endless riddle, each of his answers leading to another question. She curled in her fingers to avoid reaching for his mask. "How many languages do you speak?"

He blinked slowly as if entranced. "Five." From the sweep of her hairline to the curve of her chin, his gaze took in every part of her. "English." (Her brow.) "Español." (Her nose.) "Hindee." (Her cheek.) "Eurbaa." (Her mouth.) "And Russkiy."

Gravity dissolved.

He angled his jaw closer. "I think…" His sigh tickled. "They're gone. We can slip out now."

"What? Oh, right"—she turned away—"I mean, good."

Holden pushed against the door. It remained shut. Mave twisted and pressed alongside him with the same result.

"What's going on?"

"Hang on." He leaned forward as far as he could with her squished on his lap, and shoved with both palms. "Shit."

"Holden." She leaned her shoulder and pressed her entire weight onto the door. "It won't budge—why isn't it—oh my god—"

"Okay, listen. Everything's fine. It's probably latched because of the power outage."

"*What?*"

"I can get us out. Just give me a second." He felt along the door. "Happy thought, Mave, remember?"

The hallway lights chose that moment to shut off. Not that it mattered. Her wheezing had reset itself regardless. She squeezed her eyes shut.

"Mave listen to… happy…" His Zippo clicked and his whisper drifted in and out of her hearing.

She tried, she *tried* to keep out her paranoia and imagine the beautiful snow globe. But sweat beaded her skin and her heart rammed like a bird battering against glass. *Trapped. Trapped.* She shook. Faster and faster. Not enough (the tourniquet around her chest grew tighter) air. Stifling. This coat. Her fingers yanked at the collar. A ringing built in her ears. It was thinning already. She'd die in here. She'd (her head lolled sideways onto his shoulder) run out of—

In the back of her mind, she registered the press of his lips. But she was drowning—without oxygen. Just as quickly Holden coaxed her mouth open and exhaled. Sweet, smoky air filled her chest. Her eyelids fluttered open. Her lungs bloomed. What was—?

She strengthened her hold on his arms and pulled in another deep breath through his mouth.

Holden was feeding her air. She blinked in disbelief.

Wrong. He was kissing her.

She froze, coursing with shock and wonder. The ends of his lashes pressed together through the eyeholes of his mask. Whatever he was doing, it was working. She was no longer hyperventilating from fear. If anything, she was losing her breath for an entirely different reason.

She lifted her trembling fingers to his jaw, dragged them along the smooth edge of his mask. Want and fear warred within—everything outside, everything inside. It was more than she could handle. She gave the slightest push.

He broke away and tipped his head back. The flame of his lighter danced. There was no space to hide. "Sorry," he rasped, as if she hadn't been the one to need resuscitation. "It's just—"

"Uh-huh."

"Won't happen again."

"Okay," she exhaled, incapable of thinking of anything else to say. She couldn't recall ever being so lightheaded.

"Okay," he repeated. He suddenly flinched and cocked his ear to the door.

A shuffling sounded in the hallway. It felt as if a bucket of ice-water had been dumped over her head. Someone was there. Just outside the dumbwaiter.

She barely had a second to consider what she would do if it were Tag when the door swung open.

TWENTY-ONE

She squinted as a spear of light cut into the dumbwaiter. The cool draft from the hallway rushed inside the carriage, sobering her. Mave couldn't move quickly enough. It didn't matter anymore who was out there—Tag or the sheriff or the boogeyman—it only mattered *what* was out there: air.

She untangled her limbs and stumbled out. Behind her, the weighted door swung shut before Holden could follow. Mave caught herself on the wall and blinked, body crouched to flee or strike.

"Bastian!" She straightened as a wave of relief washed over her. "How did you—?"

"Katrina called us," he said, squinting past her shoulder. "Heard you inside and came back round once I lost Tag. You okay?"

She nodded and touched her lips. Why wasn't Holden coming out? What just happened in there? *Nothing*, her inner voice piqued.

Bastian seemed preoccupied, aiming his flashlight and peering down the dark hallway. "I should go before he notices and comes to get me."

"Who?"

"Tag." He finally looked at her. "He's pissed you got away, has Hendrick convinced you're dangerous. Do yourself a favor and keep away from the north and south stairwells for another hour."

Mave nodded though she had no idea which direction was which. Bastian gave her arm a small pat. "I'll keep working on

Hendrick and distracting Tag. Stay safe." He loped off, disappearing around the corner before she could arrange the questions cluttering her mind.

She stood there a moment, doubting everything. Ever since the incident in the library, her senses felt unreliable. Foggy. Had Bastian really even been there?

Holden exited the dumbwaiter. The sight of him rattled her nerves.

"Let's go," she whispered, straightening her coat and shoving aside her conflicted feelings. She turned away and marched in the opposite direction Bastian had gone. This was neither the time nor place to sort through her strange infatuation with Holden Frost. What was it she felt anyway? A connection with another outcast? An energy more than lust?

Her hands that had touched him seconds ago made fists at her sides. Mave didn't have to glance down to confirm it. Birdie's blood stained the beds of her nails.

They snuck into the gloomy studio, and Holden swiftly locked the door behind them. No sooner had Mave heaved a sigh than raw fear overtook her.

Suite twenty-three-oh-one. The murder site. She remained unprepared to relive the violent memory held within these walls. How long could she last here?

However long it takes, Cain replied. His strict tone temporarily stemmed her panic.

Holden sparked his lighter and moved to the nearest table overflowing with jars and pigments. He began poking around again. The flame of his lighter caused his porcelain cheeks to sink into sharp shadows.

"You shouldn't touch anything," she whispered. Less than a day ago, Tag had issued the same orders next to Birdie's corpse. Her eyes stung and shuttered. *Corpse.* It was an awful word—reminiscent of overturned graveyards and zombie parts. She concentrated on Holden.

"Never know," he said. "Could be secret information scattered in this stuff."

"Secret information would be…" *locked up. In files marked confidential.* She fished out her phone, suddenly provoked by Katrina's accusations.

Holden twisted his neck and stared at her. "What?" He edged closer.

"Those blueprints I told you I found in Hendrick's desk. Take a look." They stood shoulder to shoulder as she scrolled through the pictures she'd taken earlier.

"That's the basement level," he murmured. "Table games. Machines. Theatre. It looks like—"

"A casino," she finished. "It seems he's planning to redevelop the hotel's closed off lower levels into some kind of club."

"Fucking hell."

"You didn't know?"

"No I—" He scratched his head. "Before you, no one had come down in years."

A major renovation kept secret. But why? "He had tons of correspondence printed out, too. I managed to snap a few pictures." She zoomed in on a snippet of emails, followed by an excerpt of a legal document. "Plaintiff: LGT Construction," she read aloud. She scanned the images more than once to make sure she was piecing everything correctly. Because Edward Hendrick was being sued.

The fragment from his paper trail implied the hotel director owed over a quarter million dollars to LGT for planning and design services already rendered. A rep from the company claimed it wasn't the contractor's problem if there was red tape around a legal endorsement and the property owner's signature.

("It sounded businesslike. Something about a missing signature and a deadline?")

Mave's eyes widened. "Wait, does Birdie *own* this hotel? Is she the red tape being discussed in this email?" Birdie was well known for her stubbornness. If Hendrick had ambitions for the property—investments that involved millions of dollars—Birdie could have acted as an immovable roadblock.

"Huh," Holden sighed. "No wonder he wants you caught and arrested. He's using you to cover up his own motive for murder."

"Wait." She shook her head. "On the tapes, Mr. Hendrick was seen in the hallway *after* it happened. That means he couldn't have been in Birdie's bedroom earlier. The cameras would have caught him leaving, then returning." And how would he have cleaned the blood off himself so quickly? "This still doesn't make any sense," she muttered.

Think back. What am I missing? How had Hendrick behaved when he'd walked in? Except she'd been so disturbed at the time, it was impossible to judge with any certainty. Mave rubbed her brow. Her senses felt scattered—unreliable in the enclosing mess. She craved order, sunlight.

Stop, Cain instructed. *Make order. Go over what you know. Slowly.*

"Okay." She pulled in a deep breath, acutely aware of Holden's body standing an inch from her own. She stepped away and paced in a narrow circuit. "First Bastian—who by the way, I'm pretty sure is protecting someone—points the finger at Birdie's art dealer, Dominic Grady."

"Right, you should talk to him next."

After her exchange with Katrina, Mave needed more time before attempting another interview. "Second, Tag lied about me cutting the power and, for whatever reason, he's hellbent on my arrest. That might mean he's working with Mr. Hendrick. Also, Mr. Hendrick supposedly thinks I'm a deadly risk worth a thousand dollars to control during his precious gala weekend. And according to these papers, he'd want Birdie out of the picture if she was standing in the way of his plans for a casino.

"Then, there's Katrina. She seemed upset, but more about

having to leave the hotel. Then she outright lied about her whereabouts on the night of the murder. Why? Why lie about leaving your room?" Mave was dizzy from the countless questions and random leads. Her brain was looping itself into a giant knot. "Is she covering evidence? In on it, too? How does she fit into all of this?"

Through the eyeholes of his mask, Holden's gaze tracked her like she was a goldfish swimming back and forth in its tank.

"Does she know something about the renovations she shouldn't? Or did Birdie make one too many demands, push her in a fit of rage to commit murder?"

Wrong. Do it again, Cain drilled. *Do it right.*

She stepped over a dirty paint rag. "Except the killer staged everything. It was planned. Having me there, using my boxcutter and the glass muller with my fingerprints—it all points to premeditated murder."

Holden reached to stop her as she passed. "If that's the case, then we're going at this all wrong."

She flashed him a baffled look.

"Everyone knows Birdie was a prickly woman, right?" His choice of words triggered her guilt. The woman was lying murdered next door, and here they were judging her. "Thing is, she lived a long life and pissed off folks along the way. But not you. You're nice."

She didn't feel so nice at the moment. "What does my personality have to do with anything?"

"A lot. If someone's set you up, it's not Birdie's enemies you should be looking for. It's *yours*. Your list is considerably shorter."

She glanced at a distant point over his shoulder, drawing the connections. "So instead of asking who'd want to murder Birdie," a chill pebbled her skin, "I should be asking: who'd want to hurt me?" Her thoughts twisted in a new direction and a rock formed in her stomach. "You forgot one thing."

He raised and dropped his hand like he'd wanted to touch her again. "What?" His warmth radiated. She had to resist leaning into it.

"My father. In prison." Four years and she still hated saying it aloud. The pain and disgrace of the blow had yet to ease. Maybe it never would. The back of her throat swelled. How had it come to this: alone and running, tainted in guilt? Just like him.

"Mave?"

She sucked in a breath. "I may not have enemies but Cain sure does. Like a lot. My entire life, he's done everything he can to protect me from them."

(Thirteen years old. She sobbed and choked back her panic.

"Keep quiet or they'll find you." The bullet hole he'd shot in the top of the trunk allowed for a spear of light to enter. And air.)

She snapped her elastic once. Twice. "In his own messed up way, he did what he thought was best."

(She wiggled closer to the bullet hole. Jumper cables dug into her spine.)

"And now, someone may be using me to get to him."

Holden drew her hand into his, tethering her to the present. His thumb slipped beneath the elastic band and drew a circle on her wrist, on the angry welt there. "We'll find the killer."

Tingles shot up her arm. Their eyes locked and bridged a current in the dark.

"No one will hurt you." His thumb continued its feather stroke, igniting her skin with tiny shivers. It wasn't enough. She needed more to outrun her past. The rules. The killings.

With a rush of blood, her lips parted. Before she could talk herself out of it, she lifted her hand and placed it on his chest.

His teeth clicked together. "What are you doing?" Though he didn't sound entirely pleased, he didn't push her away.

Slowly, she slid her palm to the side of his neck. It was one of the few real parts of him she could see, touch. His throat moved up down. In out. Faster. She studied his quickening pulse, leaned in, obeying the gravitational pull between them. Closer. Who was the man beneath the—

He exhaled a curse in Russian, jerked back, and bumped into the worktable.

The spell broke. Awkwardness hung thick between them. She might as well have been a live wire threatening him with electrocution.

He pulled a deep breath through his nose and blinked away his dazed look. "Listen, about—"

"No it's fine. Good," she said, half cringing, half begging him not to utter another word. She folded her arms, embarrassment quick to fill the hole in her chest. They were near strangers. And all the chemistry in the world couldn't erase the ugly truth: she was a hitman's daughter. Even a man living like a hermit in an underground tunnel wouldn't touch her unless forced—unless his safety depended on it.

Mave looked away. "I'm stalling, I know," she whispered, grasping for an excuse, fearing the full force of her voice would betray her humiliation. She swallowed. "But I have to do this. So let's just get it over with. Okay? It's fine," she lied. "I'm fine." She stepped back as if to prove it, restoring some margin of personal space and sanity between them. Deep down though, she knew she'd fooled no one. Least of all herself.

TWENTY-TWO

"Where is she?" he asked, returning them to harsh reality. "Birdie's body—where did it happen?"

Straining to filter out the crawling shadows, Mave touched her neck. She suppressed another shudder. "Bedroom." Her reply was barely audible. All that gore. Witnessing the post-mortem effects of the executed man in the tub when she was twelve was horrific enough for one lifetime. Now she had to go through it again with Birdie.

It was my idea to come back here, she chastised herself. *And it may be my only chance to retrace my steps.*

She bit her inner cheek and did her best to ignore the glare of the portraits—the naked mannequin in the corner with its pale eyes. Something felt off, not in its rightful place. Someone had drawn open the curtains. Yet that wasn't all. She tried to pinpoint what troubled her, but the harder she focused, the deeper the niggling suspicion burrowed into her subconscious. The surrounding mess wasn't helping matters. She fidgeted with a button on her coat.

Start over. Her father's prompt from every lesson until perfection could be attained: restage it, recite it, re-solve it.

"The door into the studio was unlocked."

What did you hear?

"A voice—I thought it was Birdie's—told me to come inside. But there was no one here. I called out and" (*a muffled cough through the wall)* "someone was next door."

(*Mave Mm—!*)

She flinched and crossed her arms. "Sorry, it's just—I need a minute."

"Yeah, sure." Holden put his hands in his pockets and glanced around the room.

She stood stiffly amid the clutter as he relit his Zippo and rifled papers strewn on the nearest table. "Sketches everywhere. Maybe she drew something useful."

"A red book," she replied, unblinking.

"What?"

Birdie's final moments crashed into her thoughts again: her lined jaw twitching. *A book with a burgundy cover... leather-bound... it was murky and dusty....*She'd been so overwhelmed coping with one horror after another, she'd almost forgotten the third lead she'd scribbled on her list. She shifted next to Holden, a zing coursing through her veins. "It was her last thought. Like a dying wish. She wanted me to find this red book."

"When?" Holden asked, watching her poke a paper with her sleeve to avoid leaving prints. "I thought when you found her she was dead."

"Almost." Nothing remotely resembling a book existed on the table. Mave sighed. "She was"—bleeding out—"just hanging on when I walked into the bedroom."

"And she spoke to you?"

"Not exactly. She sort of gave off..." Mave tucked her hair behind her ear. It was always difficult to describe the sensation. "...a strong thought." She avoided his gaze. He didn't know about her hound-dogging. A part of her dreaded his reaction. Would he think her too weird, mentally unhinged, or worse, a phony?

She pretended to inspect a drawing while inwardly steeling herself for his judgment. "I have this extra sense. I can find things." She tried and failed to sound nonchalant. He held his stare on the side of her face. "Like a clairvoyant," she whispered when he offered no comment.

"For real? You're saying—you're a psychic?"

She gave the slightest nod and caught sight of a box of disposable black gloves. Birdie must have worn them to protect her hands from paint.

"Then what the hell are we doing here? Can't you just grab the murder weapon and intuit what happened? Identify the killer?"

"No. I'm not that kind of psychic." She helped herself to a pair of gloves. "I can't see into the past or the future. I can only sense lost things in present-time. Inanimate objects." Mostly junk, she wanted to add. No lost pets or people. And nothing she'd misplaced herself.

"Wow. Okay. That explains the Walt Whitman question."

She glanced up and caught him smiling. She couldn't decide whether or not he was teasing her but it didn't matter. A weight lifted.

"What's it like? How does it work?"

She considered her answer before giving it. No one had ever asked her to describe the experience. Strangers were either too impatient for their possessions to be found or too unnerved by the process to enquire. "I suppose it's like reading a person's unconscious, their connection to a belonging—like a frequency that I inhale."

"You breathe it in?"

"Sort of." She twirled a lock of hair behind her ear. "Imagine a cord between them: the owner and lost item are linked. And that cord transmits a distinct energy. I can follow it, trace it. The stronger the sentimentality, the easier the read. But the person has to be close by, ideally in the same room for it to work. That's why the connection with the red book broke when Birdie, well…"

"That's incredible." An inflection a lot like awe threaded his voice.

She brushed her neck. Her ears warmed. "Well, if Birdie lost a red book, it's unlikely to be lying around a table in the studio. I'm pretty sure it's packed away someplace." Her first visit replayed in her mind. *The trunk next door.* "This way." She was grateful for an excuse to get away from the creepy portraits.

With Holden shadowing, she followed the inky trail of her footprints from yesterday and tiptoed into the sitting room next door. The salon was just shy of pitch-black. Her eyes darted from the tufted couch to the bedroom door. Tag or someone must have shut it. Trying not to bump into furniture, she carefully inched her way toward the trunk from memory. Holden swept by her with ease, clearly accustomed to moving in the dark.

Before she even reached the trunk, he'd found and lit a pair of candles on a bar cart. "Here." He took one flickering taper for himself and offered her the other. "There's a lot more to this suite. This place is huge." His silhouette melted as he wandered deeper inside.

A quick inspection of the trunk showed it to be merely decorative. Mave pursed her lips and tried to picture the space Birdie had channeled—*somewhere dark*—but a scent of ash startled her. She flinched, pulse soaring. The backs of her knees hit the trunk.

It's just a fireplace, she noticed. She cupped her face. No ghost lingered in the penthouse. She inhaled a ribbon of musty air just to be sure. *No ash. See?* It was a symptom of stress—a warning. She couldn't put it off. She had to see the body. The longer she stalled, the more likely she'd give in to fear.

She gazed into the dark for Holden but he wasn't there. Of course. He was probably having a field day exploring this massive suite for "loose change." Mave set her shoulders and shuffled to the bedroom door.

Don't be a baby, Cain coached. *And watch you don't smudge any prints on the knob.*

She toed the door open. The hinges clicked. *Deep breath.* She forced her focus beyond the flame of her candle and stepped inside.

The balcony doors remained sealed. She gathered the lapels of her coat, anticipating the cold. *Step by step, M&M. Do it exactly like you did the first time.*

She slowly rounded the king-sized bed. Her shadow trembled against the floor, folded against the footboard. The phone was on the carpet where she'd last seen it. Thankfully the stink of decay wasn't noticeable. She blinked. Neither was Birdie's body.

Mave knelt on the carpet. She couldn't possibly be imagining this, too. She squeezed her eyes closed and counted to three, but a second glance didn't break the illusion.

Birdie's body was gone.

How?

She reached out with her candle. Her gaze traced the dark bloodstains and streaks that told of injury—of violence—from the floor to the bed.

There—where Mave had wiped her hands. *And there*—where her heels had gouged dashes into the pile of the carpet. She even looked under the bed and noted the muller and boxcutter from the giftshop. So where was the body?

Mave stood and circled the room. She surveyed corner to corner but Birdie's corpse was nowhere to be found. She was at a loss. Perhaps Mr. Hendrick had moved her for preservation until police arrived. But that, too, seemed illogical, and in violation of law and safety protocols. Tag himself had demanded that no one handle anything inside the suite. Surely moving the primary source of evidence—the body—would be considered tainting the crime scene.

Short on theories, Mave flattened onto her stomach and rechecked under the bed from the opposite side. *A different viewpoint*, Cain would say; *sometimes just changing your position can help*. Except in this case Birdie still wasn't visible.

A book was.

She would have missed it altogether had she not been worried about the boxspring catching fire from her candle. She stretched out to touch it—confirming she wasn't dreaming the book sandwiched between the bed slats and the mattress. Her fingers brushed the leather-bound cover. It was the wrong color, green rather than red.

She shifted upright and pried it out anyway—a slim photo album. Mave opened its cover. Inside was a sheet protector, yellowed and crinkled with age. Shadows of portraits were visible beneath the translucent paper. She turned the page.

A glamorous, black and white image of Birdie showed her in her early forties, brows arched and smile sultry. She was arm-in-arm with a handsome, younger man with a cleft chin and thin mustache. Her son Charlie, perhaps? They were posing alongside another couple dressed in formalwear. Birdie appeared every inch the stunning, sophisticated socialite. Mave's focus slid to the next page.

A yellowed newspaper clipping showed Birdie posing with the same young man as earlier, though both appeared a few years older in this shot and the latter had traded his mustache for a goatee. They were standing in front of a large painted portrait and a sign announcing Birdie's solo exhibition. Mave squinted to read the journalist's caption beneath the image, expecting to confirm Charlie's name beside Birdie's. But the caption identified him as Dominic Grady—*the* Dominic Grady.

Mave nearly pressed her nose to the print. The familiar way he had his arm around Birdie's waist, she wondered if the two of them had been more than friendly professionals. Birdie wouldn't have been the first wealthy woman to take a younger lover and tote him around as arm candy. She flipped another page.

A pair of eyes stared back at her, frozen in time and identical in shape to her own. Mave's heart faltered and her lungs emptied of breath. She gaped at the photograph dated thirty-two years ago: a black and white graduation picture of her mother.

TWENTY-THREE

FROM THE RED BOOK OF THE DEAD

MAY 22ND, 1991

Hola Abee-cakes!

¿Cómo estás? I'm writing this from south of the border and lord knows when you'll get it. You're not going to believe this. Where to begin! The most AMAZING thing has happened. I've met someone. His name is Cain. And I think I'm in love.

TWENTY-FOUR

JANUARY 1ˢᵗ, 2021

Mave seemed to float outside of herself. She stared at the picture. Uncomprehending. Unaccepting. What was Birdie doing with a portrait of her mother in an album hidden beneath her bed? *What. What. What.*

YOU KNOW WHAT.

It was, in fact, spelled out in handwritten captions beneath several photographs: *Valeria Elizabeth Everhart.* Birdie's elongated script was memorable—same as on the notecard delivered to Mave. And the old woman had recorded the name more than once.

Mave's mother's name had been Valeria. Valeria *Francis.* Cain had minimally shared that much with her. But not her middle or maiden name. She was having difficulty consolidating the former with the latter.

She read it over and over. It was impossible to refute. She knew each angle and idiosyncrasy of her mother's face as if it were her own. The doe-like eyes. The cupid bow's mouth. The small beauty mark beneath. She had spent hours studying them in the picture taped to her bathroom mirror. And here they were—in dozens of additional prints.

Valeria was featured in candids taken at Christmases, birthday parties, school portraits— one where she looked about six or seven with a missing front tooth. Another captured her as a toddler in a frilly dress and bonnet, squished between the laps of a girl and boy. *Everhart children at Baptism,* the caption read.

Mave's throat squeezed and her eyes clouded with tears. Stabbing pain clamped her heart. Before she had become a Francis, Valeria had been an Everhart. The mother she had pictured all these years had led a life completely unimaginable to her.

All those mornings Birdie had dropped by the giftshop and drilled her with questions about her past—she must have suspected they were related. *Known. She must have known.* Now scanning multiple photos, Mave's resemblance to Valeria was startling even to herself. So why hadn't Birdie said anything? Why had she kept something so important a secret? Questions licked like wildfire, quick and hungry burning brighter, hotter. She would never know. Birdie was no longer here to offer the truth. Newfound grief cinched her chest as the revelation settled over her.

Valeria Elizabeth Everhart.

Birdie had been Mave's *grandmother.* She hadn't even been given the opportunity to get to know the woman properly, ask her questions about Valeria and her missing family. Her roots. Stolen. All of it: her history, her bloodline, her memories of what could have been.

Mave slammed the album shut and shoved it beneath the mattress. She wiped her palms across her cheeks and stood. Her legs shook. So many secrets. So many lies. She'd played along, ignorant of too much, too long. She'd allowed others to keep her in the dark, had paid the price. From haters who'd assumed she'd abetted in her father's crimes, to manipulators who continued to treat her like a child, she was done playing their games. Her gaze fell on the balcony doors.

(*Tag snorted. "You expect us to believe someone climbed the walls outside? Twenty-three stories up, on tonight of all nights?"*)

Mave pinched off the hurt—or tried. It was like a gushing artery. But one perk about having a hitman as a father was fluency in suppressing emotion.

Compartmentalize. Focus outward, not inward.

Cain was right. Her breaths were shredded. She was falling apart. She couldn't deal with this now. Here. She sniffed and made an effort to inhale slowly—in and out. In and out. Again. She wiped her face a few more times. She was neither a pawn nor a murderer. And she'd prove it.

She'd glimpsed the killer's flight when she'd first run in to help Birdie. She was now certain. No matter the blinding ice storm or how absurd it seemed, the person responsible for stabbing Birdie had to have escaped through the balcony. It was the only other way out of this godforsaken bedroom.

She marched toward it. Though the handle was frozen, the French door swung inward with ease. Frigid air skimmed her face and tunneled into the room. The flame of her candle thrashed and extinguished in a wisp of smoke. Lashes fluttering against the current, Mave abandoned the wick on the floor and stepped onto the icy terrace.

She began to venture across, taking care not to slip. Footprints were crusted in both directions as if someone had paced back and forth. Mave crouched. A sheet of ice had preserved tread marks. They seemed too large to belong to Birdie. Perhaps a woman with big feet. Or a smaller to average-sized man. It was hard to be certain. But, if her hunch was correct, these were the killer's boot-prints.

She moved along, expecting to reach the balcony's peripheral limit, but it soon became clear none existed. Her brow puckered. The balcony curved past the bedroom. No divisions were anywhere in sight, implying the terrace extended the length of the suite. With every step, realization crystalized in Mave's thoughts.

Yesterday when she'd walked in on Birdie bleeding, the dark figure she'd mistaken for a trick of the eye had been real. At the time, Mave had assumed the glass doors had led to a Juliet balcony like the ones on the Château's front façade. But a wraparound terrace meant the killer could have slipped outdoors and reentered the suite from another room of their choice, as long as the door was unlocked from the inside.

Planned. Premeditated, Cain whispered. *Every step.*

The killer would have left her with Birdie bleeding to her death, fully aware security was minutes away from bursting in on them. Incriminating Mave.

If you're going to commit a crime, you do it right. One opportunity. No room for mistakes.

An escape route around the balcony was a start. That still left in question the main exit to the suite itself—the camera fixed in the hallway. If the perpetrator slipped through the balcony unnoticed, then came through an alternate room, they still would have needed to access the studio doors to flee the suite entirely. Tag had been correct about one thing: exposed in yesterday's storm, even the stealthiest mountain climber couldn't have scaled twenty-three flights from the Château's exterior. How did the killer sneak in and out from the corridor without getting caught on video? The unanswerable riddle vexed Mave as she reached the windows that looked in on the studio.

She paused, imagining she was enacting the exact flight of the killer. Her breath fogged the glass as she stood before the door. The latch pressed—no ice or resistance—and Mave crept into the dark studio without trouble. The perfect crime.

She shut the balcony exit. Wind whistled through a crack and a bite of frost lingered on her skin. Where had the killer disappeared to next? Where had the victim, for that matter?

Holden shuffled ahead, and Mave released a loud sigh. "There you are." She squinted into shadows. Finally, she could share part of her burden. It already felt overwhelming—the missing body. The photo album. Her tears threatened to spring again. "Holden?" Her voice cracked. An overhead spotlight flickered from another power surge and her mistake illuminated.

A bottle dropped from his hand and smashed on the floor. "*Val.*"

She stiffened at the stranger's sigh—at the reek of liquor and ash swamping her senses.

A man other than Holden had entered the studio. And that same man was now staring at her. The monstrous ghost inches from his neck.

TWENTY-FIVE

Mave's muscles engorged with blood rushing, roaring: *run*. But her knees jammed. Her bones calcified into stone, anchoring her to the spot.

Hovering beside the man, the apparition from the library turned her head toward Mave. Those strange filthy hands remained strapped to her face, one pair atop the other, masking her of voice, breath, sight. Yet she seemed to stare straight into Mave's eyes—just like the stranger who'd dropped his bottle of liquor. Didn't the man see the ghost, too? Didn't he want to get away from it?

"*You*," he said, addressing Mave. His chest sagged as if he'd used up all his air. They stood there a moment—he seemingly as terrified as she. He was balding and lanky, all elbows and knees beneath his clothes. "Witch." His whisper carried in the howling wind. His weak jaw quivered. "Did…did Mother send you to haunt me for my sins?"

The faulty spotlight above blinked on and off. Mave's gaze flitted back and forth between the stranger and the ghost. He must not have felt it there, lingering over his shoulder. It was the only explanation. He reacted only to Mave through his startled, dewy eyes—even as the ghost leaned toward his ear.

The premonition grew like soured fruit in the pit of Mave's stomach. She *alone* could see it—this man was oblivious. What's more, Mave was picking up traces of meaning. She could *scent* her rage. The creature was a prisoner plagued, trapped by those dirty hands clutching her face. A low harmonic wove in the draft. Through the seam of knuckles, she was struggling to communicate.

Mave released a sharp breath. Terror marbled her body—crawled like ants trapped beneath her skin. *Who are you—what are you?* she wanted to ask. Her lungs hitched, their sacs coated in bitter ash.

The strange man's eyes suddenly sparked like he'd solved a riddle. "Or was it Annabelle! Have you finally come to save her from me?" A garble erupted from his throat, a manic stutter caught between laughter and despair. He cradled his stomach and hacked violently. He was crazed. And yet Mave knew, she *knew* in her bones he'd said something true.

It was her: Annabelle.

No, not exactly. More flashes transmitted.

She didn't like to be called by that name. She preferred… *Abee… Ab-Abs…*

Mave gasped. Where were these thoughts coming from? She'd never experienced this type of psychic encounter. She channeled inanimate objects. The mere idea of communing with the dead—this creature—brought a surge of bile up her throat. She staggered back a step and cupped her mouth.

The monstrous ghost seemed to sense her rise in panic. She seeped through the man's flesh and advanced on Mave.

RUN.

The nerves along Mave's spine jolted painfully as her muscles shocked to life. She careened sideways and lunged wide around a worktable. The spotlights above snapped and died.

"Val, no—wait!" the man cried after her.

Sprinting wildly over the broken bottle, Mave thrust and flailed her hands in blackness. She made it all the way to the door of the studio. It even unlocked and swung inward for her, and for a ludicrous second, she considered it divine intervention. She would make it. She would get away.

Just as quickly she collided into a solid form—too stunned to process what—rebounded, fell, and purged the contents of her stomach onto the floor.

"*What the fuck,*" a woman's husky voice griped above her. It hadn't been god who'd opened the door after all. "Dammit, Charlie, you can't be in here!" The door creaked open its full width as the newcomer shifted. "Edward, how many people have a key to this suite?" Her whip-like demands conveyed her authority.

Replies were blurted over top of each other, battling to be heard. Mave's pupils contracted into pinpricks under the beam of a strong flashlight. Drooping on all fours, she managed to wipe her chin on her sleeve.

"Well, well. Mave Michael Francis I presume?"

Mave blinked at the speaker's military-style boots, their tips stained in salt—navy trousers. "Quite a few people are looking for you." The owner of the voice—perfectly human and smelling of no ash whatsoever—crouched down for a better view. She circled her flashlight onto the remains of Mave's breakfast and cringed. "Rough day?"

Mave met the sheriff's shrewd brown eyes.

Part III

BLOOD LOSS

TWENTY-SIX

She'd repeated it enough times to trigger a headache: receiving the notecard; finding Birdie; leaving Birdie. *It wasn't me*, she'd restated in every which way. *I didn't kill her. I didn't return to move her body. I didn't destroy any evidence.*

Mave's stomach growled. How many hours had passed since she'd been caught inside—*rescued from*—the studio and brought to the Oasis Spa for questioning? She was hungry, thirsty, tired. It had to be well past noon though the candlelight made it feel far later. The navy canvas wallpaper in the plush lounge doubling as her interrogation room wasn't helping matters. Nor the gloomy new age soundtrack of chimes and bowls that played from a tablet nearby. Mave silently cursed its lithium battery life.

Still no power. Still no roads. The sheriff, apparently, had hiked miles *alone on snowshoes* to reach the Château—an endeavor that Mave found shocking. The snow was still falling thickly, making the landscape inhospitable, disorienting. In current conditions, it must have taken Morganson hours on foot to cross that distance—the better part of a day, if not overnight. How had she managed?

Who's to say she did? Cain needled. *Who's to say she hasn't been here all along, secretly rubbing elbows with the rich and the affluent? Always remember, M&M: The higher the rank, the deeper the pockets, the greed. Better question: who pads the sheriff's wallet?*

Her stomach cramped. Cain's warnings only made it worse. She crossed her arms, bounced her knee, and waited for Morganson to return from a radio meeting with her deputy. Various staff tiptoed around her. All went about their business—flitted their eyes away each time she glanced in their direction—stocking towels, assembling lotions and gift baskets as if Mave didn't exist.

What's happening on the twenty-third floor? she wanted to yell. *What've you heard? Seen?* Why hadn't anyone spotted Holden? Or Birdie's body?

Or Annabelle's ghost?

Mave squeezed her eyes shut and dipped her head to her knees. *No, not that part.*

She stuffed the incident down, down with the rest of the unmentionables. Whatever rumors were currently running wild among personnel, she wasn't privy to them. It didn't take much to imagine.

Witch.

Bastian could only do so much damage control. She'd been marked. The sheriff hadn't read Mave her rights. *Yet.* But that was only because Birdie's body was temporarily missing. Whether or not an official arrest was coming now or later, it didn't look good for her. All that running from security had backfired, made her seem even guiltier.

Mave had never before felt more like hitting something. Screaming. Begging. But her colleagues' glares when they thought she wasn't looking spoke volumes. She'd been on the receiving end of such stares before. During Cain's trial. Afterwards. It didn't matter if Birdie herself resurrected from the dead and confessed the truth. The jury was set. So was the mob. They would neither accept reason nor offer mercy. Not to Mave: the disgusting daughter of a convicted hitman.

Familiar shame swelled in her gut. She gripped her forehead as a lifetime of prejudice burned in her ears. A murderer—that's all they'd ever see. A voice in her head whispered they were right: all those years she'd kept Cain's secrets and lived off his blood money. This was her doing, her blameworthy karma.

Why had she bothered? If anything, she was worse off than when she'd first run away from security. Everything had continued to go wrong.

(*"Two types of people in the world,"* Cain recited, *"the type who think police will help them, and the type who think police will get them. Now listen good, M&M: which group you belong to has nothing to do with guilt."*)

Cain's indoctrination wouldn't be easily undone. She had to force herself to change. From now on, she'd cooperate. She'd be the first type of person: pro-police. At least superficially. She might not trust Morganson, but that didn't mean she openly had to resist the investigation. Cain could scold her and throw tantrums in her mind all he wanted. She would remain seated in her pillowy chair like a good little witness until Sheriff Morganson returned. She gripped her knees tightly as if to prove it to herself. She could do this. She could resist Cain's training. "Don't run. Only criminals run," she whispered. "Trust the system." She didn't. The words felt false in her mouth.

She rubbed her eyes, determined to do this her own way. She was skilled at finding things. From now on, she would use all her senses, as *legally* as possible—beginning with logic. She pulled in the surrounding scents of lavender and eucalyptus like a tonic.

The man upstairs, it had been Birdie's son, Charlie Everhart. He had mistaken Mave for his long-dead sister. *Val,* he'd addressed her twice. It was short for her mother's name, Valeria Francis, née Everhart. At the time, Mave had been too overwhelmed to pick up on the mix-up. No wonder Charlie had reacted insanely to her sudden appearance in the studio. Even she was having difficulty believing her relation to the Everharts.

Maybe my brain concocted that, too. Maybe I'm haunting myself, driving myself into a shock-induced, permanent psychosis. Repressed trauma is hidden for a reason. Maybe I was better off completely oblivious about my maternal side.

But in her heart, she didn't wholly believe that. In fact, she now wished she'd held on to Birdie's secret album. Anger had made her act rashly. In the moment it had been easier to reject the images of her mother, the history denied her for so many years. The pain of the discovery had been unbearable—it still was. But hours later, heavy clouds had shifted. Like fresh raindrops into cracked, thirsty earth, reason seeped into Mave's mind. If she wanted to save herself from this mess, the entire truth had to be endured—even the ugliest parts that threatened to wound the deepest.

She kneaded her temples. It was connected: being recruited here, the evidence stacked against her, her estranged grandmother's murder. She'd been wrong. The missing links had never stemmed from her father. Everything led back to her mother.

She thought of the tourism officer who'd recruited her over the phone three months ago. Joseph something-or-other. He'd claimed he'd obtained her contact information from her old manager from her summer stint in a giftshop in Seattle. Too busy hiding from Cain, Mave had never bothered to check out his story. It had been so easy, so convenient: a full-time gig, room and board in an old romantic château. God, how could she have been so gullible? She pushed down on her sternum—on the ache—and blew out a long, measured breath. Who else had known about Valeria's past? Had Cain? Obviously Charlie Everhart had been aware.

That was my uncle up there.

Hollow laughter threatened to bubble from her mouth. Mave cleared her throat and straightened as Edward Hendrick scurried into the spa with a stack of papers clutched to his doughy chest.

The hotel director flinched upon noticing her there—alone—and dropped a sheet.

She stood, her hands fisted at her sides. "Mr. Hendrick, please—wait."

He ignored her and scooped up his paper from the floor. He was treating her like the others were: like she was a monster.

"Why did you offer that thousand-dollar bonus? Mr. Hendrick—"

He quickened his stride to escape.

"I know about the casino."

That got his attention. He froze before the glass doors of the lounge, shoulders tensed.

"I know about the lawsuit," she said in a hushed voice, "LGT Construction." She'd expected him to respond with anger, but when he faced her, his expression seemed closer to panic.

"Who've you been talking to?" he rasped. "That's private—none of your business."

"It is my business when Birdie was unsupportive of your plans and you're framing me for her murder." Though it was a longshot, he took the bait.

His jaw went slack. "You think I—are you seriously saying…"

"Did you kill Birdie because she wouldn't sign off on the renovation?"

"No! I—" He checked his voice while shooting a nervous glance around to make sure no one could overhear them. "That you could even *think* that is absurd."

"Okay. Then where were you yesterday when Birdie was killed?"

Mr. Hendrick's meaty cheeks seemed to be cycling through various shades of red. "You have some nerve, lying about who you are and now—" He clicked his jaw shut and inhaled deeply through his nose. "How dare you stand there and question me."

"Would you prefer I express my concerns to the sheriff?"

He scoffed though his features remained stained with anxiety.

"Please Mr. Hendrick, I just want to understand." She tried a softer tone. "It would help me to place everyone, okay? If you're innocent then it shouldn't matter."

"Look, if you insist on—Morganson already knows where I was," he spat. "Loads of people do—they all saw me circulating the ball, making sure everything was running smoothly. And it was, until I was paged about the goddamned *disaster* upstairs."

"Fine. If that's true, if you had nothing to do with Birdie's death, then why did you evict her maid less than a day after? What does she know?"

"What does she *know*? Do you hear yourself? This isn't a conspiracy. I asked Katrina to leave because of asbestos in the walls."

"Asbestos?"

"Yes," he snipped with his eyes and chest puffed. "Despite Birdie's objection to my contractors 'disturbing her peace,' about a week ago I booked an inspection for the hotel's neglected spaces—penthouse included. Even offered to relocate her and Katrina to the presidential suite while we assessed the problem."

"And she wasn't concerned?"

"No. She flat out refused. Nearly took off my head when I said it was covered in the costs of inspecting the basement; then she went over my head, fired my contractor and ordered me to put it off for another year—a *year*," he vented like he had to get this off his chest, "as if she's in charge and the world revolves around her. Meanwhile, I've got a deadline as of tomorrow to fix this mess or my investors pull and the entire reno is—"

"Oh, good, you're both here."

Hendrick gave a start as Sheriff Morganson strode into the lounge. Freshly melted snowflakes glinted atop her short hair and her hawk-like features gave away nothing.

Mr. Hendrick was likely wondering the same as Mave: how much had the sheriff overheard? Was she finally ready to arrest her?

"Edward, how'd it go?" she said instead.

"Excellent." Mr. Hendrick offered the sheriff a paper from his stack. "I had Jordy write all the copies, word for word, exactly like you asked. Just finished distributing the memo myself."

"All guests and staff? Every single one?"

"Mm-hmm."

"I didn't get any memo," Mave interrupted.

"Right, well, I assumed..." Mr. Hendrick puckered his mouth and summoned another shade of pink to his ears.

"Here. Take mine." Sheriff Morganson passed Mave the paper she'd just been given. It was a handwritten notice on hotel stationary, signed on behalf of Sheriff Louise Morganson. The memo barred all guests and staff from leaving the premises of the hotel prior to a police interview. No exceptions whatsoever.

"We're locked in?"

"*Snowed* in," the sheriff corrected. "Equally true and sounds a lot less scary. It's standard procedure," she informed Mave. "If Birdie's body was stolen from the crime scene, as you all claim, that can only mean it's hidden somewhere on this property. And if that's true, I'll need to speak to everyone here so I can find the victim and the persons responsible. Speaking of which, if you don't mind," she pivoted to the hotel director with her hands on her hips, "Edward, I'd like another word with Mave. In private. And if you could turn this shit off on your way out." She gestured overhead to indicate the new age soundtrack.

"Consider it done." Mr. Hendrick bowed his head awkwardly. "If you need me, I'll just be…" He retreated with the extra copies of the memo like a frightened weasel. A moment later the hymn of ringing bowls came to an abrupt stop. Given the sudden silence, Mave suspected Mr. Hendrick was just beyond the glass doors, listening in from the spa's reception desk.

The sheriff turned to Mave and gestured at a sofa chair. "Please, sit."

Despite the itch in her feet, Mave obeyed.

"Thanks for waiting so patiently." She took the seat opposite Mave and stretched out her stout legs. "*Oof*, these are comfy, huh?" She ran her palms along the velvety upholstery. "Could use a chair like this back at the station. Now then," she punctuated the end of pleasantries with a slap to the armrests, "I have some news."

Mave held still under Morganson's sharp gaze. She preferred it when her attention was fixed on the furniture.

"First, I questioned Bastian and he verifies your statement about the note. *But* he still hasn't found his cellphone with the alleged message from Birdie."

Mave bit her lip to avoid blurting out a useless tip about some-place with peach and green fabric. She allowed herself a tiny glim-mer of hope. The written invitation wasn't worth much without the voice recording, (she easily could have forged the note herself), but it was a start.

The sheriff watched her with a neutral expression. Whatever thoughts were running through the woman's mind, she hid them well. "That said, we can at least head to your room to collect the note."

Why? So Morganson could get rid of the evidence herself—as-suming Tag hadn't beat her to it? (*"Morganson wouldn't say noth-ing...called a buddy of mine upstate..."*) They knew each other, se-curity, police—one big happy "law and order" family.

Reluctantly, Mave nodded and leaned to get up.

"There's more." The sheriff signaled for her to stay put. "My deputy managed to track down Ms. Everhart's lawyers—another routine precaution. The firm just sent us all the details on her es-tate." There was a pause in which Mave felt she was expected to say something. "I assume you know?" the sheriff added.

Mave swallowed. "Birdie Everhart owns—owned—the Châ-teau," she offered, hoping it was enough to prove her cooperation.

"I have to be honest. It doesn't exactly help your case."

Mave shook her head. "I don't follow..."

The sheriff's aloofness finally slipped. She narrowed one eye. "Mave, you *are* aware that Elizabeth Everhart has named you her sole heir and beneficiary?"

"I'm sor—I'm *sorry*...?" Her croak trailed off and her hands grew sweaty in her lap.

"She ordered the change from her lawyers a few months ago. Right around the time you starting working here. Everything to you—the whole kit and caboodle," Sheriff Morganson said. "With Birdie's death, you stand to gain millions of dollars worth of in-come, stocks, and property. Even the deed to the land this hotel stands on is—"

The muffled clatter of an object falling cut her off. The sheriff spun at the sound.

Edward Hendrick had most definitely listened to every word.

TWENTY-SEVEN

Money. The killer had set her up over Birdie's inheritance. Mave's brain felt like it might rupture from Morganson's news.

If either Charlie or Parissa Everhart had been aware they'd been cut from their mother's will—that everything was going to a stranger—surely, the human response would be outrage. Drastic actions could cause drastic *re*actions—like murder—especially when millions of dollars were concerned. But why? Why leave her everything?

The more she considered it, the more essential it became she retrieve Birdie's note. It wasn't just evidence that could confirm her whereabouts during the crime—proof she wasn't lying. Its message and signature were possible clues into the killer's identity. And the killer had the answers Mave now desperately needed.

Her feet climbed the spiral staircase on autopilot, spinning higher and higher. Behind her, Sheriff Morganson's trailing steps vibrated through the iron handrail. The sheriff asked no more questions as they made their way to the fifth floor. It made Mave nervous. Either Morganson recognized her baffled state, or she, too, needed the time to think. What would she do when they entered her room?

Through the darkened hallways, Mave imagined suspects one by one dropping off the note: first Katrina, then Dominic Grady, then Tag, Charlie, or Parissa, or even her husband Nicholas Vaughn.

They reached the staff quarters, and Mave slowed to a stop in front of her room. "This is it," she said, though she had a feeling the sheriff knew exactly behind which door she slept. Her heart thumped unreasonably fast as she turned the lock and pushed.

I've got nothing to hide, she reminded herself. If she thought it enough times, maybe she'd begin to believe it.

The glow from her phone skated across her bed, dresser, nightstand. Everything seemed perfectly as she'd left it: tidy and organized. The exception was a silver tray from catering deposited next to the door—her dinner presumably.

She stepped across the creaky threshold, ignoring the food despite her empty stomach, and led the sheriff to her bathroom. There wasn't enough space for both of them to fit without bumping into one another. As Mave reached down to draw out her wastebasket, a fresh pang of anxiety turned her stomach. If Tag *hadn't* stolen it when he'd stopped by yesterday, could the note somehow be used against her—carry only her prints like the glass muller?

A killer who went to all this trouble would've worn gloves.

Before Mave could backtrack, Sheriff Morganson's flashlight reflected the bin's contents. The edge of the manila card was visible within. The anxiety squeezing Mave's chest intensified. She reminded herself, Birdie had not written that invitation. A forensic handwriting expert could prove it. There was chance, no matter how small, that Morganson would process the evidence and the forgery would backfire and expose its true author. That was assuming she wasn't a dirty cop. That was assuming her surprise arrival *wasn't* part of the set-up.

The sheriff hooked out Birdie's invitation with the end of her pen. After closely inspecting it, she snapped a photo of the card. She seemed neither pleased nor displeased. "You realize as the last person who saw Birdie Everhart alive, you'll likely have to answer a few more questions tomorrow." She shot Mave another ambiguous look. "In other words..."

"Don't disappear again." Mave gave a curt nod. "Got it. And

like you said, we're snowed in. Where could I disappear to, right?" A strained smile tugged her lips.

"Uh-huh." Morganson continued to watch her without giving anything away.

Like I'm a potential flight risk? A wolf in sheep's clothing? The woman was impossible to read. At least she held her light on Mave's chest versus her face.

"Who's in the photo?"

"What photo?" Mave crossed her arms. She couldn't bring herself to acknowledge Valeria's image taped to her mirror. Her eyes stung as she bent over and tucked the wastebasket into its rightful place, next to the toilet.

Everything's in order. Get it together.

"This one."

The flashlight swept sideways. There was no need to glance up to know where it now pointed. "My mother." Her voice sounded stale to her ears.

"She looks just like you."

"*Mmm*, I've been told." By Cain. And, more recently, by Charlie.

"Where is she now, if you don't mind me asking?"

Of course Mave minded. Of course the sheriff knew. Why was she making her say it?

It's what she wants—to break you.

She worried a hangnail on her thumb and drew blood. "She died when I was three."

"I'm sorry." Morganson wasn't studying the photograph, but Mave. "How did she die?"

"Drunk driver." She swiped her thumb across her bottom lip. "He ran a red light and hit her."

"And your father?"

"What about him?" Her voice was too sharp. This type of judgemental ambush was exactly why she didn't invite people in. Not into her private quarters. Not into her past or into her present.

"Just that it must have been hard. Man like him, raising a young daughter all on his own."

Mave was clenching her jaw so tightly her temples hurt. What did Sheriff Morganson know about men like Cain Francis. She was one of Them. Another supposed defender of the good who would sleep better at night knowing her team had one less piece of human garbage polluting their streets. She could hear the jeers outside the courthouse like they'd happened yesterday.

("—monster you killed my—")

"—you help him strip the bodies and wipe—"

"—blood on your hands, you filthy bitch—")

"Yeah, well," Mave shrugged and beat back the impulse to defend and curse Cain simultaneously. It took all her effort to steady her tone. "Can't pick your family."

"No. That you can't." Morganson finally broke her stare. "Realize you're tired," she said while reconsidering Valeria's portrait. It almost sounded as if she were saying it to the photograph. Mave wondered if she'd yet discovered the album beneath Birdie's mattress. "One last thing and I'll leave you to get some sleep," the sheriff placated, "I'm going to need you to give me your dress."

"My...?" Her stomach dropped as the sheriff snapped her flashlight onto her hem. Bloodstained. Beneath her poker face, Morganson was biding her time, gathering information—evidence to build a case against her. And why wouldn't she? Once Birdie's body turned up, a prosecution would be easy.

"Am I under arrest?" Miraculously, her voice didn't shake.

"Mave ..."

The sheriff's practiced demeanour of patience was familiar. The detectives who'd questioned her for eighteen hours straight after her father's arrest had worn that same look. Until they hadn't. It was all an act. Her pledge to trust the system suddenly felt entirely foolish.

"...need I remind you this is an official police investigation. It would serve you well to cooperate."

"I know my rights." To hell with being a good little witness. Who was she kidding; she'd always be a dirty suspect in the eyes of the world. Cain had made sure of that. She straightened her spine and crossed her arms. "Unless you have a warrant or are charging me with something…"

"Look," the sheriff sighed, seeming as exhausted as Mave with their charade. "I'm going to be straight with you. Witnesses have already placed you inside Birdie's suite. I found you poking around there myself."

"I wasn't—"

She raised her palm. "Traces of her blood on your dress aren't going to tell me anything I don't already know. But there could be more. Hairs or fibers trapped in the sequins. Hell, those blood-stains could belong to the person responsible. Isn't that what you want? To find whoever framed you?"

She was clever, using her words against her.

The sheriff raised her brow. "Now, we can do this the easy way, or the hard way."

Nothing about this was easy. Lying witnesses like Tag were bad enough. She wasn't about to make it convenient for the police to build a case against her. "It's late. I'd like to rest."

The sheriff's lips tightened. "Don't do anything stupid, Mave."

"I won't, goodnight."

Morganson's jaw twitched. After a pregnant pause, she gave a stiff nod and glided to the hallway in shadow. "I'll be back first thing in the morning, you understand?" The unspoken words *with a warrant* hung in the air. "If I wasn't clear earlier, let me repeat myself: don't go anywhere I can't find you. And word to the wise: lock this door behind me."

Mave wasn't sure what to make of her comment, whether it was a safety precaution intended for the guilty or the innocent. She heeded the warning either way.

Alone in the dark, she released a shuddering sigh and fell against the wall. Her legs folded like they belonged to a marionette.

Seated on the floor, she clutched her head in her hands and tried to loosen the tension that felt permanently coiled in her shoulders.

She hadn't been arrested. She was safe for another few hours. Overnight, if she was lucky. And Holden? Lord only knew where, when, or how he'd managed to disappear again. Like a ghost.

Like Abs.

Mave thumped the back of her skull. She would not think of that—she would not summon her name as if she were real. Yet the memory of Annabelle's apparition slipped beneath the surface of her thoughts with or without her permission. If it wasn't a figment of her imagination…

What did she want? Why was she haunting the hotel—or showing up in Birdie's suite in front of Mave? Why now? Bastian had been the first person to tell her the Château was haunted. She ought to find him and ask him. But they hadn't crossed paths since the dumbwaiter incident.

Exhausted from the endless unknowns, Mave pried off her tall boots. Rubbing the arches of her feet, she moaned in pain. She fumbled with the clasps on her coat next. In her rush to unfasten multiple buttons at once, her impatience grew, and she was soon tearing off every last bit of clothing.

She sat naked next to a heap topped by her sullied gown. Nearly all of the clothes were borrowed. Stolen. Another step closer to becoming Cain. She drew up her knees and wrapped herself into a ball. The ripe scent of her sweat hung about her like a familiar cloud. The last time she'd been this filthy, it had been the week after the trial. Mave closed her eyes and crawled to the bathroom in darkness.

Thumping on the door woke her from a dreamless sleep. A crack in the broken blinds let in a blade of sunlight. What day was it? Thursday? Friday? Was the cranky motel manager back for payment? Or had another journalist found her after she'd disconnected the phone?

Mave pushed her greasy hair back from her forehead and stared at the ceiling. It was discolored from old leaks that resembled piss stains. The knocking continued.

Go away.

She'd been holed up in this dive since the verdict. Since she'd watched her father being dragged away in handcuffs.

Forever.

She shut her eyes only to see Cain's face on the backs of her lids. The stern set of his jaw, the clear pools of his eyes devoid of any fear or grief. Devoid of any regret. Worthy of a double life sentence.

Mave cursed the fresh tears tracing her temples. She swiped them impatiently with the heels of her hands and sat up too quickly—a head-rush causing her to sway back onto the filthy bed sheets.

The knocking persisted.

"All right!" she swore, her voice breaking from lack of use. Needing more clothes than her bra and underwear, she rolled upright and randomly grabbed a sweater from the suitcase: a too-big cardigan that had belonged to Cain. It had leather patches on the elbows—his professor look. Slipping it on, she bunched the lapels together and shuffled to the door. She started to slide the chain-lock and paused.

Days ago, outside the courthouse, a woman had spit on her. It had been Mave's last interaction with a human before locking herself inside this motel room. This disgusting rental for her disgusting life.

Even now, she'd forgive him if only he'd ask. Repent. What did that say about her? But Cain never would—not when he had nothing to apologize for—no wronged lives, no damaged hearts. He was incapable of feeling remorse. He'd never change—not in the twenty years he'd raised her, and not now inside the walls of his prison cell.

She rubbed her cheek with her knuckle, desperate to erase the memory of the spittle striking, and turned the knob. She wasn't sure what she'd do if it happened again.

But it wasn't the angry woman from the courthouse. Or a noisy reporter, or the manager demanding payment. Mave squinted against the harsh daylight and raised her palm to shield the sun from her eye.

"*Said you'd take convincing to open up.*" *A lizard-like man in brown courier shorts stood before her. His smile was almost as seedy as his gaze which promptly lowered to ogle her legs. When he finally bothered to glance up at her bloodshot eyes and matted hair, his grin sagged into disappointment. She hadn't showered since the day before the verdict and imagined she looked and smelled about as attractive as a sack of moldy onions.*

He cleared his throat and pressed a button on his handheld scanner, seemingly all business. "*Package for an M. Francis.*" *A parcel slightly smaller than a shoebox rested by his boots.*

Mave signed for it quickly, eager to seal herself back inside her room. The courier bent down, eyeing her thighs again, and proceeded to pass her the package with another lecherous grin. "*You have yourself a—*"

She shut and locked the door.

Returning to the bed, she sat with the box. There was no return address but she didn't need one. For five long minutes, Mave rubbed her temples and debated whether or not to open the package from her father. In the end, need won over dread. One last contact and she'd be done with him. She could part with Cain Francis for good.

She carefully peeled the tape from the cardboard. Opening the box with trembling fingers, she removed the wadded paper stuffing and blinked at the gun beneath.

It had a daunting black barrel and grip with a cylinder attachment. Ridges that suited him. Serrated. Cold. A postcard lay beneath the weapon: GREETINGS FROM ARUBA. *As if he were on vacation. Swallowing the ache in her throat, Mave slid out the card, flipped it over, and read her father's elegant script:*

Never forget what I taught you. Take care of yourself. Take care of my gun.

I'll be back for both. Till then, I'm watching. —C.

She stared at the final two words until their letters were permanently burned onto her retinas. She didn't want this life anymore. She wanted to live by her own rules. To be free from the clutches of her father's sins. She collected the packaging strewn around her. One by one, she pressed the creases flat and folded each sheet into a crisp square. The tidy pile brought order, made everything better.

She rose, approached the dingy mirror across from the bed, and tucked her father's postcard into the corner of the frame. Her mind cleared. She had a plan.

Never forget what I taught you. *Like how she had no family.*

She would ditch her surname. Rid herself of Cain. Start over. With a last glance at the gun, Mave left for the bathroom to wash herself clean.

She took a scalding bath, making quick work of lathering and rinsing off the memories. Now wrapped in new troubles and a towel that chafed, she swept her hands down her face. Her gaze involuntarily drifted to the smoky mirror—to the photograph of her mother. Its frame of postcards was a blur of warnings. She'd never be free of him.

GREETINGS FROM ARUBA.

PARIS JE T'AIME.

HONG KONG AT NIGHT.

Maybe her mother had been lucky. She'd found a way to escape. A high-pitch ring from her bedroom broke up the depressing thought. Bottling up her disillusionment, Mave staggered toward the electronic warble.

A floundering inspection revealed it was coming from a landline shoved beneath her bed, next to the nightstand. She slid out the phone as if it were a grenade. The normal response would be to pick up the receiver. Instead, Mave stared at the yellowed plastic base, her paranoia running high. No clock. No digital display of any sort. Its only feature was a red light blinking in unison with its blare.

Four rings. Five rings.

In over two months, no one had telephoned her room directly.

Not a soul. Prior to now, it hadn't occurred to her that the landline might be anything more than a relic for emergency outbound calls.

Send help. I need help.

(*Mave Mm—!*) She thrust her hands through her damp hair and muted the internal echo of Birdie's cry. If she didn't pick up now, it would keep ringing indefinitely. The endless peal travelling into the hall and drawing attention to her room ultimately caused her to answer.

Mave shoved the handset to her ear, grasping it so tightly her palm stung.

A single breath revealed a speaker on the other end of the line. Waiting. Neither one of them said a thing. Silence grew. Her knuckles whitened.

Please be Holden. Please be Holden.

But her instinct knew better. Only one person could perceive precisely where she was and how to reach her. Only one person could have the persistence and intuition to grasp she would eventually respond after countless rings.

Stop it, she warred with herself. *You're stressed out and letting fear get the better of you.* Yet her mind was already racing through the questions she'd ask him.

Did you get out? Though her lips formed the words, her voice never managed. A million worries jammed her throat. *Is it really you? Do you know what's happened to me? Are you here? Are you mad at me? Is this another test?*

"Listen very carefully," Cain Francis growled, "and do exactly as I say."

If it weren't for the mattress catching her, Mave would have collapsed onto the floor.

TWENTY-EIGHT

Multiple symptoms assaulted at once: nausea, dizziness, hyperventilation. Mave couldn't decide if she should gag, lie down, or lower her head between her legs. In the end she did none of these things and merely choked out a plea. *Is it—*

"—*really you? Are you—*" Too many words needed to be said. *Are you out? Here? Angry? Watching?* But Cain didn't allow her the luxury of gathering her thoughts.

"On borrowed time here." It was her father all right. Always brusque. "Connection won't last. Need you to focus, M&M. Hear me? This isn't a catch-up call."

Mave nodded before realizing he couldn't see her. "Okay. All right," she gasped.

"Good girl. You need to be at the southwest exit at midnight."

"Wait!" Why on earth would—she didn't even know—"I don't even know where that—"

"On the ground floor past the main lobby elevators," Cain interrupted, "there's a long hall called Hunter's Alley. Look for signs. It'll lead to a coffee bar and conference rooms further along. Follow the hall all the way down and you'll see a fire door. That's the southwest exit. Its alarm is disabled. Go through it. A man, goes by the name of Stratis, he'll be outside to pick you up and take you somewhere safe. He'll wait for one minute. Sixty seconds. Twelve oh-one and he's gone. Got it? Repeat it back to me."

"Midnight. Hunter's Alley. Southwest exit. Stratis." Her voice sounded cool, collected, suited to the daughter of Cain Francis. But inwardly Mave couldn't believe what she was saying. This plan—this *conversation*. A trickle of logic seeped through her shock. There was no way her father could have been released yet— released *ever*, she reminded herself. He must have been using a smuggled cellphone.

"Good. Keep your eyes and ears open. Stay off the radar. And stay away from the Everharts, understood? They're dangerous. Whatever you do, *don't* trust… Remember: no one helps you… free… of all … den Frost."

"What?" Did her father just name Holden? Warn her? About what? "Wait Dad, I couldn't hear." How did he know all this— about Holden—about Birdie? Had he butted heads with the Everharts years ago over Valeria?

"No time … into … Frost is …ber the slayer rule…"

She definitely heard it this time. *Frost.* First Bastian, now Cain. Why was everyone alerting her without a reason? And what about the Everharts was dangerous? "I can't—Dad—you're breaking up. Dad!"

"…for…"

"Can you hear me? How do you know about Holden Frost? What about the Everharts? Do you mean they killed Birdie? Dad!"

A double beep announced the failed connection.

The silence was deafening.

She didn't move a muscle. Even when a clunking switch broke the line and the dial tone whirred. It wasn't until the telephone signal stuttered for her to hang-up that she finally lowered the handset from her ear.

Four years since she'd spoken to him. Four years since she'd reciprocated any contact.

Mave lay on her back, interlocked her fingers over her waist, and stared at the ceiling. The tiny swing of the dangling bulb was barely discernible in the dark. But if you looked for it… All around her, the ancient hotel pulsed. Secrets scuttled along its baseboards, crept into the crevices of its moldings. And the cogs of Mave's mind turned and turned.

The common law of inheritance. That's what Cain had said before getting cut off: *remember the slayer rule.* He must have known, then. About Birdie. About the money. The slayer rule prohibited Mave from collecting a penny of Birdie's fortune assuming she was tried and found guilty. No one could profit by murdering their benefactor. No one could profit, say, by leaving behind their bloody boxcutter with their fingerprints and engraved initials like a calling card. That was common sense, murder 101; certainly, a legal hiccup the daughter of a hitman would be aware of. Mave was starting to think maybe this hadn't been the perfect crime.

Because if everything had gone according to plan, she never would have slipped through security's clutches. Birdie's body never would have disappeared from the scene of the crime. And most definitely, Mave would have been in police custody by now. With murder charges stuck to her, Birdie's fortune would have been held by the state under the slayer rule, and after considerable red tape, redistributed to the victim's remaining blood relatives: Charlie and Parissa Everhart.

Cain's second warning about the Everharts being dangerous replayed in her head. Either one of them could be behind framing her. But what about Cain's mention of Holden Frost? And what about Tag's warped agenda to see her punished? Or Katrina's lies about leaving her room after the murder took place? Cain had said nothing about the security guard or the maid. Nor had he mentioned the art dealer Bastian suspected—a man whose photographs Birdie had also kept hidden beneath her bed with Valeria's pictures. Why? How were they connected?

Mave's mind manipulated theory after theory, angle after angle, but nothing seemed to fit. She couldn't say how much time passed before the order came.

Get up.

She rose from her bed, blinked away her mental static, and

stared at the silver tray on the floor.

She crouched next to it with a candle lit, her mouth already watering. She'd been so preoccupied when she'd first returned with the sheriff, she hadn't stopped to question how or why catering had dropped off the food.

Someone on staff must have let themselves into her locked room—again—deposited the tray, and left. And now that she was examining it, it wasn't just any ordinary tray.

Lined with a linen napkin, the crowded platter held three plates hidden beneath silver cloches, a bottle of chilled white wine, and a glass with a Spanish rose.

Mave instinctively plucked up the bloom by its stem. A note fluttered onto her lap. She hesitated and focused on the strange, bold handwriting.

Sorry had to split—urgent work matter. Meet me in library at midnight.

Btw, if he's who I think, DG has gone for swim every evening @ 9 for past few days.

Keep safe. Eat & drink. And happy birthday. (Wish for something good.)

It was unsigned. Neither her father's script nor his modus operandi. (Cain would never serve her alcohol.) And she hadn't divulged to anyone at the hotel about her birthday. Except for…

How had he known she'd come here after being apprehended in Birdie's suite? How had he slipped in and out of staff quarters without anyone noticing? Holden Frost continued to bewilder her.

She lifted the cloches one by one, unveiling his surprises. With each reveal, a troubling sentiment washed over her—it was like trying to push a cork underwater—a nameless emotion that she tried fruitlessly to resist and suppress.

The first plate had a matchbook at its side and featured a raspberry dotted cupcake with chocolate shavings. A birthday candle was perched in its swirl of frosting.

The next plate overflowed with an assortment of mouth-watering epicurean sandwiches cut into rolls and triangles. And the last plate contained no food at all. Mave put her hand to her mouth, her eyes watering.

Her father's pistol was tucked inside a napkin. Beside it, a snow globe with an ornate silver pedestal sat atop another note. In the center of its floating sparkles stood a perfect miniature of the Château du Ciel. Pressure building beneath her breastbone, she slid out Holden's second message.

No time to wrap. Hope you like your happy thought. (You may have mentioned it once or twice in the vent.) P.S. Gun was on your dresser. Figured you'd prefer it someplace less obvious.

Her heart skipped. Cain's gun. Tag had probably left it out in the open after searching through her drawers and blabbing everything back to Hendrick—and the sheriff. Yet Morganson had never seen the weapon.

She exhaled a clipped laugh and wiped her nose on her wrist. She reached to stroke the glass of the snow globe and paused over the gun. Whatever threads had been holding her together snapped. Abandoning her gifts, she curled onto the floor and wept in misery.

TWENTY-NINE

FROM THE RED BOOK OF THE DEAD

JUNE 1ST, 1991

Dear Abs,

I just got back home and read your last few letters. I feel so guilty. You must think I'm the worst friend ever. Please tell me you're still confiding in Rahul. It's bad enough Mr. Law has forced Caroline into this prison like solitary confinement. You shouldn't have to suffer it, too. Listen, I know I've been a horrible friend but hopefully, I did something that will make it up to you.

It's a small world. It turns out I know a guy who knows someone with a sister who goes to the same school as Caroline. I very *very* quietly looked into BP. (I promise, there's no way Mr. Law will ever know we're digging into Caroline's past.) So I found out the initials on Caroline's tattoo stand for Benjamin Prath—Benji for short—and you were right Abs, he was her boyfriend.

According to my source, Benji was a senior. He was Caroline's first in every way. Apparently, Caroline was a wallflower, never went out. Hardly anyone knew her name. But then Benji took notice of her and asked her out. Before long, he'd bumped her up the pecking order. He introduced her to partying, the drug scene, and after just one hit, got her hooked on the hard stuff. They used to shoot up together after parties.

Now here's the strange and tragic part: last January Benji never came back to school after the holiday break, and then a few weeks later, it was announced that he'd died in a skiing accident. Horrible, right? That must have been around the same time Caroline found out she was pregnant.

As for her addiction, I wish I could be more shocked. I've been to enough parties. Hardcore stuff happens. No parents, no rules. Unlike what most outsiders think, money makes a lot of people miserable and deluded into thinking they're immortal. Girls like Caroline, being an only child, there's a lot of pressure and competition. Impossible standards. The temptation to say fuck it and escape reality is huge. I get it. Birdie drives me crazy with her demands that I be perfect. A rigid control-freak like Immanuel Law must be a hundred times worse. Can you imagine? Also, can you tell I'm having my very own crisis? Compared to Caroline's though, it feels pretty petty. I guess that's a good thing. I wouldn't want to trade places with her for anything.

Here it is: the guy I mentioned falling for in my last letter, Cain, he's in town. Mother knows about him. And she doesn't approve. Like at all.

I know what you're thinking, and yes, normally I wouldn't give a shit. But Birdie hired a private investigator to follow us around on our date last night. Not a very good PI. Cain spotted the tail pretty quick. We had the best time leading him into this dive bar and then losing him. Cain knows all the tricks. Honestly, he's so amazing. He's a bit quiet and intense at first, but beneath that, he has this wild abandon. I've never met another man so in control and uninhibited at the same time. His energy is addictive. He gets in this mode where he pretends he can do anything—be any-thing—he wants. Except it's not pretending exactly. I can't explain it. He *becomes*. I feel so free around him, Abs.

Cain is showing me all sorts of new things about the world. It's like seeing through brand new eyes. Humans are so ugly-beautiful. It makes me want to cry.

THIRTY

JANUARY 1ST, 2021

Mave picked herself up and shut down the pain. She inhaled her dinner without tasting anything.

Be at the southwest exit at midnight.

Meet me in library at midnight.

The risk and reward of each destination circled nonstop in her head. When the hour struck twelve later tonight, she could either run for her freedom or stay to prove her innocence. Once more it came down to survival instinct: fight or flight. Except her senses were stunned. One strange occurrence after another had knocked her intuition sideways. She found herself dressed in her uniform and ready. But for what? She stared at the snow globe, refusing to accept that her sanity was slipping. There had to be a reason for all this horror. She only needed to find it.

With a calm bordering on manic, Mave pulled out her emergency kit. The hair bleach. The bullets. Cain's pistol. She arranged them all in a row on her dresser next to the snow globe. Anxiety twisted in her stomach. The clock ticked. She loaded the gun.

While the majority of guests wandered the heated upper lobbies sipping mimosas and snapping selfies with the hashtag *snowed-in*, down below, not a soul existed. Mave's throat pinched. This was an awful plan. The sanctuary of the giftshop beckoned. One switch in direction, and she'd be there. Everything would be in its rightful place: floral silk scarves, quaint souvenir spoons. Yet logic insisted hiding was foolish. Hiding would only lead to a false, temporary sense of security. And Mave was the furthest thing from safe. The sheriff had made that clear.

She couldn't afford to wait until midnight. No, if Holden wanted to meet, then she would find him *now*. She'd demand he be upfront with everything. How was he on Cain's radar? Did he believe the ghost was real? Was he profiting by posing as the Spirit of Dead Poets? It seemed the reasonable explanation. But then why didn't he fear the ghost, too? What made him so different than others—than Mave?

She forced her feet into the library before she could overthink what monsters awaited her inside. Tag. Penn. The ghost of Annabelle.

Mave's pattering pulse couldn't deny the haunting no matter how much her brain resisted. *This is her retreat—her favorite place.* She crossed her arms, squeezed the panic, and snaked between the towering bookstacks.

"Hello?" The bordering novels soaked in her call. Silence thickened. "Anyone here?" Maybe she'd been foolish after all. The library felt deserted, just like the galleria.

Odds were slim. It was hours before his invitation. But she had to check. Even with the risk of reencountering the ghost, searching the library for Holden was simpler than wandering the underground tunnels. It seemed she had no choice, however. Each empty row of bookstacks confirmed no spirit, dead or alive, lurked inside. No one did.

Mave slumped against a shelf and blew out a long breath. If Holden was supposedly working, he'd be in his secret hideaway below. She eyed the floor vent they'd travelled earlier that morning. Shadows animated its grate of vines. Mave swallowed and approached it. She knelt and held her lips above the cover. "Holden?

Can you hear me?"

She shut her eyes, knowing what she had to do—dizzy at the mere idea. "I can't. Please, I can't." She slapped the vent, her palm smarting against the metal. "Don't make me. It's too—"

Closed in.

How would she find her way? It was her worst idea yet. "Holden," she cried into the void, "where the hell are you?" She curled her fingers around the grate and ignored the vines knifing into her knuckles. "Holden!" It was no use.

Waiting on others gets you nowhere in life, Cain whispered. *You want something, you go after it. Play your own cards, deal your own luck, you remember?*

Mave nodded in the dark. "Except I can't this time, I—"

Yes you can and yes you will. You crawled it once. You can crawl it twice. It's a straight line. Not even that far.

She thought back. It was true: Holden hadn't made any turns when he'd carried her. She would have felt him bend.

Quit being a baby. Get it done.

She eyed the hole in the floor. She could try. Turn back if the panic pressed too much. Nothing was trapping her inside or threatening her from the outside. *It's not like the dumbwaiter. Or the trunk of the car.* She snapped her rubber-band bracelet and lifted off the vent cover. It scraped along the floorboards. Her stomach clenched.

What if she lost her sense of direction? Crawling aimlessly in a vent, the fear alone would kill her. If she was going to risk this, she needed breadcrumbs to guarantee her path back to the library.

So make breadcrumbs. Use what you have.

She straightened. What did she have... Books? Candlewax? Then she remembered: tucked in the corner next to her favorite armchair, covered in an inch of dust, someone had left a knitting basket. She hurried to it now.

In no time, she'd returned with a skein of yarn in her hands and another two stuffed in her pockets. She unravelled one end of string and tied it to the grate. "I can do this," she sighed, digging her fingers into the wool for comfort.

Mave lowered her feet into the vent.

The mistake became apparent as soon as she dropped down, caught her breath, and checked her relief. A flash of her phone revealed an unknown tunnel. No milk crate anywhere in sight and the walls were coated in barmy filth. She grimaced and held the yarn to her chest. This wasn't the route Holden had used.

Doesn't matter, she appeased herself. She was inside—had made it this far. She held the dwindling skein tightly and assured herself her knots were holding. One last ball of wool remained in her pocket, ready to be tied on when this one ran out. *Okay.* She could afford to venture a few more yards—as far as the string would reach. Then if she was still disoriented, she'd turn back. It was simple. Nothing gained, nothing lost.

She stepped forward and unspooled the yarn. It didn't matter that she'd walked the tunnels hours earlier—had experienced the whistling pipes and press of walls overnight. Coldness burrowed in her flesh. She shivered and hurried on, unsure whether she was more eager to find Holden or to run out of string and return aboveground. Another two-hundred yards deep, and the latter excuse was prompted. Her final ball of yarn came to an end. Mave stood on the rotting railway ties and ground her teeth. Out of string. Out of luck.

"Holden!"

Darkness swallowed her flashlight, black filth making everything seem dimmer. She waved her phone uselessly. She'd wasted all this time, suffered crawling the stupid vent, and for what? "Where are you?" She was ready to give up when the smell of bacon glanced her nose.

Her jaw jerked reflexively toward the scent. Was she imagining it? She sucked in a ribbon of applewood and caramelized smoke.

"Holden?"

The tunnel remained indistinct and unfamiliar.

She tentatively placed the yarn on a track where she could still see it, and took a step farther inside. And another. "I'm here!" she called to him. "If you can hear me, please come out. I need to see you." She cocked her ears for any whispered poems. He had to be near. The scent of his bacon was a sure bet—even stronger than when she'd encountered it in the morning. "Waiting gets me nowhere," she murmured to herself. She checked over her shoulder where the yarn lay on the track, as good as any signpost. *It's okay. Just a little farther. He's probably steps away.* She pointed her flashlight into the unknown and advanced with her nose leading the way.

As a sinking feeling grew in her stomach, she dismissed it as a symptom of her phobia—a weakness to be overcome. The scent led to a narrow opening: a man-sized pipeline. Mave furrowed her brow. Holden must have been in the tunnel running parallel. A wall was all that stood between them.

She ducked inside the pipe. *A bit more. Just a bit...*

A distant part of her warned she was venturing too far, forgetting all about her plan, her breadcrumbs. But the deeper she got, the more the scent smothered her reason with a physical *want*. She was a hound on a scent. She needed to track, to hunt, to uncover... what? It was fuzzy at best. An acidic desperation she'd never before felt radiated throughout her core, ordered she keep going keep going keep going.

The pipe was a blur. Everything but the scent, the pull, the agony to locate something lost. Nothing else existed or made sense or fed her starvation.

After what could have been a minute or an hour, she reached a deadend. Mave found herself in a state of wired agitation—chest heaving, skin damp and cold. Somewhere along the way, the scent of bacon had transformed into a metallic bite. It flaked against her tongue. She pointed her flashlight, squinted and blinked.

Before her was a cubic-foot steel door framed with bolts. Its rusted surface resembled an industrial furnace with a wheel-handle. *Not quite.* It wasn't a century-old furnace. With her hand trembling, she reached forward and stroked the letters that stood out in relief: BALDWIN VENTILATION CO. An old air valve.

She clamped her light between her teeth and grasped the wheel. Her body anchored its quiver. An energy hummed, connecting her to the cold site, the rough steel—sharp, sentient. It told her what to do, promised her it would be over soon: her burning itch would be salved.

Mave's breath exited her lungs in dashes. She turned the rusted wheel, palms blistering, muscles straining. Only when she saw the human bones inside did the cord of energy snap.

The scent released her. Mave sighed, dropped to her knees, and cried for the forgotten.

THIRTY-ONE

If anyone had asked her how she'd managed to return to the library, she would have lied. She would have said she'd memorized the turns, had relied on her flashlight and intuition. In truth, she had no clue.

Dreamlike snippets teased: rubbing her nose until it chafed, her feet stumbling over train tracks, red yarn winding round her fingers until her circulation pinched. All the while human remains lay forgotten in an air duct underground. A wrong. A defilement. The shock rattled her reality and, at the same time, forced it into focus. Her freedom was her priority—*not* seeking the rightful burial for a bygone stranger. Not unless she hoped to be next—locked up and left to rot. Maybe that's why she'd been drawn to the air duct in the first place. A wake-up call.

Holden Frost was not who he seemed. Bastian and her father had tried to warn her. He was trouble of the worst kind, a contradiction, a riddle of good and evil. Just like Cain himself. What did he have to do with those bones? With Birdie's death? Mave shuddered. Attraction had blinded her. She couldn't go to him for answers any more than she could go to the sheriff with her discovery. She was under enough suspicion as it was. The last thing she needed was to link herself to another dead body—no matter how old. Besides, there were others at this hotel who might talk. Others who might fill in the gouged-out blanks of the past.

She swung open the interconnecting door and was met with warm humidity and a tingle of chlorine. From the echo of splashing water, he was inside swimming, just as Holden had predicted.

Oil lamps framed the pool and the deck shimmered in shadow. Intricate deco tiles patterned the floors and walls. Under ordinary circumstances she would have admired the century-old craftsmanship but now wasn't the time. Mave waited at the foot of the deep end for the swimmer doing the front crawl.

As he slowed his stroke, Dominic Grady bobbed upward. He wore a swimming cap and goggles and was in good shape for his age. Thick biceps.

Sturdy enough to carry Birdie's body.

She wiped her expression. Noticing her, he neared to a stop and leaned on the edge of the pool. He repositioned his goggles onto his forehead and shook the droplets from his trim grey beard.

He looked different. Unsurprisingly. He was decades older than the young man in Birdie's photographs. He was also puffier around his cheekbones and temples. Odds were good he'd had a facelift or two over the years.

"Dear lord," his voice was winded and leathery, "you must be Mave."

How did he—?

"Birdie told me, but...." His jaw hung. "Sorry for staring. It's just, you're every bit as stunning."

As Birdie?

He must have perceived her yearning to know more—to know everything. "As Valeria," he qualified.

Mave searched his face for any falsity and found none. She tucked a lock of her newly-dyed hair behind her ear. She could change from brunette to Strawberry Sunset all she wanted. Valeria was imprinted in her bones.

He pulled off his cap. His thick hair beneath was a damp shade of silver. "Pardon my manners, my hand's wet. I'm Dominic Grady, old friend of Birdie's." He smiled to reveal a row of perfect white teeth.

She stepped back from the pool's edge and crossed her arms. "You knew my mother?"

"Of course. We met years ago, through Birdie." He cleared his throat. "With everything that's happened, I gather you've heard by now that Birdie... well, she was your grandmother. That's why you're here, isn't it?"

It felt stupefying hearing someone say it aloud. Maybe coming here had been another mistake. Dominic Grady sounded almost as if he'd been expecting her. Her eyes flicked to the changing room door. She regretted leaving Cain's gun in her room; but in the end, she'd been too terrified to carry it—to concede what arming herself would signify.

He sighed. "Was wondering when you'd find out." He climbed out of the pool and put on a robe. "Please." He gestured to a nearby group of chaises. Mave perched stiffly on a teak chair while the older man ruffled a towel through his hair.

"She told you... about me?"

"Only a few months ago. After she manipulated Edward into hiring you."

"*Mr. Hendrick* knew about me?"

"Christ, no." Dominic was quick to assure her. "Edward's about as sharp as a turkey. No, Birdie kept you a secret from everyone. Except me. She and I are"—his lips twitched into a frown—"*were* very close."

Though she was burning with questions, she kept quiet. Cain's rules were hard habits to break. ("*Never seem desperate. Never give up your hand.*")

Dominic carelessly tossed aside the towel onto the pool deck and sat on a facing chaise. He must have been accustomed to staff cleaning up after him. "When the sheriff broke the news to me earlier..." He closed his eyes and tipped his head back. "Ah, I can hardly believe it. Losing her. It's not right. Fair." His jaw pushed forward. "Life never is." He ran a hand down his beard.

She remembered their photo: his arm around her waist. "You

loved her." Her words trailed up like a question.

"I did," he said simply. "Since the first moment I laid eyes on her. We shared a lot good times, working and laughing together."

Except for the other day when they'd fought loud enough to alert Bastian.

Poker face, M&M.

"Mr. Grady—"

"Please, call me Dominic."

"Dominic. Birdie obviously confided in you. What do you think happened to her?"

"I think," he wrinkled his brow, "Birdie was an extremely talented and successful woman, but she also… marched to the beat of her own drum. Unfortunately that made others jealous of her. Her refusal to listen to anyone other than herself got her into trouble every now and again. She must have finally gone too far."

"But how? Too far for who?" Did he mean cutting her children out of her inheritance, refusing to sign off on Hendrick's casino, or something else? Mave watched him closely. He seemed somber but otherwise entirely at ease. Either he didn't consider her Birdie's killer or he hadn't run into the gossip.

"Who, indeed," he uttered while staring off into space. "I'd give anything to know." The intensity of his words shone in his eyes. He shifted and blinked. "Truth is, as much as I cared for her, Birdie angered a lot of people on a regular basis. And I'm not one to spread slander, you understand. A man is only as good as his reputation."

He was avoiding giving a straight answer. It was possible Birdie had confessed to him about changing her will. It must have stung Dominic to have been left with nothing after all their years together. Who knew if his love had been reciprocated. Bastian's suspicion circled her mind. "You two had a bad argument a few days ago."

His face flashed an emotion too quick for her to read. "Heard about that, did you?"

"A lot of people did. There was a noise complaint."

"Yes, suppose things got too heated. I regret it now. More than anyone could know." He swallowed. "Birdie always knew how to push my buttons."

"Sorry for prying, but what were you two fighting over?"

"You."

Mave gave a hard blink.

"I was trying to convince your grandmother to tell you the truth."

If she'd expected an answer, that hadn't been it. "Why?"

"Because what she was doing was cowardly. And cruel. I know firsthand what it's like to be denied family. I grew up not knowing my father. You, on the other hand, had a chance to reconnect and make up for lost time. You deserved to hear the truth from Birdie. I tried convincing her of that but," he spread out his palms, "she was set in her ways." He smiled again, though his eyes brimmed with sorrow.

"I still don't understand. Why did she refuse? Why lie to me?" It cost her to ask. Her vision threatened to blur with tears. She bit her bottom lip.

"It's complicated. She was afraid you'd hate her if you found out."

"Why on earth would I hate her?"

"How much do you know about Birdie's relationship with your mother?"

Mave didn't answer—couldn't answer without losing her composure. Dominic had the grace to pretend not to notice. He laced his fingers together and regarded the still pool water.

"Many years ago, before you were born, your mother and Birdie had a terrible falling out. Birdie never spoke of it after it happened—not even to me. But I'd seen and heard enough.

"Back then, Val was secretly seeing someone. Birdie never revealed who it was, but there were rumors of course. An opportunistic and dangerous outsider, I'd heard—a con artist."

Cain. Her pulse quickened.

"Birdie was convinced he was after the family money. But Val refused to break things off, and your grandmother, well—she was used to getting her way. She was appalled by Val's rebelliousness." He shook his head, lost in memory. "Birdie was always too passionate for her own good. Extreme in her ways."

"What do you mean? What did she do?"

"She cut Val out of her will. I think in her mind, she thought it would force Val to come to her senses. Birdie imagined Val would end her fickle romance once and for all. Or it would force the gold-digger to give up on Val when he found out she was worth nothing. Either way, your grandmother saw it as a win-win. She didn't take into account Val's stubbornness. They were perfectly matched in that way, both bullheaded and unwilling to compromise."

"My mother kept seeing him." *My dad*. She gripped the edge of her chair with both hands, her elbows locked.

Dominic nodded. "And not long after, I don't know what exactly passed between them, but Birdie disowned Val completely. She erased her youngest daughter from the family—pretended as if she didn't exist. She instructed everyone—Parissa, Charlie, me—that Valeria was dead to us."

The injustice of it all rocked through her. Her mother had been punished for refusing to leave Cain. Mave had difficulty accepting it. "And you were okay with that? No one reached out to her?"

"Like I said: your grandmother was a strong woman. She seldom didn't get her way. Back then, Birdie—god bless her—she was furious at Valeria for defying her. And with Val gone, she misdirected her anger at those closest to her. She threatened us. Looking back after all these years, I can understand. I think she craved to regain the control she'd lost with Val."

Mave dug her nails into the grain of the wood. "How exactly did she threaten you?"

"Please, you can't repeat this to anyone." Dominic finally seemed to realize the severity of the secrets he was sharing. "I'm only telling you because it's the right thing; what Birdie should have done herself had she not been"—his frown deepened—"stolen from us."

"You don't have to worry about that. I'm not here to cause anyone trouble. Please…"

Dominic offered her a sympathetic look. "After she disowned your mother, Birdie told us if we disobeyed her instructions and contacted Val, she would make sure we'd be financially ruined and left with nothing. Birdie wasn't known to bluff. Val was proof of that. She could make your world miserable. No one wanted that. Certainly not me." He rubbed the back of his neck, head hung. "I'm not proud of it. I told myself I'd wait for everything to cool down. But one month quickly turned into one year, then two years. Before I knew it, it was too late. For any of us."

Her throat grew thick. "You mean because my mother died."

Dominic seemed a shade paler than when he'd first starting speaking. "No one could have predicted that tragedy," he whispered. "When the police contacted Birdie and told her Val had been killed in a car crash, she was never quite the same. She never said it outright, but I think she blamed herself."

"And she assumed I would too?" Resentment squeezed her heart. Dominic had been right. Birdie should have given her the chance to make up her own mind. He'd described Birdie's actions as cruel. So many people had. Mave finally understood why.

"Maybe not for Val's death, but for the rest," he sighed, "abandoning her—you—yes. She told me as much. After Val's death, she searched for you. She hired and fired countless private investigators over the years. They couldn't find a single trace you existed. Nothing."

Of course not. (*"Stay away from the Everharts, understood? They're dangerous."*) Cain would have kept her hidden away. Especially if he'd known Birdie had disowned Valeria.

"But all this time, Birdie never gave up looking." Dominic leaned forward, imploring her with his grief-stricken eyes. "Never. It wasn't until recently that she learned of your whereabouts. But by then, so many years had passed. She was afraid. She arranged for your recruitment to the hotel under false pretenses as a way to test the waters."

"And then what?" Mave snapped. "Was she ever planning on telling me the truth?"

"Eventually. I think so. It was her cockamamie plan to get to know you first, win you over, I guess, before rehashing the past. It wasn't easy for her, you understand." He must have loved her, to defend her even now.

Mave stood. "No. I don't understand."

"Listen, I realize it's not my place but… I never got the chance. With my father. Birdie may have been misguided in her ways, but she did what she thought was best. She was trying—no matter how backwards it may seem to you. And Charlie and Parissa, they're still here. And they never knew. Birdie never told anyone Val had had a daughter.

"If and when you're ready," he looked up at her with a mixture of kindness and regret, "odds are good you'll find Charlie in the cigar lounge."

Mave realized she ought to thank him but she couldn't find her voice. She left before Dominic Grady could witness her tears break.

THIRTY-TWO

His words wouldn't stop nagging her: *They're still here.*

If she fled the hotel at midnight, she might never get another opportunity. Her hunger to know Valeria had been merely inflamed by Dominic's advice. He was right. She'd regret passing up the chance to meet her estranged blood relatives—whether or not they were behind framing her. All the more reason to confront them.

She hurried to the cigar lounge before her nerve could abandon her. Head down. Eyes up. Her mind replayed her last encounter with Charlie and prepared for the worst: Annabelle's monstrous ghost hovering over him again; Charlie making a scene, mistaking her for Valeria, blaming her for murdering Birdie in front of others. But apart from random guests socializing in a haze of smoke and twinkling tealights, there was no sign of the gangly, balding man she'd seen inside the studio. She asked the bartender, and he informed her she'd missed Charlie by about twenty minutes. Parissa Everhart had summoned her brother up to the game room on the mezzanine level.

When Cain had instructed Mave to lay low and avoid the Everharts, he probably hadn't intended for her to crash a family meeting. But Cain didn't understand. If she wanted to rescue her future, she had to make sense of her past.

She skirted around a rowdy group of guests playing charades in the upper lobby. Farther along, a string quartet played. The music barely registered. What would she say to either Charlie or Parissa when she barged in on them? What would she do if they lashed out? As if her nerves weren't enough, the cloying perfume of candles in every space was making her nauseated. She slipped into a dark vestibule that led to the game room. A soft glow and voices drifted through the open doorway. Mave instinctively stilled. Her brow crimped.

A massive mirror offered her a preview of the room's occupants. True to the bartender's tip, Charlie Everhart was inside. He was sunken in a sofa chair, knees spread and one heel bouncing with nervous energy.

"…told you," he said in a flat voice, "don't know anything about Mother disappearing from her bedroom. Never went in."

Unnoticed in the vestibule, Mave tilted her head, adjusting her view of the mirror. A woman in her early fifties was seated on a couch near Charlie. Mave stared in fascination.

Parissa Everhart. Her legs were crossed, her head braced by her manicured fingertips like she had a headache. She was an attractive woman with sandy blonde hair pulled into a low ponytail, a pink nose, and a girlish figure that told of discipline and low-fat meals. Beside her, cropped in the reflection, Sheriff Morganson hovered. "But you were searching for your spare key," Morganson said. "Why didn't you look in the bedroom, too?"

"He's grieving," Parissa offered, "hasn't slept since—"

"Wasn't thinking straight, okay?" Charlie growled over his sister.

"You mean because you were drunk," Morganson clarified. "Tell me, do suffer from blackouts?"

His glazed eyes snapped to the sheriff. "What's that supposed to mean?"

"Listen," Parissa sat forward with her arm extended to her brother, "we're both in shock here. Charlie had a little too much, headed to the penthouse automatically, right? Like a pigeon to a nest. Yes, it was a stupid mistake, but harmless."

The sheriff shifted and checked her notebook. "Did Birdie mention anything to either of you about a recent argument with her former art dealer, Dominic Grady?"

Parissa tilted her head. "Dominic's here?"

"Mother added him to the list months ago," Charlie replied, his voice flat again. "With the cancer—"

Parissa scoffed. "Of course she did."

Mave was taken aback. Dominic had cancer?

"So she said nothing about the fight?" Morganson pressed. "The noise complaint?"

"No," Charlie grunted. "What noise complaint?"

"I only arrived yesterday morning," Parissa said. "I hardly even spoke to Mother before—"

"Why, what'd Dom say?" Charlie's eyes narrowed into slits as he stared at the sheriff. "You know, when I heard he'd checked in, I paid him a visit. Felt the bastard on the other side of his door but he wouldn't answer. You think he was avoiding me because he had something to do with—?"

"Oh, come on," Parissa scowled. "Dominic Grady, really, Charlie?" She turned to the sheriff. "The person you should be focusing on is that fraud from the giftshop."

"Your niece?"

Mave's ears sharpened, tuning out the string quartet, laughter from the mezzanine—everything but Parissa's reply.

"Let's get one thing straight: I have no niece. Just like Mother had no long-lost granddaughter." After Dominic's openness, Mave wasn't prepared for the bluntness with which Parissa dismissed her existence. She dug her nails into her palms and kept quiet. "Nick and Tag already told me everything," Parissa continued. "It's a blatant lie that girl's using to scam millions from Mother. She's a criminal just like her father."

Mave instinctively backed farther into shadow. Her pulse pattered uncomfortably in her temples.

"Were you aware your husband left the card table yesterday during the timeframe your mother was assaulted?"

Parissa shut her eyes a moment, as if having difficulty processing the sheriff's words. "You aren't suggesting he's responsible for this nightmare."

"Answer the question, Ms. Everhart."

She mumbled under her breath too low for Mave to hear.

"Ms—"

"*Yes,*" she said, "he came upstairs for a minute to check on me. He wanted to know if I was feeling well enough to join him in the ballroom."

"What time would you say this was?"

"I don't know. I explained already, I had an intense stomachache. The last thing on my mind was checking the time."

"Not much of a New Year's gal, huh?" Sheriff Morganson paused to jot a detail in her notebook. "How long would you say Nicholas stayed upstairs with you?"

"About a quarter of an hour, maybe longer."

"A moment ago you said he came up for a minute."

"I was using a figure of speech."

"Was his visit before or after you dialed for room service?"

"This is ridiculous." Parissa wadded a tissue and looked to Charlie for backup, but he seemed to be battling his own inner demons, his lashes fluttering and jaw rolling. "Look, Nick knew Mother's diagnosis as well as I did," she told the sheriff. "If he wanted her dead, why wouldn't he just wait a few months—maybe weeks—for her to die of natural causes? You're wasting everyone's time here!"

Mave's mouth popped open. *Birdie* had been dying of cancer?

The sheriff cocked her brow in warning as Parissa pinched the bridge of her nose and took a deep breath. "Rather than question my brother and I—or double-checking my husband's alibi—you should be interrogating that con who killed her in cold blood. Tag *saw* her." Her eyes welled as she leaned forward. "She had her pinned to the ground! Tag saw her toss her boxcutter when they caught her. What more do you need? Why the fuck haven't you arrested her?"

Mave's stomach turned. If that was Tag's statement then he'd outright lied to the police.

"Ms. Everhart—"

"She's looking to take everything from us—everything! First our mother, now our—"

"—I need you to calm down and control yourself. We're gathering all the facts, considering every angle. Once we locate your mother, we'll be able to—"

"Don't you see? This girl clearly got desperate after she was caught. She ran from security then broke into the suite this morning and stole h-her—" Tears flooded her eyes as her shoulders sagged against the sofa's backrest. "You have to find Mother," she wheezed, "please." The pink of her nose brightened. Next to her, Charlie rubbed his eyes. Parissa pressed her balled-up tissue to her face again and again until it was reduced to soggy shreds. Mave felt sick but she couldn't bring herself to look away.

Her aunt shook her head as if silently arguing with herself. "My poor—" she hiccoughed. "And that sick *freak*, pretending to.... We won't let her get away with this. She thinks she can steal from *us*?" She barked a laugh. "Nick already promised he'll hire as many lawyers and investigators as it takes. We don't care what it costs. This Francis girl is going to pay for what she's done." The hair on the back of Mave's neck rose. She had seen and heard enough.

She reversed silently from the vestibule into the mezzanine's main hall and backed into a human wall. Before she could react, a pair of thick hands wrapped her shoulders. Annabelle's face flashed before her—those strong male fingers entrapping her.

"Well, well." A honeyed voice broke the illusion. "Just who do we have here?"

Mave spun with her forearms flung wide, and his grip released.

"Uh-oh." A six-foot-something man old enough to be her father grinned down at her with his palms up. Some would have found him handsome, no doubt: well-tailored suit, broad-boned and chiseled. To Mave, he looked every bit a lazy lion waiting for his prey to fall at his feet. He puckered his lips with a disapproving look. "Didn't anyone ever teach you it's impolite to listen in on other people's conversations?"

Cain had taught her the opposite: only the ignorant were willingly deaf.

"I was just leaving," she said, her mouth gone dry. She took a few steps to pass but he easily blocked her in.

"*Uh-uh*, not so fast."

Mave angled against the wall as his gaze slowly travelled the length of her body. She kept still under his scrutiny, debating whether it was worth drawing additional attention to herself.

String quartet at nine o'clock. Guests clustered at eight o'clock. A punch to his trachea would surely erase his noxious grin, but it would also cause him to croak violently. She stared at the exposed wedge of his throat and chest. Even under weak candlelight, its tan suggested winters vacationed in St Barts, Fiji. Sailing in a yacht.

"I don't believe I caught your name."

His sense of entitlement irked her. Too many men considered it their right to know any and all women's names. "Kennedy," she replied meekly, slipping into the role he'd assigned her.

"Well, Kennedy, my wife and I don't take kindly to eavesdroppers."

His wife. Mave's blood spiked. Along with Charlie, Parissa must have called Nicholas Vaughn to meet her here. "I wasn't—"

"You know, I'm a bit disappointed." His barreled chest was invading her space. She wanted to retreat but the wall behind her limited her options. He leaned closer. The peppery scent of his aftershave made her cringe. "I expected better lying from the offspring of a convicted felon."

She held her breath.

"Then again, your father couldn't have been a very good liar himself. He was caught and put away for life. With all the other animals. And you will be, too," he whispered, "once I'm done with the daughter of Cain Francis."

Mave could endure no more. She flinched, slipped from his reach, and fled the mezzanine short of running. Once or twice, she peeked back. Each time, Nicholas Vaughn was tracking her retreat with his gaze. And beneath his fake smile, the sincerity of his threat was unmistakable.

THIRTY-THREE

FROM THE RED BOOK OF THE DEAD

JUNE 20TH, 1991

Dear Rie,

I've been holding this in for days. I can't go to Rahul. It has nothing to do with Caroline and it's just too humiliating. I want you to hear it from me, okay? In case either Charlie or Birdie ever mention it to you, I want you to hear the truth—my truth.

Four nights ago, Charlie's shouts woke me up. It was around two in the morning. He was knocking and rattling my doorknob. I could tell from his slurred voice calling my name that he was drunk. I waited about five minutes and, when he wouldn't stop, I got up to tell him off. By the time I rose and got to the door, though, he'd finally shut up and wandered away. I was annoyed but relieved, and went back to bed.

The next morning, I went to go find him. He needed to know his middle-of-the-night, drunken-frat-boy act was *not* cool. Rahul told me he was staying in one of his mother's suites on the penthouse floor. So I charged up there ready to give him a piece of my mind.

Well I found him, all right, except he was passed out in the hall, right in front of the doors to Birdie's studio. I don't know. I guess I hadn't expected that. He looked really sad and pathetic, crumpled up in the fetal position. My irritation was already duller by this point, so I decided to put it off. I'd confront him later when he'd slept it off. Or so I thought.

By noon, Mr. Law had returned to the hotel on one of his dreaded visits, and I grew distracted. The day flew by. Before I knew it, it was two a.m. again, and Charlie was back. He was banging on my door and hollering my name, on and on.

I shouldn't have opened the door. God, that was stupid of me. I should have just pretended I didn't hear him and waited him out. But I was angry and half-asleep. All I could think of was Mr. Law a few doors down. I was worried Charlie's racket would wake him and everyone else in the damn hotel and cause problems for me, maybe even get me fired. So I unlocked the door. I was going to tell him off. Stupid. Stupid. Stupid.

Of course he immediately barged in. He was all over me in no time. Grabbing and hugging. I tried pushing him away. I told him to stop again and again, but he wasn't listening. He had me trapped against the wall. He said awful things—whined I was a cock tease—that he'd seen me staring at him all these weeks when IT'S THE OTHER WAY AROUND. He's the creep who stares! I had no idea it would come to this.

He yanked up my nightshirt and tried to kiss me. I reacted. I bit his ear and kneed him as hard as I could. It's horrifying and ironic, right? Because in the end, it wasn't Charlie's shouts that woke Mr. Law. It was mine.

That was the whole reason I answered the door in the first place—to avoid drama. But apparently I'd been screaming from the moment he shoved himself inside of my room. I can't really remember. It all happened so fast.

At one point I looked up and found Caroline watching us from our shared doorway. Before I knew it, Birdie was there too. Mr. Law must have called her down. She handled Charlie, whisked him out of my sight while Mr. Law assured me I'd done nothing wrong.

I'd never seen this side of him. He was so incredibly gentle and caring. He brought me my robe and ordered warm milk to my room. I was pretty shaken. I went to go clean myself up in the bathroom and saw I had a bit of blood on my mouth. I couldn't even make it to the toilet. I threw up in the sink.

I know he's your brother but what Charlie did was unforgivable. I never want to see his fucking face again.

JUNE 26ᵀᴴ, 1991

Dear Abs,

I'm beside myself. I'm so devastated and sorry for what Charlie did. I've always considered him to be a bit desperate for girls, but this—this is so much worse. He's a disgusting fucking troll and I'm ashamed to call him my brother. God. I'm tearing up just imagining you going through this.

Listen, you did everything right, okay? Answering the door—how could you have possibly known he'd do something so horrible. It's not your fault. Don't ever think that, not even for one second, okay? What a mess. Are you pressing charges? Really, why am I bothering to ask. I know Birdie. There's no way my Queen mother would allow charges to stick. She'd either, (a) talk you out of it, or (b) sign a healthy check to shut you up. I'm so mad right now. I seriously want to beat Charlie up myself. How dare he fucking do this to you! I'm dying to give him a piece of my mind.

I tried phoning him more than once, but either his line is disconnected or he's not picking up. He probably realizes what a colossal fuck-up he is. The asshole. I swear if I wasn't stuck doing these summer courses, I'd come up there myself. I know you said Mr. Law has been helpful, but I need to make sure you're seriously okay—safe with that creep still lurking around the hotel. So I have another plan, a guarantee that Charlie never dares touch you again.

I might not be able to come up there, but Cain can.

Thirty-Four

January 1st, 2021

Cain's offer to take off at midnight was sounding better with each passing minute. Mave tried convincing herself that Sheriff Morganson was handling the investigation but her innate mistrust of all law enforcement wouldn't let up. Tag, Nicholas, Parissa—they were sharpening their pitchforks, spreading toxic lies. Morganson "gathering all the facts" could easily end with Mave in handcuffs.

She had a little over an hour before Stratis would arrive outside the southwest exit. Her mind pictured Holden waiting for her simultaneously inside the library. What urgent work matter did an online translator have to attend to? Would Annabelle's ghost show up again? A shiver passed through her body. Answers—she needed answers. Bastian hadn't been at his desk, so Mave sought the only other person with information willing to help her.

Uncaring of the hour or the DO NOT DISTURB sign hanging from the doorknob, she rapped with urgency for the guest inside. A moment later, the door creaked open.

Dual surprise and concern rippled over Dominic Grady's face as he squinted into the hallway. "Mave. Is everything—?"

"Did you know Birdie was dying?" She had neither time nor energy for small talk.

Although the furrow of his brow remained, Dominic no longer looked surprised. He tightened the belt on his robe, his pleated pyjamas visible beneath. "I take it you spoke with your uncle."

"Well, did you?"

He poked his head into the corridor and glanced around. "Not here. Come inside. Please."

She followed him into his suite. It was massive in comparison to staff's quarters, with multiple doors leading off from a living room and a separate dining area. She waited as Dominic shut the door and lit a set of vintage oil lamps. His eyes were red and puffy, reminding her of his grief. She crossed her arms.

"Why didn't you say anything earlier?"

Dominic sighed and shuffled to a bar cart. "Guilt I suppose." He poured himself a drink. "Cognac?" Mave shook her head as the older man swilled the liquor in his glass. He seemed deep in thought, his eyes unfocused and unblinking. "I'd already gone against so many of Birdie's wishes. And while everything else I shared with you concerned your mother, Birdie's illness..." His brow caved in. "Well, it wasn't my place. That was Birdie's secret to keep." He sunk into a recliner, obviously tired, and she mirrored him on a musty sofa.

"Mr. Grady, I'm sorry if I woke you, but I need to know. How exactly was she dying?"

"Breast cancer." His voice scratched and he shot back his drink. "It had spread. Too advanced for treatment. Said she'd rather die than do chemo anyway. The doctors had given her under a year."

"Who else knew?"

"As far as I know, only her children."

"And Nicholas Vaughn."

His expression darkened. "Yes."

"Did Nicholas ever meet my mother?" What she really wanted to ask was if he'd crossed paths with Cain.

"Oh, I doubt it. Parissa only got together with Vaughn after graduating college. That would have been well after Val left the family."

"Are you sure?" The formal way Nicholas had addressed her

as the daughter of Cain Francis, it had sounded a lot like an old vendetta.

"Yes. Why do you ask?" He regarded her now, his eyes reflecting his curiosity.

Careful, M&M. No one is this helpful without an ulterior motive. Stop and ask yourself: what's in it for him?

She took a deep breath and reminded herself not to be Cain—not to see everyone as evil. Yet trusting Dominic Grady made her even warier. "When I went to find Charlie, I bumped into him—Nicholas. He made it clear he holds a grudge against me. I thought maybe it had to do with the past, something that might have happened years ago between him and my mother." *Or Cain.*

"Ah, I see. Well, my dear," he set down his empty glass and crossed his legs, "I'd wager any resentment he holds has less to do with the past and more to do with the present."

She considered his theory. "You mean Birdie's inheritance?"

He nodded. "Look, I shouldn't say anything but your vulnerability, you remind me so much of—" His eyes glistened and drooped.

"What is it? Please, Mr. Grady. You're the only person who's been honest with me about"—the words *my family* stuck in her throat—"everything."

"All right, but this can't leave this room, you understand? If it were to get back to Parissa…"

Mave nodded. "I promise."

"Nicholas Vaughn," his nose puckered, "hate to say it, but that man is no better than a vulture. He was banking on Birdie's illness. I think no one was more pleased than him when she was diagnosed with stage four cancer."

"That's awful. Why?"

"I wouldn't have believed it myself if I hadn't been there that night. A fluke, really. It happened about a year ago. I have a client who every now and again attends a private club of high rollers. Very elite, players by invitation only. I don't normally attend these things but I was trying to close a sale on a painting so I agreed to tag along. I was shocked to find Nick there. The club, well, it's not entirely aboveground, and one of its rules is never to speak of its members"

"Sort of like a fight club."

"Exactly: absolute privacy. Nick was playing poker with some dangerous men—men who I wouldn't want to share one round at the table with, much less owe money to. And you can guess the rest."

"He lost."

Dominic nodded. "Millions. It was nauseating to watch. He wouldn't stop. I have every reason to believe he's an addict—the way he played, the money he bet. The fool is now bankrupt. He was relying on Parissa's fortune to come through to settle his debts and save his kneecaps."

"Oh my god, and now…"

"His wife's fortune goes to you instead." He gave her a meaningful look. "That's enough for a grudge I'd say."

And assuming Nicholas had known Birdie had changed her will, it was enough to frame Mave for murder—before time ran out and Birdie died of cancer. Only by way of Mave's guilt could the inheritance legally return to Parissa. The slayer rule. That's what Cain had been telling her. Mave rubbed her forehead.

"You're upset. Of course you are."

She opened her mouth, but her mind was too busy absorbing Dominic's information to organize any coherent reply. What if Parissa had discovered her husband's crime that evening? ("…*he came upstairs for a minute to check on me.*") What if, afraid Nicholas would be caught, she'd recruited Charlie to get rid of Birdie's body? How many of them were involved? Paranoia gripped her. She needed privacy to mull over everything.

"I…it's late. I should go." She pushed into the sunken cushion to rise. "Thank you for everything you've told me."

Dominic's mouth bowed like a horseshoe. "You sure you're all right? Safe for the night? I can speak to Edward for—"

"No, please," she shook her head, a lump in her throat. "I'm okay. I promise."

His kind smile did little to reassure her. "For what it's worth, I'm glad you came to see me. Birdie would have wanted that." He rose ahead of her with his empty glass reclaimed. "Only wish there was more I could do to help."

As she shifted to get up, a small button on the couch dug into her thigh. Not a button. Mave pinched a gold charm between her fingers and inspected it under the lamplight.

She'd seen this little Russian doll before—in Katrina Kovak's mind.

She climbed the dark stairwell and absently thumbed the charm in her pocket. In a split decision, she'd confronted Dominic about the jewelry. It had been clear from his disinterest that he'd never before seen the charm. He told her it must have fallen into the cushion from a previous guest. He was more than fine when Mave offered to take it to the hotel's lost and found.

Likely there was a simple explanation. For all Mave knew, Birdie could have lent Dominic Katrina's cleaning services. Still, something wasn't sitting right. She couldn't guess why Katrina had lied about leaving her room on the night Birdie was murdered. And now that the maid's charm had turned up in Dominic's suite, Mave's suspicions were doubled. What was Katrina's story?

It became clear after a minute of waiting outside the maid's door that she wouldn't get the chance to ask her. Either she wasn't inside her room or was refusing to respond to Mave's knocks. It was well past eleven. No vacancies on any floor. Had she found someone—another maid to take her in? Then again, she could have a routine of leaving her room late each evening. It occurred to Mave she should have taken more time to review the security tapes when she'd had the chance.

She tried knocking again. As she leaned her ear against the mahogany panel, the hallway's emergency lights switched off. She stood in darkness, her frustration morphing into anxiety.

Great, just great.

She fidgeted with her phone and the drained battery icon flashed and disappeared. No power. No flashlight. The sound of her breath swelled in silence.

She groped for the wall and tried convincing herself she wouldn't get lost. This was her second visit. She could retrace her way back to the main staircase from memory. Eyes closed. Blindfolded. No problem. It only took one step for her heart to rise into her throat.

The smell came first. Overpowering. Saturating her sinuses and coating them in soot. Mave hunched, coughed. She shielded her nose with her elbow as a single sconce buzzed back to life. Its glass flickered and pinged like a moth was trapped inside. Color shifted and the corridor tinted violet. Mave lifted her head, dazed and speechless. Everything felt spun on its head. The floor was the ceiling. Left was right. She back-stepped reflexively and collided with Katrina's door.

Her eyes sprung wide as the patterns on the wallpaper in front of her grew animated. Cockles stretched, fanned, flocked like blackbirds sweeping in unison across a twilight sky. And through the avian dance—through solid wall and amethyst light—the ghost of Annabelle took shape.

Up close the skin on her neck was candescent. Her hair draped like black velvet down her slender shoulders. Their beauty made the thick fingers shuttering her face all the more violating. Mave gaped helplessly, her body trembling, her tongue stuck to the roof of her mouth.

The braided knuckles on Abs' face flexed and whitened as if she were sucking beneath, pushing to be released and heard.

"*What—*" Mave's lungs spasmed. "What do you,"—*breathe*—"want?" The doorknob dug into her spine.

Abs slowly stuck out her chin. Her unnaturally long neck craned closer and closer.

Though she perceived her intent, Mave didn't have time to put her hands to her ears.

Annabelle moaned.

The light shattered.

And the knob digging into Mave's spine twisted.

She stumbled backward into the darkness of Katrina's suite.

THIRTY-FIVE

The surreal moment was there and gone like a shiver.

A votive candle flickered on the coffee table. The door was shut. As if it hadn't spontaneously unlocked for her. As if she hadn't just toppled through like Alice down the rabbit hole. She rolled to her feet, knees down, knuckles out. Her blood pounded between her ears.

The room was silent, empty. No ghost or maid or murderer awaited her inside. She wasn't sure what she was supposed to do. Intuition told her she'd been thrust inside Katrina's suite for a reason. Or had she broken in—hallucinated the haunting as a means to justify her crime?

Get a hold of yourself. Act now. Worry later. All that matters is that you're inside. She put a hand on her chest, lengthened her breaths, and ordered her heart to slow.

She plucked the votive holder from the table. Its heated glass stung the chill from her fingers. Time was short. The wick was almost burned down to nothing. Mave began to search for anything that stood out as strange or suspicious.

Why was she here—to find the charm bracelet, the red book? Inky shadows leaked across her sight. The small sitting room had changed since her first visit. No pashmina shawl or picture frames. No radio. It seemed sparser, free of personalization. As if Katrina had already moved out. *Or fled.* She couldn't have gotten far with Morganson's orders and the roads shut. Mave wandered into the bathroom and, sure enough, no towels, toothbrush, or soaps were stored anywhere. She moved on to the bedroom.

Like the modest sitting room, there were no windows here. Mave guided the candle over the space. A water glass with a lipstick stain on its rim sat on the nightstand. Wilted flowers hung from a standing mirror. A few clothes hangers littered the floor. She paused her survey on the unmade bed. Her pulse skittered. It felt familiar. She'd encountered this space before. Except...

She rushed to the foot of the mattress where a comforter lay bunched up. She pulled it smooth. Even through darkness, the peach and green floral print was recognizable. Adrenaline laced her veins. The description she'd offered Bastian in the morning recited in her mind: ...*sandwiched in a soft place... peach and green... someplace up high. No windows.*

This had to be it. The bed had a gaudy pleated skirt. Mave hurriedly frisked the edge of the mattress. She could mentally scent it. Bastian's lost cell phone had been jammed along this bedframe. *Had.*

Five passes proved it was no longer stashed here. Katrina must have moved it along with the rest of her belongings since this morning. Mave sat back on her heels and groaned.

She'd been so close. That must be the reason she'd been pushed into the abandoned room. So why deny her the phone; what was the point in knowing Katrina's involvement without the evidence to back it? Suspicions twisted and turned with logic.

A stolen phone implied the maid had known about Birdie's voicemail. She was withholding evidence, telling lies. It seemed probable: Katrina delivered the note to Bastian. Impersonated Birdie's handwriting—her voice. Lied about her whereabouts hours later. Maybe she'd stolen the phone then, at midnight, when Bastian would have been distracted with the countdown.

Probable. Not one hundred percent certain, M&M.

She pushed her hair off her forehead, feeling one step behind. *Why.* Why frame her?

(*"...caught and put away for life. With all the other animals. And you will be, too...once I'm done with the daughter of Cain Francis."*)

Muddled glimpses of truths and lies teased her unconscious. Someway, somehow, she had to reestablish order. Except order in this hotel seemed impossible. It was the single irrefutable fact: between Birdie's murder, the killer's machinations, Holden's games, Annabelle's haunt, and staff and guests' countless secrets, the Château du Ciel was a breeding ground for mental chaos. Before she could subdue her frustration, a creak carried from the sitting room. Mave's attention snapped to the bedroom's doorway. Her pulse leapt.

Another creak. Footsteps. Someone was here.

Katrina? Had the maid forgotten something and returned?

Mave blew out her candle and stiffened in the encroaching darkness. The reflex to duck into the closet tempted for only a second. She refused to hide. She'd get answers once and for all. She crept forward in shadow. But her chance to take control of her visitor never came.

"Hands where I can see 'em!"

Mave's heart lurched and her legs nearly gave out.

A gun pointed directly at her chest.

THIRTY-SIX

She did as she was told and raised her arms. *It's just a candle*, she wanted to cry, but her tongue had seized. *Gun.* Even while squinting away from the flashlight, she could make out the shape of the Glock.

"*Jesus*, you again." Morganson blew out a breath and lowered her weapon. Her flashlight remained aimed at Mave's eyes. "What are you doing in here?"

"I—" Her jaw clicked shut.

Calmly, M&M. Pull yourself together.

Morganson cocked her head, eyes narrowed. "Breaking into rooms a habit of yours?"

"I didn't"—she swallowed—"she let me in." *Pushed me*, was more like it. Her lungs were still heaving, a step behind her brain. *It's okay. Everything's okay.*

"Let you in, huh?" Morganson sounded less than convinced. "If that's the case, then where is she?"

Mave shook her head. *The ghost?* Unless it'd been *her* hidden in the suite all along… Had the sheriff opened the door for her?

Morganson must have read the disorientation on her face. She holstered her Glock and slid her flashlight lower so it wasn't stinging Mave's eyes. "Katrina Kovak. No one has seen her since this morning."

She'd meant the maid. *Where's the maid. Right.*

"I don't…" Mave lowered her hands and helplessly glanced

back to the bed as if Katrina might materialize from beneath the blanket. "She left. I mean, she took all her stuff. She's not here."

"I can see that," Morganson said without inflection. "So I'll ask you again: what are you doing in here? And try not to lie this time."

"I'm not—" She inhaled a quick breath. She needed an excuse to buy herself time. "I just dropped by to give her this." She cautiously set down the votive holder and removed the Russian doll charm from her pocket. "See?" Her palm trembled as she held it out.

The slash in Morganson's brow deepened.

"She lost it," she added as if that might clear up this entire misunderstanding. "It's a charm from her bracelet."

"Where did you get that?"

"From—"

Say nothing, Cain whispered.

"You and Katrina know each other well?"

"What?"

"How long have you two known one another?"

Mave shook her head again. It suddenly occurred to her how this must seem. "No, I barely—we met for the first time earlier today. I swear, I didn't even…" Her plea trailed off. "This isn't what it looks like," she breathed.

Morganson didn't so much as blink. "And what does it look like?"

Like I'm working with Katrina—like we're in on Birdie's murder together.

"Mave, when I instructed you not to do anything stupid, this is exactly the kind of behavior I was referring to. Now, I'm going to have to ask you to put your hands behind your head."

"Wh-what?"

"Don't make me repeat myself."

Her entire body shook as she raised and clasped her fingers together.

Morganson advanced and steered her to face the wall. "Legs

apart." She nudged them with her boot.

The ground seemed to drop from beneath her. This was it. Morganson was frisking her. A distant part of her thanked god she wasn't carrying Cain's gun. Not that it mattered. She was going down for a crime she hadn't committed. In the end, it wasn't the revelation that she would follow in her father's footsteps that tipped her over the edge—it wasn't Cain's shouts in her head or her need to retch. It was the rattle of the handcuffs.

"Mave Michael Francis, you're under arrest for breaking and entering, altering evidence, and interfering with—"

Morganson never got the chance to finish her list of crimes.

As her fingers glanced Mave's wrist, Mave pivoted low like a boxer dodging a blow. She shouldered Morganson's hip along the way, throwing her off-balance, slowing her from redrawing her Glock. And she ran like the devil that burned in her blood.

Twelve oh-one and he's gone. Got it?

A sheen of sweat pierced her skin. She nicked a candlestick from a console table and struggled to push the deadline from her mind. Escaping Morganson had been relatively simple given the blackout and the hotel's sprawling floorplan. But luck was a fickle thing. Here today, prison tomorrow. Her eyes flitted to guests roaming the lobby.

Who else knew? Would an APB have reached Tag already? It hadn't sunk in—not entirely. *I did it again. I ran.* In the past few minutes, she'd gone from being a material witness to a key suspect in a murder investigation. And once Morganson located Birdie's body, then what? The sheriff had all but prophesized her arrest. She'd requested her clothes as evidence—promised to come back for her in the morning. Mave had merely sped up the inevitable.

("*Stay away from the Everharts.*")

If only Cain had shared the truth sooner—all of it. Even now, she felt him concealing more pieces of the puzzle. *Makes no differ-*

ence, she reprimanded herself, *you're out of time.*

Last she'd checked, it had been ten minutes to twelve. Ten minutes until a life-altering decision. As much as she hated to admit it, Cain's offer was her last chance to keep a sliver of her freedom. One desperate weekend and she'd already behaved in ways that horrified her. Lying, stealing, blackmailing, breaking and entering, resisting arrest. A life in prison would corrupt her permanently. With a bitter taste in her mouth and a heaviness inside her chest, she hurried to the southwest exit where she would begin her life as a fugitive. Stratis waited.

As she cut across the lobby, Hendrick's winter wonderland seemed to be in full swing. A number of guests were still socializing in the common areas. Jazz played from a phonograph. Couples cuddled under fur blankets, sipped mulled wine and hot toddies by the fireplace. *Bobs*, Cain would call them. Witnesses. Liabilities. *Read the room.*

Perimeter soft. Cameras out. One fire extinguisher. Three exits.

How many Bobs, M&M? Count them all.

She did. There were too many. Avoiding eyes would be tricky but not impossible. She wandered to the edge of the room. Limbs loose. Head lowered.

When her steps crossed onto the carpet of the wing marked Hunter's Alley, she released a heavy breath. Decorated with dusty credenzas and stuffed animal head trophies, the hallway proved dark and uninviting—an ideal escape route. She gave up her relaxed act and darted ahead.

She reached a fork, hastily swung right, and thirty to forty feet beyond, encountered a wall sign that told she should have ventured left. Mave cursed and hustled to backtrack. Her pulse ticked like a timer about to expire. She was so fixated on approaching the turn, meeting Stratis, that the beam of light registered a second too late. She couldn't stop her momentum.

"Oh!" She bumped into a tall figure and stepped away with her hand on the wall to steady herself.

"Mave!" Bastian stood with his flashlight fisted. "Thought that was you in the lobby. Been looking everywhere for you."

Why—what had he heard?

"Nice hair by the way. You all right? You look a bit pale."

"Sure. Fine. You just," her smile twitched, "startled me." Her heart felt like it had jumped out from her throat and landed a few feet away on the matted carpeting.

Bastian eyed her suspiciously. He pointed his light further down the hall. "What are you doing out this way all alone?"

She turned, hoping to draw his attention away from her escape route. "What? Oh…" A nervous giggle escaped her lips. *Get it together. It's only been a few minutes since Morganson tried to arrest you. He doesn't know.* "Following signs for the coffee bar," she lied, "but it's already closed for the night. Duh." Miraculously, her voice was level and sounded halfway sane.

"Coffee at this hour?" His words were edged with doubt. "Better off visiting the kitchens, yeah?"

Mave's smile grew brittle. She fumbled for another topic. "You said you were looking for me?"

Bastian tilted his head as if anticipating something. "It's nearly midnight, remember?"

He knew? Whatever blood remained in her face drained to her feet. She opened her mouth, but no witty reply came out.

"The master key? Please don't tell me—"

"Oh, that!" She laughed, hoping to pass off her relief as humor. "No, of course, I have it here." She dug into her pocket with more enthusiasm than necessary.

"Great. Thanks. Had me worried for a second." He tucked away the key. "Come, I'll walk you back."

"Oh, that's—" *not necessary.* "Thanks." They strolled side by side at a leisurely pace toward the lobby. Bastian's two-way radio crackled static, giving her another small start. *Relax or he's going to suspect something.* She crossed her arms and concentrated on acting casual, natural.

Bastian threw her a sidelong glance. "I heard about Birdie going missing. You okay?" He must have been misinterpreting her nerves for what had happened earlier.

She shrugged, suddenly worn out from lying. "As much as I can be with most people assuming I stole the body. Speaking of theft, did you find your cellphone yet?" Even as she redirected the conversation, she was only half-listening. Her focus lay ahead where Morganson or security could be patrolling for her arrest.

Bastian snorted. "I wish. Haven't even had the chance to search properly. I've been too busy coordinating Hendrick's ridiculous itinerary." He checked his watch sighed dramatically. "Midnight wine tasting starts in seven minutes in the upper lobby."

Mave's tinny laugh bounced from the walls. Seven minutes till Stratis came. Eight minutes till Stratis left. She tried not to trip over her feet.

"Well good and bad news, I figured out where your phone *used* to be."

"What?" He turned to her. "You mean someone found it and took it?"

"Sort of." She finally bothered to look at him. "The place I described this morning? It was Katrina's bedroom."

The deep hood over his eyes returned. "Birdie's maid? How did it get—"

"Bastian, I have to ask," she'd had her fill of guesses and hints, "are you covering for her?"

"Huh? Who?"

She inhaled and prayed for more time. "Katrina."

"Why would I be covering for …?"

Mave stopped him at the mouth of Hunter's Alley. Though he seemed genuinely confused, she still didn't trust he wasn't hiding something. "I have no idea," she said in a low voice. "Just like I have no idea why she'd have your cell stashed in her room. Look, I have to be honest: I got the impression this morning there was more

you weren't telling me. When I asked you about Birdie's enemies…
you seemed to be holding back."

He wiped his forehead and blinked nervously. "Okay, okay. I'm
sorry. I shouldn't have. But that was before I heard about Birdie's will. I didn't know about the money, I swear." He fidgeted with
his radio, avoiding her eyes. "And it wasn't Katrina Kovak on my
mind," he mumbled, "that's for sure."

"Who then? Please Bastian, whoever's behind this," frustration
funneled from her throat like coarse salt, grinding and quickening
with each word, "for whatever reason they're out to destroy my
life and see me locked up for a crime I didn't commit and if there's
anyone who—"

"It's Tag."

Her mouth stayed ajar.

"Look, I don't want to lose my job." His eyes flicked toward the
lobby. "You can't let on I told you anything, okay? He's got seniority
over me."

"Told me what?" Even now, the security guard's hostility toward her stung—just like all the haters outside the courthouse,
jeering, spitting. "Why does Tag *hate* me so much?"

"It's not a question of hate. It's who he loves that matters."

"Huh?" She caught up to his meaning. "Tag loves Birdie?"

"Right family. Wrong lady. *Parissa.*"

Mave's eyes grew into saucers.

"Tag's been obsessed with her for years," Bastian whispered,
"ever since he first started working here and she came to visit."

All the pieces belong to the same puzzle, Cain whispered. *Flip
them. Spin them. Lift them for another angle.*

"So you're saying Tag's blaming me to protect Parissa? Or he's
working for her?" A seed of anger bloomed in her belly. Tag had
marked Mave as a murderer, lied about her holding down Birdie
and hiding the boxcutter—all to serve Parissa Everhart.

"Maybe. All I know is he goes out of his way to fawn over her,
get her attention. Seems desperate."

A flashback of the offices came to her: how quickly Tag had offered to deliver Parissa wine to soften the news about Birdie.

"Remember," Bastian went on, "he's done two tours, seen a lot of blood and who knows what else. That shit does things to a man's head. Then you throw money into the mix…" He shuddered. "Listen, I should've been up front before. But like I said, I hadn't heard about the inheritance—and that library creeps me out. Makes me feel like I'm being watched all the time. I can't think straight when I'm inside that place."

The clock was ticking but Mave couldn't stop herself. Her brain was already rushing to flip the puzzle pieces, to lift them for a new angle.

"Bastian, what do you know about the Spirit of Dead Poets?"

THIRTY-SEVEN

FROM THE RED BOOK OF THE DEAD

JULY 5TH, 1991

Dear Rie,

I love you to death for all your support and faith in me—but please, please don't get Cain to come up here. Don't get me wrong—I'd love to meet this special guy who's stolen your heart, and, believe me, it's tempting to see Charlie get his face pounded in. But I have to do this my way. Please. It's finished ... at least I want it to be.

I'm not reporting Charlie. I realize I ought to but just the thought makes me sick. I can't live through that horrible night over again with police, you know? It's my word against his. What if they don't believe me? Or say I asked for it? I could barely confess it to you in a letter. I'm not ready, Rie. Maybe someday... For now, I just want to put it behind me. Is that so terrible—to want to go back to worrying over Caroline and not myself? Caring for her feels right somehow. Like it's healing. Yesterday, when I felt the baby kicking in her stomach, it gave me hope. Honestly though, if it hadn't been for Mr. Law, I would've quit the morning after.

He's left, but he checks in regularly, makes sure I'm well. His concern has made a world of difference. He keeps reminding me that I'm safe. I can defend myself. And he's right. If Charlie comes near me again, I swear I'll do something much worse than just kick and bite him. Mr. Law even gave me pepper spray. Plus Birdie promised that Charlie would keep away, and so far, she's kept her word.

The asshole has stopped his creepy stalking. He doesn't wait for me on my walks each evening. In fact I was starting to think Birdie must have sent him away; but just the other morning, I caught a glimpse of him. It made me want to throw up. He was leaving the restaurant after breakfast. I hid behind a plant as he slunk past, oblivious. He looked like shit. His cheeks were hollowed out like he'd lost weight. His eyes had yellow bags and were dull, almost lifeless. If I didn't know better, I'd say he'd been popping some serious downers. Good. He could be sedated into a coma for all I care.

Also, this is going to sound terrible, but I got a raise from Mr. Law. After what you wrote, I suspect Birdie might be the real person behind it, but I'm not exactly in a position to turn down money. Anyway, Mr. Law made it sound like I was invaluable to him and Caroline—made me feel really appreciated. In hindsight, I may have been too quick to judge him. Did you know he and Birdie weren't just old flames, but each other's first love? He told me they used to be sweethearts! Said he trusted Birdie deeply, and I could rely on her when he's away. He's been wonderful. And the silver lining? The vibe has changed between Caroline and me. I think her being there that night, seeing me hurt like that, it bonded us. She's much more accepting of my care, and I finally got her to trust me with her past.

Since you told me her boyfriend's name, I commented on her tattoo again. She still wouldn't say who BP was, so I pretended to go through random names until I hit on Benjamin. It worked. Caroline was afraid at first, but then she started to talk and it all spilled out. It's so heartbreaking, Rie. She told me all about Benji's death and, get this, it wasn't a skiing accident at all that killed him. That's just the rumor his family spread to cover up the ugly truth: an overdose. And the worse part? Caroline thinks it might have been intentional. Benji knew Caroline was pregnant and was freaking out about the whole mess. He was super worried what everyone would think, say—especially Mr. Law. According to Caroline, Benji was terrified of her father.

JULY 16ᵀᴴ, 1991

Dear Abs,

How are you holding up, for real? I know you say we judged Mr. Law wrongly—that he's been watching out for you—but I'm still worried. I mean, now that you've told me the real reasons behind Benji's fate, it made me remember how when I was a kid, Mr. Law seemed scary to me, too. Whenever Birdie left the room, he was stern and snarky like he hated kids. But then Mother would return and he'd be this different person. Maybe it's just what you said, first love… it changes people. But if you need more support, you just say the word, okay? Screw my summer courses. I'll gladly come up there and while I'm at it, I'll confront my jerk family members face to face.

Birdie's latest maneuvers have me tearing out my hair. Rather than hire another PI, this time Mother has sent her favorite little lap dog. Even as I write this, Dominic is in town sniffing around, tapping his sketchy art contacts and trying to dig up dirt on Cain. Birdie is convinced Cain is manipulating me. Isn't that hilarious? Cain is supposedly dangerous because he's a drifter with no ties. Imagine Birdie's horror: no annual membership to the country club, no ivy league legacy or uncle on the board of the Yachters Society. She keeps insisting Cain is ill-bred and only after me for my money. I swear—all that time cooped up in that hotel, inhaling her paint fumes—my mother's lost it. Cain might not be blue-blooded but little does Birdie know he has plenty of cash from doing private contract work; security wiring and consulting, odds and ends. He's so handy and smooth with money, though you wouldn't think it just to look at him. He's not flashy like Dom with his Rolex watches and yuppy suits. He's real. He's so much more. And the way he treats me, like I'm this surprise gift under the tree on Christmas morning…

He's the one, Abs. Nothing Birdie can possibly say or do will ever break us apart. Nothing. If she keeps pushing like this, she's going to regret it.

❖

JULY 27ᵀᴴ, 1991

Dear Rie,

Don't worry; I'm perfectly okay. So is Caroline. Her abdominal measurements are on the smaller side, but apart from that, all's well. With her due date around the corner, mind you, Caroline is growing more and more devastated about having to give up her baby. I'm telling her she has a choice. It's her right to decide—morally, legally. But she's convinced it's impossible and she'll forever lose her baby like she did Benji. I honestly don't know how to give her faith. Listening to her fears last night, I was crying right alongside her. This girl has been through so much already. She deserves a happy ending. I'm praying. Rahul has rubbed off with all his talk of a higher power.

Speaking of the old sweetheart, I caught him talking to himself the other day. Did you ever see him doing that? I was part entertained, part worried. He was at his desk with no one else around and seemed to be chatting with shadows. Like, not just mumbling thoughts aloud, Rie—I mean he was having a full-blown conversation with hand gestures and everything. At one point, what he was saying sounded like total gibberish. But then I remembered he's super humble and smart and speaks a bunch of languages, right? For sure I've caught him reading books in Hindi and Arabic.

As soon as he noticed me, he stopped and smiled. It was like nothing had happened. I felt weird bringing it up and just went with the flow. I don't want to insult him or anything. It might be a bit pathetic but, he's the only true friend I have up here. I'm sure I'll miss him in a couple weeks when this is all over. Sadly, I can't say the same about this hotel. Once the baby is born and Mr. Law pays me, I won't be sticking around. As much as I've grown to really care for Caroline, I don't ever want to come back to this château. Ever.

THIRTY-EIGHT

JANUARY 2ND, 2021

"The Spirit of Dead Poets will drive you to madness."

Bastian's dire warning rang in her head.

"You'll get sick—grow paranoid. You'll experience hallucinations. And the voices." *He licked his lips.* *"If you stay too long in the library, the voices will make you do terrible things."*

"What do you mean? What kinds of things?"

"Murder."

The decision had made itself. She'd missed her chance. Stratis was gone. And for the first time since this nightmare had begun, clarity had resurfaced. She was neither sick, nor paranoid, nor losing her mind from too many breaks spent reading in a haunted library. Bumping into Bastian had been an awakening. It had stopped her from making the biggest mistake of her life.

Only criminals run, she repeated. *I'm innocent.* She wouldn't flee and cower because of horrific, misunderstood lies. Katrina had set her up, along with Tag or Nicholas. They were playing her for a fool, laying traps to make her act guilty again: the vile daughter of Cain Francis. Even Cain himself underestimated her. Well she'd stay and prove them wrong. She'd expose the truth with everything in her.

Most people were incapable of understanding the invisible threads that twirled from human psyches. But not Mave. For whatever reason, she'd been born with a sixth sense others lacked. Logic could be stretched. Brainwaves emitted patterns, energies. Echoes of electrical pulses could reverberate in a space for years on end. Isn't that what a haunting was? Now that she'd been forced to analyze it—to accept that Abs wasn't a symptom of her fears—how different was encountering a ghost from her own hound-dogging?

Bastian may have believed a ghost existed in the library—enough to trade a key with him out of terror—but only Mave had recognized the Spirit of Dead Poets was a masked mole named Holden Frost. Only she had been invited into the cursed library, or had channeled the ghost of Annabelle, or had sensed the bones hidden in an air vent below.

She thought of Holden's hot-and-cold cooperation and Abs' repeated attempts to communicate. They were connected to Birdie—everything was. Mave had to get Holden to confess the entire truth. He'd been born here. What else? What secrets about the hotel's dark past was he harboring?

Mind set, she snuck down the grand staircase. The temperature dropped as she descended. With all the entertainment raging upstairs, the galleria's corridors were soulless, just like before. Her heart pounded in time with her feet. If Morganson spotted her now, there would be no reprieve, no hesitation. Her Glock would aim and another escape would be impossible. Mave's mouth grew dry. She mentally recited questions for Holden to distract herself. She didn't get far, however; he was headed straight for her like a billowing storm cloud.

"What's going on?" He jerked to a stop less than a foot away. She opened and closed her mouth. Whatever lines she'd been rehearsing flitted from her mind.

He leaned forward and back as if caught between the urge to hug her or shake her. "You're late. What happened to your hair?"

"I—" She brushed a flyaway strand and gathered her voice. "I got lost." It wasn't a lie. Not really. As if she might get lost again, he took her by the hand.

"Come on. Let's go."

Sparks shot into her chest. She'd almost forgotten about the effect of his touch. Her stomach tightened with every step they took closer to the library. "Holden, I—" He towed her through the French doors before she could complete her protest.

She slowed steps ahead of him and blinked at wavering shadows. She wasn't sure which dreadfulness she'd been waiting to re-encounter. Another mouthful of ash. More lights flashing, crystals clattering. A pair of filthy male hands sprouting from her vertebrae, wrapping her face.

"Hey—"

She flinched as he cupped her shoulders.

"Mave?" He faced her and rubbed the warmth back into her arms. "You're shaking. What's happened?"

Nothing had happened. In fact, the library appeared as it always had before this weekend. Beeswax dripped from candelabras. Logs snapped in the fireplace. A knot formed in her throat. Over the past few months, whenever she'd visited during her breaks, it had been the same. Holden must have lit all those fires. He must have anticipated her daily visits and readied the room for her. Waiting. Watching.

All her doubts rushed back in a heartbeat: Why did he run off earlier? How did Cain know about him? Whose bones were—

"Mave?"

She stepped out of his reach and crossed her arms. "I need you to be honest with me." It came out sterner than she'd intended. He stilled like a statue, either nervous or held in attention. It was impossible to tell with the mask hiding his face. "What do you know about Annabelle?" She waited but he offered no reply. "The *real* spirit," she tried.

His breathing grew animated. "Who's Annabelle?"

"Please don't pretend."

He returned to his controlled, frozen state, and she had to stop herself from lunging forward and ripping off that mask once and for all.

"You claim no one except for me ever comes in here, right? Because it's your library. But you and I both know that's a lie."

He gave a hard blink.

"I saw her," she challenged. "I know this place is hers and not yours."

"What are you—" He drew closer, his scent of earthy smoke filling her head. She squared her shoulders, holding her ground. "What do you mean, you saw her?"

"More than once." She raised her chin. "She even tried speaking to me but I could only pick up a bit. Those horrible hands suffocating her all the time muffle her—"

"You mean..." He cocked his neck forward.

"Yes, exactly." A part of her feared saying her name too many times might conger her.

His eyes widened and volleyed between her own. "She showed herself to you, and she *spoke*."

Her confidence wavered. She swept her bangs behind her ears. "'Spoke' may be a bit much. More like I accidentally interpreted a few sounds."

"Holy fuck." He raked his hands through his hair. "I mean, I suspected with you coming in here, unaffected all these months..." Lost in thought, his stare grew unfocused.

"What's that supposed to mean? *Holden*." Their eyes met. Mave shifted and touched her neck. "Why are you looking at me like that?"

"Like what?"

"Like I'm about to unfold some wings and flap around this library like a bat."

"Sorry, it's just, no one's ever seen her, much less heard her."

"Abs?" she whispered, just to be sure.

"*Jesus*." He laced his fingers behind his head and rocked back. "That you even know her name is incredible. Don't you see what this means?"

She shook her head in confusion.

"Mave, you can channel the dead. You're a *medium*."

"What? No." She huffed. "No, absolutely not. I can't even find my own—"

"Listen to me. Yes, most people who stay here for a few weeks or more end up tuning in to her presence, but they feel sick when that happens. You're right. She keeps assholes like that security guard who was chasing you out of here. If trespassers manage to barge in, she has this way of making them irrationally sick or afraid. Unless she invites them in. Like you." He regarded her with that same hint of awe as when she'd first told him about her hound-dogging.

"No, uh-uh." She crossed her arms. "I've spent months hanging around this library. If I were a medium, I would have seen her here on day one. Not after Birdie's death."

"The murder..." His eyes sprung wide. "Shit, that's it—that must have been the trigger."

Her frown deepened. "Trigger?"

"You didn't know what you were capable of. Neither did she. Not until Birdie's murder shook up both of you."

Until she was spooked into believing.

I do—I see you, she'd whispered in that strange dream. It'd been the first time she'd sensed the ashes. Mave recalled all too well: though blurry during that initial contact, Annabelle had reacted with surprise. It was as if Mave had accidentally picked up on her longing for something lost—something forgotten—a longing that according to Holden's theory, had been provoked and grown wilder by Birdie's murder. It was possible. Except what lost possession would a ghost suddenly crave?

She took a deep breath, struggling to process Holden's revelation. "What about you?" she thought aloud. "You know about her, too. And you spend all this time in the library and don't get sick."

"Maybe because I was born here?" He shrugged. "Suppose I'm immune. I can only vaguely guess when she's around, and more so in my dreams. When I was younger, it was more often. She sort of hovered like a shadow on the sidelines. Never spoke—or maybe she tried and eventually gave up when I couldn't hear. I remember she was angry, burning hot and cold,"—he cupped the back of his neck—"and sad. A long time ago, something really bad must have happened to her. I think she may have been in a fire. I don't know how exactly. But she doesn't want to leave here. Or she can't."

A grievance. An offense so strong, its resulting emotional frequency remained trapped in spiritual form. Mave pictured her candescent skin against the dirty fingers and a shiver rippled down her body.

"Hey," he brushed her shoulder, "what's going on in your head?"

She struggled to gather her thoughts. This place—with its drafty halls and whistling pipes, it was easy to let your imagination run wild. A rundown grand hotel inspired dark dreams. The uncanny seemed to breathe in every nook and cranny, conjuring monsters.

"I know it's a lot to take in," Holden said. "I've never spoken about her to anyone. But you"—his voice dropped—"you're different. Not like the others. I saw it. *She* saw it." He made her oddness sound like a good thing. Mave gently pulled away and backed against a bookshelf.

If grieving spirits were real and she was a medium, then where was her mother's ghost? Where was Valeria Francis's longing for her lost daughter? Without warning, her wound threatened to crush her. Her eyes stung.

"You're quiet." He leaned his weight onto a desk, seeming to sense her need for space. "Listen, I can help. Don't be scared. Maybe we can try conjuring her in—"

"There has to be more." She stared at him without apology. "I realize I've got an extra freak-sensor or two, but how come you don't and you're still on her good list? Besides being born here, what aren't you telling me?"

He looked to the floor and shrugged again. "Nothing..."

"Have you been here your entire life?" Something wasn't adding up. "Were your parents long-term residents like Birdie?"

"No."

"But they must have met her."

"I don't—"

His leg jittered. "They died young. I never knew them."

His parents?

"Then all that stuff about your dad being a junkie, was that a lie to make me feel better about Cain?"

He rolled his jaw. "I never lied. I just don't—" He pushed his hands in his pockets like he was struggling to keep something down.

"Just don't what? Did your abusive grandfather raise you?" Is that why he was so jaded with life?

He shut his eyes and mumbled to himself. She leaned forward to catch the tail end of his words. "…of that matters."

"You're wrong, Holden. Please just answer me."

He swore under his breath. "Rah—Rah looked after me, okay, an old concierge." He bit down and looked to the ceiling. "We done talking about—"

"No." She swallowed. She couldn't quit until he gave her the link to the puzzle. "I need to know everything. What happened to Rah?"

He focused on a candle burning next to him and grew still. She could sense him shutting down again. Her teeth tightened. "Hol—"

"He was sick." The reply was monotone and gravelly, surprising her. "Lost his job. Couldn't look after me anymore. So he sent me away."

A pang of empathy squeezed her chest, curbing her frustration. "Away where?" she asked softly. "To the tunnels?"

"Tunnels were home," he whispered. "No, I had to survive the big bad world. Didn't care for it much so I came back. I always came back." His sorrow swelled without release. "We were together in the end."

The air between them shifted. It was her turn to comfort him—one outcast to another. She approached slowly, fearing his pull even now. She touched his chest and he inhaled sharply, his attention held on the candle. "Holden..." Beneath her palm, his frenzied pulse confirmed what she already knew. It didn't belong to an innocent person. She pressed with her hold, her voice. "There's more. What are you hiding?"

He danced his fingers through the flame. "Nothing."

No more games. Her own pulse raced to match his heated beats. "Then why...why does my father know your name?" His gaze flicked up, eyes like black maelstroms.

"Mave, *don't*—"

"Who are you?" she breathed.

He tremored, emotions shimmering off his skin. Torment. Sadness. Desire. "You already know." Both their chests heaved. Without looking away, he raised his hands and lifted off his mask. It clattered onto the desk. "I'm a villain."

THIRTY-NINE

She stared in shock at the man beneath the many faces, processing him piece by piece. He wasn't ghoulish beneath his mask. Quite the opposite. His face matched his body: lean and angular. Aquiline nose. Brooding brow. Deep-set eyes that sloped at the corners as if he were forever bored. She fixated on a small scar that cut through his left eyebrow. *A villain.* It still wasn't right.

"What"—her voice caught and she dropped her hand from his chest—"are you saying…you had something to do with Birdie's murder?"

Confusion lit his eyes. "No."

"What about—" She stopped for breath, relief quick to bloom with her lungs. "What about Rah? Or Annabelle?"

The tension about him seemed to loosen. His lashes lowered. He studied her mouth. "Rah was like a father to me. And I never even knew Annabelle."

She hesitated, weighing his words.

He trusts you—removed his mask for you, a voice inside her whispered. *Don't be a hypocrite. Trust him back.*

The strangest thing was, Mave wanted to—even with all the uncertainties still racing through her mind. She had to give him a chance.

She studied the dip between his collarbones. He no longer felt like a near-stranger. Even if he was one. She lifted her gaze, caught in his spell. Resisting seemed impossible now that he'd taken off his mask. She tentatively reached up and traced the white scar that bisected his brow. "And this?"

He closed his eyes, his shoulders tight. "Fell off a bunk bed when I was seven."

"A bunk bed here?"

"Foster care."

She tried picturing him as a boy. "Did you have to go to the hospital?"

He shook his head. "Ran away. Found Rah and he stitched me up with a mini bottle of rum and a needle from a sewing kit—both complimentary from housekeeping." His smile was melancholic. "I begged to stay but… he could hardly look after himself."

Emotions she'd rather not name fluttered inside her. She dropped her hand to his chest, overcome by a connection she'd never before experienced. He'd been lonely as a child—had suffered a complicated upbringing. Like her. Yearning burned. For a moment, they would pretend. They would be an ordinary set of people, a woman and man without secrets, without damaged pasts or bleak futures.

"Holden?" She waited until he met her stare. His pupils had dilated into pools of onyx. "Is all this real?" She made a fist over his heart. It thumped a mile a minute, echoing the knocks beneath her own breastbone.

The cords on his neck stood taut. "Yeah," he sighed, "it's real."

Heat gathered into a twister inside her belly, climbing higher, siphoning lower. She leaned up and pressed her mouth to his.

The electrical jolt between them bordered on stunning. His breath hitched as he stiffened. She feared he'd turn her away. But a second later, he pushed into her with a moan that rippled through them both.

She threaded her hands into his thick hair, deepening the kiss. His beard chafed. She didn't care. She needed to fill herself with his smoke and edges. He tasted heady and sweet with a tannic bite— orange and tobacco and oakwood and cinnamon. His hands slid to her behind and she arched, writhed. He lifted her. They rocked sideways, knocked into a bookshelf, tangled together. Thighs to waist. Ankles to hips. He held her steady even as the remainder of the world spun off course.

"*Mave*—" He broke for air. The want in his gaze made her stomach flip.

"I know." Lips swollen, foreheads touching, they had to stop. Her mind spiraled downward from its high. Whatever this was between them, it was too intense. The perfect storm. It would sweep her up and devour her whole. She wiggled out of his hold and pulled down her shirt. The absence of his warmth prickled like a warning.

Sheriff Morganson was coming for her. Or Nicholas. Or Tag. Maybe Katrina. The possibilities were finite. Sooner or later, one way or another, the mud they were slinging would stick. She grazed her knuckles across her mouth, thoughts torn between two things at once: his arms, her arrest.

"Go on," he said, once again correctly gauging her need, "tell me."

She tucked a stray lock behind her ear and spoke quickly. "The bones hidden in an air vent—do you know anything about them?"

Without his mask, the bafflement on his face was easy enough to read. "What bones in what vent?"

She inhaled deeply through her nose, then confessed to him about her failed attempt to find him underground.

Holden swore under his breath. "They sealed off the tunnels fifty years ago, but this place is way older than that—and construction of those pipes would have been even earlier."

"So you're saying someone could have hidden the bones as far back as a century ago?"

His frown deepened. "Only forensic testing could answer that. I could probably help you find the exact vent though, if you describe your path. We could figure it out together."

Mave fiddled with her cuff as she contemplated his offer. She wasn't sure how that would help her case. She needed to secure evidence aboveground—tangible proof to clear her name. Like Bastian's phone or Katrina's whereabouts or Birdie's red book. *Or the green album.* Her chest constricted. The old photographs of Valeria Francis tugged her thoughts…

"There's something I have to do," she said to herself. She turned to leave.

"Hang on." He grabbed her hand. "Where are you going?"

She'd been wrong to stay in the library for as long as she had. The clock was winding down and with it, her potential freedom. "Wait here. I'll come back," she said, deliberately vague so he wouldn't involve himself. Not only did she need solitude to untangle the knots in her head, but now that he'd opened up to her, the real reason terrified her. She slipped out her hand from his in an attempt to ignore her heart's admission. Holden mattered too much.

Don't let them in. New meaning colored Cain's warning. She had weakened herself. Had potentially given her enemies more leverage by caring for someone.

"Mave, you're safe here. With me. Nothing bad will happen to you as long as we stay to—"

"I can't hide." She stepped back, determined to see this through. "I won't. Don't you understand? My entire life, I've been doing it. And I'm done." A clipped snort escaped her throat. "The real kicker? Cain in all his twisted glory taught me the answer from day one: you need to fight for what you want. Not hide. I need to pick myself up and gather whatever scraps I can before my fate is sealed." She took a big breath and nodded, needing to convince herself as much as him. She had to go back, one last time—retrace her steps before more police arrived and crawled the hallways and suites. Then if—*when*—they caught her, she could turn in whatever scant proof she'd assembled. Anything was better than uselessly running or hiding.

"Okay. I'll come with you."

"No!" Too much could go wrong.

A look of hurt flashed in his eyes.

It was clear he wouldn't accept being left behind. But neither could she allow him to fall on police radar. As it was, she'd barely dodged Morganson's initial questions about her escape. If Holden stayed with her now, the authorities would surely learn all about his underground home. They'd charge him with grand theft, criminal mischief, trespassing, unauthorized access—who knew what else. Mave glanced away. It had to be done. And only a lie would stop him from following her into certain danger.

"This was a mistake," she blurted before her nerve could leave her.

"*What?*" The sting in his voice was unmistakable.

She avoided his gaze, regret quick to thicken her throat and weigh down her stomach. *I have no choice,* she argued with herself, *no chance.* Birdie's blood remained on her hands. They were coming for her. Only her. He couldn't be there when that happened. The backs of her eyelids heated.

Holden held his arm across his chest, his expression crestfallen.

She bit her cheek and fisted her hands to stop from reaching out to him. Her knees shook. If she touched him, she doubted she'd ever find the strength to leave. "I'll come back," she whispered though they both understood it was a false promise. Her voice sounded like it belonged to another person. Someone cold. Her heart clenched. "I'm sorry." The apology fell flat.

She slipped away before he could call her a liar.

FORTY

The corridor leading to the staff quarters was too dark. Mave rubbed her eyes and swerved to avoid a potted fern. The witching hour. The majority of staff and guests would be sound asleep, having finally retired for the night. It was worth the risk, she assured herself. She'd be quick—in and out. And if she spied security or Morganson creeping near her door, then she'd abort. Simple.

She groped her way to her room and, with her path clear, entered in haste. Every sound was amplified in her ears: the bolt's clack, the floor's creak, her pounding pulse and ragged breath. *Fast. Faster. Go.*

She shifted to the dresser, her hands moving with a precision that belonged to a stranger—a person with neither the fear nor the panic she was bottling inside.

Everything was in order: the soft pocket holster in the back of the third drawer, the gun, loaded and ready. Nicholas Vaughn's threat looped in her ears. She'd be a fool to leave behind her weapon a second time. Her fingers wrapped around the cool metal.

Inside the waistband, Cain whispered, *carefully*.

She holstered the pistol, closed her eyes and shivered. *Don't stop now.* The time to second-guess herself was long spent. She twisted to exit and was stopped short by the shrill ring of the landline. With a yelp, Mave clapped her hands to her mouth and froze. The ring ripped through the silence. Her initial fright wearing off, she scrambled to answer it before its chime woke half the floor.

She banged her knee on her bedpost, bit back another cry, and flailed for the handset. She found it by the fourth ring. "Hello?" she hissed. "Dad? Hello?"

"—failed to follow my instructions," Cain rumbled. "I specifically said for you to—"

"Dad, I know. Stop."

"—ruined your *only* shot. You think it was easy for me to—" Cain Francis was a man of few words. She'd never heard him so upset.

"Dad, please." She concentrated on what she needed most and held in all her other burning questions, (like how he'd timed his call perfectly again, but then, he could have been phoning every half hour for all she knew). "I need you to listen. Hello?"

"Speak. Make it quick."

"Dad, is there any reason why Nicholas Vaughn would hate you?"

"Nicholas Vaughn? Christ. You know nothing," he uttered beneath his breath. "That's the problem. If you did, then you wouldn't have missed your one chance to escape."

His tone rankled her already-sensitive nerves. "That's so unfair! The only reason I know nothing is because you've kept me in the dark all this time. You should've told me about Birdie. You should've mentioned she was my *grandmother*. You think this is easy for me? The sheriff's here, okay? She tried to arrest me and Nicholas Vaughn's threatened me. Everyone is either lying or treating me like I'm"—*you*—"some bloodthirsty freak, and if it wasn't for the concierge and Holden and—"

"*Motherfucker.*" The low, uttered threat caused the remainder of her excuse to stick inside her throat. "Told you to be careful—trust no one. What the hell did Frost do, Mave Michael? That punk trying to get a free ride off you, is that it?"

Mave was dumbfounded. "What? No!"

"Did he manipulate you into staying? What'd he promise you, huh?"

"Dad, wait. I swear I have no idea what you're talking about. Holden isn't like that. He's helping to—wait—how do you even know about him?"

"He's not *helping* you. He's working you," he said, ignoring her questions.

"That's complete bull." *He cares for me*, she almost added.

"What've you done?"

"Nothing. I—" She snapped her mouth shut. She sounded guilty. Cain knew her too well, could read between the lines of her defensiveness. But so what if she'd trusted Holden? "I'm a grown woman," she reminded her father, wishing her voice sounded calmer. "Or did you forget. You've been gone for four years."

"Then you need a lesson for an adult."

Her back stiffened. She didn't dare ask him what he meant by that.

The beat of silence that followed was thick with tension. When Cain spoke next, his tone was that of a killer. "Do precisely what I say, Mave Michael: set down the phone and search your body. Under your clothes."

"What?"

"I'm going to show you exactly who your little helper is. Now, it's going to be somewhere you don't see it. Like between the shoulder blades."

A sour feeling bled into her stomach. "What is?"

"Just *do* it."

She flinched, recognizing his quiet rage. Though a part of her craved to defy him, she wouldn't get answers unless she obeyed. Hands trembling, she set down the receiver and reached around to grope her back. She slipped her hands beneath her shirt, damp with sweat. She glided her palms across her ribcage and touched nothing but clammy skin.

She picked up the handset. "I don't know what's going on but there's nothing on me."

"Check lower."

"This is—"

"For fuck's sake, Mave Michael. Stop arguing and do it."

With a huff, she set down the phone again and slipped her fingers beneath the hem of her shirt. She felt along her spine.

Lower.

Beneath her waistband, she found it.

It was on the small of her back: a bump no bigger than her pinkie nail and stuck to her like a button-sized Band-Aid. She peeled it off with effort, eyes pricked and owl-like in the dark. It didn't matter. No light was required to confirm what she held between her fingers.

The realization stung slowly, injecting her deep with venom. She tried to label the heavy, clamping sensation inside her chest. Was it anger, fear, humiliation? Everything mixed. Nausea churned. She lifted the phone. Her ear felt hot against the plastic.

"Who—" Her voice chafed her throat. "Who's tracking me?"

Trust no one.

"I am."

She gritted her teeth. The room swayed and she held the bedpost to keep from tipping into madness. "How'd you get this GPS on me? You're in prison." She scraped it from her fingers onto the nightstand like it was a small, deadly pox mark.

"Think. You know how."

"No," she shook her head, "I don't." She didn't—she didn't. Her eyes watered helplessly. *Ugly, ugly, cruel world.*

"He's been working for me for the past two months. He's my eyes and ears inside the hotel. Do you understand now?"

She pinched her eyes shut, twisted her mouth, waiting for it. And the blow came.

"I paid Holden Frost to put it on you."

No. He wouldn't. He's—he and I—he's a friend. God she was pathetic.

"A friend?"

She'd thought aloud in her shock. *Stop talking*, she wanted to yell. *Shut up shut up. No more.* But her father continued like a heartless, monotone android.

"You asked me *how* I know him. You should be asking for how long."

She couldn't bring herself to hang-up and she couldn't bring herself to hear another poisonous word from her father's mouth.

"Holden Frost has a long and impressive resume. He plays in the big field, M&M."

"What's that supposed to mean?" Dry, so dry. Her eyes had drained her. She needed water.

"He's a translator on the dark web," Cain continued, "calls himself the Spirit of Dead Poets. And he'll translate anything for a price. Anything. Not just bootlegs for the Middle East and Russia. He's a middleman for the world's most dangerous men. We're talking translations of secret online meetings between international gang members who're making deals across borders—everything from illegal guns to heroin. The Mexican cartel, the Bratva, the Indian Mafia—for the right price, your *friend* will freelance for them all."

No.

"He's their go-to interpreter. Dirty through and—"

The line went dead. No warning. No choppiness. One second her father was speaking and the next he'd been cut off.

Dad?

Silence crushed against her temples.

He's my eyes and ears...

Cain's payroll. Of course.

All this time Holden Frost had been playing her for a fool. His offer of help had nothing to do with kindness. He'd never truly *liked* her. Never cared. Months spent spying on her in the library—his behavior had nothing to do with an infatuation. He'd known all about her real identity before they'd ever met. When she'd stumbled into his underground hideout, he'd acted anxious *not* because he'd witnessed her take down a security guard, the way he'd pulled away when she'd made an advance in Birdie's studio—he'd been

251

afraid of Cain. Her father had always been the real threat.

"Think I've heard enough," she whispered to no one. She replaced the handset and swallowed bile. The voices overlapped, replayed, and shattered like glass in her mind, insistent, persistent.

—*left eye like a warm sip of cognac, your right, a whirl of cool*—

—*you already know*—

—*first person in a long while to enter my*—

—*it's real*—

—*safe here. With me. Nothing bad will*—

Lies. All of them.

She folded herself onto the floor. Her cheek dragged along the hardwood and, with a clatter, her elbow bumped the forgotten dinner tray. She shifted, fumbled and hissed as her finger caught a thorn. The rose. The gift. She ought to hurl the damn snow globe against the wall. But no. That could alert a neighbor. So instead she sat up and reached for the fallen wine bottle.

Mave broke the aluminum seal and twisted off the cap. She sniffed the tart poison funneling from inside—the catalyst of her mother's death. The added hurt was all it took. She gripped the bottle by its neck with both hands and drank.

Her throat was a siphon sucking, drowning independently of her mind. Dark thought after thought spun, collided. Cain Francis was in prison miles away, trading deals, watching through his cage—always watching. Holden Frost was using her, seducing her, pretending to have real feelings for her. When it came down to it, she was nothing more than a paycheck. And he was just another criminal, a masked man flashing fake faces to get his way. Only his crime was far worse than murder.

Heartbroken, Mave drank.

FORTY-ONE

Sometime between the bottle full and the bottle half empty, Mave's original goal took shape: the photographs of her mother. She needed them. They held answers about the past—held more than just nostalgia.

By this point, the hardest parts had become fuzzy and the easiest parts, clear. First: she was no longer thirsty. Second: this hotel was huge—impossible for one sheriff and two security guards to patrol with efficiency. And third: she had to review that green album. The shock had worn off. It may have taken her a few hours but she'd accepted it: she was guilty by association.

Cain Francis or Valeria Everhart or Elizabeth Everhart—did it matter which one? Either way, Mave's DNA was her only fault. She'd been promised millions by Birdie and targeted to pay the price for her family's sins—a past injustice. Now all she had to do was return to Birdie's suite and find whatever traces of that past remained. Assuming it was still hidden beneath the mattress. It's not like a better plan existed.

Mave lit her birthday candle and crawled to her dresser. She rifled inside a drawer for her winter gloves and pulled them on. Wobbling onto her feet, she gripped her head until the floor stopped its rocking. She would find some shred of proof if it was the last thing she did. Locating her ballet flats, she bobbed, aimed her feet and, after more than one try, managed to thrust on the shoes. Arms spread, she stumbled out into the gloomy corridor.

The patterned carpet helped guide her footing. Step left. Step right. Repeat. She ran her palm along the wall, fingers skittering, and avoided the main spiral staircase, (it would only add to her vertigo). She crawled up an emergency stairwell instead. The steps dipped and rose like piano keys under her weight. Her birthday candle became a melted stub and extinguished. Panting, she curled over and used her hands to climb ahead of her feet. She reached the infamous twenty-third floor, clutched the handrail and swayed.

The scent of ash was faint but noticeable—even from the landing. Mave tilted forward and blinked into the hallway. The backup generators hadn't timed out. She was alone in shadow, and yet Annabelle had to be close.

She followed the bitter smell, allowed it to saturate her sinuses no matter its unpleasantness. In through the nose, out through the mouth, she breathed and stumbled onward.

When the snoring reached her ears, a heavy gnarl that sawed through the silence, she barely hesitated. The alcohol seemed to numb her fear and float logic atop the chaos. *Ghosts don't snore,* her primitive brain insisted. *Humans do.* The snoring was a sign. It was all connected—her coming here. Maybe the ashes had drawn them both. She rounded the corner, her shoulder braced against the wall, and squinted.

Sure enough, her uncle had returned: Charlie Everhart, folded into the fetal position outside the doors to suite twenty-three-oh-one. A drunken pigeon to his nest—isn't that what Parissa had said? Except he hadn't made it all the way into his mother's studio this time.

Mave approached unsteadily. Charlie's head was tipped back, jaw slack and breath rattling. Up close, fumes of sweet alcohol wafted from his skin and mixed with the ashes. Mave held her face away and patted his pockets. The lift was less than smooth, but Charlie was the drunker of the two—as good as comatose. *Like taking candy from a slumbering baby.*

She slipped out his cellphone first, then his keyring. She shined the mobile's flashlight onto the lock and jiggled a random key inside. It stuck. So did the second key. But the third one slid and spun. She swallowed, turned the knob, and shoved in the door.

With each drag and tick of the hinges, she readied herself for those sick, ghoulish hands cinching Annabelle's face—for her mouthful of soot and her harrowing moan.

Dust motes floated in her bluish beam like in footage of the ocean's deep; left to right, corner to corner. The studio was vacant. She exhaled sharply and stumbled over Charlie's body. The door whined shut behind her.

Inside, ash and a metallic taste coated her tongue. But unlike Mave's last visit, Annabelle's ghost wasn't visibly lingering. Not yet. Nor was there any sign the sheriff had passed through. No police tape anywhere. No evidence markers numbering Mave's inky footprints. Before her luck could change, she scampered through the studio, cut across the salon, and headed straight into the bedroom. There was no need to hesitate, with Birdie's body stolen and rotting elsewhere.

A quick search and she found it: the green album hidden beneath the mattress. She yanked it atop the bed and leafed through its pages. Once. Twice. She blinked and struggled to focus. There had to be something—a pattern, a hint that would help unravel the mystery of Birdie's death. On the third scan, the discrepancy sharpened.

The entire album contained images of Valeria Everhart in her early years—a homage to a daughter lost. Except for the first two pages. The book's introductory images were of Birdie and her long-time lover and agent, Dominic Grady. Now that she really considered it, it was jarring.

Why include Dominic? Why curate him in an album otherwise dedicated to your disowned daughter, and keep the images secret all these years?

Mave flipped to the opening photograph and newspaper clipping. There again was the younger Dominic, handsomer and yet unworn by time, his arm around Birdie's waist at an exhibition opening; then arm-in-arm with another couple at the Château. An intuitive warning—a dire realization teased her mind but remained just out of reach. *Dammit. Think.* Why were these two memories here? Something with the Château? Both photographs had been taken at the hotel—in a hall with tilework a lot like the grand ballroom. *Queen's Hall.* The decrepit ballroom that led to the railway aisle niggled her thoughts. She pulled the first photo free and flipped it over.

~ Me, Dom, Manny and ?

Mave stared at the faded remains of Birdie's handwriting. Had she been wrong about Dominic Grady? Like she'd been wrong about Holden Frost? The reminder sent a stab of pain through her heart. No.

She shut the album and screwed her thumb amid her brow. The room was spinning again. Abandoning the album on the bed, she shoved Birdie's photo into her pocket and scurried out from the bedroom.

Red Book, M&M.

She tripped and held on to the bar cart. *Right.* Mave shook her head to clear it and managed to dizzy herself even more. An awareness of being watched tingled along her spine. She flinched and pointed the flashlight over her shoulder. Nothing. No one. She blinked rapidly. All that wine—her imagination was loopy. She plucked the elastic on her wrist and commanded herself forward. Her feet staggered but obeyed, returning her to the messy studio. The damn red book had to be lost in the clutter.

She stood with her hand on her hip, inhaled ash, and scanned all around. There was still no physical specter of the ghost. But the combination of alcohol and exhaustion must have given her new-found clarity. The answer came at once.

Hadn't she noticed the difference during her second visit? No longer staring at the wall, the mannequin in the corner had rotated. It was watching her with its milky irises whereas, on New Year's Eve, it'd been turned away. There'd been so many portraits overwhelming her that she'd missed pinpointing an additional set of eyes. But she'd *felt* it this morning: the mannequin out of place.

Mave stomped around the littered art supplies and slowed. Silly. It was just an inanimate object. But between the evening of and the morning after Birdie's death, someone—the killer—had spun the dummy. She examined it closely. It seemed to be an ordinary mannequin. Maybe…

She peeked behind it. Either her imagination was manipulating her again, or the scent of ash was stronger back here. She glanced up and down, helpless for direction. She tilted closer to the wall. Cool air kissed her cheek. She jerked her hand to her face and accidentally struck the dummy's shoulder. It lurched sideways and crashed into a pile of—

Her eyes shot to the door. Surely the noise would have woken Charlie? He'd charge inside any second now. Another. Mave stood with her hand over her heart, gnawed her cheek and waited. Nothing happened. Unless she counted the breeze. She turned to the wall and narrowed her eyes.

The draft had strengthened—seemed to be drifting through solid wood panels. She reached out unsteadily. Her gloved palms met the wall and slid across as if they had a mind of their own, searching, feeling. It took a few sweeps but she found the seam, an old border that extended from the floor. A private door. There was no handle, making the entryway invisible to the naked eye. She settled both palms at the door's edge and shoved. With a click and crackle, the panelled wall brushed inward to reveal another cluttered room.

Storage boxes were covered in an inch of dust. They seemed to have been shoved inside as an afterthought, haphazardly arranged around furniture. Everywhere she pointed the flashlight, there was red velvet and paisley silk and black leather. A boudoir. An unmade bed. Mave's eyes grew wide. Ironically, the darkness made it stand out in the haze of her beam: a sunken pillow where a head had recently rested; strips of dust erased from the floor as if freshly tramped.

She rushed toward the king-sized bed. Her thighs bumped into a box, forming bruises she barely felt. Here—someone had slept *here*. It was near-perfect. Undetectable.

The blackout. No coincidences, M&M.

The power outage had been staged, along with the note, the weapons, this room. All events had been planned. She closed her eyes and played it out in her mind.

The killer had slipped from the bedroom to the studio through the balcony, then had stowed themselves here. They'd remained overnight, and the following morning, when the cameras had been disabled, they'd sauntered out from the studio free and unseen by anyone. Her heart pounding, she opened her eyes. She was tempted to scream it from the windows.

The cameras never caught the real murderer exiting the studio that evening because the killer had never left. They'd been hiding in this storage space. Confident she'd solved the *how*, Mave refocused on the *who*. The more she considered it, the more likely it seemed Birdie's murder had been a two-person job. And at the top of her accomplice list was the recently-vanished Katrina Kovak.

She began to rummage for the red book. She frisked the mattress but, unlike with the green album, came up with nothing. She searched the floor, beneath a rug, along the backside of a nightstand. She crawled back to the bed on her hands and knees. She ought to double-check. Maybe it had been sandwiched or taped to the centre of the boxspring.

She had her head lowered, was working up a sweat as she lifted the mattress, when the creak sounded. She mistook the sound for the bedsprings. Had she been sober, things would have gone differently. She would have been sharper, her reflexes, less sluggish.

Around the time the forearm swung around her neck, her first mistake became apparent: she hadn't locked the studio doors. As she'd investigated the secret room, someone had been alerted by the mannequin's crash. They'd entered the suite behind her. Her attacker grunted and her second error sharpened into clarity: she shouldn't have pulled Cain's gun unless she was capable of using it. Her wrist wobbled under its weight and her fingers fumbled for the safety.

It came without warning, too quick for her mind to process. Her teeth snapped together and her tendons burst in shock. Pain engulfed her. Electricity burned her everywhere, scorching each and every nerve ending.

Her mind functioned fine—enough to scream that she was being shot full of fifty thousand volts of electricity. She had to resist, get away. Yet her body stiffened and dropped. She tried to cry out, crawl and escape, but every tendon, every muscle, every *bone* had constricted and locked in agony. She couldn't say how long the Tasering lasted—ten seconds, a thousand? She gasped air into her lungs as the pain disappeared as quickly as it had come.

She staggered up only to be thrown back to the ground. Her hands didn't extend in time. Her teeth smashed into hardwood. Blood filled her mouth. What was happening? She heard sobbing. She was sobbing.

A sharp pain stabbed her wrist and she found her fallen gun. *Lift it—point it!* But in which direction? Why was it so heavy? Everything spun like a rolling kaleidoscope. A knee pushed into her spine and the sudden weight on the center of her back drew a scream from her throat. Instinctively, Mave flipped her hips, thrust her legs upward, and wrapped her thighs around her attacker's throat.

Tag's startled eyes bulged from his head as she jerked, yanked him off balance and slammed him to the floor. His Taser skittered under the bed. His split second of disorientation was just enough. She scrambled to her feet and dove toward the exit. She'd escape him. She'd get—

The door swung inward, smashing into her forehead. She flew backward. Her head glanced off the foot of the bed. She would remember nothing more. Not even the sound of muffled gunfire.

FORTY-TWO

FROM THE RED BOOK OF THE DEAD

AUGUST 4TH, 1991

Dear Abs,

This will be the last letter I'm able to send you. I'm sure Caroline's baby will be born any day, and with the summer zipping by, you'll be home soon anyway. But you won't find me. Not now. Not in the fall or winter. I'm telling myself this is my biggest adventure yet and you'll understand. You'll forgive me for disappearing so suddenly. We both know you're a helpless romantic, so here it is: I'm running away with Cain.

I'll reach out if I can, but please don't try to find me. You're my true best friend—I love you to bits—but Birdie knows this. Her threats know no bounds. I don't trust she won't try to use you to get to me. Cain agrees. I need a clean break. Mother's left me no choice. You have to believe me. This is all her fault.

Birdie has done something so despicable, so horrible—I won't forgive her. Ever. And she didn't even have the guts to tell me to my face. Isn't that so like my Queen mother! She couldn't be bothered to dirty her hands, so she sent Dominic to deliver the blow.

I'm no longer in her will. I'm entirely cut out like a cancerous tumor. When Mother croaks, I'll get nothing. I'll be penniless and homeless, according to Dominic. Isn't that hilarious? All because

I'm not cowering on my knees, doing as she orders. Because I *refuse* to stop seeing Cain, the man I love. Apparently this will teach me a lesson. Well fuck her money. What Birdie doesn't realize is that she's been teaching me lessons for many, many years, and I've been paying close attention.

She wants to cut me off and take what's rightfully mine? Fine by me. The least I can do is repay her the favor and take something that belongs to her, right? Isn't that what she's taught me since day one? Strategy is everything in a game of chess. Sometimes you have to sacrifice your knight to get to the Queen. Well, I did. I risked my beautiful knight and I took the Queen. Or I will...

Mother, are you reading this? Are you intercepting my letters, you cold heartless bitch? I sure hope you are because this is all for you! Are you ready?

I fucked Dominic, Mother. And whore that he is, he took virtually no convincing. After he delivered your dirty news, your lap dog was more than eager to kiss my troubles away. It turns out, he thinks you're a shitty lay.

Goodbye.

Part IV

TIME OF DEATH

FORTY-THREE

JANUARY 2ND, 2021

She tried to lick the grit from her teeth. Her tongue felt like a strip of dried leather. The bruise on her spine throbbed. The room swayed, spun—reeked of ripe sweat. She groaned and opened her gummy eyes. Her first thought was of Cain's gun: it was still in her grip. She hadn't lost it. But her relief was short-lived.

It was wrong. All of it. Reflexively, her fingers touched a tender lump on her forehead. She hissed as the memory surfaced. The door. It had slammed into her skull, knocked her out. But even if she were unconscious, why would Tag allow her to keep the gun? An ex-Marine would disarm the enemy. Her thoughts congealed into confusion. Too much wine still burned in her gut.

She rolled her head and blinked at the gun in her grasp. Her knuckles protested as she tried relaxing them. They felt petrified, clawed around the pistol's handle. Finally managing to release her grip, she bobbled unsteadily, heaved onto her hip, and froze.

Not far from her lay a fallen flashlight, its beam switched on and throwing deep shadows inside the room. And another person. His dark suit was familiar. *Tag.*

He wasn't moving. In fact, he seemed crumpled like a ragdoll dropped on his stomach. She shut her eyes and ordered herself to retreat into the blackness once more. Anything—even a coma— was better than this nightmare she'd awoken inside. Yet her eyelids lifted masochistically and her gaze travelled to the wall.

The spray of blood resembled a single brushstroke by Jackson Pollock—wide and impressive, dripping into the shadows of the baseboard. Her brain digested the scene slowly, rationally, as if removed from her trembling figure. She looked to the gun she'd been holding. Then again at the blood.

One. Two.

Gun. Blood.

Okay. That meant she had pulled the trigger. And hit a target.

Mave turned to Tag. Motionless. As if he were…

She flailed sideways and threw up the contents of her stomach. The cramp in her abdomen only worsened. She doubled-over and moaned, suddenly aware she was sick—more than sick: terminal. Knives stabbed her head. Spiders crawled her cheeks and bit into her temples. She floundered her hands over her face, batting away the sensation. A scream built inside her throat, readying to tear her in half.

Breathe, Cain barked. *You're delusional, dammit. Breathe.*

Perhaps her hyperventilation had started a while ago—as soon as she'd gained consciousness. But it was only with Cain's prompt that she noticed her respiration had reached a critical rate. She closed her eyes, lowered her head between her knees, and forced herself to calm. Hysterics were for normal people. She wasn't normal. (*In through the nose. Out through the mouth.*) If she could withstand a hitman for a father, she could handle anything—even this.

She opened her eyes, her composure hanging by a thread. She had to do something. Now.

She wouldn't freeze up, make the same mistake as she had with Birdie. Tag wouldn't die on her watch.

Focus. You have to save him. Quickly. If you let him die, that would make you a… She blinked in rapid succession, barring her mind from finishing its last thought. Pain throbbed inside her head as she dragged herself closer to Tag. Pulse and breathing— she had to check. Except it was easier said than done.

She couldn't locate his carotid artery. She pushed on the security guard for a better angle, but his body was rigid, more stone than flesh. In the end she was forced to shove her forearms under his torso to lever him upward. Blood seeped through her woolen gloves. She swallowed and ignored the repulsive feel.

Gritting her teeth, she grunted and pushed. It took all her strength to roll him face-up. And when she did she turned away and threw up a second time.

Killer, killer.

She looked to the ceiling to avoid another glimpse of the gore.

He'd been shot through the heart. His wound was a sticky, red mess. What had she been thinking, attempting first aid? (She hadn't.) No amount of CPR would ever revive Tag. He was dead. Murdered. She wiped her mouth on her shoulder and kept her back turned to the body. She put her hands on her hips.

Handle it. You have to handle it.

Dirty killer. Like father like—

She yanked off her gloves. "No." She shuddered her head, slapped and batted the tears tracking her jaw with the heels of her hands. She had to get out of here. Her instincts screamed for her to run before the sun rose and the entire hotel woke. Tag's blood was on her clothes. Red. Syrupy. The sight of it—the acerbic scent caused her stomach to spasm. Heaving, she staggered out from the boudoir and into the studio.

She held onto a plinth and gagged. There was nothing left in her. She was empty. She'd gone and pulled the trigger. Using her father's gun, she'd killed a man. Taken a life. And she couldn't even remember doing it. She sagged against the plinth with her head hung. All her energy was spent. How could she cry of her innocence now? Who would believe her?

He attacked you first, a weak voice whispered. *It was self defense.*

But Mave couldn't say for certain what had happened—how she'd shot the gun. She strained to recall the sequence of events before she'd blacked out.

Tag had grabbed her. A sob. A fall. And then…

Doubt persecuted her. She deserved to be locked up for life. She deserved to be spit on and shunned from society. She was a murderer. Just like Cain Francis. How had it come to this? Her body hurt everywhere—wrists, throat, heart.

The spotlight overhead flickered on and off.

Never had she been more full of self-disgust. She was the product of a monster. And now more than ever, she needed that same monster to talk her through this.

"What am I going to do?" she wept, pushing the hair off her slick brow. She squeezed her eyes shut, careening slightly. The strain of containing her panic combined with her drunkenness was too much. *Cain. Anyone! How am I going to get out of this?* But for once her father's voice was quiet. No instructions came to mind. No pep talk, no matter how much she silently begged.

She wrapped herself into a ball and rocked. She was alone. Trapped. And no amount of crying could save her. Her lungs stuttered and the angry voices whispered *I told you so*. She was responsible for Tag's death. Soon, Sheriff Morganson would complete the arrest and that would be that. She'd confess everything. She was guilty. She'd *been* guilty for longer than she cared to admit.

She'd kept her father's secrets for most of her life, hadn't she? She'd walked in on Cain's hit in the bathtub and, till this day, had told no one. All those mornings and nights she'd seen him living a double-life and had turned a blind eye. The charges against her might as well include aiding and abetting for most of her youth.

For years she'd known about Cain's disguises, the fake IDs, the all-cash payments. Yet she'd never once questioned or challenged him, always afraid of losing her one and only parent. That had been her choice, her true crime: to love the father despite the killer. And though he'd clothed her with blood money, had fed her with it, his approval had meant more. It had trumped her self-loathing. Hadn't she done everything she could to avoid it—her reflection in the mirror? She'd tried to find the pieces of herself that belonged to her mother but, all along, Valeria Francis had been a stranger. So when push had come to shove, Mave had pulled the trigger just like Cain had taught her.

She massaged her temples, trying to squeeze the memory out from hiding. *It's fine*, she told herself. *I'll deal with it. I killed him. Just please, let me remember.* She would repent and forgive herself. One day at a time. For Tag. For Cain. For all the lives she could have saved if only she'd been stronger, sooner. And she would begin by stopping her denial.

Cain's pistol had been in her grip the whole time. She nodded, prodding the memory. That was right: the gun in her hand. Only the more she imagined it, the less it made sense. One second she'd flipped Tag to the ground and the next, she'd leaped for the door and blacked out. If she'd shot Tag while unconscious—how? Had it been an accident?

Cain's whisper echoed in the back of her thoughts: *Can't hit a bullseye blindfolded, M&M.*

The blood spatter on the wall—she cringed and rubbed her heart. It had to have been her.

Wrong, her inner voice snapped, gaining volume. *Do it again. Do it right.*

When she'd attempted to escape, the door had smacked her head. She'd been clumsy and rushing, and yet—it had been shoved *inward* from the studio.

Someone else had come in after Tag.

Mave waited for this new fact to settle in her mind. Her perception shifted. Not the door itself—a second person had knocked her unconscious. And if she'd been out cold, that same person could have also shot Tag using the gun in her hand. The murderer could have framed her. Again.

The taste of blood dotted her dry tongue. She knew who she was. Deep down, she had known all along. It settled over her like the eye of a storm. She was innocent. Her nerve endings were on fire. The spotlight emitted a high frequency. Mave rubbed her ears.

Stop it. Stop that ringing. Her eyes flicked upward.

Annabelle's ghost hovered on the other side of the plinth as if she'd been watching her the entire time.

Mave jumped up and a fiery headrush eclipsed her vision. She closed her eyes and waited for the stars to clear. When they did, Abs was still there. Mave slid her hands to her face and choked on a sob. Alcohol had stripped her of all inhibitions, all defenses and filters. And she felt *everything*: rage, sorrow, hatred.

("...something really bad happened to her... she died in a fire")

"My god" she whispered, "you know, don't you?" She swallowed and ground out the words. "You saw who came in, who started this all." She waited impatiently for another sign, a nod, a moan—anything. "Go on. Just tell me. Who's framing me, who killed Birdie: Parissa Everhart? Nicholas Vaughn?"

Abs merely hovered. She didn't respond. She couldn't.

Or maybe Mave hadn't asked the right question.

She licked her lips, racked her brain, and tried again. Who else had she originally suspected..."Edward Hendrick? Dominic Gra...?"

Annabelle's head twitched. The fingers on her face fluttered like the thick legs of a spider. Mave yanked her focus away from them and to the high-pitched buzzing instead—through the piercing ring...

"No."

She caught her breath. She couldn't believe she'd heard it, and yet— "No... No what?" She cocked her ears and listened. This time she knew what to filter out, how to hear through the shrill noise.

Abs' figure trembled, faded in and out with the light. Her effort to reply seemed to be draining her of energy. *"Not-Dommm"*—those blackened hands tightened and she choked—*"I'm-I'm...letterrrs."*

"What—?"

"LETTERSBONESLETTERS."

The spotlight burst and Mave fell to her knees. Broken shards of the forgotten stabbed her inner eye as a lost scent flooded her sixth sense.

—blackened bones inside a pipe—
—rats and darkness—
—deep underground—

Mave sucked in another mouthful of ash. Reality sped and rewound. She clawed at nothing and her eyes rolled to the back of her head.

—Dear Rie—
—creased letters—
—collected in a red book—
—kept hidden in the—

It left as quickly as it had come. One moment she'd been thrust into the forgotten, and the next, she was alone on the floor of the studio, shaking against the plinth, darkness swallowing everything. Mave gasped. All scent of ash was gone. So was Abs. But it had been enough.

Old letters that had belonged to Annabelle were lost inside a red book—*the* red book that had been owned by Birdie. And Mave had scented exactly where everything was hidden. She had to hurry—assemble all the pieces before Morganson arrested her.

She stumbled to her feet and rushed out from the studio in a near frenzy. The hallway was empty, the exit from the suite, clear. Wherever he was, Charlie Everhart was no longer asleep outside the doors. The distant thought passed. Charlie's absence was of no importance and muted by the larger revelation: Birdie's red book was hidden inside the library.

FORTY-FOUR

Holden had left. It was for the best. She wouldn't think of the endless depths of his eyes, his expression as he'd held her with his arms flexed. She'd waste no more time crying over him. None. She darted to the bookcase she'd sensed in Annabelle's longing.

The simplicity of it was brilliant. Where better to hide a book than inside an abandoned library—a place that nearly everyone was too afraid to enter? The red spine stood out between the other titles, seemed to glow as if begging to be plucked. She stood on tiptoe and carefully slid out the coveted text—the one piece of evidence that could link the murder with its master. At least she hoped.

The leather-bound book was untitled, its burgundy cover cracked in several spots like a scab. Mave swept away the dust and gingerly opened it, afraid its bindings might fall apart. A wrinkled sheet of paper had been folded into a square, then pressed inside like a flower preserved in a scrapbook. Her hands were sweaty. She wiped them on her hips and knelt on the ground. With the flashlight ready, she unfolded the first letter.

Dear Rie,

Arrived a few days ago. It's exactly like you described it…

She devoured every word. Somehow, Birdie had saved the correspondence from both sides: Abs' letters and Rie's replies. By the time she reached the final letter, she was in tears. The grievance swallowed her whole. Annabelle had been killed here, her bones disposed and forgotten. And she'd been her mother's best friend.

How had Abs died in a fire? *Not just died—murdered.* Mave stared at the fireplace, its embers glowing orange. The emotions Abs had transferred to her in Birdie's studio had been clear. Her spirit was festering, full of rage. Only a horrific event could have caused the spirit to remain trapped inside the hotel all these years—not to mention the gnarled hands that imprisoned her face. Whatever wrong had occurred, Mave would wager it had gone unpunished; three decades and counting unless she could figure out how to tie the murders together in the next few hours. Assuming they were linked.

No co—

"Coincidences. I know, I know," she muttered to her father. The fireplace wafted cold as always. "Abs?" she whispered. "Are you here? Can you just…?" Her shoulders slumped. It was a wasted effort. They were both too new at this. Transferring all that energy to communicate with Mave upstairs had to have drained the ghost. Even Mave felt depleted, and she'd been on the passive, receiving end. She sighed without relief. The combined tragedies wouldn't release her. Her mother's best friend had been taken too soon from this world—just like Valeria. Mave started to rub her eyes and flinched. Tag's blood streaked her sleeves. *You're running out of time.*

In her mind's eye, Morganson was returning to Birdie's suite, discovering the secret door to the boudoir—Tag shot dead. Cain's gun. Mave had been so distraught she'd left the weapon. It was as if she'd been set up all over again—only this time, no one would steal the body and keep her from— *Enough,* Cain barked.

Focus. It's all here. Birdie gave you the answers in this book. Figure it out.

She dropped her forehead to the cover as if she might absorb its truth.

A young nurse from thirty years ago and Birdie Everhart. They had both been staying at the Château in 1991. And they had both died violently, years apart. Why? Why did Birdie keep these letters hidden for thirty years? Why had she wanted Mave to find them? *Think, think, think.* Who'd been named back then—who remained here now? She'd heard next to nothing about Immanuel Law. Thirty years was a long time. He might have passed away himself. And Caroline Law was—

Goosebumps rose on her skin. She suddenly remembered her birthday gift from Holden, the snow globe. Abs had described it in her letters. The same one—Caroline's keepsake. Back then she'd been pregnant and days from giving birth to—

Mave blinked and jerked upright to check the dates. *Holden.* It made sense. He had to be Caroline's son. And Rah was Rahul, the old concierge who'd gotten sick. According to Holden, they'd all died ages ago: his mother, father, and Rahul. Meanwhile Valeria would've been too swept up in running away with Cain. She had cut ties with her past and had survived only a few years after writing these letters. So who the hell was left with answers?

She winced. As much as she wanted to deny his existence, Holden had been there in '91, at least via his young pregnant mother. But he seemed oblivious to his parentage and Mave refused to consult him after he'd used her so heartlessly. Katrina Kovak had been recently hired as Birdie's personal maid. She couldn't have been involved in Annabelle's death—couldn't possibly know Caroline Law, let alone what tragedy had befallen her nurse all those years ago. Mave flipped to an earlier letter, the incident with the broken martini glass in the cigar lounge. Her eyes fell on two names: Charlie Everhart and Dominic Grady.

Both men had been mentioned repeatedly—especially Charlie. Unfortunately, Charlie was also an ugly, unstable drunk. She was lucky she'd escaped him when she had. That left Dominic. His past infidelity and lapse in judgement aside, the man Mave had met today claimed to love Birdie. Parissa Everhart didn't seem to think he was a threat. And Annabelle's ghost had confirmed as much, cleared him of guilt when Mave had asked her to point the finger at the killer. Dominic had kept Birdie's secrets and guided Mave repeatedly when she'd gone to him. (*"Only wish there was more I could do to help."*)

She told herself she could trust him once more. If she wanted the truth, she had to.

She knocked in the dead of night, and he opened the door without delay.

Dominic seemed unsurprised to see her return so soon. "Couldn't sleep either?"

Mave shook her head.

"Well, I'm glad you're back. I could use the..." His eyes widened as he noticed the stains on her white shirt. "My god, what's—are you hurt?"

"No. Mr. Grady, please, you have to help me. It's urgent."

His eyes remained fixed on the bloodstains. "Who's...?" He met her eyes, brimming with worry, and gave a curt nod. Mave's breath hitched. He wouldn't let her down. "Come, dear, quickly."

He led her inside by her elbow and sat her down on the couch. Only one of his oil lamps remained lit, and his decanter of cognac was near-empty. "Here, drink this." He passed her a glass of water. "I'll find some towels."

Her hands shook as she tipped the cup to her lips. She swallowed quickly, only now realizing how thirsty she was. A moment later Dominic returned with dampened facecloths. Dark circles lined his eyes. "I was thinking about you, your grandmother. What happened?"

Mave took the facecloths and scrubbed at the blood on her shirt. The stain merely spread. She inhaled a wavering breath and kept her eyes on her lap. It was easier that way. "I—" *was framed for shooting the security guard.* She pinched her lips together, the confession turning her stomach.

"Is someone hurt? Did someone try to hurt you?" Dominic tried.

When she still couldn't answer, he sat on the coffee table across from her and gently touched her arm. "Mave, your grandmother wouldn't have wanted this. She wanted to protect you from any pain, and now..." He sighed. "Listen, I know for a fact Morganson's a fair woman. Whatever it is that has you so upset—whatever's happened to cause"—he gestured at her sullied shirt—"*this*, she'll listen to reason when you explain. You have to tell her before she draws the wrong conclusions. Here," he reached for his phone on the table, "cell service came back about fifteen minutes ago. We can call the front desk right now and ask for the sheriff's suite."

She chewed her lip. Though less certain of Sheriff Morganson's fairness, Mave agreed she had to tell her side of the story. "Yes—no, I'm going to—I mean, I will. It's just, before you call, I need something from you first."

His brow rose. "From me? What is it? Do you need me to come with you?" He stood before she could respond. "I'll quickly change and—"

"No, not that." She waited for him to sit again. "Mr. Grady, I need you to tell me about Annabelle."

His face froze. "Beg your pardon?"

She twisted a washcloth with both hands. (*"Not-Dom."*) He'd been there. He would help her. There was no one else she could turn to—not even Cain.

"She was a nursing student," she hurriedly whispered. "She took a job caring for a sixteen-year-old girl named Caroline Law back in 1991. She stayed here through spring and summer."

Dominic's jaw had slackened and all the blood seemed to have drained from his face. "How?" He blinked. "That name...I haven't heard it in years."

"Please, Mr. Grady," she leaned forward, "I know it sounds strange, but I think—I think Annabelle's stay here all those years ago has something to do with why Birdie was murdered."

He choked on a laugh and wiped his hand down his jaw. "Incredible." He shook his head. "You know, don't you? I have no idea how..."

"Know what?"

"*Charlie*. Birdie tried to bury his secret over and over." His eyes glazed over. "But it was the one truth that refused to rest. It took everything from her to keep quiet—poisoned her with guilt. She became *sick* with it. That was the true cancer eating away at her all these years, what really killed her. She blamed herself for what Charlie did."

(*...he was passed out in hall, right in front of the doors to Birdie's suite... what Charlie did was unforgivable.*)

Her uncle slumbering outside Birdie's suite earlier flashed before her. It seemed too similar to Annabelle's account, like he'd been compelled to re-enact the past. "What did he do?" Mave breathed. "Mr. Grady, Are you saying—" she swallowed.

("*Did Mother send you to haunt me for my sins? Or was it Annabelle! Have you finally come to save her from me?*")

"Did Charlie kill Annabelle?"

Dominic glanced up, his eyes rounded and stunned as if seeing her for the first time. He nodded. "I believe," a tear slipped down his weathered face, "he killed that poor girl and has no memory of it."

Dominic told her everything—fragments of the tragedy he'd pieced together from Birdie over the years. He had no proof, he stressed—then or now—hadn't been at the hotel that awful night. He'd only suspected what had happened much, much later. By then, too much time had already passed, and reviving old wounds seemed callous without solid proof. He loved Birdie too much to put her through that heartache.

He'd heard of Caroline Law, but as it turned out, their paths had never crossed in '91. He'd only met her nurse, Annabelle that spring. Caroline, meanwhile, had been secluded in her suite the entire time and had secretly died as such, months later, during childbirth. *An unforeseen complication. Uncontrollable hemorrhaging.* Mave's heart sunk. There'd been a funeral. The official story had been a blood clot had led to her brain, and she'd died unexpectedly but peacefully in her home. No one had thought twice. Only Birdie had let it slip to Dominic in a moment of vulnerability: Annabelle had been to blame.

The doctor had never arrived for the labor, and the nursing student had been ill-prepared, underqualified. Her negligence during the delivery had cost Caroline and her baby their lives. What followed the botched delivery attempt was unclear according to Dominic, but the gist of it was more tragedy. He had a theory, nonetheless—a suspicion he'd formed years later through his questions and devotion to Birdie. It had been too disturbing to share with anyone. Until now.

For whatever reason, on the night of Caroline's death, Annabelle had turned to Charlie for comfort. Who knows, Dominic speculated, perhaps they'd gotten drunk together. One thing had led to another, and, (from what he'd been able to guess), Charlie had made unwanted advances. It had ended ugly.

Charlie later told his mother he remembered only flashes. Annabelle had used pepper spray on him—scratched him up good. Charlie must have been furious. That much anyone could presume. The remainder, Dominic admitted, was speculation on his part.

By the time Charlie's rage had drained his body, he'd found Annabelle lying in his suite, half-naked and with her neck badly bruised. She was lifeless. No pulse. He panicked. He was still drunk at the time. That may explain—yet not excuse—the abhorrent choice he made next.

He stuffed the girl inside a large racquet bag he owned, and smuggled her body down to the library. He was desperate to cover up his crime, and the library was often empty—certainly at that hour of the night. It also had a large fireplace. So...

Charlie dumped his load inside, doused the bag with whiskey, and then... *poof.* He burned that poor girl like she'd been no more than diseased cattle.

Mave shook her head in horror. *And the bones*—the trauma that she'd discovered inside the air vent. Once the fire died, Charlie must have hidden Annabelle's remains in the closed off tunnels. Mave had heard enough.

FORTY-FIVE

"I don't understand." Dominic pulled a tissue from his pocket and wiped his eyes. "Even if my suspicions were right, what does any of this have to do with Birdie's death?"

Mave took a moment to organize her thoughts. "You said Birdie had been diagnosed with terminal cancer... that keeping this horrible secret for thirty years was killing her. Well..." She twisted the cloth in her hands, around and around. The connection formed in her mind. Hendrick's contractors poking around the basement—the deadline to renovate and Birdie adamant refusal to approve his plans. "What if the haunting got worse. Grew unbearable with the clock winding down. What if it was only a matter of time before Annabelle's bones were found, and Birdie wanted to make amends before then—before she died, set right what had gone wrong so long ago?" Mave straightened, her heart skipping. "What if she was ready to come clean about Annabelle, recover her remains for a proper burial, and she told Charlie."

Dominic blinked in disbelief. "And Charlie being guilty... he killed his mother before she could get the chance to incriminate him? Mave, you think—your inheritance—he must have known and he—"

"Framed me," she finished. "I was the perfect scapegoat: the daughter of a convicted felon who was due to get rich from the murder. Charlie would have killed two birds with one stone."

"Birdie's silence and her fortune," Dominic reasoned, his mouth gaping. "My god, this is..." He shook his head and winced. "I should have told someone years ago—my suspicions about Charlie. I should have—"

"You were thinking of Birdie," she consoled. "It was the police's place, not yours."

"It was only a missing persons case. Maybe if I'd said something, they might have, have…" He cupped his mouth, eyes watering.

"Charlie's to blame, Mr. Grady."

He drew in a deep breath. "No. You don't understand, I made it worse."

"What do you mean?"

"Afterward, he came to me in the city," he whispered, "begged, it was only the one time. He needed Valium, couldn't renew his prescription. And I knew someone. So I did him a favor." He buried his face in his hands. "Thought I was helping him treat anxiety—not forget *murder*. But soon he needed more. He'd phone at all hours of the night and cry he wasn't sleeping. The Valium wasn't enough and the doctors wouldn't listen. He wanted Ambien, Clonazepam, Vicodin. I cut him off but he just found another source. He never married. Never had children. Whenever I saw him after that summer, he was always a shell of a man, drifting through life half-asleep."

"Just as haunted," she uttered, recalling Annabelle lurking over him in the studio.

"Deep down, I didn't want to believe he was capable—not once, let alone twice. To kill his own mother in cold blood." His expression crumpled and he wiped his eyes again. "It's too awful. Birdie, Annabelle, Caroline and her baby. Just awful."

And Tag. Mave ground her knuckles into her forehead as if she could erase the security guard's murder. She shuddered. To think Charlie had been outside the studio doors—then had disappeared. Had he sent Tag inside the boudoir knowing what would happen? Pained by the notion, she rewound her attention on everything Dominic had revealed about the chain of death. Her frown deepened. There was one detail that wasn't right.

"But he lived," she mumbled to her lap.

"Pardon? Who lived?"

"Caroline's baby." She looked to Dominic. "He's alive."

"I—what?" A series of emotions too quick to read rippled across his face.

"Mr. Grady, I've met him." It was difficult to believe, even for her: there was hope yet in the harrowed past. "Caroline's son *survived*. He's here."

"What—what do you mean, *here*?" His jaw twitched back and he blinked at her like she'd lost her mind.

"Just hear me out," she said. "When I was hiding from security, I found him by accident. He lives in secret in the old train tunnels. I saw his underground home. He even told me he'd been born here, but at the time, I didn't realize what that meant. I don't know how he lived, but he did. I swear, I'm sure of it."

Dominic hung his head, his features slackened. "Impossible," he repeated under his breath. He wiped his palms across his mouth to the back of his neck. "A man in the tunnels saying—if that's true then—dear god, the implications." His gaze snapped to her with such intensity, it made her uncomfortable. "Do you think you can go underground again," he asked, "find this man posing as Caroline's son, ask him for help?"

"I—maybe. I think so." *Posing*. He still didn't believe her. "But help with what?"

"If he lives down there, he'll have a good sense of the tunnels. Go find him, tell him what you've told me, and have him help you search for Annabelle's bones. In the meantime, I'll go wake Sheriff Morganson and alert her about Charlie—this entire mess—everything. The sheriff and I will come meet you down there." He stood and Mave followed, his urgency contagious. "Hurry, Mave. Before everyone else wakes, we'll clear your name."

Her stomach was sour with anxiety. The idea of retracing her steps had seemed doable ten minutes ago, but now—

She zigzagged through stacks of chairs, debris and dust in Queen's Hall, and tried convincing herself this was the safer route. Holden knew all the underground shortcuts. The library's vent, meanwhile, would likely get her lost someplace entirely new. She didn't trust her poor sense of direction. But what if she descended the elevator shaft and *still* couldn't find Holden? Could she even face him if she did? Her only alternative was to search for the bones herself—to rely on her memory of stumbling through some blackened tunnel. She was capable of navigating a space with a map but ...

Hendrick's blueprints. The thought made her freeze.

Those blueprints could direct her through the labyrinth of the old tunnel system—could lead the sheriff to her and, if all went right, to Annabelle's bones. If Mave wanted any chance at recovering proof, then she needed to use any and all resources. Her only issue was time. Rounding back to staff quarters to wake Hendrick for his blueprints would be foolish. He was more likely to slap her in handcuffs than help her. But if Dominic told the sheriff and the police ordered the blueprints for an official investigation, Hendrick would have no choice but to cooperate.

Mave paced before the upended piano. She clicked on Charlie's phone, not entirely surprised to find her fuddled uncle had no passcode. She scanned his contacts without success, then opened a browser. Cell numbers weren't included in public directories, but if you knew where to search (and thanks to Cain, Mave did), all sorts of personal information could be harvested online. It took seconds and she had three possible matches. Her heart raced as she copied and pasted the likeliest number, one with a New York City area code. The phone caught a single bar of reception. Not pushing her luck, she held still to keep the signal. But without explanation, her thumb paused above the call button.

She stared at the screen. An inexplicable weight curdled in her stomach. Dread grew with her hesitation—a troubling premonition that a piece of the puzzle remained amiss. Disorder. A detail was incorrectly jammed. But what? She'd been so quick to follow Dominic's lead upstairs, to accept his promise. *("We'll clear your name.")* Her sub-conscious struggled to digest his words.

("I should have told someone years ago—my suspicions about Charlie. I—")

If Birdie had kept this horrible secret about Charlie's crime, how had Dominic gathered so much information based on suspicion alone? All those details: the bruises on Annabelle's neck, her body in the racquet bag. It was almost as if he'd been there on the night of Annabelle's murder. But what motive would he have to lie? *To kill?* She gripped her temples. She was paranoid again. Sunrise was approaching. Each second she spent doubting was a second closer to Charlie getting away. She forced herself to dial the number. She'd ask Dominic about it. There was probably a simple explanation.

The line crackled. "Please, come on…" she whispered.

He picked up on the sixth ring.

"Yeah…" His greeting sounded breathy and groggy like she'd woken him. "Who's this? Hello?" Mave knit her brow. "Charlie?" he said, slightly more alert. He must have checked his call display. "Fecking kidding me? Thought we were past this, man. No more." His Irish lilt, his tone—rich and musical like a radio announcer—it was wrong. She must have been mistaken about the number—but then why was this man reacting as if he knew Charlie?

"Oh, I'm sorry," she rasped, finding her voice at last. "I was calling for Dominic Grady, the art dealer."

"What?" he snapped. "Yeah, you got him. Who's this? Why do you have Charlie's phone?"

"No, I'm"—the dread rushed through her limbs, stung the beds of her nails and the stem of her tongue—"sorry, did you say—you know Charlie?"

"*Yes.* And who the hell am I speaking to?"

She blinked and replied reflexively. "It's Mave Michael."

It was the man's turn to be confused. "Mave Michael…?"

"Birdie's granddaughter," she breathed. Silence blared over her pounding pulse. "Are you—still there?"

"Yeah, I—" He coughed. "I wasn't aware Birdie had a granddaughter." He cleared his throat. "Look, Birdie and I haven't been in touch for years. What's this about?"

"I found your number in Charlie's phone," she fibbed. "Sorry to have woken you." She hung up, cradled her stomach, and sunk to the floor. Lies splintered her mind.

Something was horribly wrong.

FORTY-SIX

If that stranger on the phone had been Dominic Grady, then *who* was the Dominic Grady she'd been confiding in moments earlier? The question made it hard to breathe.

You've been fighting the truth all along, Cain whispered, *too busy trying not to think like me, move like me. But deep down you suspected, kept going back to him again and again...*

What did she suspect? Mave dug her nails into her into her breastbone. Who was the man supposedly seeking the sheriff at this very moment—the man who knew a great deal about Birdie's past—about Valeria and Mave—who was crying over Birdie like a lover. Mave scratched and scratched for answers. The bruise on her forehead throbbed.

Your pocket. Look again.

Her fingers fumbled and pulled out the photograph she'd saved from Birdie's green album.

~ Me, Dom, Manny and ?

Her eyes dilated as the resemblance she'd failed to notice earlier now glared back at her.

It wasn't Dominic Grady at all staring back at her. It was the killer.

It was the first trick Cain had taught her about disguises: context dictated perception. Wear the right mask in the right place at the right time, and you could become anyone. Isn't that what Immanuel Law had done? Mave had been so transfixed by the past—by the image of the younger Dominic—that she'd dismissed the couple posing alongside him and Birdie.

There he was, the man to the right of Birdie and Dominic, the one she'd met at the pool, in his suite: Manny. Immanuel Law. His features were less boyish, less handsome than the real Dominic Grady; and of course, the facelift, aging lines, and beard had thrown her off. Abs' ghost had tried to warn her. When she'd shared those two little words, *not-Dom*, she hadn't been clearing Dominic Grady of guilt; she'd been exposing the man Mave had met for who he really was: a murderous liar.

No. What have I done?

She shot to her feet and lurched toward the exit for the railway aisle. She slammed through the RESTRICTED door. Warning bells rang in her mind.

Caroline's father was alive, *here*, posing as another man, thinking his grandson dead all these years. And Mave had gone and told him about Holden's underground home. Who knew how he'd react—what he was planning to do with the news. He'd already tried to drown his grandson once. Mave couldn't be responsible for another death.

She followed the wind's whistle into the deep dark. The ceiling lowered as the railway ties began. Cables wound above and below, thickened like vines. Mave checked over her shoulder every few steps. A nagging unease she was being followed kept her skittish—but when she scanned and held her breath, there was no one. Her heart hammered and her stomach clenched.

Immanuel Law was a conniving psychopath. He wouldn't stop—was likely poisoning the sheriff with more lies this very second. Mave had to escape the Château before his plan to frame her succeeded once and for all, and she would—right after she found Holden and warned him about her mistake. The mental admission punched her in the gut.

Overwhelmed with lies and betrayal—so hellbent on denying Cain's voice—she'd ignored instinct and broken her promise to keep quiet about Holden's home. And now he was at risk. Thanks to her, his dangerous grandfather had caught scent of him.

A split in the tunnel appeared and she jerked to a stop. She swung the cell's flashlight from one passageway to the next. No cat appeared to guide her this time. She was on her own. The cramp in her abdomen squeezed and released. "Holden!" she rasped, short of breath.

Only the wind replied.

Taking a guess, she tried the tunnel on the right. Her feet sped up, carrying her deeper, faster into the labyrinth. She'd been running for a while, was covered in sweat. Holden's cave couldn't be far. Where was it? Instead of cigarette smoke from a crevice in the wall, another stench hit her. Rot. The air was thick with it. She shielded her nose in the crease of her elbow and scanned ahead.

Shadows stirred and a scratching noise drifted. "Holden?" This couldn't be it. She'd made a wrong turn somewhere. She ought to go back, try the left-hand tunnel. Her gaze remained glued to the playful tendrils of dark. There was movement ahead. And that stench. Had she entered a sewage drain? *Turn around. Go back.*

She crept forward a little closer. A little more. The flashlight trembled in her grip. The scratching sound grew along with the reek. "Hello?" She puckered her nose. "Who's there?" Another step. She held her breath as the light finally found the source of the scratching.

A person lay squirming beneath a blanket. A damask duvet from the Château—like the one Holden had stolen—wrapped them from head to toe. Mave crept to a stop across from the figure. Her legs shook. She had to look. To confirm.

Stop stalling, Cain growled. *Finish it.*

She toed the blanket aside quickly. Her scream was muffled against her arm and she stumbled back into the wall. Rats scattered into shadow. Mave gagged, unable to look away.

The skin on Birdie Everhart's face resembled pearly, fractured glass. Her red-rimmed eyes were cracked open and her crow's feet had deepened into dried rivers, scarring her temples. Mave didn't have a chance to manage her shock—to turn away.

"What the hell are you doing in here?"

She spun to the voice and locked eyes with Holden.

"Jesus," he cringed as he pushed up his mask. "You okay?" He reached for Mave's shoulder.

"Don't touch me," she rasped, flinching away.

He squinted away from her flashlight. "Whoa, all right. Just—let's stay calm. Everything's going to be okay."

"No." It wasn't. His duvet was covering Birdie's corpse. And no one else knew these tunnels like he did. "It was you," she exhaled. His urgent work matter—he'd disappeared from Birdie's suite to do *this*. He'd hidden the body here to delay her arrest—another twisted attempt to protect her through lies. Except it was one deception too many. She was no longer certain why she'd come.

"What are you talking about? We have to get—"

"Are you saying that's not your blanket?" A part of her was proud of herself. She'd spoken clearly. Robotically.

He reluctantly glanced down at the body and grimaced. "Yeah, but—"

"What, were you just following another one of Cain's orders? When were you planning on telling me: in the library? Never?"

He blinked, no doubt taking a moment to sort through his lies. "Look, I get that you have questions. Just let me explain. I hardly ever come this—"

"Liar." She took a step back, breathing heavily even though it turned her stomach. She kept the flashlight pointed on his duplicitous eyes. How different they had seemed a few hours ago, when his thick lashes had fluttered along her cheek and he'd gazed up, up into her soul. *Fool.*

"Mave," he tried to block the beam with his palm, "you don't look so hot. We can talk about this later. Someone's set you up and you shouldn't be—"

"Liar," she said again, a coldness in her tone. Her heels slowly led her away. *Don't trust Holden Frost. Don't trust anyone.* "You've been playing me this entire time—pretending to help me, to—pretending you don't know anything."

He moved forward as if pulled in her orbit. "I'm not pretending." He extended his palm and spoke slowly, "I swear. *It's real*—"

"Don't."

"—and I've no idea how Birdie's body ended up down here. I heard you calling my name. I saw your light and followed—"

"I don't believe you." She raised her chin.

"Jesus, Mave, you have to—"

"No. I don't have to anything." She backed farther and farther away. She couldn't stand to listen to another word. "Stop following me. Stop saying things you think I want to hear. I only came to warn you: Your grandfather's checked in. And he knows you're alive."

"Wait—what?"

She turned and left in a hurry, leaving him where he belonged: with the rats.

He must have been caught off guard. His pursuit wasn't immediate. She shut off the flashlight and sprinted into darkness with her hand tracking the wall. The tunnel had a bend. She had enough of a lead that he wouldn't be able to see her unless he was on her heels. She muted her breaths through sheer will as she reached the tunnel's split.

She made a sharp turn, pressed her back to the wall to hide in the corner, and waited. Less than a minute later, Holden rustled past.

Mave released a quick breath. She hung her head and cradled her face in her hands.

Push it down. Swallow it. Now's not the time to cry over him. A liar. A thief.

She wasn't clear of trouble yet. Somehow she had to find a way out of these tunnels without Holden's help. Risking to turn on the flashlight, she hurriedly retraced her steps to the rusted railway tracks and began to trail them. Logic insisted they had to lead outside. Eventually. What she'd do in the frozen mountainside without a ride or a safehouse, she'd figure out later.

She got as far as a few steps and jolted.

"There you are!" He stretched out his oil lamp for a better view. Mave barely contained her scream as her heart stuttered and plummeted.

"Where is he? The man down here."

Immanuel Law had followed her.

FORTY-SEVEN

"Oh!" Her mouth twitched into a tight smile as panic threaded her veins. *Act normal.*

She brushed her hair behind her ear and struggled to erase the fear from her face. "I'm so glad you're here. Did you find the sheriff?" She pretended to check over his shoulder, knowing full well he'd hunted her down here alone. "Is she with you?"

"On her way." He was winded, his temples glistening and his shirt untucked on one side. Though he was in excellent shape—a symptom of his narcissism—it couldn't have been easy for him to climb down the elevator shaft. "She went to arrest Charlie first. Came as fast as I could. You and I can find Caroline's son together." He gave her an eager look, as if challenging her to refuse.

"Uh-huh." She nodded stiffly. "It's—just this way." Her feet stayed planted. A few seconds of distraction was all she would require to escape. She pointed into the darkness, inviting him to lead or, at the very least, to inspect the tunnel she'd been fleeing. When he did neither, she added, "It's not far, actually, I was just coming back to get you."

"Were you." He studied her closely—didn't so much as pretend to glance in the direction she'd pointed.

Mave's throat clenched. "You'd be amazed," she forced lightness into her words, "wait till you see his cave. He has so many library books. Loves poetry."

A muscle in his jaw ticked. "You seem to know a lot."

Her nerve endings stung and her intuition screamed. He wasn't buying her act.

She avoided his eyes and held the flashlight with both hands to stem off her tremor. She couldn't risk having her back turned or rushing past him. Not yet. He was too close, inspecting her with too much suspicion. Her pulse soared. Why wasn't he saying anything? "Mr. Law?" She shifted her feet. "Is everything all right?"

"Ah." A dark cloud seemed to settle in his eyes. His mouth tensed. "Don't you mean, Mr. Grady?"

Time froze and the tunnel seemed to shrink.

Mave stood still, her lungs pumping with shallow sucks of air.

"Bravo," he said flatly. "What gave me away then?" His eyes were unblinking.

Stall, Cain coached in his gravelled whisper. *Do it slowly. Keep him listening—talking. Whatever it takes.*

"I called him." Her voice sounded reedy and hollow to her ears. "Before coming down here. The reception was back so I called you— him—on Charlie's phone." She shook it to remind him it was more than a flashlight in her grasp.

"Is that what you were doing in Queen's Hall?" He looked mildly impressed. "It was so dark, couldn't tell. I didn't want to startle you by getting any closer."

She ground her teeth. He'd been shadowing her from the instant she'd left his suite. Which meant she'd guided him underground and walked into another trap. She stuck out her chin in feigned confidence.

"I spoke to the real Dominic Grady, told him everything," she embellished, "right before I phoned and told the sheriff." She slipped the mobile into her pocket before he would think to demand proof in her call log.

His brow hitched skyward. "Told her what, exactly? Hmm?"

"That Birdie never threatened Charlie with recovering Annabelle's bones. She threatened *you*." She kept her gaze on his face even as she peripherally tracked his arms and legs for any sudden movement. "That's why you had to get rid of her, and use me—the inheritance—as the perfect distraction that would con everyone. And you were right."

"But I didn't con you, which makes this all the harder." He flashed a rueful smile. "I like you, Mave—I really do. We aren't so different: hiding who we are, paying for the crimes of another."

A shiver travelled her spine. "What are you talking about?"

"I thought you understood: Annabelle started this." The lines on his weathered face crimped. "She lied about her credentials, let my daughter bleed to death trying to deliver that bastard. This is all her fault. I was only cleaning up her mess."

"And what about Birdie?"

He tilted his head as if uncomprehending. "She was already sick."

"Sick from knowing Annabelle was murdered. You said it yourself. Keeping that secret ate away at her. She was haunted," she rationalized, connecting the pieces at last, "and when Hendrick pressured her with his renovation plans for the basement, she took it as a sign. She knew she'd been an accessory to murder all those years ago. Her past was catching up to her. Whether or not Charlie was involved, she needed to expose the truth. She wanted to die on her own terms with a clear conscience. And you couldn't have that."

Agitation flickered in his eyes. It gave her an idea. Emotions made people sloppy. If she could get him to breakdown, grow distracted and lose precision…

"The other night, that noise complaint, you lied," she fished. "You two were never arguing over me. You were arguing over Annabelle, weren't you? You were trying to keep Birdie quiet."

His expression tightened. She was on the right track.

"But she was stubborn," Mave goaded. "Her mind was set. And no matter her blind spot for you—her first love—she was impossible to manipulate—at least not after her diagnosis. She refused to bend, no matter how hard you tried, she wouldn't be your puppet any—"

"Birdie betrayed *me*," he barked. "I'd hardly call that love." His lips clamped, mashing the grudge. "You think I wanted to return to this shithole after thirty years? But after everything I'd done, everything I'd *sacrificed*, she was ready to drag my name through the dirt and ruin me. Just like that. And for what?" He scoffed. "Some fucking lost bones giving her nightmares?"

"What about Annabelle?"

He snorted, seemingly amused by her concern. "Annabelle was a murderer."

No remorse, M&M.

"But you were the mastermind." She licked her lips, improvising. "You must have been planning this for weeks. So many players to control. The blackout. Your con. It couldn't have been simple to take over the identity of Dominic Grady."

"Simpler than you'd think in a hotel this size." His smugness radiated. "I flashed Dom's business card along with my invitation, and told the moron at check-in he could keep the change on my cash deposit."

"But why even bother with the false name?"

"Come on," he sneered, "you of all people should know that a person's reputation precedes them."

She shook her head. "I still don't understand."

He inched his lantern higher, his scowl sinking into shadows. "Everyone knows Birdie and I were close. We had an open affair through most of her marriage and carried on for years afterward. They'd come knocking and demand answers of me, wouldn't they? It's textbook: the boyfriend did it. I'd be seen as the guilty lover. But Dom? Birdie fired and dumped him after Val disappeared, and he's been an estranged has-been ever since. No more than a routine interview."

"And even with the guest list," she deliberated aloud, "the police have no record that you're here."

"Exactly." His eyes gleamed. Deception gave him a thrill. "No name. No trace."

"Except you forgot one thing."

He blinked in surprise, and Mave now anticipated what followed: discomfort. His sense of grandeur was his weakness. He craved absolute dominance—couldn't tolerate its loss.

"That noise complaint," she reminded him. "You fell on everyone's radar, even as Dominic. And Charlie came looking for you. He suspects. You may have hidden so he wouldn't recognize you, but between him, Parissa and the sheriff, they'll poke around and—"

"That's enough," he hissed. His face was sweaty and waxen. "Nothing but words. You have no proof."

"Her bones," she whispered. "I know where you hid them." Approximately. Not exactly.

He jerked his lantern level with her face. Its heat swung in waves against her cheek. It took all her effort not to bat the lamp away. *Not yet. Wait.* If he came any closer, she'd have a clear aim at his eyes. Ears. Throat. Groin. The choreography streamed in her mind.

"You're bluffing," he said. "Just like you're bluffing about phoning the sheriff. Else she'd be here, wouldn't she? You made it all up. Oh"— he grinned—"you had me going for a bit. I almost fell for your lie about a man in the tunnels."

Mave shook her head. "It's the truth." All masks were off. "He's alive. Caroline's son is a grown man. Like I said, he lives down here."

He narrowed his eyes, his jaw flexing. She anticipated another retort but he sprung at her without warning.

She'd underestimated his speed—her exhaustion and concussion. His hands cinched her throat and crushed her breath as his oil lamp shattered on the ground. "Lying bitch! Where is he then? Where!" Madness made a man stronger. His grip stunned her and smoke reached her nose. The lantern's flame had caught on the dry wood of a railway tie. A split second was all it took. The fire set and the world lit up. The truth was there in his wrathful eyes. He'd strangled a young woman before.

Annabelle.

Heat snapped at her ankles, tripping her reflexes. She drove her knee into his groin and punched his ears with both fists. He released her with a roar, stumbled back and forward again as fire grazed his arm. She gasped for air. The warning cry was like a dream layered behind the grate of her cough.

"*Look out!*" Holden's shove came from nowhere.

She flew shoulder-first into brick. Her ears rang. Her throat scratched. But her attention was fixed on the two men standing amid the growing smoke.

Holden was a few feet away, a bloodstain blooming in his shirt. And Immanuel Law was behind him, waving a gun and batting smoke from his arm.

"Hold—!" Mave could no longer control her coughing, her shaking. In his mask, Holden's eyes rolled toward her. He swayed on his feet. All around, reality sped up and bled—sandy air, sharp sounds, blistered shapes. *Not hurt*, she tried to convince herself. Holden rocked unsteadily inches away. *He's not shot. He's pretending again. He's—*

Run. His lips formed the word even as his eyes remained glazed.

He pounced like a drunken man. His arms swung at Immanuel just as the older man pointed the gun again. They fell back into thick, billowing smoke. Another shot was fired. Mave's eyes were stinging with tears. She couldn't breathe—couldn't see through the smolder and soot. She tore her gaze away from the raging flames and reflexively lurched into the tunnel.

Heat wafted at her back. The fire was spreading along the tracks. She had to find another route. *Abs, please, where are you?* Her head spun and she flailed for balance. *Help me. Show me the way.*

The stale scent of ash came at once, pulling her forward into cooler air. One second she ran toward it, and the next another gunshot popped her eardrums. The remainder was a blur.

Mave's ribs burned in agony. She tripped. Her kneecaps scraped with fresh cuts but she hardly noticed. The piercing at her side demanded all her focus, grew wet. She gasped and careened, half-upright.

How strange, a part of her mused. *There's blood seeping from my stomach.* No longer capable of rational thought, she heard herself wailing. Was she wailing? She bit her tongue to stop the horrid vibration and splayed her fingers over her weeping wound. Wet. So wet. A man grunting loudly drew her gaze.

Immanuel Law. The whites of his eyes and teeth were bared in his charred face. He'd forced his way past Holden and the fire. His one leg dragged and his arm lifted. Snippets of understanding stunned Mave.

Mr. Law was going to shoot her. Again. It would be a fatal hit.

DIVE.

She leapt sideways as another bang rang out and a bullet hissed, slicing past her hair and missing her face by inches. She lunged forward. Dizzy and faint, her heart leaked, leapt from her throat.

"You stupid bitch," Immanuel snarled. His leg bent awkwardly and he cursed again. It wasn't carrying his weight properly, splitting his attention and slowing his stride.

Shuffling on her hands and knees, Mave clambered toward the stink of old ash. She reached the man-sized pipeline, scampered on all fours, and barrelled through the hole.

Up. You're a bipedal creature, dammit.

"Where do you think you're going?" Immanuel hollered, catching up after her. His hand brushed her ankle. Mave kicked back and heard a satisfying crunch. She pushed the heel of her palm against her wound, hunched to her feet, and stumbled into shadow.

Everything throbbed. She tried to keep a straight path but the tunnel bent and warped. Colors leaked into her vision, darkened and lit in time with her whooshing pulse. Which way? Was she still smelling ash? She had to lose Immanuel.

Divert! Cain shouted. *Create a distraction, mislead!*

She scuttled unevenly, blindly. Divert where? Immanuel's footsteps dragged and his labored breaths echoed. She'd merely delayed him with her kick. Her guts burning, she ducked into a connecting pipeline and collapsed with her spine curled against the wall. She waited for the world to slow its spin. But the sudden inertia made everything worse. Her face knotted in agony and she doubled over, biting back a moan. So much blood. Her hands were soaked all over again.

"Enough!" Immanuel yelled. "It's over! The sheriff's not coming. We're the only two down in this hellhole!" She was in too much agony to absorb his meaning. His echo played from one tunnel to the next, making it hard to pinpoint his exact location. Was he getting closer? Farther? She may have lost her vision to darkness, but she refused to sit and wait to be shot.

She sucked in her cheeks and willed herself to crawl deeper into the tunnel. Something dug into her hip.

"Did you hear me?"

Charlie's phone.

"Pretty soon you'll disappear forever like Annabelle. It's over."

Short of breath and nauseated from pain, she stopped crawling and groped inside her pocket. *Divert. Divert. Divert.* She fished out the phone and barely registered the glare of the screen before the keypad blurred and shook. Her thumb jerked over the three little numbers from memory. *9-1-1.* With her final reserve of energy, she dug into the call button and—praying for a miracle—pitched the phone as far as she could down the alternate pipe.

The plastic case skittered to the ground. Her heartbeat drummed in her temples.

"I had it all planned, you know," he called. "Morganson was supposed to arrest you."

Her diversion hadn't worked. If anything, the echo of the monster was sharpening. Getting closer.

"But then there was no fucking body. You had to go and make a simple arrest complicated. You ruined *everything*. Just like her. She did it on purpose, you know. Killed my Caroline—so concerned over that disgusting baby—and then she had the nerve to try to pin it on me. She made me do horrible things—like you. It's your goddammed fault," he cried. "You made me kill Birdie! And that fucking guard!" He was out of his mind. Deranged. His stuttered steps grew closer.

No, no, no. Mave shrunk against the pipe and choked on a mouthful of soot. She slid on her belly, leaving a thick trail of blood but unable to escape. His labored pursuit found her wherever she slunk.

"I know what you're trying to do, coming this way."

Darkness congealed like a blanket over her body.

"And it won't work. It's too late. I'll just bury your bones on top of hers."

In a matter of seconds, Mr. Law would either trip over her or shoot her. Mave had already lost so much blood. She wouldn't survive another bullet. Tears of rage dripped from her cheeks.

It couldn't end like this. It couldn't. She wanted so much more. A little house. A family. Love. To see her father again. *Cain.*

Don't give up, M&M, he rasped in her ears. *Not now. Not ever. You hear me, baby? You're my daughter, Mave Michael. You fight it. Fight, goddammit.*

Keeping one palm pressed to her wound, she rolled onto her good side, reached forward, slapped and pulled in a final effort. Through a mental haze, Mave kept crawling. For Cain. For Valeria. For the father she'd lost and the mother she'd never known, she would live. Her belly smeared and seethed into the ground. Her hand slapped the floor again, pulled and grated her guts. She choked in agony, lungs convulsing with ash.

Shh, don't quit. That's my girl. Keep breathing. Keep moving. You're almost there.

Almost where? But then she felt it.

Her fingers wrapped around the metal wheel. The clarity was a shock to her system. Her knuckles flexed into position. It was sheer wonder how the body could function without rational thought; how the survival instinct could fracture one's consciousness into tiny, operational pieces.

Now, M&M, NOW!

A wail skinning her throat, Mave cranked the wheel and released the air valve. Ashes swarmed.

The bones.

The ghost of Annabelle thundered out from the valve. She swept past Mave in a fiery glow, blind rage flickering in her wake. The filthy hands wrapping her head strained bone-white under pressure. There was a scream. The monster.

Annabelle arched her back and descended on Immanuel Law.

Her mask of fingers broke at their joints, one by one, the knuckles snapping with audible cracks. Immanuel howled in reply as if suffering the fracture of each bone—as if those disgusting hands that had imprisoned her had belonged to him all along.

His eyes popped and streamed with tears. Streaks dripped through his filmy skin, forked at his bloody upper lip. Annabelle burned brighter, closer. He tried to back away, wheezed and buckled to his knees. She paused inches away from him and, as graceful as a dancer, raised her palms. She locked Immanuel's filthy cheeks in her grip—lowered her mouth to his face. Mave didn't want to see any more. She wanted to hide, to sleep, to block out the horror and pain forever. She squeezed her eyes shut just as Immanuel raised his gun to his temple.

A shot fired and Mave's eyes sprung open without her permission.

Immanuel Law lay dead—a hole in his skull and his brains splattered on the inner wall of the pipe.

Annabelle turned.

No. Please.

Without her mask, her face was burned raw—an ulcer of bloody blisters and charred flesh. She placed a fist on her diaphragm, and with her other hand, she extended two fingers and hooked them deep inside her mouth. Then she doubled over, and she retched out the truth.

Ashes and loss. Mave fell into the past.

FORTY-EIGHT

MEMOIRS OF THE DEAD

AUGUST 4ᵀᴴ, 1991 - JANUARY 2ᴺᴰ, 2021

Clamped in the vice of his dirtied hands, there is no sight, no sound. Only pain. I relive it in flashes, over and again, white and blue like the flicking tongue of the fire. Sometimes it comes out of order. Other times it happens in sequence. First the blood, then the baby. Then the murder.

A flash of rage feeds the flame.

She gives birth to a baby boy. He's crying. He's beautiful. Ten fingers and toes. And for a moment everything is good again. Even though the doctor never made it and there's too much bleeding, it's stopped now, hasn't it?

"You did it!" I say. Tears spring in my vision. "Caroline, you did it!" I cut the cord, sweep the mucus from his tiny little nose and mouth. He tries to suckle my finger and I laugh. I scoop him up and transfer him to her breast, skin on skin, but something's not right. My breath catches.

"Caroline?"

The baby screams and seeks warmth, helpless against his mother. His pudgy fists bat. The arches of his feet curl. But his mother's chest doesn't rise. Her fingers are limp against the snow globe she palms for relief. Her eyes, like her mouth, are open. Lifeless.

Pain overtakes me.

Another flash.

"Leave it," Mr. Law snaps when I fuss over the blanket. The baby sleeps peacefully, so I step away.

"Sit down, Annabelle. You and I have some things to discuss." The severity of his expression, this crisis—I immediately obey.

Mr. Law remains standing. "You posed as a trained midwife," he says, "you said you were capable of handling the delivery. You lied about your qualifications for money. And now, well," he huffs and spreads out his hands, "you've killed my daughter."

I've both heard him and not heard him. I blink with my mouth gaping like I've been slapped. My brain struggles between processing and repressing what's happened, what's *happening*—Caroline's death—Mr. Law's accusation. I can't wrap my head around it. I don't know how to respond, so I say nothing.

His jaw slides forward. "In case I'm not making myself clear, let me spell it out: *This*," he points to Caroline's body draped beneath a bloody sheet, "happened because of *you*."

I'm holding both armrests. Letting go means running or puking or screaming. But I have to face my actions like a big girl. I asked for this experience, didn't I? When the anonymous doctor didn't show, it was my duty to step in, to help. Still, I need to think—to get out of this suite, this hotel. It's suffocating. My eyes flick to the door and he catches my train of thought.

"No, afraid I can't let you leave, my dear, not without taking a few precautions." He runs his hands through his hair, seeming dishevelled for the first time. "Now, if you say anything to anyone, break your NDA in any way—so much as breathe a word about Caroline or what happened here—not only will I deny you the money you so desperately need, but I'll hire the best damn lawyers and have you charged with criminal negligence for my daughter's death."

"What?" My blood races, throbs in my ears.

"You killed her," he repeats in all seriousness, and my stomach dives. I hear him—really hear him this time.

"I tried to—" *save her*, my head spins and my defense never comes. My mouth feels stuffed with steel wool. I try licking my lips but they just sting with cracks. "There's no phone in this suite," I manage to squeak. "I wanted to call an ambulance. When the blood began. I—"

"You didn't insist it was an emergency." His face is chalky gray like the belly of a crab. "Not once."

Didn't I? I thought I'd made it clear to phone for help, but I'm not so sure anymore.

A deep hood has formed over his eyes. It reminds me of the night he found Charlie in my suite. Only this time around, no false comfort masks his attention. It was an act. I see it now: the coldness in his eyes. The man standing before me is incapable of sympathy.

"I wouldn't let my own daughter die, now, would I?" he says. "No one will believe that. Annabelle, my dear, what you did? You've committed manslaughter. Now you think about that while I clean up your mess." He lifts the baby roughly and marches away.

I sob.

Minutes pass before the groan of the pipes breaks me from my stupor. I wipe my face of snot and tears. What's going on? What is he doing with the baby?

I get up slowly, my steps dragging, and try not to notice Caroline's body beneath the sheet. It's as if I'm struggling to move in someone else's nightmare. I follow the sound to the ensuite.

Mr. Law is inside. He hunches with one arm dunked into the bathtub. He catches sight of me. "I'm in charge!" he cries over the gushing water. "Me! Not this act of sin, this poison—you remember that!" His shoulders shake.

"Mr. Law!" I call over the groan of the pipes, "what—what are you doing?"

"Told her to be good," he drones. "Said it would end bad but she defied me." The bath is full to the point of overflowing. "Went whoring around with that little prick behind my back, poisoned her mind, her body, and now look: I'm left having to wash that fucking poison out."

I wander closer. I scream.

He's holding the baby underwater.

I yank on his arm. He releases the infant, and Caroline's baby bobs into my hands. He's at once slippery, pale, and limp, his lips like a crushed grape.

Mr. Law stares at the wall tiles. "It's a sin," he repeats. "A dirty sin you used to kill her. But understand this, Annabelle: I won't be stained."

I'm the only one crying as I cradle the drowned baby to my chest. "Okay. Please. Leave it to me." My plea is a high-pitched croak.

Mr. Law seems too far gone to notice or care. His knuckles are white, gripping the edge of the porcelain tub. Water rushes, spills. He remains on the floor, his knees soaking in a puddle that grows.

I reverse a step, careful not to turn my back to him. "I'll get rid of it. Wait here." Whether he hears me, I'm not sure. But right before I exit the bathroom, he snaps his head toward me.

"You'll bury it and come straight back here," he grunts, "if you know what's good for you."

His threat leaves me speechless. My feet can't move fast enough.

Does he mean to press charges? What will he do if I don't come back? I rush the baby to my room next door and lock it for privacy. I check his vitals and when the faint patter of his heart reaches my ears, I swallow a yelp. He's alive—there's still a chance!

I do everything I can, first, to drain his tiny lungs, then to stifle his whimpers.

Mr. Law cannot know. That man is a monster.

The sorrow of losing Caroline—the pain that punches deep in

my chest—switches to something sharper, brighter. It slices along my spine.

Once it begins, the razor of fear never releases.

I can tell Rahul is not one-hundred percent by the way his eyes twitch. Every now and then he mumbles gibberish, but I have no one else I can turn to. It takes more than one try. I manage to articulate the horror. He's skeptical I've done anything wrong, yet he agrees to leave the police out of it. He won't chance my arrest. He promises he will keep my secret, hide the baby and protect him with his life until I return. I believe him. Rahul may have his odd moments, but he's an honest person, a good soul.

My legs feel weak and my entire body trembles. I'm tempted to run. If I do, Mr. Law will come looking. He's a powerful man. His threat is a promise. I must finish my part, do damage control, if not for myself, then for Caroline's baby. I must convince him the infant is dead, that I've gotten rid of his body. The drowning I witnessed—he can never suspect or look for his grandson. Ever. I will make sure of it.

On impulse I stumble to the kitchen. It's dark, inside and out. No one is awake to ask questions. In the walk-in fridge, I grab the closest match I can find—flank of lamb, pork, rabbit—I'm too distraught to distinguish. It only matters that its little ribs are intact. Somehow I make it to the library, light the fire amid my choking sobs, and return upstairs. I repeat to myself: it will work. I broke up the remains and the char did the rest. He won't know the difference.

I expect to find him by the bathtub frozen in rage, but when I enter the ensuite, he's no longer there and the water's shut off. A part of me naively hopes it's a sign: he's returned to reason. In truth, it's simply my coping mechanism to keep from running. Caroline's baby needs me. What Mr. Law's done—there's no going back.

I find him in Caroline's bedroom. He's seated in the armchair I vacated with his legs crossed. Nearby, his daughter's body remains cold beneath the sheet, the snow globe a bulge against her hip. I hold in a shudder and mirror his calm. Inside, I am screaming.

In the time it's taken me to smuggle the baby to Rahul and stage proof of his death, Mr. Law has changed into a fresh suit and combed his hair.

"Did you take care of it?" he says robotically. I nod, grateful the lights are dim and he can't see my chin quivering. I bite my lips together.

"Where?" The word is less a question and more a command. But I'm ready.

"Cremated in the library's fireplace," I lie. "Hardly anything left. Swept and cleaned up."

He raises an eyebrow, assessing me coolly. "Cremated?"

I attempt to say yes but my voice frays. I clear my throat.

"My, my," he drums his fingers on the armrest, "how you've tricked me."

I stumble two steps and drop onto the nearest ottoman. The alternative is to fall to my knees. He knows. He will demand I take him to the baby and finish what he started.

"You're anything but wholesome," he says instead. "Cunning, to burn proof. Maybe I underestimated you and should have you locked up after all."

"What? No, I—" I stand. It's impossible to contain the adrenaline shooting through my body. Or my burst of toxic outrage. "I did everything and you—I *caught* you drowning your grandson to death."

He tilts his head and blinks but all I can see is Caroline's body a few feet away—all I can hear is her orphaned baby's cries ringing in my ears.

"What do you mean 'caught?'" His voice is too quiet. Too close. He has risen from his chair, approached me in my bewilderment. My mind's warning comes too late. I've barely considered a way to back pedal when his hands are squeezing round my neck.

"Think you can threaten me? Who do you think you are"—his face reddens—"coming here and spreading your lies, killing my daughter?" My eyes grow round as panic rattles through me. His hands pinch and throttle. There's not enough air to scream. "What are you planning, eh? Think you can hold this over me? Blackmail me? That I'm stupid enough to let you walk away with the upper hand? You're nothing. A *nobody*."

The more I resist, the harder he squeezes.

"Got greedy—is that it?"

Pain extends down my body, reaches my extremities and constricts them like invasive ivy, crawling, coiling. My toes cramp and sickle. I claw his wrists, but they won't budge. My mouth pulls, desperate for breath. I wheeze in the vice of his powerful grip.

Please.

"No one threatens my name." The madness in his eyes is unbreakable.

Veins burst in my temples. My vision scatters, darkens.

I struggle to move toward the white light, but I can't. No matter how hard I yell at myself to let go, my anger rages and anchors me to my bones.

He must pay. He must pay.

I am weightless and heavy at the same time. I can't leave. I can't stay. So I just howl and drift.

He drags me by my wrists. I want to recoil even though I can't feel my flesh. He rolls me, lifts me with grunts and curses. I scream for him to stop touching me with his filthy hands—try hitting him with both fists to no effect. He folds me in ways I don't want to bend, cricks and crams me limb by limb inside a large canvas bag. It reeks of sweat.

The world rocks for a while.

The next thing I know, I'm in my favorite place. I can't see it but I can smell it—paper and ink and wax. Wood smoke. It's a distinct scent that belongs to the library alone.

I swing and fall on a hard surface. Metal or stone or both at once. It's so dark, so cold, my body is together bruised and vacant. As if in a faraway dream, my skin dampens and the oaky licks of whiskey follow. Seconds later, the fire ignites.

I scream louder and louder for no one to hear. I burn and burn, too much and not enough. My skin curdles and melts but my bones merely blacken.

My bones, they are a problem that won't go away.

Flashes fester, canker and bubble black until a crust finally forms and a mask of marrow smothers my fury.

I wail. I wait. I cackle and cry outside of myself: *he will pay.*

He lugs in a man's body and drops it inside the suite where mine used to lie. Charlie. Though I rage in his face, it's hopeless. He can't hear me. No one can. So I watch without eyes.

Charlie is drugged. Asleep. There's a clink and rustle.

Mr. Law has unfastened Charlie's belt and shimmied down his pants. He leaves and returns a moment later with the pepper spray he'd given me. Charlie's eyes are closed but he sprays them anyway. Charlie moans in his sleep. Mr. Law responds by clawing the younger man's face. Pink streaks cut through his patchy, five o'clock shadow, but he doesn't wake.

Mr. Law tosses the pepper spray, and it's only now I sense the leather gloves he wears. He pauses with his hands on his hips, assessing the tableau before him. He sniffs, walks to the nightstand, and backhands the items on top. The lamp smashes to the floor.

He leaves again for a longer stretch, and when he returns, a woman accompanies him.

"What's he done?" Birdie hisses. She covers her mouth, taking in the scene.

"I think," Mr. Law says, "when Annabelle couldn't deliver the baby and they both died at her hands, she turned to Charlie for comfort. He confessed to me before he passed out. There's no easy way to put this…" He drags his palm down his mouth. "He forced himself on her. Again. When Annabelle fought back, he lost control. Accidentally strangled the poor girl." A heavy silence follows.

"I—I moved her body," he stutters. "I didn't know what else to do. I didn't want you to see the violence but—it's not good, Birdie." His voice is so emotional, so pained. "The security camera will show him entering her suite. His fingerprints are everywhere, and look, she must have scratched him." He indicates the scored cheek. "Even his handprints are bruised on her neck." He swallows and shakes his head. "I can't guarantee he didn't rape her. Sweetheart, this kind of hard evidence will be irrefutable in court."

"What are you suggesting?" Her chest heaves and her stare never leaves her unconscious son.

"I'm saying what happened here tonight was a terrible, unspeakable tragedy. I can see that. You can see that. But others won't. Unless you want your son locked up for committing murder, we have to hide Annabelle's body where no one will ever find it. You know this hotel, Birdie, there must be someplace no one would think to go. Please. Enough lives have been destroyed for one night. Charlie was just sucked into this horrible event—at the wrong place at the wrong time. I thought—I couldn't let that happen to you. To lose your child, I—" His face crumples. He begins to cry and his shoulders shake. The performance is so real, I'm almost tempted to believe it myself.

"Someone will come looking," Birdie's voice tremors, "her family."

Immanuel scrubs his hands across his temples. "Her single guardian is an oblivious stepmother and nobody knows she's here."

"What about the maid—the staff."

"I'll—I'll call a taxi round back," he says. "She left. No one will be the wiser. Sweetheart, it only matters that we get rid of the body. Now. Without it, no one will think twice or draw any connection to the hotel. And Charlie will be safe."

There is a long pause when I think she'll see through his disgusting lies. Call him out.

"The abandoned train tunnels," she whispers. "You take her there. I'll handle Charlie." She doesn't wait for his reply. She gets straight to work. She pulls up her son's pants and refastens his belt without batting an eyelid. Only I can hear the three words that silently form on her lips.

God help me.

She searches my room. Each time I try to touch her, I taste her acidic thoughts. She's afraid, frantic, looking to rid evidence that could be used against her son. She opens and shuts the nightstand drawers, yanks the sheets and frisks the bed. When she discovers Rie's letters stuffed at the bottom of my backpack, her heart trips. Her fear is salt-ridden and familiar, like a leash I can grip through the endless agony. But as she reads, there is more: anger, doubt, betrayal. Their intensity keeps me close. I follow and follow, and every now and again, instinctively reach to stroke her cheek.

In the penthouse, her hands shake as she dials a long-distance number. A man answers. She orders him to search her daughter's room in her apartment and forward her any letters he comes across. She is a pack rat—he must dig through her belongings but use discretion, she stresses. An unspoken threat lingers on her terse lips.

I extend my flaming tongue. I lick and swallow.

She's read the words more than once. Suspicions torment her day and night, but she's too frightened to raise questions—not when it could land her son in prison. He must be protected at all costs.

She thinks to burn the letters but then I pass through her skin. Again. And again. She curses, sweats and shivers. She will hide the correspondence as collateral instead—should things go sour with *him*, she can use it as proof of his daughter's pregnancy, her heroin addiction. Tit-for-tat, she will even the playing field. But only if she must.

Until then, she vows to keep silent and forget the nightmare. Except it won't be forgotten. Not so long as I burn. And not so long as I kiss her through my mask and sense her choke in the dark.

He will pay.

FORTY-NINE

JANUARY 7TH, 2021

Mave had been rushed to the town hospital where she had been asleep for five days. Five whole days since she'd faced off with the monster. She'd also undergone emergency surgery while unconscious.

A middle-aged woman who'd introduced herself as Doctor Zaheer told her she was being treated for a gunshot wound to the left lumbar, along with a concussion and other minor injuries. Zaheer assured her they'd operated in time and her prognosis was good for a full recovery. She was a lucky woman. She'd initially lost a lot of blood, but the bullet had passed cleanly without hitting any major organs, and under the circumstances, Mave's injury was non-life-threatening.

When Mave asked how she'd made it out of the tunnels, all the doctor would tell her was the EMTs had arrived in time. She advised her not to worry about the past. Now that she was awake, she needed to focus all her energy on her recovery. Mave had a difficult time resting, however, plagued by dreams of Annabelle's murder. The strangling. The burning. Her door swinging open a few hours later was a welcome sight. Until she focused on the sheriff.

Morganson greeted her with a brisk nod. She was with another uniformed officer, a younger cop with pockmarked cheeks and a long nose that looked hammered along its bridge. He introduced himself as Officer Rawlings. At the sight of them, a rock formed in Mave's stomach. She'd run from Morganson—Tag—she'd left him dead inside Birdie's suite.

Mave found herself feeling lightheaded. Her underarms were damp with sweat. It had come down to this moment. Tag was dead. And they believed she had fired Cain's gun.

"I didn't do it," she croaked.

Morganson frowned and paused a moment. Her face was stern but otherwise unreadable. She sat down. Officer Rawlings remained standing.

"Mave, we're not here to arrest you."

"You—you're not?" Hope skipped through her heart.

"We know about Immanuel Law," she said.

Mave released a sharp breath. "You know?" she repeated, her voice scratching.

Morganson nodded slowly. For the first time since they'd met, her brown eyes seemed to let down their guard. "We have some questions for you. We're hoping you can fill in some blanks."

"How much do you remember from the tunnels?" Officer Rawlings asked. His voice had a pleasant drawl. The corners of his lips were turned up, encouraging her trust. He held his pen and notebook ready for her statement.

Mave could hardly fathom the nightmare was over. She took a moment and blinked at the ceiling tiles. "I was lost and he followed me. He had a gun and …" She rolled her head to the sheriff. "How did I end up here?" *Alive.*

Morganson regarded her with a hint of curiosity. "We received two anonymous 911 calls, back to back. Strangely, both were connected through an untraceable IP address." She paused for Mave to absorb this news.

An untraceable IP address. Mave couldn't believe it. There was no satellite reception underground. Her desperate attempt to divert Immanuel by dialing 911 must have defaulted to internet data—Holden's WiFi.

"The first caller managed to inform us of a fire raging inside the tunnels," Morganson said, surprising her further. "He didn't sound well. We can only assume it was Immanuel Law having a mental break but it's hard to be sure. There was a lot of coughing. He referred to himself as a madman with a gun, chasing after you, claimed he'd started the fire. The connection was lost after that."

Mave's breath hitched.

Rawlings took a small step forward. "Do you have any recollection of Immanuel making that call?"

Her mind throbbed as she processed the question. He would have been the last person to phone the police, and no one else had been down there except for her and—

Mave's vision pooled with tears. Holden had saved her life twice: first by taking a bullet for her; then by alerting police. Lost for words, she gave the slightest shake of her head.

"The second caller never spoke," Morganson said, "however, our dispatcher was able to overhear a person yelling in the background. Again, we believe that person was Immanuel Law."

"I dialed—I made that call," she stammered. Still, a part of her remained unconvinced. Whether or not she'd gotten through to emergency services, it was impossible: how had she escaped the tunnels—the fire?

As if sensing her doubt, Morganson continued, "The fire department has a trained dog. She's a miracle worker; led us straight to you and the bodies. You were extremely smart to find that open air vent."

A lump had formed in Mave's throat. She was afraid to ask but at the same time, she had to know. "The bodies?"

"Once fire fighters managed to put out the flames, we found a lot of destruction down there. Hardly anything recognizable. Entire sections burned to ash. But with the help of Leia....."

Mave raised her brow.

"...the fire dog," the sheriff filled-in, "we were able to recover the remains of three persons. The first two have been positively

IDed as Immanuel Law and your grandmother, Birdie Everhart."

"Do you know how"—her voice failed and she swallowed and tried again—"how Birdie ended up down there?"

Officer Rawlings seemed to look to the sheriff for permission. "It's not public yet, but," he cleared his throat, "Charlie hid her there post-mortem."

"Charlie?" Mave blinked. "Why?"

The sheriff leaned on her knees, her palms together. "Well," she squinted upward, seemingly having trouble picking her words, "he claims a ghost made him do it." She cocked an eyebrow. "More likely though, he was suffering from hallucinogenic side effects. He tried to flush them, but we recovered a dangerous cocktail of antipsychotic drugs from his room."

Mave's mouth stayed ajar as another piece of the puzzle snapped into place. Birdie had disappeared on that same morning when Charlie had broken into her suite—and Abs' ghost had whispered in his ear. Holden had been telling the truth: he'd never hidden the body on Cain's orders. The theft had been orchestrated by Annabelle. She'd wanted to draw Mave deeper—to thwart Immanuel's plan to frame her, while allowing Mave more time to solve both murders. And she'd used Charlie's intoxication and weakmindedness to manage it.

"You said you found *three* bodies." Dread ballooned her lungs. Her hands gripped the bed sheet. "Who was the third?"

Morganson tilted her head. "An unidentified woman," she said.

Mave sucked in a breath, relief sweeping over her. *Not Holden.*

"Amazingly enough, it seems years ago, someone sealed her bones inside that same ventilation pipe—the one that saved your life by feeding you clean air—and we've only now recovered them."

"Annabelle," she wheezed.

Both Morganson and Rawlings stiffened to attention. "Who's Annabelle?" Officer Rawlings asked.

The simple question unlocked something inside of Mave. She couldn't hold in the truth any longer. It spilled from her. Her hound-dogging. Annabelle's ghost. The letters in the red book. How Immanuel had tricked her into seeking the bones and had trapped her inside the tunnels. With a concerned look, Morganson asked her to slow down and to start from the beginning.

Despite more than one scolding from the nurse, the interview lasted a good hour. It was liberating to finally voice the secrets she'd uncovered. Mave spoke of her first meeting with the supposed Dominic Grady at the pool. She told of how she'd been unwittingly recruited to the hotel under false pretenses, and how Immanuel had used that, combined with his knowledge of Birdie's inheritance, to frame Mave. Officer Rawlings scribbled in his small notebook, while the sheriff patiently listened with creases lining her forehead.

"If it's of any consolation," she said, "the real Dominic Grady is cooperating. He gave us his statement. He received an invitation for the gala months ago and RSVPed no. He had no idea Immanuel intercepted and took over his reservation." The sheriff's affirmation merely urged Mave to reveal her side of the story.

She confessed to overhearing Parissa's resentment, experiencing Nicholas's threat, and being further misled by Immanuel about the Everharts. She told them of Birdie's hidden photo album with the younger photographs of her mother, Dominic, and Immanuel, and the red book of old letters hidden inside the library. With a nervous flutter in her chest, she described how she'd discovered the secret room connecting to Birdie's studio where Immanuel must have hidden overnight after killing Birdie; and how that had led to Tag's attack and her blackout.

Mave's throat closed up. She couldn't put it off forever. "Did I—was Tag…"

The scratch of Rawling's pen stopped.

"He was patrolling, sent by Parissa to look for Charlie." Morganson's look of disapproval was brief yet palpable. "You should have contacted us immediately when you came to and found him shot. But under the circumstances, extreme duress can hinder a person's decision making."

Mave rubbed her eyes and hung her head. "I thought you wouldn't believe me."

"Mave, you're not the bad guy," Morganson reminded her. "Your father said as much. He was right."

Just when Mave thought the sheriff couldn't possibly shock her more. "You spoke with Cain?" Her voice cracked and the tears she'd been holding back trickled over her temples.

A small smile lifted one corner of the sheriff's mouth. "He had a lot to tell me about the Everharts. How your mother, Valeria was disowned and ran away from home to escape them. Funny," she got a distant look in her eye, "he sure does care a lot about you, your father. Sounded like he'd move heaven and earth to protect you." Mave heard the sheriff's unstated words behind her wonder. Cain loved her.

She turned away and blotted her face with the starchy bed sheet. Cain wasn't perfect. He wasn't immune. He was human and he'd been caught. He understood firsthand what it meant to be behind bars. It would kill Mave. Maybe she knew now, too. The postcards. Hiring Holden, Stratis. Cain had been scared for her. Desperate to save her. She drew in a long breath.

She wasn't ready to forgive him but she could start by forgiving herself. She could be upset about the life he'd chosen. And she could still care for him. Where her heart was concerned, hating and loving her father weren't mutually exclusive. And that was okay. All the running and hiding in the world couldn't change her past. So maybe it was best she stop fighting it.

"Mave," Officer Rawlings said softly, interrupting her reverie, "thanks to that 911 call you placed, emergency dispatch recorded a live audio of Immanuel's confession. We know you weren't the one who murdered Tag Whitaker—or your grandmother." Hearing those words, Mave didn't know whether to laugh or cry. Officer Rawlings transferred his weight from one foot to the other. "Between the recording and the confessions, the DA's having a field day."

"Confessions?"

"Since your time recovering in the hospital," Morganson said, "Katrina Kovak has admitted to working with Immanuel Law. He allegedly fed her false information and coerced her into abetting in his crime."

"You mean…"

"He had it on good authority Katrina's visa had expired," Rawlings said. "He blackmailed her with deportation."

The Russian doll charm in Immanuel's suite. "She was behind Birdie's fake invitation," Mave croaked, finding no satisfaction in having her suspicions confirmed, "and that voicemail Bastian received."

Morganson nodded. "And the power outage. I had a hunch when Tag kept insisting he saw a woman's footsteps in the snow. We found her and took her into custody a few days ago."

Thoughts spinning, Mave was no longer actively listening. She pleated and unpleated the edge of her blanket, avoiding their gazes.

"Rest assured," Rawlings added, misreading her anxiety, "we're doing everything we can to hold the persons responsible for your grandmother's murder accountable."

But she wasn't worried about finding justice. Holden's chest bleeding flashed in her inner eye. Somehow she had to protect him—keep from dragging him into this mess. Yet she couldn't live with herself if his body had been missed in the ashes. The gunfire still rang in her ears. Nerves getting the better of her, she snuck a glance at the sheriff. "What about a man?"

Morganson shook her head. "What man?"

Her need to confirm his whereabouts burned beneath her ribcage. She struggled with how much to tell them. "A friend of mine. He was helping me."

"You mean, another guest or staff member?"

Mave began to shake her head and stopped, the motion making her nauseous. "Holden Frost," she whispered.

A look passed between the sheriff and the officer—a silent exchange. Morganson extended her hand to the metal bed frame. "Mave, you've suffered a major trauma, a concussion and gunshot wound. That can be disorienting." She shifted in her chair. The silence grew thick.

"What do you mean?" Her heart monitor pierced her hearing. "Please, just tell me."

The sheriff pursed her lips. She seemed to be inwardly debating something. Mave held her stare, imploring her to relieve the stress eating away at her mind. Morganson shared another look with her officer before returning her attention to Mave.

"While you were out," she said, "you kept uttering that name in your sleep: *Holden Frost*. I thought he might be someone close to you, so I looked into him." She leaned forward, sympathy crinkling the corners of her eyes. "Years ago, Holden Frost was a local. He'd been in and out of foster homes since the age of five and had a juvie record. Since then, well, I'm sorry to be the one to tell you this—especially after everything that's happened—but your friend," her expression slumped, "he's listed as deceased. He died in a suspected drowning fifteen years ago."

FIFTY

Mave spent the next few days in a medicated haze. She gazed out from her window at the falling snow. Morganson's words kept replaying in her mind—followed by the memory of Holden in the library—the scrape of his jaw, the push of his lips. The knot in her heart tightened.

He hadn't died fifteen years ago. He'd been real. It had all been real.

Her mind clung to the tiny detail: *suspected* drowning. His body had never been recovered—then or now. She mentally wrestled with the facts of the man she'd met in the abandoned train tunnels.

He'd been contracted by Cain to keep an eye on her. He'd been shot during the fire. He'd managed to place a call during that same time. So where was he? Dead or alive, how had he disappeared without a trace? Why hadn't she been the one lost to the flames? Why not her? (*Keep breathing. Keep moving. You're almost there.*) Her final thoughts in the tunnel echoed loud and clear. She sucked in sharply.

That voice in her head—the one that growled, scolded, and kept her functioning in times of crisis—it had taken a near-death experience to hear it properly, but she recognized it now. It belonged to *her*. Doubling as Cain, she alone had coached herself through that fire. It had been her own mind, her own instincts keeping her alive.

She barely noticed when a knock came.

Without waiting for permission, Parissa Everhart whisked into the room with a large, elegant bouquet. She wore sunglasses and a floral scent that blended with the freshly-cut lilacs. She set the vase on the window ledge, turned to Mave, and stowed her sunglasses in her Birkin bag. Her eyes were a clear, cornflower blue—the same color Mave imagined Valeria's had been.

Parissa cleared her throat and spun the solitaire diamond on her ring back and forth. "We haven't met yet." She spoke softly—nothing like the tone she'd used with Morganson a week ago. "I'm Parissa Everhart."

Mave was unsure how to reply. A simple hello seemed insufficient.

"You've probably heard by now…" She broke eye contact and glanced out the window. "I'm your aunt." The declaration sent a wave of uninvited emotion through Mave. She needed her to confirm it.

"How long have you known," she whispered hoarsely, "about me?" Her hands balled up on either side of her.

"Since last week. Morganson told me. After informing me about Mother's will." Her tone was collected, as if she'd rehearsed this encounter more than once. "I'm ashamed to admit I didn't believe her at first. It was easier to think you were pulling a scam than admit my own mother had…" She shuddered and faced her, her gaze reflecting a fusion of regret and wonder. "But then I saw you." Her resemblance to Valeria.

Mave swallowed. Her ears felt hot. "I didn't have anything to do with Birdie's—"

"Oh, I know," she sighed. "That's not why I'm here. I'm just—" She absently chafed her purse strap. "I wanted you to know how terribly sorry I am for everything you've been through. What Immanuel did, murdering my mother," her gaze hardened and she sucked in her cheeks, "manipulating and victimizing so many people…" She stared off into space.

A headache began to build. Mave had been having intense migraines since she woke. She stretched her neck, wishing for the auto-button that would raise her backrest. Parissa seemed to notice her discomfort.

"Do you need me to call the nurse?" She glanced around for the intercom. "It's too soon. I shouldn't have mentioned—"

"No," she looked up even though her eyes hurt from the movement, "it helps me. To talk about it."

"Well," Parissa replied with a hesitant smile, "there'll be plenty of time for that later."

"Later?"

She sat in the visitor's chair, appearing out of place against the cheap linoleum. "Truth is"—she nervously smoothed a pleat on her thigh—"it wasn't just Immanuel in the wrong. My mother made a lot of mistakes. With Valeria. With you. And all of this horror, it's forced me to take a hard look at the past." She paused, studying the heart monitor with undue concentration.

"You need to understand," her voice dropped, "when Val left all those years ago, I didn't entirely get it. I'm not sure any of us did. It seemed like a spoiled and melodramatic reaction Mother had baited her into." She blinked rapidly, trying and failing to suppress the grief in her eyes. Mave's throat pinched. "But I finally see. Val left and never looked back, not because she was acting out. She did it because she had to break the chain—the pain and dysfunction." She shook her head, her mouth twisting. "You never met your great-grandmother. Whatever you've heard about Birdie, that woman made her seem like a saint by comparison. What I'm trying to say is"—her chest rose as if bearing the weight even now—"enough people have been hurt. God knows I don't want to repeat Birdie's mistakes and end up like her. Growing up, Val and I weren't very close. Still I have to believe it's not too late. I know it won't be easy…" She inhaled a shaky breath. "But I'd like for us to get to know one another."

A lot more remained to be said, old scars that had to heal for them to move forward. Bottled-up question after question itched. All those years wondering, dreaming: what had her mother been like? Had she loved to sing, read novels, watch movies? What had been her favorite foods? Her hobbies? Maybe Mave's roots weren't lost and forgotten after all.

Tomorrow, she thought, feeling her eyelids grow heavy with exhaustion. Tomorrow she would ask. For now, Parissa Everhart's unexpected olive branch would have to be enough.

FIFTY-ONE

Mave was crouched over a box when the bells jingled. She straightened slowly, her stitches itchy and sore, and dusted her knees. Seeing the sheriff removing her hat, her heart sped in eager anticipation. "Thanks for coming so soon."

"Worked out well." Morganson eyed the open cigar cabinet she'd been restocking. "Had to come anyway, some loose ends from the investigation."

Mave followed her gaze. "You smoke?"

"Quit seven years ago." A subtle longing drew out her tone. She blinked and refocused. "Gotta say, surprised when you phoned and asked to meet here." She glanced around the giftshop with open curiosity, as if trying to understand its appeal. "Just figured you'd want a fresh start." She wandered to the magazine stand, her back to Mave. Mave didn't have to peek over the sheriff's shoulder to know she was browsing the newspapers neatly arranged on the bottom ledge. The headlines.

Online and in print, news of the disaster had gone viral. Forensics had identified the bones of a missing persons cold case from thirty years ago: Annabelle Leandro. The entire town buzzed with gossip. The latest, (according to Bastian), was Charlie Everhart was being detained in a health and wellness center for psychiatric evaluation.

Mave picked a hangnail, her pulse pattering. "Well Hendrick's quit…" Plans scrapped, he'd fled with his blueprints the day after the fire broke. "So when Parissa offered to work it out with new management, it just"—she shrugged—"felt right." She cleared her throat. "Dr. Zaheer said routine was good for me, to get back to normal. Within limits." She held in the rest. Beyond the tranquility of the shop, her motivation to return was a bruise in her heart too sore to articulate. So she told herself she was simply tired of running. It was true enough. Even a damaged home was better than no home. After all, a damaged home might be fixed.

The sheriff returned to the counter across from Mave, her shrewd gaze taking her in. "Got your belongings here." She reached into a bag she'd left by her feet and pulled out the books: one green, the other red. She slid them to Mave and paused. "Way I see it, once the tape clears in a month or two, all this stuff is yours anyway." Mave had yet to wrap her head around the inheritance. One day at a time. "You'll have to sign a bunch of official papers," Morganson added, "but uh, till then, maybe don't mention how you got a hold of these, yeah?" She patted the books and Mave nodded.

"Appreciate this. Really." She swallowed and stared at the albums. The memories of her mother. "Parissa's been helpful but…" *She also believed me a murderer a few weeks ago.* Though her aunt continued to make an effort to make amends—phoning Mave more than once and going as far as to invite her to lunch next week—Mave couldn't bring herself to hope for too much.

"After tragedy, forgiveness is tough." The sheriff leaned on the counter and casually spun a rack of silver earrings. "Take it from me: I've seen plenty of families broken apart. And most folks, well, they aren't exactly objective when they're mourning. Scared. Pissed. Parissa was wrong to accept rumors at face value, but in her shock and all… well, if it'd been me, it would've been easier to blame a stranger than face the truth. That's all."

Mave hung her head, mulling over the sheriff's advice. Morganson nodded and put on her hat. "You need anything else, you find me. Take care, Mave Michael." The bells jingled as she left her with her troubles.

Mave inhaled a deep breath and opened the green album. She flipped its pages until she reached a picture of her mother and aunt. The sheriff was right. She was sick of wondering about people's hidden motives. She was sick of being suspicious, crying and screaming questions into a void.

Messed up family or not, from now on, she would put her energy into positive things. No more moping or feeling sorry for herself. No more agonizing about the past and running from her identity. She would wear an arm's length of rubber bands if she had to, but from this point forward, she would live in the clarity of the present. She was in a position to help others by reuniting them with their belongings—not just lost junk but meaningful objects. She traced the edge of her mother's photo. Remembrances. Channeling Annabelle's bones and feeling that suffering, it hadn't been a curse. Her hound-dogging was an untapped gift. And she could choose to grow it slowly, on her own terms. Just like her relationship with her aunt.

By the following week, she talked herself into purchasing a postcard of the hotel. Before her courage could escape her, she scribbled her first reply to Cain in four years. It wasn't much—she couldn't bring herself to express any deep sentiment—but it was a start. She stamped it, addressed it to the prison, and openly tossed it into Bastian's outbox for the world to witness. She was Mave Michael Francis, daughter of a convicted gun for hire. With a weight lifted from her shoulders, she headed to the library for her break.

Since her time in the hospital, she'd thought of Holden Frost constantly; sometimes with inexplicable anger, other times with uncontrollable tears. It'd been one month. There'd been no more news. No trace of another body in the underground debris or breakthrough arrest of a criminal translator for the dark web. He was a ghost all over again.

("*Tunnels were home...I always came back.*")

He'd return. She didn't need clairvoyance to confirm it. It was a promise that shivered along her skin, that whispered on her eyelids while she slept. Holden had to be alive. She brushed her fingers across book spines as she made her way to the fireplace. The shadows twirled and the draft danced. She wrapped a blanket around her shoulders and glanced at the portrait she'd asked Bastian to hang over the mantle. It turned out Birdie had made several paintings of Annabelle Leandro over the years. This one, a close up that captured her warm, almond-shaped eyes, was Mave's favorite. She picked up the book she'd left face-down on the mantle during her last break and skimmed the verse by Walt Whitman.

The smoke of my own breath;

Echoes, ripples, buzz'd whispers, love-root, silk-thread, crotch and vine;

My respiration and inspiration, the beating of my heart, the passing of blood

and air through my lungs…

Her eyes pricked as she pictured the same verse climbing Holden's forearm in the shape of a branch. The poem was unfinished.

Mave wandered to her favorite wingback chair and curled up in its seat. She had no clue how to harness her unresolved feelings for Holden Frost. They chafed her heart day and night. And if she was being honest with herself, she had no desire to suppress the ache. She'd found an odd comfort in it—in the truth. Maybe you could take the criminal from the girl but you couldn't take the girl from the criminal. Maybe she was okay with that. For now.

Mave turned the page.

ACKNOWLEDGMENTS

Thank you for picking up this book, lovely reader! It means the world to me, and I'm still pinching myself. Writing and publishing *The Hitman's Daughter* has been a dream come true, and I had a ton of help along the way...

Thank you to my wonderful agent, Ann Leslie Tuttle for believing in my writing. I couldn't have done this without your talented eye and insight! You saw the potential of this story from its rough beginnings, challenged me to make it better, and found it a perfect home at Agora Books. Reading and loving fiction is such a subjective experience; when an editor clicks with your work, it truly feels like a bit of magic. Thank you for taking a chance on me and welcoming me to Agora, Chantelle Aimée Osman! You're a superstar editor, and I couldn't have asked for my debut to be in better hands.

I owe a debt of gratitude to my friends at the West End Writers' Group; you helped me plant and water the seeds for this mystery. Kristen Kolynchuk and Sarah Robertson, your critiques have made *The Hitman's Daughter* insurmountably better, and I'm ever-lucky our paths crossed at the Humber School for Writers years ago. A heartfelt thank you to Megan Starks who read a first, messy draft of Mave's story and told me how much she loved it and needed it—and that Holden was her new book boyfriend. A huge thanks to my fellow 2021-22 debuts and to my P2P friends; your continuous cheer and comradery are one-of-a-kind. A big shout out to Casie and Tara for their edits and feedback, and to Holly for swiftly connecting me with her "gun expert." Anne, thank you for all our creative exchanges; you're an amazing human and writer that I'm blessed to call friend! Thank you to Tammy for giving me the insider scoop on hotel procedures with guests who croak—I was captivated by your morbid adventures in hospitality services! Thank you to the incredible Pitch Wars community, including Lisa Leoni and Megan McGee who generously read early drafts, and Remy Lai who helped me with my pinyin translation (any mistakes are 100% mine).

Last but not least, my love and gratitude to my friends and family for their support. You are dispersed all over the world—Toronto, Ottawa, Montreal, Bathurst, Dubai, Athens, London—too many places to list here; though I hope to tell you thank you in person someday soon! To my sister, *merci* for helping promote my debut! Likewise, a mountainous *merci* to my parents for working so hard to give me a life where I could pursue my dreams—*sirtov shad shnorhakalem*. Thank you to my kids for gifting me their laughter and buoyant positive energy. And thank you to Jason; without your patience, encouragement, and belief in me, this novel wouldn't exist.